I0576053

WHEN THINGS
GO MISSING

by
Deborah J. Brasket

This is a work of fiction. Names, characters, places, and incidents are the product of the author's imagination or used fictitiously. Any resemblance to actual persons, living or dead, events, or locales, is entirely coincidental.

Copyright © 2025 Deborah J. Brasket. All rights reserved. No part of this book may be used or reproduced in any form without express written permission from the author, except for brief quotes, approved excerpts, articles, and reviews. For information, quotes from the author, or interview requests, contact the author.

Sea Stone Press
Paso Robles, California, USA
www.DeborahJBrasket.com

Cover design ©Owen Gent
Painting *Colorful Architecture* by Paul Klee

Paperback ISBN 979-8-9920103-0-5, 979-8-9920103-2-9
Hardcover ISBN 979-8-9920103-1-2, 979-8-9920103-3-6
eBook ISBN 979-8-9920103-4-3

Library of Congress Control Number: 2024925880
Printed in the United States of America

Praise for *When Things Go Missing*

"If this novel were compared to an art form, it would be Kintsugi, the Japanese practice of repairing broken pottery with gold, embracing imperfections as part of the piece's beauty. This philosophy of resilience mirrors the painstaking healing of Franny's flawed yet deeply relatable family in *When Things Go Missing*. Deborah J. Brasket's eloquent, intimate prose draws readers into an introspective journey. . . Part mystery, part engrossing family drama, *When Things Go Missing* is a poignant reflection not just on what leaves a mark, but on what binds us back together.
—**Nicky Flowers, *Indies Today***

"A powerful novel about losing yourself in order to find a way home, *When Things Go Missing* by Deborah J. Brasket is an achingly poignant exploration of femininity, responsibility, and liberation from societal expectations. Featuring sharp, emotional storytelling and painfully flawed characters traversing profound developmental arcs, this subtle but profound novel is a testament to choosing your own path, no matter how strange the road." — **SPR Review, ★★★★★**

"*When Things Go Missing* is catnip for book club readers. Brasket is a gorgeous writer who explores complex family dynamics in a raw yet sympathetic way."
—**Dianne Emley, *Los Angeles Times* bestselling author**

"*When Things Go Missing* will stay with you long after you've read the final page. To me, this is the mark of a powerful and authentic story. You may find yourself reflecting on your own life path, the choices you've made, and the choices that await you. *When Things Go Missing* is a beautiful unfolding – a tender, loving portrait of a family contending with grief, loss, and regret, while fully embracing all the joy that life can hold. —**Valorie Grace Hallinan, *Books Can Save A Life***

"Deborah Brasket's *When Things Go Missing* is a must-read, a beautifully crafted story about the kaleidoscopic facets within families. With characters expertly drawn, "*When Things Go Missing*" expresses the power of giving space and creating distance in order for individuals— flawed as we all are—to flourish. As a licensed therapist with years of experience assisting others with mental health and addiction challenges,

I was struck by the power of Brasket's prose. . . . As the reader learns about each compelling character, their voices and perspectives are distinct: Real and raw; engaging and endearing."
—**Dr. Vicki Atkinson, Ed.D, LPC, author of** *Surviving Sue*

Deborah Brasket exquisitely captures minute moments of human interaction and emotion. Amid the chaos is welcome humor and recognizable nuances of family life. —**Dana Isaacson,** *Career Authors*

"I absolutely loved *When Things Go Missing*. Every part of this thought-provoking novel was engaging, and the voices that told the story really captured me. . . . I really enjoyed seeing each of the three main characters grow into different versions of themselves. Many thanks to the author for letting me read the advanced copy. I have already recommended it to several people." —**Valerie Tingle,** *Rockin' Riverview Book Club*

"*When Things Go Missing* is an excellent read . . . one of the first novels I've wanted to keep reading through in ages. Brasket has such a rich, immersive style of writing. With scant softening around the edges, she writes with grit and grace. She shows how people and relationships are always evolving, but the desire to stay connected with those we love is an ever-present driving force."—**Laura Bruno Lilly,** *classical guitarist, composer, poet www.laurabrunolilly.com*

"Wow, just wow! I adored this book. Each POV feels real, raw and reads powerfully true-to-character. *When Things go Missing* is a wonderfully written gem that inspires readers to dig inward towards the most authentic versions of ourselves."
—**Stasha Birdsey,** *Reader from Creede, Colorado*

"I loved *When Things Go Missing*. I was hooked right from the start and enjoyed the talk of art, archeology, and finding passion after everything seems lost. . . . What a satisfying conclusion! I'm so happy I had a chance to read an advanced copy of Brasket's book."
—*Barbara Morningstar, Artist and Writer, San Luis Obispo, California*

To all families who fall apart and struggle
to find their way home again.

*I have loved thee with an everlasting love: therefore,
with lovingkindness have I drawn thee.*
—Jeremiah 31:3

CONTENTS

Prologue – Franny, September 1997 9

Part I - Scattered to the Ends of the Earth

1   Kay - Let Me Count the Ways 15
2   Kay - All the Little Lambs 20
3   Cal - This Is My Brain 33
4   Cal - Band of Brothers 41
5   Kay - One Hot Thing 48
6   Kay - Forced Feedings 53
7   Cal - Night Like Damp Ashes 59
8   Walter - Good Girl 66
9   Kay - The Scent of Rocks 72
10   Kay - Split Wide Open 80
11   Cal - Running With Wolves 88
12   Cal - Don't Mean Shit 99
13   Walter - To the Far Ends of the Earth 104
14   Kay - Scattered 109
15   Cal - Suck of the Unborn 114
16   Cal - King of the Castle 123
17   Kay - Flying 131

Part II - Making New

18   Walter - Luther, Alaska 141
19   Walter - Weight of Gold 150
20   Kay - Eyes Like Hands 155
21   Kay - Drowning 163
22   Cal - Give & Get 174
23   Cal - Wide Awake 181
24   Kay - Fitting In 186
25   Walter - Damn Weather 191

26   Cal - Drinking the Kool-Aid 202
27   Kay - Mother of All Mountains 209
28   Cal - White-Hot Flow 216
29   Cal - Tats 221
30   Walter - Lighting a Fire 230
31   Cal - Keeping the Lights On 237
32   Cal - Lost & Found 242

Part III - The Gathering

33   Walter - The Deer 251
34   Kay - Couches on Curbs 260
35   Kay - Door Number Three 271
36   Walter - Something Unseemly 276
37   Cal - Rocks & Ducks 280
38   Cal - Pearl & Bailey 288
39   Cal - Wings & Claws 297
40   Walter - Ghosts Among the Ruins 307
41   Walter - Dawn Again 313
42   Cal - Hanging On & Letting Go 316
43   Kay - Little Raft of Love 325
44   Kay - Getting to the Heart of Things 331
45   Kay - The Gathering 340
46   Cal - Seeing & Being Seen 347

Reading Group Questions and Topics for Discussion 348
Note From the Author 350
About the Author 351

Prologue

FRANNY
September 1997

A few weeks after Franny turns fifty, she finds a large plastic tub hidden behind a pressure cooker on the bottom shelf of the kitchen cupboard. It's filled with old recipes she collected when the kids were still young—scraps of yellowed paper torn from old newspapers and magazines, index cards stained with tomato sauce and fudge frosting.

She kneels on the cold kitchen tiles, sifting through these half-forgotten memories as if they are fragments of some other woman's life. When did a recipe for lamb chops and lima beans ever seem special enough to cut out and save? Why did she ever think she would make her own yogurt or have the patience to build a gingerbread house from scratch?

Who was this woman?

One by one, she holds up the strips of paper to the light streaming through the window. She lets them slip from her fingers and float to the floor as if she were peeling away fragile layers of sunburned skin, the way she used to when she was young and bored, fascinated by how something that had been such an intimate part of her was so easily stripped away and discarded.

All week long, she goes through the same shedding process, opening closets and cupboards, ridding herself of everything she no longer needs, stripping away all that's not essential. She's amazed by how much she's accumulated over the years, how easily she lets go, how freeing it feels. Sometimes she opens cupboard doors just for the pleasure of seeing how spare it all is now, how clean and simple.

The following week she finds a stack of old journals in the bottom drawer of her nightstand. She sits cross-legged in the middle of her bed, surrounded by half a dozen spiral-bound notebooks, skimming lightly over the surface of a life that no longer captures what's essential. One by one, she tears out the pages that fail to ring true. Scattered chads from the spiraled edges drift about like debris floating at the bottom of a sea. Sunlight filters down through a haze of dust motes from the skylight overhead. A pool of shimmering blue beckons. She imagines herself swimming up toward the light, pushing through the glass, melting into the widening sky.

The next day Franny heads toward the grocery store, her weekly shopping list and a handful of coupons tucked in her bag on the Bronco seat beside her. But instead of turning into the lot, she glances sideways at women walking carts to parked cars and keeps going. She passes Carson Elementary School where her children once went, its parking lot now overflowing with portable classrooms. She drives by the Oak Hill condominiums where she and her husband lived when first married. Then she turns onto the freeway heading south. The golden hillsides of the California coastline flow past. She rolls down the window, letting the cool air untangle her hair. The road ahead is wide open, endless.

In the late afternoon she pulls over for gas at a small Pemex station outside Ensenada, Mexico. She's been driving seven hours straight with only the occasional stop for fuel and food: apples and granola bars and tall bottles of cold iced tea. Her thin cotton blouse is plastered against her back. She pulls it loose and stretches as she leaves the car, looking across the desert. A warm breeze blows along the ground, gathering little dust devils that spin with sudden passion and dissolve just as quickly. She shields her eyes with her hand and looks out against the glare of the sun. Lavender hills rise above shimmering pools of heat.

An attendant fills her gas tank while she calls her daughter from a pay phone, but there's no answer. The phone rings and rings. When the beep comes, she leaves her message.

"Hi, Sweetie. Don't worry about a thing. Everything is fine, just fine. Tell Dad and Cal I love them. I love you all. Kisses."

The gravel crunches beneath the Bronco as she pulls forward. The road curls along the edge of the cliff as she heads south again, the sun slanting toward the sea.

PART I

Scattered to the Ends of the Earth
September 1997 – June 1998

Turning and turning in the widening gyre
The falcon cannot hear the falconer;
Things fall apart; the center cannot hold;

Surely some revelation is at hand;

—William Butler Yeats, from "The Second Coming"

1

Let Me Count the Ways

When the call comes, Kay is sitting cross-legged on the living room floor, lost in a swamp of paper. It's another hot blistering September in the valley. Santa Ana winds are blowing desert air through the canyons, fanning fires in the Los Angeles forests some thirty miles away. Drifts of smoke and ash taint the air. And here she is, cooped up in her dark, stuffy apartment, the blinds pulled tight against the day's glare with nothing but a portable fan to relieve the heat. A blast of hot air stirs the edges of the papers strewn across the carpet, looking like whitecaps on a stormy sea. Loose strands of dark hair from the knot twisted on top of her head whip around her.

She's looking for the last article she needs to complete a grant report about an archaeology field study she's been working on in Baja these last two years. She'll have one more visit to the site before she graduates with her master's in May. Sometimes she wishes she could be a lifelong student. She loves research as much as time in the field, digging through the earth like a treasure hunter or time traveler. What she doesn't love is the vast number of articles assigned each semester that she barely has time to skim through, let alone read with the kind of depth they deserve.

"Karl, can you get that?" Kay shouts over her shoulder when the phone rings. But apparently Karl doesn't hear. Or he's decided to ignore her. He's too cozy propped up on their pillow-top mattress in the next room, slurping down a bowl of Ben & Jerry's ice cream, watching Larry King on CNN. The Clinton's Whitewater scandal is all the rage now and, of course, Karl finds it riveting—another way they don't connect. He's been living in her apartment for four months now, a fellow grad student at CSUN. Four months too long, she thinks now.

When the answering machine picks up, Kay hears her mother's voice. Her face softens, and the tension in her neck and shoulders eases. "Breathe," she can almost hear her mother saying, and she does, pulling back her shoulders and taking a long, deep breath from her diaphragm the way her eighth-grade chorus teacher taught her, letting her power rise from a place just behind her belly button.

She can barely hear her mother's message above the whirr of the fan—something about Dad and Cal. What has her brother done now? His bright face and cocky smile fill her mind for a moment, then abruptly disappear as she remembers what he's become. Her stomach twists. She slams that door shut. Poor Mom, having to deal with that. Already the calming effect of her mother's voice has disappeared.

She turns with a sigh to the mess surrounding her, and that's when she sees the missing article, "Aspects of Hunter-Gatherer Complexity in the Cape Region of Baja California Sur."

"About time!" she says, snatching it up with relief. She grabs a cold apple from the fridge before punching play on the answering machine. Then she pauses mid-chomp as she listens to her mother's message. She presses replay, but it still makes no sense.

"Karl!" she shouts again, although he's still only a thin wall away. He's carrying his bowl, scooping spoonsful of ice cream into his mouth when he enters the kitchen, wearing only a pair of purple and yellow-checkered boxers.

She looks at his pale, knobby knees and grimaces. He looks so much better tucked into his faded Levi's and black T-shirt, or even a tie and jacket—a clown's costume, for God's sake—anything but this.

They met in a biology class Kay was auditing. She liked how he challenged the professor, identifying Karl as a kindred spirit. "Another cranky grad student" is how Donner, her mentor and thesis advisor, tagged Kay and others like her—always reading against the grain, demanding and arrogant, prone to streaks of brilliance, yet all the while as critical of themselves and each other as of everyone else.

She invited him out for coffee after class, wanting to pick his brain about carbon-dating plant remains found at archaeological sites. He was surprisingly funny and attentive. She liked his cocky confidence, his tendency to prattle on in a self-mocking, acerbic way on almost any topic she introduced. But mostly she liked the way he looked at her, the desire she saw as his eyes feasted upon her, like she was the most delicious thing he'd ever seen. When he finally took her to bed, she had an orgasm almost before he finished undressing her.

Soon after, he invited her to move in with him, but she declined. If they were going to live together, it would have to be in her apartment. If things didn't work out, she wanted him to be the one to move, not her. Now everyone thinks they are a couple—Kay, too, most of the time, she must admit. Except for times like this, when standing before her in his boxers slurping ice cream, she's ever so sure they are not a couple and never will be.

Sometimes she thinks she should send him on his way so they both can be free to find what they really want, but he's so convenient to have around. Besides the savings in rent, he's an excellent cook and housekeeper, two tasks she detests. And then there's the sex. She blushes, remembering how good he is in bed, this scrawny, pale, prematurely balding man shuffling toward her.

O, how thou dost annoy me, let me count the ways, she sings to herself and is tempted to sing it out loud as she watches her lover approaching. But then there's this message from her mother she must deal with, so she represses the urge. First things first. Her mother.

"Listen to this," Kay says, punching replay.

He listens and shrugs. "So, it's your mother."

She glares at him. "I know it's my mother. Listen to what she says." She plays the message again. "What does she mean 'tell Dad and Cal'? She lives with them, for Christ's sake, a four-hour drive from here. Why would I be giving messages to them? Don't you think it's strange?"

"Well, yeah, but like I said, it's your mother. We all know how she can be—how shall we say it—a little spacey?"

Kay draws a sharp breath. "Spacey? Why on earth would you say that?"

He raises his spoon as if to fend off an attack. "Hey! You asked. I always saw your mother as a little trippy, you know. Like the way she went on and on about the stars, and string theory, and multiple universes, and all that pop science crap last time we visited. Remember?"

"Oh, that," she says, remembering how they sat on the patio as the first stars began to show, her mom and Karl bantering while she and her brother looked on, feeling left out. Who knew where her mother picked up all that stuff? "I never pay attention when she goes off like that. I'm not interested in those kinds of things."

"But your mom *is*. That's my point, Doll. Your mom is. And you don't see it. You don't see *her*. You just see *Mom*."

Kay glares at him. If he calls her "Doll" one more time . . . .

"Go away, Karl," she says, shooing him off with her hand. "You're no help."

She picks up the phone and dials home, drumming her fingers on the counter.

"Dad! Where's Mom?"

"What do you mean?" asks Walter. "Isn't she there with you?"

"Why would she be here with me? Would I be calling you if she was here with me?"

Has the whole world gone crazy?

2

KAY
All the Little Lambs

It's nearly noon when Kay pulls her Volvo into the driveway of the small tract house in San Domingo, the small town on the central coast where she grew up. She's come home to confront her father and brother about their missing mother, seeing as how, after a week's absence, no one has heard from her and neither seems motivated to do much about it.

Someone must rally the troops, she thinks—form a posse, do whatever people do in a crisis like this when someone goes missing. Do what Mom would do if one of them went missing. This is the kind of thing her mother was so good at. She was always the family cheerleader, the one who could pull everyone together and get them to do what was needed, even when they resisted. Now there is no one to do it but Kay, and she doesn't know where to begin. How can you make Cal or Dad do anything they don't want to do? She doesn't have that kind of strength or patience.

Kay has played her mother's message over and over, trying to decipher its meaning. Her mother's voice sounds happy—like she always sounds—not like someone who has lost her mind, who has abandoned her family, who has decided to wander off into the world to do God knows what with no clue how to live on her own. Mind you, for all her inner resources, this is a woman who has never held a full-time job, never lived on her own, never stepped more than five yards away from someone who loved her, who could dash to her rescue if needed. This was her mother!

These thoughts wind through her mind, growing tighter and tighter as she tries to pull them apart and make sense of it all. It's like a tourniquet twisting around her. She has a sudden, surreal image of herself standing alone on some desolate battlefield as if she were a wounded soldier, stunned, wandering helplessly about. Her head is tied up in a bloody bandage, and she's dazed, bewildered. It hasn't quite registered that her arm has been blown away. She just knows something is missing. Something vital is missing.

She sits in the car, trying to push away these morose thoughts. The house before her is small but neatly kept. It was built in the fifties, a starter home they called it back then. A small home on a big lot with plenty of room to grow. Land was not the commodity it is today. Wide open spaces and carefree living full of promise were the norm then. People drove cars with muscles, sans seatbelts or airbags. Infants sat snugly in their mother's arms rather than strapped alone in the backseat.

It was when fresh-faced men dressed in white stepped with cheerful optimism onto the moon. Not like today when the moon rocks they collected lie in dusty obscurity on museum shelves, and abandoned satellites orbit the globe in concert with the gigantic garbage patches circling the oceans.

A starter house was a bright promise of something better.

Kay gathers herself and steps out of the car. The sun has burned off the last of the morning fog, leaving a dazzling sheen on the wet lawn and purple leaves of the plum trees lining the street. But you'd never know that when you stepped inside the house. The blinds are pulled so tight she must pause a moment in the doorway to allow her eyes to adjust.

Cal, her big brother—twenty-eight going on eight—is slumped on the couch, his leg bouncing a mile a minute as it always does, the light from the blaring TV flickering over his face. He jumps, startled, when he sees her then pops up and bounces toward her, grinning like a star quarterback coming to greet his fans. Only football was never his sport. He never bought into the whole team vibe. Surfing, wrestling, that's where he excelled: one on one, board on wave, body on body. Primal. Elemental.

She's surprised and pleased by how much weight he's put on—Mom's home cooking on top of all that jailhouse food, she supposes. She wishes he could stay like this, like the brother she remembered when they were both in high school, the one all her girlfriends had crushes on because he was so cute and funny and sweet. He made people feel special when they were with him, like some spotlight that surrounded him fell on them as well. The last time she saw him, he was a dim shadow of himself, all skinny and wasted, the way he always gets when he's strung out on the street. A heroin addict, for God's sake! Cal could never do anything by half measures. Her stomach knots thinking about all he's lost, all he's put Mom through. She's sure that's why she left, to get away from him. And the thought sickens her.

"Hey little Sista', how ya doing," he croons, throwing his arms around her. At nearly six feet, he towers over her, enveloping her in that heavy-handed, suffocating way he has, the weight of his body melting on top of her, nearly driving her to the floor. She smells the sweet, pungent scent of beer on his breath, weed on his clothes, and pushes him away.

"How do you think I'm doing? Have you heard anything yet? Has she called?"

"Has who called?" he asks, looking genuinely clueless.

"Mom, of course!"

His face darkens and he turns away. "Fuck no, she hasn't called. Why would she call? She's glad to be rid of us."

"Stop it. That's not true."

"What else then? Why else would she leave like that, out of the blue, without saying anything? Don't be stupid, Kay. She's done with us." He's back on the couch again, staring up at her, incredulous, like she's the one who's clueless.

She can't speak, she can barely think and pushes his words away.

"Where's Dad?" she asks finally, her voice choked and spongy.

"The garage, where else," he replies, reaching for the remote, his eyes fixed on the TV.

But Dad's not in the garage. He's in the backyard watering the hanging fuchsias, their pink and purple petals the twirling skirts of ballerinas. She watches him through the French doors. He's small and dark like Kay, more taut than muscular. He's talking to himself beneath his breath, a habit he's had forever—one that she and Cal interpreted, along with his whistling, as a sign to stay far away. She steps out cautiously onto the patio. He turns, and his face softens.

He puts his arms around her and pats her gingerly on the back, the way he always does in greeting, as if he's not quite sure how hugs are done or for what purpose, but he knows it's expected, so he tries. She senses in these hugs and pats not only his awkwardness but the genuine affection he feels for her that comes more naturally through twenties pressed into her palms than through physical contact. How this man ever fathered two children, she'll never know, for his body language nearly shouts stay away.

He's always seemed like the unwitting partner in a family life that mystifies him, that moves around him, carries him along, but never pulls him in. He stands on the far side of some invisible barrier, remote, aloof, and unaware.

Mom was the one she and Cal counted on, the one who helped them with homework, attended school conferences, took them out on Halloween nights, and read them fairy tales at bedtime.

Where was her father when all this was going on? What role did he play in their lives? The only times he made a real impression on either of them was when he was irritated, upset, or angry: his grunts of dissatisfaction, sighs of disappointment, and angry grabs on their shoulders and arms as he led them where he wanted them to go.

Cal bore the brunt of his displeasure. The image of her father with his hand on the back of Cal's neck, steering him into a room or out the door, was imprinted on her mind. Worse were the times he lost control of himself, or Cal, or both. It wasn't often, not enough to get used to, or learn to expect or prepare for. And that made it worse somehow, the unexpectedness of it. The hand reaching out, coming down too hard, too fierce, and Cal flying through the air or flung against a wall—a torrent of angry slander slamming down upon him, ricocheting off the walls and catching Kay where she stood by silently watching.

The memory of that violence, that inexplicable rage, lay at the back of her mind, breathed down her neck, all the time they were growing up. Even in the good times—and there were good times—even when basking in his smiles, his rare hugs, his nods of approval, his corny jokes; even when they grew up and moved away, in his presence the breath of danger, the shame of disapproval, the sense of betrayal silently lingered. Mom was the only one who seemed not to fear him, who was able to calm and contain him, to shout him down when necessary or pull him back when needed. She was the one who stood between them and their father, who bridged that gap and had the uncanny ability to translate each to the other.

Now, there is no one to breach the distance between us, Kay thinks. He looks lost and lonely out here. When she questions him about her mother's disappearance, he seems mystified but not particularly concerned.

"Why haven't you filed a missing person report like I told you?" she asks.

"She'll come home when she's ready," he tells her.

"But what if she doesn't? What if she's suffering from a brain aneurysm or having a midlife crisis?"

"She left you a message, right? Said she's fine?"

Kay nods.

"Well, then. She'll be back when she's ready." He reaches up to water another fuchsia.

"But what if—" She isn't sure she can say this, and she feels heat rising from her gut to scorch her face. "What if her message was like a . . . like a suicide note or something?" Her eyes burn, and she blinks hard.

His head snaps toward her. "She's not like that. Don't you know her at all?"

He sighs, and his voice softens. "She was telling you the truth, telling you not to worry, telling you everything was fine. That's your mother, not the other."

And it's true, she knows. Her mother was always saying everything was fine, as if thinking makes it so.

"But if everything is fine, why did she leave?"

Her father looks at her and then turns to his watering without a word.

"Dad?" she says. But there's no answer. She's lost him, or he's tuned her out. It drives her crazy, the way he turns his back on people and acts like he can't hear them, or their words require no response. Even more maddening is his unwillingness to act. Nothing will budge him from his conviction that her mother will return when she's ready, and their only recourse is to wait.

Cal's reaction is even worse. Every single time Kay mentions their mother, his nose flares, his eyes grow hard, and his fingers dig into his fists.

"Screw her. She doesn't want us, doesn't love us. It's her loss. To hell with her. I don't need her anyway."

Which is total bullshit. Cal has been living with his parents since he got out of jail four months ago, holed up in the back bedroom, sleeping all day and emerging at night to go carousing with his buddies or, more likely, looking for his next fix. "He's depressed. That's why he sleeps all day," Mom claimed the last time she called, making excuses for him like she always did. Kay hated those conversations, anxiously waiting for a lull so she could change the subject.

She doesn't know how her mother survived all these years, worried sick about a son who seemed so lost, taking him in from time to time, trying to help him sober up, getting him into rehab after rehab until he finally convinced her they were all scams to get government grants.

Four years ago, Kay took part in an intervention for her brother that her mom and the director of a sober living home organized. Some of Cal's old girlfriends and high school buddies participated, taking turns telling Cal how much they cared for him, how much they missed him, all the great things they loved about him, and why his drug use was so hurtful. Kay was dabbing her eyes as they went around the circle, and when it was her turn to talk, she wept openly.

But Cal sat there dry-eyed and stone-faced, furious they ambushed him this way, bringing in people he hadn't seen since graduation, humiliating him like that. Kay warned her mother how this might backfire and make it worse, but she insisted they had to do something drastic. And so, they did, all to no avail.

After that, Kay wanted nothing more to do with Cal and his addiction or her mother's efforts to save him. Dad felt the same way. He didn't even attend Cal's intervention. Not his scene, apparently. Same as Cal, it appeared.

All Kay wanted after that was to shut her eyes to all that was happening to her brother. It was too painful. They can't save him, and he won't save himself. Yet she didn't want to be like Dad either, who checked out long ago when it came to Cal, letting Mom take the lead and do what she thought was best, even allowing him to live at home if she insisted. Yet what could Kay do? She didn't want to get sucked up into her brother's disastrous life. She had her own problems and her own way to make in the world. It was a relief when she started grad school and moved out of the area—easier to put the whole thing out of her mind.

Kay spends the rest of the day wandering around the house, looking for clues about her mother's disappearance, opening closets and cupboards only to find everything looking barren and unfamiliar, almost as if someone had gone through and cleared everything out. Isn't that what people do when they get ready to commit suicide? She's sure she read that somewhere. Or have they always looked like this? When was the last time she opened the hall closet or peeked beneath the bathroom sink? She can't remember and has the sudden, sickening feeling that something precious has been lost forever.

This is the only home she's ever known. Every stick of furniture, every picture, every rug is permeated with memories of her mother. The house seems ghostly without her here, like seeing the shape of her shadow everywhere while she is nowhere in sight.

*****

Later that afternoon, Kay joins Cal on the back patio where he sits smoking a hand-rolled cigarette, tapping the ashes into an empty beer can. She looks out at the yard where they used to play together. A swing set once stood between the two birch trees. She loved swinging when she was little, pumping her legs and going higher and higher, the thrill of the wind in her face while imagining herself letting go, sailing over the house and up to the moon. But she never could let go, like her brother. He swung for the pure pleasure of letting go, seeing how far he could jump. He pumped so hard Kay thought he was going to wrap himself around the crossbar. He never did, of course. When the swing reached its peak, he jumped, flying with arms spread.

"Come on, it's fun!" he'd say. "I'll catch you. I won't let you fall." But still, she couldn't.

Cal was the fearless one, the risk-taker, not Kay. Swinging was never enough for him. He was too restless and too joyous in his restlessness, climbing all over the swing set and doing tricks none of the other kids in the neighborhood would dare.

Kay remembers the first time he climbed on top of the crossbar and slowly stood up, walking half-hunched with his arms held wide, tipping from side to side to balance himself. Reaching the end, he yelled, "Watch this!" Then with a shout of glee he flung himself toward the birch tree, grabbing hold of a branch. He hung there for a second, the branch creaking beneath his weight until it broke, tossing him into a pile of leaves, where he sat laughing his head off.

She thought her brother was the bravest person in the world back then. There was nothing he couldn't do. He paid dearly for the broken branch later. But that leap of faith and laughing among the leaves seemed well worth it to both.

What happened to all that?

"You okay?" Cal asks now, looking intently at her, the smoke curling around his face. She glances sideways at him. He's always had a way of tuning into her feelings, knowing when things aren't right, when she needs him. He hasn't done that in a long while.

She gazes out at the birch trees, the low sun filtering through leaves starting to yellow. "I can't stay here tonight."

She can feel his eyes studying her. He taps his ashes in the beer can.

"Why, you sick?"

"Yes, I'm sick!" Her eyes flash as she turns toward him. "I thought this would bring us together. I thought we'd all be rallying together to find Mom and bring her home."

Cal laughs. "Rally? Really? We're not the rallying kind of family, Kay. When did we ever rally about anything?"

"If we can't come together for this then . . .?"

"Then what? We're doomed?"

"Then there's no hope."

"Hope for what?"

She looks away and shakes her head.

Cal is quiet, and she can feel him studying her again. When she turns to look, he's shaking his head too and squeezing out a sad smile. He grabs her neck in the crook of his arm and pulls her close until their heads touch.

"Kay, Kay, Kay," he sighs.

They sit like that in silence for a moment, and it reminds her of old times, when her brother would come to her rescue and try to cheer her up when she was upset. But now all she feels is sadness. She pulls away and rubs the back of her neck.

"So, what are you going to do now, now that Mom's gone," she asks. "Are you going to stay here with Dad?"

Cal sucks in a long, hard drag and lets it out slowly while his knee jiggles a hundred miles a minute.

"Why not?" he says with a snort. "Make the bastard kick me out if he doesn't want me here, if he has the balls to do it." But she can tell from the way he juts out his jaw and grinds his teeth that it's eating him up with worry.

"That's your plan? Wait till he kicks you out?"

"That's my plan, Sissy," he says, squeezing the tip of his spent cigarette and flicking it onto the grass.

"And what then?" she asks, resisting the urge to retrieve the butt, knowing how the sight of it on the lawn will irritate Dad.

"Then," he says, leaning back with his hands behind his head, grinning at her like she's a girl who needs charming, "then it's back to life on the mean streets of San Domingo. A junkie's dream come true if there ever was one."

"You're sick. You know that, don't you?"

"And lovin' every minute," he says, his leg jumping like a machine gun out of control.

*****

They eat pizza in the living room huddled around the TV. Kay opens the blinds to let in at least some semblance of cheer but closes them halfway when Cal complains about the glare on the screen.

Dad leans forward in his green recliner with a paper plate in his lap. Cal is on the couch hunched over the coffee table, his plate piled three slices high. He folds the edges and pushes the ends into his mouth. Then he washes it down with a huge swig of milk from a beer mug, which he slams down on the coffee table afterward.

Kay watches her brother, the unconscious enthusiasm with which he consumes his meal. If you didn't know he was a junkie, you'd never guess it. He has that square-jawed manly look with a little-boy grin that has won the hearts of countless girls and women everywhere. Few can resist him when he turns on the charm. She and her father grew immune to his wiles long ago, but her mother always saw in him the boy she loved and the man she knew he could be.

"For God's sake, Cal! Put something under your plate if you're going to eat like that."

"Sure thing, Pops," he says with a mouthful of food.

Kay hands him some newspaper lying on the floor to tuck beneath his plate. Then she sits back in her armchair, her knees pressed together, the paper plate balanced on her lap while she picks off anchovies and peppers. After a couple of half-hearted bites, she gives up, unsatisfied.

Dad and Cal have their eyes glued to the TV screen where the History Channel is playing. It's one of the few things they have in common, their love of documentaries. Kay tries to watch but fails to see what's so fascinating about herding and sheering sheep in Australia. One fat, furry creature bleats pitifully while being held by its head and hoofs. Electric shears screaming loudly graze its body, removing thick layers of wool that fall in soft heaps to the ground. Eventually, nothing is left but the scrawny, pink body naked beneath. The lamb looks so vulnerable. Bewildered. Betrayed.

"All the little lambs . . .," Kay says without thinking.

Cal and Dad turn to stare at her quizzically, waiting to see what comes next.

"I think I'm going to be sick," she says before bolting from the room.

*****

Kay's fingers clutch the steering wheel as she backs down the driveway, leaving her brother standing alone on the front stoop, looking forlorn and abandoned, hunched in the shadows, the orange tip of his cigarette glowing in the gathering darkness.

She planned on staying longer, but she couldn't stand the oppression she felt within those walls: her father's pathetic apathy, her brother's rage and helplessness. She made excuses and left at dusk. Now, as she drives away, the fear and anger that was feeding on her brother begin to nibble at the edge of her mind. She pushes against the threat of tears rising in spasms from her gut, pushes them beneath the anger and fear so she can drive, just drive. Get past the traffic and maze of freeways so she can curl up into a ball on her bed and let it all out.

She'll be happy if she never sees Cal or Dad again. It's her mother, only her mother, she wants, needs, misses. The one person she could always count on to be there for her, for all of them—and now she's gone, inexplicably gone.

Maybe Karl is right. Maybe she never really knew her mother at all.

3

CAL
This Is My Brain

The sun is gone, leaving a dull glow smeared along the horizon. Cal stands on the front stoop of his parent's home as dusk settles like ashes over the neighborhood rooftops. He watches Kay back her Volvo down the driveway, heading back to Northridge or Norwalk or wherever the hell she's living these days. She came home looking for a little comfort since Mom went missing. Fat chance of that. But he's sorry now he didn't try harder to cheer her up. Or at least say he loved her. Or asked her for a loan, for fuck's sake! He's missing her before she disappears around the corner.

A cold breeze swirls a few dead leaves around his feet, and a damp chill seeps into his skin, goosing it up. The fog will be rolling in soon. He doesn't want to go in yet but has no excuse to stand here any longer. The house behind him crouches small and dark like a cave, offering shelter but filled with things he'd rather not face. The night before him grows darker, wide open, endless. He takes a long last drag on his cigarette, squeezes the tip, and drops what's left into his shirt pocket to save for later. Then he turns toward the front door.

It feels weird walking into his parents' house without knocking, even though he grew up here, even though he's been living here off and on over the past ten years since he graduated from high school. He's acutely conscious of the fact that this isn't his home and never really has been, even when he was a kid. He sucks on the fact like a sore tooth, teasing it, testing it with his tongue. It's like he was born homeless. Like from the day he was born, they were all waiting for him to move out again. The thought fills him with a peculiar sense of satisfaction: He doesn't need a home, doesn't need anything. Anyone. Ever.

Dad is nowhere in sight as he enters the house, thank God. With Kay gone, he's probably in his bedroom, where he always goes when Cal's up and about. Muted sounds of Fox News coming from behind the closed door confirm his suspicion. He grabs a Corona from the fridge and settles on the couch, feet crossed on the coffee table, an old chest his mom rescued from some dust heap and gussied up.

He used to go treasure hunting with her back in the day, before the bad times rolled in, searching through thrift stores and flea markets for under-appreciated treasure they could bring home. He really got into that, picking through the clutter and the piles of junk. Hours rolled by like minutes. He was good at it too—had a great eye his mom told him, the ability to see beneath the rust and tarnish what was bright and valuable. They talked about opening their own thrift store together someday. He always wanted to be his own boss, like Dad was when he opened his own welding shop before returning to the grind of the construction site.

Cal hated working for people, couldn't stand being bossed around, made to feel like a fool or a fuckup. Like a kid again, under his dad's thumb, nothing he did ever good enough.

But being his own boss, running his own business? He could do that.

When he got excited about something, his mind was razor-sharp. When he felt all that energy and passion running through him, he could stay on task for hours, days, like he did when he started that recycling business as a kid, going around collecting beer cans and soda bottles from the neighbors or stealing them from garbage cans. That was back in the 70's when recycling was something new and exciting. Back when that littering campaign on TV featured some old Indian chief with a big tear running down his cheek while the stream behind him filled with trash. Recycling was something noble back then. Something you could wrap your heart around and feel good about.

Mom said Cal was an entrepreneur at heart, someone with vision and drive. A risk-taker, not afraid of leaping out ahead of everyone else. Like that Kinko guy she told him about who started all the copier places. He had ADHD like Cal too, which, contrary to popular belief, wasn't only about an "attention deficit" but, on the flip side, about "attention overdrive" too, an uncanny ability to hyper-focus, to latch onto something and beat it to death or spin it into gold. Mom said it like she was proud of him, proud of a son who could latch onto something and not let go.

Only who knew back then what else he might latch onto and not be able to let go, even when he wanted? Who knew that addictive drive could take hold of your life and shake it loose of everything good and worthwhile you ever were or ever wanted to be? Who knew?

Dad was the one who ended his recycling career, embarrassed of a son digging through trash cans and bothering the neighbors. He seemed to hate everything about a son who was nothing but trouble, who could never sit still, never stop talking, never do anything right. The simplest thing Dad asked him to do fell apart under his stern gaze and turned to shit.

Mom and Dad, what a pair. One pumped him up; the other tore him down. Better to sit back and do nothing, he figures. Watch the world roll by, like now.

He grabs the remote and surfs through the channels—never stopping long enough to see what's playing, only to get a sense of movement, passing images, passing time. All the while, that fist in his gut is clenching and unclenching with each thrust of his thumb on the remote, each thought ricocheting through his brain like it doesn't know which way to go. Trying not to think about her. Where she went. Why she left.

Actually, it might not be too bad having Mom gone. If she were here, she'd be frowning at his beer, telling him to find a channel and stick with it or, better yet, start working on that pile of job applications she helped him get. He'd be feeling that as much as she claimed she wanted to help him, what she *really* wanted was to have her house back to herself, tired of having to pick up after him all the time, seeing as how Dad never leaves anything out of place.

Cal's always been the slob in the house, even worse than Kay, and she's bad. Although truth be known, he can't help it. He appears to be missing whatever's needed to look after himself like that, another product of his ADHD. *Attention deficit* and *hyperactivity* all rolled into one like some superbug. It's not something you outgrow either, like they once thought, or fix. You feel the buzz of the world, all pervasive, all around you, all the time.

It isn't just the way he leaves his dishes, clothes, and tobacco pouches all over the place either. Or the way he dribbles food down his shirt, all over the coffee table, along the floor, and onto the walls he passes. Or the way everything he touches gets upturned, pushed sideways, knocked down, or screwed up. It's everything. He can't find anything he wants, loses track of time, never knows where he's left something last, never remembers appointments. And it frustrates the hell out of him, living in constant chaos with his mom following him around, picking up after him. Like he's some charity she has to champion, some fool she has to suffer.

Why is it these do-gooders sometimes make you feel worse than the guys kicking you in the balls? His thumb hitting the remote aims straight and true, like shooting BBs at the heart of a bird.

After a while, he puts down the remote and starts scratching at his body. The bane of opiates. First, it's the arch of his left foot, then his calves, his balls, his neck, his scalp—his eyeballs, for god's sake! He's a twitching mass of itches. He wants to jump up, rip open his shirt, and howl like a wolf—to escape the madness or enter it, to beat it or become it, he can't tell which.

Either way, he's sorry now for every thought that passed through his head minutes ago, sorry for not missing his mom, not appreciating her, not being the son she wanted. For doing whatever the hell he did to drive her away—the only good thing left in his life.

This is the way his mind works, Cal realizes, never settling on one way of thinking about things. Just when he's ready to write off Mom and everything else, including work, or having a life, or being anyone, and feeling good about it, like it's a decision he's carefully considered and made for himself, to be nothing and nobody, to have nothing and no one, and liking it that way, truly digging it, he gets sideswiped by this opposing flood of thoughts that gushes through his mind like his mother's conscience. That's how he sees it too—not *his* conscience but some uncomfortable and undesirable feeling that drifts in from his mother's looks and sighs and follows him around like a fucking rain cloud. Hell, if she isn't still doing it, even now when she's disappeared.

"Damn her anyway," he mutters, and then, quick as a beat, a queasy sense of shame rises from his belly like a bad case of heartburn. For of all the people on God's sweet earth, saying there is a God, and he's certain there isn't, his mother's got to be his one true angel, the only one he can count on no matter what.

Until now, of course. Until now.

Don't that beat shit. His thumb hits the remote again like it's a fucking machine gun and he's going to kill them all. He throws the remote at the TV, but it hits the wall and falls apart. The bedroom door bangs open.

"What the hell!" Dad shouts from the hallway.

Cal scrambles to his feet and rushes to pick up the pieces of the remote.

"Sorry, Dad, it's nothing, just something I dropped. I'll clean it up."

The bedroom door slams shut, and Cal slumps back onto the couch, rattled by the close call, thankful his dad didn't come out, but all the same irritated he didn't, and even more irritated by his own panicked reaction.

I wish to hell he had come out. I wish he'd come out and seen what I'd done and come after me. I would have thrown him to the floor, and . . . and . . ..

But the rest won't come. For as much as he wants to pounce on his dad and pummel his face into a bloody pulp, when he tries to picture it, when he sees himself straddled across his body, lifting his fist for the first blow, he knows what he really wants is that explosive, intimate contact—just some contact, for fuck's sake.

Some goddamn, face-to-face, skin-on-skin, touching, contact.

*****

Cal knows it's the drugs. The drugs or ADHD—both, maybe. Either way, he's certain other people's minds and emotions don't roller-coaster around in their head and gut the way they do in his. He's used everything you can imagine for so long—heroin, coke, speed, meth, Vicodin, whatever's handy, whatever's available—it's affected the way he thinks, scrambled everything in his brain. It's like that public education commercial that shows someone frying eggs in a skillet and then slamming it against the wall: "This is your brain on drugs," it says.

It's like that. That's me, Cal, my brain, smashed against a wall. And he takes a perverse kind of pleasure in that, in knowing that's him. His brain. On drugs. All the time.

He turns on the shower in the bathroom and opens a window so he can smoke a bowl of weed, hoping like hell his dad doesn't smell it or, if he does, hoping he ignores it because he doesn't want to have to deal with it, with Cal, ever. And the truth is, sometimes he likes it like that, like now, when he can sit on the john and smoke his bowl in peace without interference. Heaven, right here, right now. Bliss in a bowl. Sweet.

If he had an unlimited supply of pot, he'd never have to shoot up again. It's all he needs to feel better, see clearer, slow his brain enough to concentrate on stuff, to actually watch a whole goddamned show on TV without the irritating habit of flicking through the channels, letting the flickering images match the flickering thoughts in his head that won't leave him alone, won't give him any rest. If only he could figure out how to get a doctor to prescribe it for him. They passed that law last year making cannabis legal for people suffering from pain and arthritis and stuff like that. Hell, he was in pain all the time when he wasn't using.

This occupies his thoughts for a long time until he crashes into the wall, having drifted asleep and fallen off the john, spilling the weed on the floor. By now the room is so full of hot steam from the running shower that the walls are dripping, and he can barely see. He turns off the faucet and opens the door to let some of the steam out. Then he closes it again, liking the feel of the hot, sweaty air.

He clears out a space on the bathroom mirror so he can look at himself, the image blurry in the wetness, surreal, with the steam all around, his face ringed by a bright halo of light. He thinks if he stares at his face ringed with light long enough, hard enough, deep enough, he might catch a glimmer of who the hell he really is or was supposed to be in another lifetime. Whatever it was, he knows it was good. Whatever could have been, whatever he blew away, it was all unbelievably good.

4

CAL

Band of Brothers

Cal drags himself out of bed the next day at three in the afternoon, but only because the pain in his bladder, which has been building for hours while he lay awake unable to move, is threatening to explode. Even so, it's a struggle to get up. His body feels like lead and the mattress like a magnet holding him down. Only after he manages to roll to the floor and stumble into the bathroom, feeling the force of his stream pumping out fast and furious, does his brain start buzzing again, all its bells and whistles going off full tilt.

The thing he's got to do, the thing he's got to figure out, is how to survive living here alone with Dad now Mom's gone. How to deal with the uncertainty, not knowing where he stands or how long he'll be able to hang onto his free room and board. He feels that crackle of tension building between them, never knowing when it might explode, and Mom not here to diffuse it. Which means, how can he melt into the walls, so his dad doesn't know he's still here? Because once Dad realizes how, with Mom gone, he doesn't have to put up with his loser son anymore, Cal knows he's a goner.

He paws through a pile of clothes on the bedroom floor to find something halfway clean to wear. Then he calls a buddy to pick him up so he can get the hell out of Dodge before Dad realizes he's slept away another day.

Mikey's not really a buddy. He's another derelict like Cal, as he likes to think of them, but they team up now and again for mutual benefit. Mikey's got a car, Cal's got connections. Mikey will give him a ride into town in exchange for the last of his weed. At least, that's what Cal tells him.

He waits around the corner from his house where his dad won't see him. It's damn cold out. He stamps his feet and blows on his hands, waiting and waiting. He wonders if Mikey's gone missing too, like everyone else. If so, he's in deep shit. Because even though they may not be buddies, Mikey is part of the matrix that holds everything together. He's part of that little band of brothers, the losers and users and dealers, that food chain of commerce and convenience he's part of and depends on, which makes life on the street possible. Or at least tolerable. And even though he's not actually living on the streets right now, he lives with one foot out the door because it's coming. You know damn well it's coming.

So, he's careful to keep his little band of brothers intact or at least as intact as something as shifty as all that can be. Still, it's not like they're real brothers, not like in the military where they all have each other's backs. The brothers in this band help each other out when they can and use each other when they can't. They're more like a gang of pickpockets, he thinks, remembering that show *Oliver* he and Mom watched on TV not that long ago. There's safety in numbers, so they stick together, but they aren't above stealing from each other if they must, if it's a matter of survival. It's who's fittest. You have to know where you fall on the food chain.

Now Mikey's way down there, about as low as you can go. He's barely holding on by his fingernails, and if he didn't have a car or his auntie's couch, he'd be done for. He couldn't survive on the streets, not without hustlers like Cal helping him out. Mikey doesn't have his connections or smooth talk, his bravado, his pure holy-shit balls, or his devilish good looks, the latter of which, Cal must admit, is his saving grace.

He glances down the street and, seeing that Mikey, the little fuck, is still nowhere in sight, continues the monologue reeling in his head to keep from flipping out from waiting so long.

So, in his little band of brothers, there's Mikey, his little buddy, this little turd ball hanging on by a hair, who might not be hanging on at all if he doesn't get here soon. Then there's Eddy, his dealer, who is farther up the food chain, ahead of Cal, but not by much, seeing as how he works the lower end of the drug trade. But Eddy's almost like family and treats him like a little brother because he dated Kay once and is still half in love with her. Cal's the way he keeps track of her, like she's some celebrity, a movie star whose poster he's tacked up on the wall of his heart that he's eager to hear the latest gossip about.

"Archaeology! No shit! I knew she was brainy, but I thought, you know, she'd be a teacher or a nurse or some such shit. A model maybe or one of those weather girls on TV, like Nicole Kidman in *To Die For*, you know. Not something fucking hardcore like archaeology!"

Then there's Stewart, his buddy from high school. They were on the wrestling team together before Cal got benched permanently for smarting off too much. They were tight even after high school when they both actually had lives—you know, jobs, cars, girlfriends. A future. They shared an apartment once, where Stew still lives. His dad owns the complex, and Stew does odd jobs for him whenever he gets out from under that cloud of smoke he lives under. His place is where Cal gets most of his pot. But he can't hang out there because Stew's dad hates his guts and won't let him on the premises.

So, Stewart, well, he's still part of his band of brothers, but he's pretty low on the food chain these days. He works the fringes, like Yolanda, where he's headed now if Mikey ever gets his ass in gear and shows up like he's supposed to.

Then there's Wanda. She's one wicked bitch—queen of Abel's Mall. She rules the streets, the hardcore homeless, the homeless by choice. He's not sure where she fits on the food chain. It's more like she's got her own food chain, and she's at the top. She's hard as nails, but she gets a kick out of Cal, likes having him hang around, hearing his sweet talk, and giving him a hard time. He helps her out too—runs errands, boosts stuff, chases the bad guys away. He hangs with her when his other prospects have dried up, when he's been reduced to hardcore street living. Which could be soon, he thinks, as he blows on his hands and wonders where the hell Mikey is.

He's about ready to stomp back into the house to call him again when Mikey comes careening around the corner in a 1974 Lincoln and pulls up to the curb.

"About time! What took you so goddamn long?" Cal turns the heater on full blast. "I about froze my nuts off out there."

"Hey, man, my auntie, she says I can't leave till I pick up all that dog shit in the back yard, and there's a ton of it. You can't believe how two little Yorkies can crap up the place like that!"

"You can't let her run you around like that. Show her what's what. Who's the man?"

"Yeah, right! You show her. She likes you. She thinks I'm some retard taking up couch space."

Cal can understand that. Mikey's not too bright, skinny as a screwdriver and about as sharp. Plus, his aunt's one of those broads who likes to throw her weight around. Literally. She's a big woman. Somehow, though, she's taken a shine to Cal, thinking he's got more going on upstairs than her nephew and hoping some of it will rub off. Besides that, like so many of these old broads, he reminds her of someone special back in the day, and more than once he's caught her giving him a look that's soft with regret. He has that effect on lots of these old gals who've seen hard times but who still harbor some unquenched longing for some young Romeo who got away. It's a different story, though, with the ones whose smooth-talking Romeo *didn't* get away, the ones who hooked them instead and reeled them in real tight. Those are the women who hate Cal at first sight. He can tell who they are right away. Their eyes dilate a fraction before their lids half close. Then they either give him a sly grin as if now it's their turn to reel him in and burn him slowly over hot coals, or else their mouths flatline like they just tasted death and want nothing to do with him. At all.

They're halfway to town before Mikey thinks to ask for the weed he was promised. Cal stalls him until they get closer to where he wants to be, fumbling through his jacket and pants pockets, then saying, "Shit! Guess I left it at home!" Mikey screeches to a halt and kicks him out after driving halfway up the curb and almost hitting some old granny walking her dog.

Cal's cool. Yolanda's apartment is only a few blocks away. He ducks into a liquor store and pinches two Debbie Cakes, stuffing them into his hoodie. Then he throws a couple of crumpled bills on the counter to pay for a pouch of tobacco. Outside, his breath is smoking from the cold. But the low-hanging sun at the end of the street spreads a cozy glow over the gray sidewalk. He likes the feel of the chill on his warm cheeks. Likes walking along the street in that golden glow knowing where he's going.

"Hey, girlfriend!" he says when Yolanda opens the door.

She's not really his girlfriend. It's what he calls all his young female friends, and they seem to like it. He knows Yolanda would like to be his girlfriend, and they have hooked up a few times, but mostly their time together is casual and impermanent. She's part of his band too, or used to be, back when she was doing blow. When she got knocked up with Gabby, she went into rehab and got her act together. They still smoke a little weed together now and then but nothing harder. Even so, she's always there for him. He still sees that yearning in her eyes when she looks up at him. Like now.

"Hey, Sweetie, what you doin' out here in the daylight—not gonna melt like a vampire, are ya?" She gives him a smooch on the cheek, welcoming him in.

He grabs hold of her, leaning her back over his arm and biting her neck with relish. She squeals and squirms loose, laughing. Her little daughter peeks around the corner to see what's going on.

"Gabby!" he says, getting down on one knee so she can run into his arms. "How's my favorite little monster doing?"

"I'm not a monster," she tells him.

"Well, that's good, 'cause I got a little something for you. See if you can find it."

She searches through all his pockets until she finds a Debbie Cake and tears off the wrapper. She's about four, small for her age, with honey brown skin, honey brown hair, and great big black eyes with the longest lashes. His heart squeezes just watching her—all that beauty and innocence rolled up together.

Cal loves kids, always has, loves looking at them, playing with them, listening to their laughter. He loves everything about them, their freshness, fearlessness, spontaneity. He loves rolling on the ground with them, getting down to their level, becoming a kid again himself, being goofy and loud, making them laugh.

How could you not like kids? How could anyone not like kids? Which always leads to that critical question: How could his dad not like kids? Not like Cal when he was a kid like this, young and innocent?

He rolls the question around in his mind, but he can find no satisfactory answer. *How could you not?*

Cal feels most like himself when he's around kids. He can drop all pretenses and defenses, all the hardness, the bitterness, the frustration, the attempts to be what he's expected to be but never can, and simply be what he knows in his heart he really is—

just a big, goofy kid, lighthearted and carefree, open and giving— when all the hard, crusty layers fall away.

He spends the rest of the afternoon with Yolanda, helping her wash dishes and fold laundry, and watching *Barney and Friends* on TV with Gabby. Then he falls asleep on the couch, the first real sleep he's had in a long, long time.

5

KAY
One Hot Thing

Kay rarely attends class now, and when she does, she wears dark glasses to hide her puffy eyes and a scarf wrapped around her neck to hide her quivering chin. She stops wearing makeup and stops washing her hair, which she rolls up inside a woolen cap and pulls down over her forehead. She's sure she looks like a terrorist, schlepping around the university with her head down, leaving abruptly when anyone approaches.

She's in mourning, she tells herself, mourning a mother she thought she knew who she now realizes she may never have truly known: A mother who always was the still center of comfort she could turn to in times like these, who is there no more. A mother who held her dysfunctional family together, a family she now fears will fall apart. The grief isn't only about losing her mother but losing everything her mother represented: family, home, security, unconditional love. It's like her mother's absence blew a hole through the center of her universe and everything is flying apart, including Kay. There's nothing left to hold onto.

But no one else is mourning. Her father's in denial, her brother beyond caring. And the grief she bears, she bears alone. Tears well up tirelessly from some deep, unknown, unplumbed source, spilling down her cheeks, her neck, her breasts. Ceaselessly. And there's nothing she can do about it.

Kay tries to staunch the grief by assuring herself her mom is fine like she said. Maybe she's taking a break from Cal. Maybe she's out having the time of her life. Maybe, as Karl suggested, she's on a cruise ship with a forty-year-old investment banker. Maybe, maybe . . .. But if any of that was true, why wouldn't she tell Kay?

When Kay was young, she thought her mother was perfect. She felt sorry for other children with their imperfect mothers who nagged and complained, who were too controlling or too smothering, the ones who worked all day and never had time for their children. The ones who were too whiney, too anxious, too critical. But her mother was never too anything. She was always just right, always what she needed when she needed it.

That's also why all this is so impossible. Women who've been married to one man their whole lives don't do this. Mothers who stay at home and play dolls with their daughters, who read them poetry and paint their toenails, don't do this.

*****

Kay avoids Karl as much as possible now. Her annoyance with him, with everything he does or says, is pushing her over the edge. She wants to scream and throw things at him. She wants to pummel him with her fists. She wants to drive him from her home. But she knows it's unfair to take out her craziness on him. So, instead, she tells him she needs some space, meaning he needs to move out until she clears her head.

Instead, he starts sleeping on the couch. He rarely talks and leaves the room when she enters. He stays late at the library studying. But he doesn't take seriously her requests for him to move out, and she finds that maddening.

One day near the end of the semester when he enters the bedroom, she's sitting in the middle of the bed surrounded by books, trying to study for her midyear exams. Instead, she's obsessing over her mother, how she may be lying in a ditch somewhere, alone, un-mourned, unburied. She eyes him, lids lowered, and scowls.

Karl takes one look at her face and squirms.

"Hey! I'm just getting my slippers!" he tells her, reaching toward where they lay beside the bed. "Then I'll disappear into the walls of the living room like a good boy."

But it's too late. By the time he rises with the slippers, she's lost it, screaming at him.

"What are you doing here? Didn't I tell you to stay away? Didn't I tell you to move out? What's wrong with you? Why are you *here!*"

As he backs away, she throws a book at him. He ducks and stumbles against the wall while she jumps down from the bed, tears the slippers from his hands, and beats his chest with them. Then she jerks open a drawer and hurls his clothes at him.

He stands there, mouth wide, speechless for once. That's when she shoves him from the bedroom, through the living room, out the front door, shouting the whole time, "Get out, get out, get out, get out, get out!"

Karl moves out the next day. She helps him pack, apologizing the whole while. She's mortified by her behavior, but beneath that, she's angry. If he had moved out on his own, she wouldn't have had to go postal.

As Karl gathers the last box in his arms and steps outside, he turns to face her.

"Look, Doll, I know you don't want to hear this, but you've got to let go of your mom. You've been dragging that big, fat umbilical cord around with you forever. To save your sanity and your career, you need to cut her loose right now."

She stares at him.

"Not her, Karl. You!"

Then she slams the door in his face.

But as she turns to look at her apartment, half empty and disheveled with his things gone, she knows he's right. She can't go on this way anymore. She has to let go.

That's when she sees the light flashing on her answering machine. Someone must have called when she was helping Karl take boxes out to his car. She hears static at first, as if the call is coming from far away, then a few blurred words, and then . . . her mother.

"Hi, Darling! Guess where I am? In Baja at that campground by the sea where we stayed when you were little. Remember? I swam out into the bay this morning when the sun was rising, swimming through swaths of pink and coral, the water like silk on my skin, weightless within a world of wonder. It was magical. Everything about this place reminds me of you—how much I love you and always will." The words feel like cool raindrops on scorched skin. Kay sinks to the floor as the tears rise, crying now not with hot heavy sobs like before but a gentle rain of relief. Her mother hasn't left her. She's still here.

A message like that comes every few days for the next two weeks, each one with soothing, healing words. Her breathless messages share choice morsels of what she sees and senses: A hawk circling and crying overhead. Lavender mountains wavering in the sunlight. An overripe papaya, hot from lying too long in the sun, melting in her mouth when she eats it. The excitement she feels crossing the Sea of Cortez on a ferry to mainland Mexico.

More than anything Kay longs to be there when the phone rings so she can talk to her mother, but it never happens. The calls always come when she's in the shower, or at the mailbox, or late at night when she is sleeping, or dreaming, or too tired, too slow, too afraid to ever answer. How can this be?

But when the calls stop, the old worry and grief return. She manages to make it to school for her midterm exams, but after that, when winter break arrives, she retreats to her apartment. She lies in bed, in the airless, semi-dark room, and cannot force herself to get up, let alone get dressed. And besides, she has nowhere to go. She wonders vaguely if she's clinically depressed and if she should call someone. But who? Her mother was always the one she called when she needed cheering up. Her best friend, stoic, practical Bethany? She'd never understand. Besides, why trouble her with all this?

She sits in bed with a box of Kleenex at her side, soggy tissues tossed everywhere. The blinds are drawn tight. Slivers of sun pierce through the edges of the narrow slats, laying razor-thin slices of light like hot knives across the crumpled bed.

The memory of her mother's voice—the slight lisp, the soft inflections, the hushed breathlessness, the wonder and reverence for all she's experiencing—is all she has to comfort her. The grieving and the comforting become one hot thing.

6

KAY
Forced Feedings

"Kay! Kay! Are you there?"

Bethany is pounding on her apartment door.

"Go away," Kay yells from her bedroom, her voice scratchy from disuse. They've known each other forever and now attend the same university. Bethany is the kind of friend who doesn't stand on ceremony, who will badger her mercilessly if she believes it's in her friend's best interest to do so. And Kay's not ready for that.

All she wants to do is sleep. She can barely force herself to get out of bed to choke down a carton of yogurt. Christmas has come and gone with no family, no celebrations, no calls from Dad or Cal—or Mom. Bethany left a message saying she and Bill were spending Christmas with his family this year and she'd see Kay when she got back. But that was it.

"Open the door!" Bethany yells now.

"Go away!" Kay answers, flopping onto her stomach and pulling the pillow over her head. But now Bethany is at the bedroom window, scratching at the screen and forcing it off. She tugs at the window, sliding it open. A leg comes through, rattling the blinds.

Kay sits up. "Are you crazy? What are you doing?"

"Damn, I'm stuck!" Bethany tells her.

Kay knows that if she tries to help, it will only encourage her, so she stays put.

"I'm stuck I tell you! Get out here and help me right now or I'm going to . . .."

Kay groans and throws back the covers. By the time she opens the front door to help her friend, Bethany has managed to wrestle her leg loose and stands there on the other side of the door, her pink face flushed with fury—till she sees Kay. Then her eyes grow wide.

"My God! Is this Kay? My Kay? What have you done to yourself?"

Bethany throws her arms around her and then thrusts her away to better examine the damage. Kay knows how she must look. Her eyes are nearly swollen shut, her lips chapped and beginning to crack, her greasy hair matted to her head.

Kay pushes her away with a groan and tries to return to bed. But Bethany won't let her. She spends the rest of the afternoon taking care of Kay, drawing a bath, washing her hair, spoon-feeding her tomato soup, and airing the apartment. When it's time to leave, she's afraid to go.

"You're not . . .?" Bethany asks, eyeing her oddly.

Kay's in bed now, her hair still damp, a cup of tea and plate of whole wheat toast on the nightstand beside her.

"Not what?"

"You know."

"What?"

"Never mind," Bethany says, taking her hand.

Kay pulls it away. "Suicidal? You think I'm suicidal?"

"It's just that . . . this isn't normal. This is too extreme."

"No! How can you think that?" Kay flings aside the covers and slips out of bed, pushing past Bethany and pacing.

"God no! I'm just . . . sad and confused and, I don't know, depressed. I finally know how people can get so severely depressed that they can't get out of bed!" She sinks down cross-legged onto the floor, burying her head in her hands.

Bethany sinks down beside her. "I know. I won't go."

"No, go. Really. I'm okay."

"You sure?" Bethany stays there beside her while Kay assures her that she's fine. Then she kisses the top of Kay's head as she rises. "I'll be back tomorrow."

"I know."

She pauses before leaving the bedroom. "You have to get up," she tells her.

"I will."

"Really."

"I will!"

But when the apartment door closes, Kay pulls down the comforter from her bed and curls up in it, liking the firm feel of the floor beneath her.

*****

Bethany returns the next day and the day after that. Each day Kay's tearful bouts are fewer and, eventually, she starts feeling more like her old self.

"Bethany, I don't know what I'd do without you. I don't think I would have made it through this. Honestly." They are in the small laundry room tucked beneath the stairwell of her apartment building, washing her bed linen.

"What are best friends for if not to force-feed them?" Bethany grins.

Kay is quiet as they fold a clean sheet into quarters and then eighths.

"Dad and Cal have no one. Dad is in denial. Cal is too angry to realize how worried he is. He must know, or suspect, that he's the reason Mom left. That's the only explanation. But how awful to know that. The guilt . . .." She feels the hot flush of tears behind her eyes.

"Well, I feel sorry for your dad. But Cal?" Bethany makes a face. "Whose fault is it if he has no one? There was a time when he could have had anyone he wanted."

Including you, Kay thinks, remembering the bad crush she had on Cal and thinking she's always been especially hard on him because of that.

"It's a sickness, Beth," she says, parroting what her mother always told her as she pulls another sheet out of the dryer. "Addiction is a sickness. It's stolen everything from him, and now you won't even give him a little compassion?"

"People recover from addiction, Kay. You have to work at it. Cal doesn't."

"You sound like my dad."

"You sound like your mother."

"She may have been right," Kay says. "Maybe she wouldn't have left if I'd helped more with Cal instead of shutting him out the way I did. Because I knew I could. She had his back. I could let go because I knew she never would."

"Well, then, where is she? If her son is so sick, so needy, where is she?"

"Don't!" Kay says, yanking the sheet from Bethany's hands and hugging it to her chest.

"I'm sorry, Kay. But you can't take over where your mother left off, enabling Cal because she's not here to do it anymore."

Kay's eyes fill with tears. "He's living on the streets, Beth! He eats from garbage cans!"

"You don't know that! There are soup kitchens, for God's sake. Don't do this to yourself. It won't help him. Besides, I thought he was still living with your dad?"

"Yeah, but for how long? Without Mom there, it can't last."

"It's not your problem."

"Maybe it is. Maybe now she's gone I should do something to help him, like you're helping me. I mean, he was always looking after me when we were little. Maybe it's my turn now to look after him?"

Bethany rolls her eyes and shakes her head.

"Let's not talk about this anymore," Kay tells her. She loads the folded linen from the counter into a laundry basket and picks it up, ready to leave.

"Okay," Bethany agrees, but instead of leaving she pushes herself up on the empty counter to sit. "Can I say something? It's not about Cal. Or your mother." She pats the space beside her, inviting her to sit too.

"What?" Kay asks cautiously, shifting the basket to her hip.

"I'm glad you dumped Karl! He was such a know-it-all and so cocky about it! He wasn't right for you."

"You never told me that!" Kay puts down her basket and scoots up beside her friend.

"I wanted to, but then I thought, would I want to know if you couldn't stand Bill? Of course not. You do like Bill, though, don't you?"

"Of course I do!"

"Well, don't tell me if you don't. It could get ugly."

Kay laughs. "You know I love Bill."

"I know, I know. Karl wasn't in his class. You need your own Bill. I don't know why you always end up with someone you know you're going to dump eventually. It's like you want to start a relationship with a built-in reason to end it."

It's true. Kay likes being in control of the relationship, knowing she's able to let go whenever she wants. She can't imagine being with someone she really cares about, leaving herself vulnerable like that. She stares glumly at the bare wall before her. "I don't want anyone. Ever."

"How can you say that? You don't mean it!"

"I *do*! How could I ever trust anyone to stick around? Especially now. After mother."

Bethany sighs and takes her hand. "Don't do this. You've got to move on. Aren't you supposed to go digging in Baja with Donner during winter break? You should be getting ready for that."

Kay pulls away her hand. "Don't you start too! Donner's flooding my inbox with emails about the trip, but I keep telling him there's no way. I don't even want to think about it!"

"Why? You always love it out there in the field. It will help get you out of this funk."

She knows Bethany's right, but the thought of leaving her apartment, leaving the landline that her mother leaves messages on, seems impossible.

That night when Kay checks her email there's another message from Donner. She types back, "I'm sorry. I can't. I'll go over spring break instead." Then she hits send, hoping that's an end to it.

When the phone rings, she jumps, knowing it's him.

"Look, I haven't been mentoring you all this time for you to bail on me. Gillespie already pulled out, and Clark is waffling. I'm shorthanded, and I need you. We leave next weekend. I'll be at your apartment on Saturday. You better be ready, Kay. I'm not kidding. Don't make me come in after you!"

7

CAL

Night Like Damp Ashes

Cal stands in the dark kitchen bathed in the cold damp light of the refrigerator, eating the last of the pizza left over from when Kay was here. Yolanda dropped him off at his parents' house before starting her midnight shift at Denny's, but he's not ready to go to bed. Instead, he's thinking about his missing mother.

Funny, he doesn't miss her like he thought he would or probably should. He's certainly not all broken up about it the way Kay is. He's reacting more like Dad—the cold-hearted bastard— indifferent and undisturbed. But he's never thought of himself as a cold person, so this surprises him. He sees himself more as the warm and sensitive type, emotional, like Mom. Maybe her disappearance hasn't struck home yet. Maybe he's still in that stage of disbelief, like his dad, thinking she'll walk through the door any day now, so you might as well take advantage of her absence while you can.

But her absence does make life more complicated. When she was around, he could always weasel a few dollars out of her or pinch a bit from her purse if he had to. He'd sweet talk her into driving him into town to buy some tobacco or to run by the day labor agency to see if anything turned up. On the way home, they'd stop by a friend's house who owed him some money. He had a shitload of friends who owed him money, or so he led her to believe. She'd be waiting in the car, fuming or praying or whatever the hell it was she did out there, while he'd be inside bullshitting with friends, getting high on their dime, or haggling for pills on spec.

When he got back in the car, there she'd be waiting, yelling at him for taking so long and swearing never to take him anywhere again. And he'd tell her he was sorry, so sorry, for making her wait, but . . . and then the bullshit would fly, always with the intent of convincing her this trip wasn't a waste of time after all. Maybe that job tip he got would pan out or maybe his friend's offer to let him move into the back room when his cousin cleared out would come true. Maybe, maybe . . . ..

Sometimes she believed him. Yet even when she didn't, he could tell she wanted to. She wanted to believe that all the time and tears she spent on him would pay off someday. And her face had that look, all open and innocent and pure, like she was created for this very thing, to keep taking all he could dish out, all his lies and his love and his bullshit. That's what a mother's heart was made for, wasn't it? To keep giving and taking and hoping as long as she had to. Because you know, you just know if you do, it has to turn out right in the end. Doesn't it?

He slams the fridge door shut and stands there in the dark, waiting for the hot, slick, sickening feel of self-disgust pass through him.

Maybe he did drive her away. Maybe it was all his fault. But it was her choice, too. She could have kicked him out anytime. Maybe if she wasn't always there for him to lean on, making the downside of addiction a little more palatable, he would have been forced to take rehab more seriously.

Or, maybe if she had kicked him out, or refused to take him in when he was at his lowest, when he had no hope left and no desire to stay this side of the grave, if he'd looked around and could not find one pair of loving eyes staring back at him, not one single soul who had not turned his back on him or thought he was worth a second thought, he'd be dead by now.

He's lost track of all the times he overdosed or come close to it. He's seen it happen to others, too—some guy lying on the floor in a pool of vomit, gray as dust. *That could be me*, he thought when it happened. *Me*. But it didn't make a bit of difference. Cal was shooting up again the next day and the dead guy was just dead.

No. It's better this way. Dad gave up on him years ago, if he ever had his back to begin with. And Mom is gone now too, clean of him at long last, as she should have been long ago.

He shakes his head and heads down the hallway. What he wants, needs, is to go to bed and forget about all this shit. But retreating to his room with nothing but his thoughts to keep him company has no appeal either.

His room. Yeah, right.

Well, it was his room once, when he and Kay were kids. Now, it's just the spare room where he's allowed to crash on an air mattress when he's in between jobs and rehabs and jail. Now it's another reminder of all he's lost, a place he dreads—no TV, no music, nothing but silent walls and the deep night beyond bearing down on him—sleepless nights filled with waking nightmares. "Night terrors," some call it.

These are nothing like the nightmares he had as a kid—a witch cackling on her broom and chasing him through a pumpkin patch or some evil-eyed vulture grabbing him by the scruff of his neck and dropping him over a cliff—nothing like these waking terrors.

Unless you've experienced this, you have no idea how terrifying it can be. It's not like you're asleep at all. It's like you're walking around in a fucking Freddy Krueger movie filled with demons and goblins and putrid filth spilling down the walls, body parts strewn across the floor, and tortured beings screaming their heads off. And you're just one of them, one of the screamers. But no one's listening, no one's coming to your rescue, and you know there's no way out. You're stuck here forever in this heart-curdling horror show. It goes on and on until you're kicking and thrashing about, and your mom's shaking you awake, and you see you're in your room again, in that flophouse that passes as a room, and only then do you know you're awake.

But *that*, my friend, is no nightmare. *That* is a living hell. And you know you're condemned to go back there again tonight if you can't manage to stay awake this time. But you will, you tell yourself. You bloody fucking well *will* stay awake.

*****

Most of October goes by with Cal managing to avoid his dad completely, leaving the house when he's out and returning when he's in bed. Sometimes it feels like he's living in some sci-fi flick where his parents have disappeared into the walls of the house, waiting and watching, while he's stumbling around in the dark, trying not to bump into and wake them. Careful, careful, he tells himself, and he is.

Other times, he's thinking he's got this licked: he and Dad in a groove, making space for each other, working it out, biding time till Mom returns. Or doesn't. Who the hell knows?

When November rolls around, he's feeling good, productive. He's spent the last two weeks painting some guy's house. Lou is one of Yolanda's big tippers looking for cheap labor so he can put his house up for sale. Some executive type who's gone off the wagon, his life crashing down around him, living way up here on the bluff with a wall of glass overlooking the valley with just a glimpse of the ocean, the tiniest whiff if you squint in the right direction.

When Cal's done for the day, he strips off the paint-spattered overalls that Lou loaned him and washes up in the bathroom. While he's there, he pokes through the medicine cabinet, looking for anything interesting, and pockets a pair of cuff links he finds in a drawer. He doesn't wear cufflinks, but hey, you never know when they might come in handy.

When he comes out, Lou is standing in front of that wall of glass, looking out. He turns when he hears Cal, like he's been waiting for him, and hands him some cash and a Michelob.

"Why don't you hang awhile tonight? I've got people coming and some nasty shit someone brought up from Tijuana. Says it will blow the fuckin' daylights out of you."

"Don't mind if I do," Cal says and lifts his bottle, clinking it against Lou's. "To the nasty shit!" he adds. Lou laughs.

Lou's a little guy with a big nose and thick glasses, but he seems to like Cal. Sees him as streetwise and savvy, someone he should stay in touch with now he's on the way down. Figures Cal must be on his way up, based purely on appearance, his Calvin Klein profile and Marlboro Man swagger, and maybe some shit he fed him about his prospects in the drug trade.

When Lou leaves to get ready for his other guests, Cal stays. He looks across the valley toward the ocean, or where the ocean would be if he could see that far, and watches the sky turn tropical colors like an ad for Bacardi Rum. He imagines a couple lying under a cabana with their feet stretched out, their toes backlit by turquoise seas. But it's Lou's face he sees there, not his.

When the sun finally goes, a sprinkling of lights flicker in the dark below to mirror the ones overhead. He stands there looking out while a party gathers steam behind him. The house is lit bright now. He can feel all that light, all that music, all that laughter, breaking behind him, like it's going to blow him away—he and the glass, splintering across the sky.

*****

Cal's not sure who gives him a ride home that night, but he waves as they drive away and then stumbles on the curb and crashes. He sits there in the damp grass, laughing at himself, at how a fucking curb could become Mt. Everest when he's totally wasted. The crystal-clear sky from earlier in the evening on the bluff is gone. The valley where he lives is covered by a thick gray blanket. The cold fog on his face feels like something physical, like flecks of damp ashes plastering his skin or wet goose feathers fluttering around him.

The house is dark and seemingly lifeless, ghostly in the fog. He figures it must be two or three in the morning. A few houses down the street already have their Christmas lights up, and it's not even Thanksgiving yet. The red and green glow is shrouded in fog.

Cal heaves himself to his feet and tries to be quiet as he grabs the latch on the front door and pushes, not wanting to wake Dad. But it's stuck. He pushes on the handle again and again, but the door won't give.

The one crazy thing about his parents, and especially his dad, him being so cynical and practical and all, is that neither ever bothers to lock the doors at night. They've lived in the neighborhood nearly their whole adult lives and never found a reason to lock up, except when they went away for the day. His mom gave Cal several keys over the years, but he could never keep track of them. Besides, he never saw the need.

He grabs hold of the cold metal handle one more time, pushes long and hard, and then stands back, staring at the door.

Fuck me! The old man finally got up enough nerve to lock me out.

Somehow this strikes him as hilarious. He can barely smother his laughter as he stumbles around the house in the dark to the side gate but finds it locked too. He nearly breaks his neck scrambling over the fence, landing on his ass in the backyard. He tries the sliding glass door, but that's locked too. Same with the French doors. Every damn door in the house is locked!

The motherfucker.

He's stone sober now. He tears off the screen on his bedroom window with his fingernails, yanks open the window, and crawls through. He grabs a backpack from the closet and starts throwing in clothes. Then he sneaks into the kitchen for beer, granola bars, and anything else he can find that's small and compact and will fit into his bag. As he's leaving, he spies the binoculars hanging by the back door and grabs them, thinking they're something he can pawn that his dad will never miss. Fuck that, he thinks again, grabbing his dad's favorite sunglasses too, knowing he'll miss those.

He decides to wait till daylight to make his escape. No sense going out into the dark and the cold with no place to go. He sits on the kitchen floor with his back against the wall and his backpack between his knees, wide awake. His mind is racing, on the hunt, planning the next move, liking the fact he's moving on, that he doesn't have to deal with Dad anymore or worry about what he's thinking, what he'll do, now that Mom's gone.

Poor little Mama. Out there somewhere. Alone in the dark and the cold. Wonder where she is?

Tears well up, hot and slick. He feels a huge swelling in his heart rising to his throat, threatening to choke him. "Fuck that," he mutters, pushing his heart down into his gut, making it a hard, tight ball, small enough and hard enough to spit out any time he wants. He scrambles to his feet, not waiting for daylight now. He flings open the front door and walks out into the night, tall and proud like a man. He leaves the door hanging wide open where any motherfucker could walk right in and steal everything in sight. "Damn right!" he says as he steps off the front stoop and disappears into the cold, damp ashes of night.

8

WALTER
Good Girl

The first credit card bill comes in October, three weeks after Franny disappears. Walter slits it open with his pocketknife like he does all his mail, sitting at the dining room table with a cup of black coffee steaming at his side. He's been up for hours. Can't sleep. Never could. Some restlessness that keeps him moving, keeps him awake.

By now he's hosed off the patio and its smoked glass table and wrought-iron chairs, hand-watered the hanging plants and boxwood bushes that line the fence, as well as the birch trees whose long limbs sweep the ground. He's refilled the hummingbird feeders, dodging the long, thin beaks that swoop at him like kamikaze pilots.

And he's stood motionless in the middle of the damp grass while the sun raised a watery face above the fence line, a face as pale as an old moon in a new sky, trying not to think of Franny.

At first when he sees the balance on the statement, he's stunned. There must be some mistake. He reads through the charges to see what's wrong. That's when he finds her. Franny. He laughs out loud—at her, at himself.

He should have realized she'd need something to stay alive, to keep gone this long. Where else would she get the money? He shakes his head.

Good girl, he thinks. Smart. Always was.

She could have cleaned out the savings account by now, but she didn't. She put it all on credit instead, knowing he'd pay it off. It's her way of staying in touch, letting him know where she's been, that she's okay, letting him know she trusts him to keep taking care of her like he's always done.

"Good girl," he says aloud now, softly. A weight that's been crushing his shoulders, which he hadn't realized he was carrying until now, begins to lighten.

He studies the bill. She starts by filling her tank in Ventura then again near Ensenada. She stays a few days at a hotel there, where she takes out three hundred dollars in pesos. Then she stays a day or two each in San Quintin and San Ignacio, then another week in Mulegé. It looks like she's headed south where it's warm, like she likes.

She loved that time they went camping at Conception Bay in Baja. The kids did too, but it was too damn hot for him. Only the early mornings and evenings he enjoyed, being out there on the water fishing in that little skiff he rented. Even Cal seemed to like that the few times he let him tag along—all that pent-up energy contained in the anticipation of catching another fish. Who knew Cal could sit still and be quiet that long? He was a puzzle, his son. Maybe more fishing would have done him good, like it did Walter when he used to go out with his granddad up north, where it was cool, before he died. Sometimes Walter thinks he and Cal may be more alike than you'd think at first glance: both restless, easy to rile, no patience. Only Walter learned to contain all that, for the most part, and Cal never could. That's what frustrated, and at times enraged, Walter—his own inability to still his son, to make him do what he wanted, what he knew was right. It was hard enough to keep himself stilled, contained, without another person to worry about. Better to leave him in Franny's care and step away. Safer for all of them.

But where is she now? He digs out an old National Geographic map of Central and South America and pins it on the garage wall. He sticks push pins into each place she's been, drawing a line with a red marker to connect the dots. He stands back to survey his handiwork.

Over the next few months as each new bill arrives, he tries to guess where she'll go next. Sometimes he's right, but mostly he's wrong, and she turns up in places off track, or even backtracked, traveling in circles. He wonders if she's lost or even if it's Franny he's tracking. Maybe it's some maniac who stole her car and credit cards, leaving her lying somewhere beside the road. But no. The camera purchase, the film, the books, even the backtracking, circling—that's Franny all over.

Somehow, it's comforting, knowing where she's been, guessing where she's headed, and wondering what drives her to leave one place and go to another. He pays each bill on time and makes sure there's plenty of credit for her to draw on. It never occurs to him to cancel the card.

But he worries about her—mostly about her getting lost, stranded somewhere along the side of the road, trying to get her car fixed and nobody there to help. He's been taking care of Franny since she graduated from high school, and he got home from Vietnam. He put her through college while he worked as a welder and even had his own shop once. Sometimes she helped in the shop, answering the phone, keeping records. When she grew bored, she went back to what she did best, minding the kids and the house.

He never minded that she didn't work. Why should he? He earned enough on his own. She worked part-time at a bookstore once and helped fundraise for an animal shelter. Sometimes, she took classes at the local college—art, photography, cooking. She always had something new to show for her efforts—a watercolor of lemons in a blue bowl hanging in the dining room, black-and-white photos of the Grand Canyon she took when they visited there, matted and framed, lining the hallway walls.

She's a dabbler. That's how he sees it. He's always been proud of the way she takes an interest in things beyond anything he cares about. That was her world, that and the kids. The shop was his, the cars and yard.

In a way, he sees this little adventure she's taking as more of the same. She's farther away from home—that's a fact—but still it's more evidence of her curious nature about the world, wanting a taste of this, a sip of that, trying it all on for herself to see how it fits. At least, that's what he tells himself. What he tries to hang onto when her absence starts to rattle like a skeleton in a cage trying to get out.

But in the end, she always comes home to him, doesn't she? He knows there's no stopping her, and why should he? He's never tried to stop her before from doing anything she wanted. He just has to keep letting the rope out more, giving her as much lead as she needs, and then, when she's ready, she'll find her way home again. It's what he tells himself, what he needs to believe to get through the day.

He was only twenty when he met her, a young Marine on leave from Vietnam with one more year to serve. She was a senior in high school on spring break. He borrowed a buddy's Yamaha 360 so he could ride her up into the hills above Highway 1, where the wildflowers were spreading carpets of gold and lavender across the fields. They parked beside the road and climbed a fence, wading hand in hand through the wild poppies like they were parting seas of gold. They climbed until they reached a spot where the purple lupine showed through the green grass. He lay against the hillside, all that blue overhead, and shut his eyes. There was nothing but stillness and a warm wind stirring the grasses, stirring the hot, spicy scent of the lupine baking in the sun. She sat beside him, her fingers lightly brushing his forehead, making trails through his hair, sending electric sparks through his scalp. He reached up and brought her down on him, her head lying on his heart, the sweet scent of her hair overcoming all else.

Through all the battles that lay ahead, when the scent of sulfur from burnt carbon was thick enough to choke a man, and the rat-a-tat-tat of gunfire fell all around him, the buzz so close he was sure it must have shot straight through his brain, he felt her, her head on his heart.

"Not now," she told him when he tried to turn himself upon her that day in the poppies. "When you get back," she said, lying there beside him, her fingers tracing his face. "I'll wait for you."

He provided for her the best he could when he got back—a home, a living, security. He did so feeling, even then, it would never be good enough, not for someone who deserved better than him, even if she never knew it. Or maybe she always did know? Maybe that's why she left? Looking for something that isn't him. Anyway, she's gone now.

It's his turn to wait for her and take care of her the best he can in the meantime.

*****

The first package arrives in December: a flat, padded manila envelope that says "Photos—do not bend" in red ink. It's addressed to Cal, written in big, blocky, childlike letters—Franny's hand. He would know her handwriting anywhere, the worst he's ever seen. If she didn't print, no one would be able to read it. He chuckles. Then he puts the package on the table, smooths it with his hand, and lifts it to his face to better read the postal stamp. La Paz, it looks like. She's still heading south. He weighs it in his hand, gives it a long, hard sniff, then checks the back seals and tests it with a finger. Tight. He puts it down. He can't quite tear himself away from it, sitting there on the table. He wonders where Cal is so he can open it. Same place as his sunglasses and binoculars, he supposes.

Cal's gone missing too—around Thanksgiving, he thinks. One day he looks around and can't remember the last time he saw him. Not that they saw much of each other, even when he was here. They learned the hard way it made for a more peaceful coexistence when they gave each other plenty of room. It's better this way, his leaving, being on his own. Franny always coddled him too much. And look how that turned out.

Franny. He sure misses that girl. Sometimes he envies her, out on the road like that. He's been contemplating an early retirement for some time now. With the cash in his pension, he could go into business for himself again. He liked that, having his own welding shop, watching something he built himself grow. But it never brought in as much as his union job as a foreman, so he gave it up. Or maybe he'll keep the pension and sell the rental he inherited from his grandma. Maybe he'll move up to Alaska, build a cabin and go fishing again where it's cool, not hot. That's where his grandpa took him on their last fishing trip before he died—Moosehead Lake, not far from Luther, Alaska. He still remembers how clean and fresh it smelled up there in the pines, the dark trees reflected in the cold water where he dipped his fingers.

He puts the package on the fireplace mantel where Cal's likely to find it, should he ever come home again. By the time he does, there's a pile of unopened envelopes, one arriving every week or so over the next three months.

9

KAY
The Scent of Rocks

Kay leans against the backseat of Donner's station wagon, gazing out the side window. Freddy is sleeping beside her, his head thrown back, his snores coming in little huffs and hiccups. In the front seat, Donner and Raymond carry on a low-key conversation that blends with the hum of the engine. Following behind them in a pickup is the rest of their team, Clark and Robin, carrying the camping gear and equipment needed for the dig.

They've been driving since early morning, watching the city rooflines and freeway snarls of southern California give way to the hillside slums and congested streets of the border towns. Eventually, these fade away, too, and long stretches of desert and the distant hills of Baja Sur open before them.

She's glad Donner insisted she go on the dig now. She still hates leaving her landline in case Mom calls, but at least her dad is keeping track of her through her purchases. As long as they keep coming, she knows she's alive. She leans forward eagerly as they travel deeper into Baja and looks out the window between the shoulders of the men in front of her.

Did her mother pass this way, too, before crossing to the mainland? Has this winding road, that abandoned ranch house, those barren mountains melted into her mother's memories as they will hers? Just the thought of her having seen all this too steadies Kay, allows her to breathe more deeply, and makes her mind grow easier.

She watches the road and the surrounding desert unfurl before her as if she's looking at a map. The Baja peninsula is narrow and jagged like a knife, splitting the tranquil waters of the Sea of Cortez from the energetic upheaving of the Pacific Ocean. Humans migrated here from Eurasia on a land bridge soon after the Ice Age. They traveled from Alaska past her home on the Central Coast and into Baja, leaving bits and pieces of their lives scattered from one end to the other.

For Kay the most interesting archeological sites are the burial caves and rock paintings. Mother-of-pearl ornaments, coiled baskets, wooden ceremonial tablets inlaid with shark's teeth, among other artifacts, have been found in the burial caves along with the bodies—elongated skulls wrapped in palm fronds or animal hides and skeletons with red, ocher-stained bones. The bodies were de-fleshed so the bones could be painted, but no one knows why. Some think these inhabitants may have migrated from as far away as the Melanesian Islands because of similarities between skull findings. But no one knows for sure.

The same is true for rock paintings. Most are simple geometric designs—lines and dots, ovals with slashes drawn through them. Some are handprints, sometimes single prints widely spaced, sometimes multiple prints overlapping each other. But further south from their destination are huge, elaborate black-and-red murals with oversized images of animals and humans. Local tribespeople told the early Spanish explorers that these were drawn by giants from the north. Today archaeologists are no wiser in their speculations.

So much in the study of archaeology is speculative, open to revision, provisional at best. Like everything else, Kay thinks. You can gather all the bones and artifacts, all the hard evidence of someone's life in your hands, but what do you ever know of their heart or mind? You can piece together some of the puzzle and speculate about what's missing—but that's what it remains—

pieces, not the whole; speculation, not the truth. And even then, what they piece together is slanted by the perspective of those searching, limited by their life experiences, the questions they ask and fail to ask, the depth of their quest and reach of their vision, the keenness of their need to know and their fear of what they don't know.

Their destination is the Piedra Pintada, a rock painting deep in the heart of the cape at Cabo de San Pablo. They opened an excavation pit beneath the ledge of the rock two years ago, and now they will go deeper. Donner has staked his reputation on this site, and Kay has helped with the research.

Kay has entered a new area of archaeological research for her thesis project—the identification of carbonized plant remains. Donner will give her a few days before they leave to continue her work of collecting flowers, fruits, seeds, nuts, and other native plants in the area to press. Later she will char them and compare them under a high-powered microscope with the pollen fossils found buried in ancient campsites and earthen ovens. This will reveal not only the diet of these ancient people but also, and perhaps more importantly, how the vegetation and therefore the climate has changed over time. It's not as sexy as studying rock paintings and burial sites, but it's an emerging field that will help boost her credentials and opportunities for employment when she graduates.

When they reach Rancho Viejo, their dig site, Don Pablo and Doña Flora welcome them back. They live here with a large extended family—brothers and sisters, nephews and nieces, cousins and grandchildren. They grow most of their own food and raise pigs, goats, and chickens. The stipend they receive from the university for access to the dig site is an important part of their income. In addition, Donner pays them to prepare their evening meals during their stay. The two men greet each other with hearty hugs. Donner speaks fluent Spanish, but Kay's is woefully limited. Doña Flora smiles warmly at Kay, taking her hand and squeezing it affectionately. Coming behind her grandmother is Martina, one of the twins Kay befriended the last time she visited. Martina practices her English on Kay as they link arms and head up the hill toward the kitchen, where her sister Marta is making something special for dinner.

Sides of pork, rolls of homemade sausages, and strips of drying venison hang from the kitchen rafters as they enter. A rich, chocolaty aroma rises from one of the pots simmering on a tripod above the fireplace where Marta is stirring. Shyly, she lifts a spoonful of the sweet and spicy sauce for Kay to taste. "*Mole poblano*," she tells her. Kay moans with delight, and the girls giggle.

After a restless night beneath the orange dome of her pup tent, Kay wakes, weary and groggy. The weak coffee Freddy hands her does little to rouse her. She nibbles a dry granola bar and watches the mist rise from the arroyo below them while the men fry up bacon and eggs on a camp stove. But by the time she's helped uncover the pit and climbed inside the five-foot hole, beginning the slow, meticulous process of brushing back layer upon layer of earth, her weariness evaporates.

Whenever she's at the rancho, she feels like she's stepped back two hundred years. But here, deep in the pit, alone, as she is now, slowing brushing away centuries of packed earth, she loses track of time itself, as if it's peeled back and floated away. Thousands of years roll by while uncovering, as she did last year, tiny beads made from oyster shells by women who lived here before Caesar ruled Rome. She wouldn't be surprised to find when she looks up to that square patch of sky overhead the painted faces of Martina's ancestors staring down at her or the helmeted heads of Spanish explorers.

A time traveler is what she is, uncovering fragments of people's lives, most of them from the dust heap of their days, trying to decipher who they were from the things they threw away, lost, or abandoned—from the absence, not the presence, of things.

But this sifting through forgotten fragments, piecing together competing possibilities, isn't limited to archaeology, Kay realizes. This endless, tedious, tenuous effort to piece things together to make sense of our lives and each other is what we all do all the time. We fill in the blanks and blind spots and absences with questions, hypotheses, educated guesses—theories strung out and glued together from fragments of our past and shifting memories.

After an hour in the pit, slowly, meticulously brushing away the earth, the surface of a smooth, round stone emerges. Her heartbeat quickens. It might be something significant, part of a circle of hearth stones perhaps, or a mano for milling grain, and she's tempted to tease the stone loose quickly to see what it is. But she can't. She must slowly, patiently brush away the earth until the stone is completely uncovered before examining it further.

At last, she holds the stone in her hands—round, unmarked, like any stone you might come across in some dry riverbed. She lifts it to her nose to sniff, remembering when she and Cal used to gather stones like these near their home.

One summer when they were still in grade school, Mom took her and Cal to a rock and mineral show at the fairgrounds where they walked between long lines of tables filled with all sorts of colorful gems and rocks—blue agate, ruby sapphire, dark green jade, gold pyrite. Kay was fascinated by how rocks that looked dull and ordinary on the outside, when cracked open, revealed hidden treasures: brilliant veins of red and green, silver and gold, dazzling flecks of light. Some were filled with bright, sharp-edged crystals like Superman's cave of Kryptonite. Others contained the skeletal remains of creatures that lived long ago—delicate etchings of butterfly wings, tiny grasshopper legs, scalloped shells, and the fine cross-hatchings of fish bones. Who knew the insides of things, of plain gray rocks of no distinction, could sparkle like stars or gleam like a deep-sea garden? She was entranced.

After the show, she and Cal spent that summer rock hunting in the dry riverbed near their home, searching for hidden treasure. Cal led their excursions because he was ten, three years older than Kay, and besides, he had the hammer and chisel stolen with much trepidation from Dad's garage, so it was his due. She trailed behind him in her flip-flops, carrying a large tin pail and shovel she used on outings to the beach. She wore oversized sunglasses with heart-shaped, hot-pink frames, the kind cute little girls wore back then to make people smile and think she's got attitude. Wearing them made her feel special and grown-up.

Cal was the serious hunter—no cute sunglasses or flip-flops for him. He wore high tops with serious soles like tread on a big rig, no socks, cut-off jeans, and a stretchy tank top. He looked like a bloodhound the way he raced along the riverbed, nose pointed to the ground, sniffing and grunting, leaping over fallen logs or dodging boulders tumbled down from high in the hills.

They'd dig along the riverbanks and bottom for promising rocks of a particular size and heft, then gather them in a pile and sit cross-legged, taking turns cracking them open. First Cal, and then Kay, would put a rock between their legs and place the chisel just so—the way the man at the show showed them—then tap, tap, tap with the hammer on the chisel until *crack*! The rock split open. But one after the other, time and time again, there was nothing to show for their effort but disappointment. The insides were no better than the outsides, and some rocks crumbled in their hands like clods of dirt rather than proper rocks at all.

"This is stupid," Cal said after spending a week out there in the riverbed, gazing at the pile of rocks between them. "We might as well give up."

Kay hated seeing him look so dejected. "There's only a few left. We might as well try those."

He sighed and took up one more rock. Tap, tap, tap, he went, his nose stuck down close to the business at hand until the rock fell apart. Then his head shot back.

"Whoa!" he said, throwing her a startled look. "Smell this!" He thrust the stone beneath her nose.

For the briefest moment she caught a scent like sour apples.

"Did you smell it?" He sniffed again. "It's gone!"

She tried too and, sure enough, the smell was gone.

He took another rock from the pile, cracked it open, and gave it a strong sniff, quickly passing it on to her.

"Not apples," she said.

"No," Cal agreed. "More like—"

"Burnt toast!"

"Yes!"

It became an obsession after that—roaming through the riverbed, hunting for rocks to crack open and sniff, like it was their own little high, like they'd become addicted to the smell of rocks. Sometimes they agreed on the scent—cinnamon, hot tar, pine trees. Sometimes they couldn't tell—it was just sweet or metallic or pungent. Each was distinct. Each lasted only seconds.

It was like a whiff of air when the world was new, like the scent of a new car before it gets used up or the smell of sun-dried sheets before they get laid on. They were trying to hold onto something never meant to last more than a few seconds. So, the only way they could try to grasp it, to get that holding-onto feeling, was to do it over and over as quickly as possible, creating an illusion of duration for as long as the rock pile lasted.

Their fascination with the fragrance of rocks lasted much longer than that one summer. For Kay, finding the wonder of things hidden in the earth led to her interest in archaeology, in digging deep into the earth to discover hidden treasures, clues about people who lived long ago.

But Cal's obsession took him in a different direction. When the summer passed, he graduated to smelling moldy leaves, old socks, gasoline fumes, and paper glue. If the fragrance of rocks could create such a sensation of elation and wonder, what might other smells elicit? Soon it wasn't the smell of things he was addicted to but the hunt for that knock-your-socks-off whiff of something new and exciting, like the scent they first shared.

She should have known, Kay thinks now, leaning back on her heels in the pit, her brush still in her hand, that Cal, once obsessed with something, would never curb his appetite for it. There were obvious hints she should have seen, like that tap-tap-tap of the hammer, no more, no less. He tapped the light switch three times before turning it off and on, touched the doorknob three times before opening or closing, kissed Kay three times before going to bed—first on the right eye, then the left eye, then the nose, always in that order. If she tried to run away before he could complete the cycle, he'd chase her down and deliver those missing kisses with a vengeance. If Dad pulled him up by the elbow before he touched the door three times, he'd be in a fury the rest of the day, touching everything in sight three times as if to make up for it, but it never worked. The panic in his eyes then was something serious. This compulsive behavior—needing to do everything three times—only lasted a few years, but the addictive aspect of it never ended. In the end, it wasn't the craving for the new and unexpected, the ultimate high, that was self-destructive. It was the inability to cease some comforting habit once started.

How strange that magical summer would become a defining moment in both their lives and lead them in such different directions—her to archaeology, him to heroin—both searching incessantly for that mysterious something hidden at the core when things cracked open fall apart.

10

KAY

Split Wide Open

By the end of the week, Kay is exhausted, her back and knees sore. Donner gives her the next two days to work on her carbon-dating project before they head back to the States. Miguel, one of Don Pablo's grandsons, will be her guide and lead a pack burro loaded with the plant press, pup tent, and provisions up the canyon. Kay immediately likes Miguel, a young man in his early twenties. His sweet smile and soft laugh remind her of Marta, the shyer of the twins.

As they leave camp and head up the arroyo, Kay's exhaustion gives way to exhilaration. At first Miguel leads with the burro beside him. She watches them as they climb, the young man's broad back, the burro's rhythmic rump, short tail twitching. The canyon walls rising above the creek are high and rocky, peppered with cactus and thorny succulents. But the path upstream is lined with wild fig and date palm trees, fragrant spears of blue lupine, and spiny redberry. Soon she takes the lead as she searches for plants, cuts and bags them, and marks their locations.

When they stop so she can press the plants before they wilt, Miguel sits on his haunches watching her as if fascinated. She tries explaining in her broken Spanish what she's doing, and then apologizes that her grasp of his language is so poor. He politely disagrees, saying her Spanish is excellent. She laughs and tells him that's not true. He insists it is with a look of mock offense that softens into a grin. She grins back, liking the way he looks at her, open and attentive.

As they continue hiking up the canyon, she's acutely conscious of his presence behind her, watching her now as she watched him before. He's always there, a few steps behind, like a shadow self who, when she turns to look, is gazing at her—his wide, round face like a reflection in a dark pool. His silent presence becomes a constant conscious awareness—the feel of him there behind her at the periphery of her vision.

Soon, it's not only him she feels. A hyperawareness envelops her and accentuates everything around her—the crunch of her boots struggling up the rocky gorge, the pungent odor of the prickly leaves she gathers and presses, the warmth of the hot sun on her face, and the slipperiness between her breasts, her thighs, her knees when she kneels. All of it—these sensations and the surrounding scenery, even the wide watchful sky bending over her—presses upon her like a larger skin.

The creek has broadened now, filled with mammoth boulders and deep still pools between rippling cascades of cold, sweet water. They stop often to refill their canteens. As the sun sinks behind the canyon walls, darkness descends quickly. Miguel scouts out a place to camp and pitches her tent beneath a tall, spreading oak. He cobbles the burro and unpacks the provisions. Kay takes a towel and bar of soap from her bag and shows Miguel, pointing to the river. He nods and turns back to his work.

She sits on a low, broad rock near the bank, removing her boots and socks and soaking her hot feet in the cool water. She wishes she could strip and immerse herself but resists out of modesty for Miguel's sake. Instead, she splashes the water up her arms and down between her breasts. When she turns to leave, she's startled to find Miguel standing on the bank behind her, his face turned away. Has he been here all this time? Thank God she didn't strip! But she's disappointed in him too. She frowns as she moves past him. He grabs her wrist, stopping her.

"*Venga*," he says, motioning for her to follow him as he turns upriver. He paces near the bank, searching for something, and then squats. There in the mud are huge paw prints.

"Jesus!" Kay cries, hand flying to mouth. A mountain lion, it must be.

She looks up at Miguel. He's been standing guard, not spying but protecting her. Looking at the paw prints, he nods solemnly, saying something she can't understand. Then he grins and says something else. She only understands the words "*no dinero*," no money. By the twinkle in his eyes, she guesses he's making some kind of joke at her expense—maybe something about how, if she were eaten, he would not be paid. She smiles. He's trying to lighten the mood, so she won't be afraid.

When they return to camp, he builds a small fire and heats the stew Marta packed for them. They eat their meal in small tin bowls with hunks of bread he has broken from a loaf. Later, he makes coffee. By then it's nearly dark, the sky a deep violet between the dusky green oak leaves. A sudden exhaustion settles over her, and she excuses herself, crawling into the small pup tent, slipping out of her clothes and into her sleeping bag.

She listens to Miguel moving around outside, doing whatever he's doing, washing dishes, she supposes, repacking provisions, making sure the burro is safely tethered for the night. She imagines him rolling up in blankets and sleeping outside her tent to protect her from any lingering mountain lions.

She listens to the river now with its continual rushing. Everything sounds so much louder in the dark than in the day: the haunting hoot of a nearby owl, a raucous twittering in the tree branches overhead, and something else. What is it? Miguel! Snoring already. She almost laughs, considering how comforting the sound is coming from her protector.

His soft snores and the rushing river, the rustling of leaves and creaking boughs in the breeze wash together in her mind. Before she falls asleep, she realizes she hasn't thought of her mother in days.

*****

The next day they move away from the river into the foothills to find the rest of the plant specimens she needs before heading back to the ranch. The climb is steep, but the burro seems to know how to find the easiest path, so they follow him. They reach the ridge, and she stops to catch her breath, looking down at the steepness of their climb and the winding river winking in the sun far below.

Miguel stands beside her, surveying the land.

"*Venga*," he tells her, gesturing for her to follow. They hike along the ridge and then descend through a gully that opens into a small rocky enclave. He heads toward the largest live oak Kay has ever seen.

As she walks below the tangled branches, her feet sink into the earth beneath, covered with who knows how many layers of decaying leaves. The canopy spreading above her head is so high and dense it blocks the sun. Thick, massive branches reach out in all directions, curling upward like the waving arms of some giant, upended octopus. The trunk is huge. Her arms spread wide cannot span the width of it. She read somewhere how the hug-spans of ancient oaks reveal their age. This one, five hug-spans at least, would make it one of the oldest oak trees on record. She presses her cheek against the rough bark, breathing in the strong, musky scent and imagines she hears the rush of centuries passing through its sap. Its roots are spread so wide they must have touched the roots of the other, more ancient, oaks from which it sprang, the ones that sheltered it as a sapling, going back to a time when the people she is studying still roamed these hills. She pictures them here now, gathering the acorns that sustain them and looking out across the hills and down to the river below, as Miguel does now.

But he's impatient, his face tells her. Apparently, this ancient oak is not what he's brought her to see after all. What could be more marvelous than this giant tree? He leads her to the large rock outcropping, where one tall monolith stands next to a mammoth stone whose hunched back is rough and scarred. They walk around the edges of the stones, holding onto the sides, for the way is steep here as it leans downhill. Soon they pass beneath a small ledge that opens into a deep cave. She reaches for a flashlight in her pack, but Miguel already has a torch of sap-soaked rags wrapped around a thick branch, prepared, no doubt, while she was busy marveling at the ancient oak. He lights the torch now and ducks beneath the lip and into the belly of the cavern. She follows.

The cave is higher than she imagined it would be but not as deep as first thought. He leads her to the far wall and lifts the light. Red ocher handprints climb the wall and spread onto the ceiling. The lower prints are no larger than her own—a woman or youth. But as they climb higher, the handprints grow smaller, half the size of her own, the prints of a small child. A shiver tickles her spine, realizing at once what an extraordinary find this is.

She laughs and claps her hands, turning toward Miguel. She's so happy and grateful, she grabs him by the shoulders and kisses him hard and fierce on the lips. She's surprised by the softness of his lips, the sharpness of his teeth. He jerks back, startled. His hand touches his mouth, as if to cover her indiscretion or hold the kiss closer beneath his fingertips. For a moment, she doesn't know what to do. She's as startled by the kiss as he is yet still reeling with excitement from the find.

"I'm sorry! So sorry!" she says, wringing her hands. "I'm just so happy," she explains.

He laughs. "*De nada,*" it's nothing, he tells her.

Relieved, she turns back to the handprints on the wall and presses her hand against the surface, as if to capture the thrill of it. She tries to imagine how these handprints must have been created. She pictures a young mother leading her child by the hand into the cave, dipping her tiny fingers into the red ocher, and then lifting her into her arms and onto her shoulders. There the child presses her hand against the cold stone over and over until only the ghost of an imprint remains on the last one. All the while, the mother is whispering into her daughter's ear whatever mothers say when initiating their children into the mysteries of the world.

Kay pulls a notebook from her backpack and sketches their findings. Then she leaves the cave and sits on the hillside, looking down at the river and up toward the ancient oak, triangulating their position and drawing a small map so she can lead Donner back here. How excited he will be, even though it will be years before they have the funds, let alone the necessary approval, to excavate this site. Miguel kneels beside her, watching. Then he places his hands on hers and looks her in the eye as he slowly draws the notebook away and tears off the map.

"What are you doing?" she asks, even though she knows already. He doesn't want her to share this find with others.

"But why?"

He rolls the paper into a scroll and puts it into his back pocket.

"*Porque?*" she repeats in Spanish, but he only shakes his head and says something she cannot understand. He takes hold of the burro's reins and heads down through the thicket toward the river. She has no choice but to follow.

How will she be able to find this place again without Miguel, without a map? What will she tell Donner? Should she say anything at all? Does she have the right to show others what Miguel showed her in confidence? Maybe what they found today should remain hidden here in the hills, guarded by the ancient oak, undisturbed.

They head back toward the river now, retracing their steps down the hillside and into the canyon. She can't let loose the feel of that young mother's hand holding onto her daughter as she led her into that cave so long ago, or the thought they might have trod this very path on their way there, breathing in the same scent of lavender and sage, hearing the wash of the river against these very rocks.

Kay has taken the lead now and feels Miguel behind her, his eyes rubbing against the small of her back, the metallic taste of his tongue still in her mouth. She feels spread out, elastic, like there's no end to her, no hard edges to hold back the world. It's all folding in around her, all melding together.

They come to a deep pool backed by giant boulders, some standing upright like silent sentinels, others lying on their sides like sleeping giants. The sun is low, skirting the top of the canyon wall, and when she looks at Miguel, he's all dark shadow pressed against the light behind him.

Sitting on the bank of the pool, she removes her boots and socks and wades out into the cool water, leaning forward to splash it on her arms, her face and neck. Then she wades further, thigh deep. She feels Miguel watching her and turns to look, but he's only a dark silhouette now, one leg thrust forward, hand on hip. She watches him as he watches her and then wades deeper into the pool. She unbuttons her shirt and removes it, unclasps her bra, leans against a tall rock to step out of her shorts, peels away her panties, and lays her clothes on a flat boulder.

She glides through the cool water, swimming slowly, each breaststroke long and languorous. Then she dives under, down to the cool, smooth stones lying at the bottom of the pool, slick with moss and leaves. She holds her breath for as long as she can as she glides through the cool grasses growing along the bottom of the pool.

She wishes this could last forever, this stillness, this deep, abiding peace where she feels part of everything around her. Her mother always gave off a scent of this, like she tapped into it somewhere and carried it home with her. Kay wishes she could do that too. Maybe it's not her mother she needs, but to find what she found.

When she surfaces, Miguel is no longer there, sweet Miguel with the shy smile and laughing eyes. Everything has been shed of its past. Only rock, river, man, woman remain. He has shed his clothes, too, and is gliding toward her. He touches her shoulders tentatively at first, then his hands slide down her arms, around her waist, over her hips. She wraps her legs around him. Even in the cool water, his flesh feels hot beneath her fingers, his shoulders and arms thick and hard.

He carries her to a flat rock and lifts her on it. The rock, still hot from the sun, cools beneath the wetness of her body. His dark face and shoulders rise above her, silhouetted against the sky. Overhead a hawk is circling, circling, its sharp wings cutting through the air. Man, woman, hawk. Sky, river, rock. All roll into one.

As he enters, she breaks apart. Something ineffably sweet rises out of her.

11

CAL
Running with Wolves

Cal shivers. Rain drips from his nose as he gazes across the street at the house he once called home. It's been raining for weeks now, sometimes a soft drizzle like today, sometimes a steady drum like that's the nature of things, the way things are and ever will be for time out of mind. And sometimes the rain whips the world so hard you think everything will break loose and blow away for good.

It feels strange standing here, looking at the old homestead through this grainy haze of drizzle, as if watching a home movie of his childhood. He can see himself there now, tearing up the sidewalk on his big wheel, wrestling with his friends on the lawn, pulling Kay in that little red wagon she loved so much.

He remembers a photo his mother took of them back when they were young and innocent. She must have been standing right here, where he is now, to fit them all in the viewfinder. He sees them now—Kay in her wagon with her skinny pale knees drawn up to her chin, that grin on her face, that short dark hair like a helmet on her head. And him, freckle-faced and rowdy looking even then, pulling the wagon while looking across the street at his mom. His head is cocked and mouth flap open, spouting some sass, no doubt. His skinny little body pulls at that wagon, straining, as if what he carries behind him is a mighty heavy load, leaning so far forward as to fall flat on his face if the handle slips. And he doesn't know now if the wagon really was that heavy or if he was making it seem so for comic effect.

Standing behind them on the lawn is his dad with that perpetual beer in his hand. The one he always seemed to have when they took family photos, holding it up to the camera, as if saying, *Hey there, here's us having a good time, and don't you forget it—* the happy family at home.

Only his father didn't look happy wearing that horseshoe mustache, the ends dragging down his face like a perpetual frown. He wore it all through the 70s and 80s, the whole time Cal was growing up. It comes as a revelation to him now how, as a kid, he could never tell when his dad was smiling, when he was happy or sad or mad, because that damn mustache hid half his face.

He got so he watched his dad's eyes to see what was going on in his head. Were his eyes dark and cold, or tired and empty, or brown and warm? Was the light on or off? What was really weird was when Dad finally shaved off the mustache, it was days before anyone noticed. They all knew something didn't look right but couldn't figure out what was missing.

Cal reaches up to his face now and realizes for the first time he's been growing the same kind of mustache his old man had when he was young like him.

How did he miss that? How did he miss so much?

*****

Cal's been living on the street for three months now. Thanksgiving, Christmas, New Year's Day—all gone. All the holidays that meant so much to Mom, that enabled her to pretend they were all one happy family together, now gone.

At first it wasn't too bad being out on the streets again—it's not like it was his first time. He knew the ropes. There's something exciting, almost primal, about being here again, the adrenalin pumping through his blood, not knowing when his next meal would come, where he'd lay his head down that night, who he'd bump up against, and what the exchange might be. Always sniffing the air for hints of danger and opportunity, gauging the situation and becoming whatever was needed to turn things to his advantage—the hunter on the hunt.

People like him with ADHD are hunters at heart, from the old school before people started domesticating things. He read that somewhere. You needed to be hyper back then, always scanning the horizon, seeing everything at once and not zeroing in on anything unless it posed a danger or an opportunity. People like him were the dominant race then, the ones who survived— until the farmers took over and ruined everything. Built tiny houses to suffocate you, schools to teach you to be drones, to keep you hobbled, keep you still in your seat where you can't move, can't breathe, can't think, and all you want is out. Out into the fresh air and the wind, running with the wolves, pulling down deer and rams, gutting them and drinking with holy relish the life-giving blood.

After he left home that night his dad locked him out, he called Mikey, asking if he could lay over at his home for a while.

"Shit, I'm living on my auntie's couch! How I'm supposed to put you up?"

"Your auntie loves me. She'll let me stay a few days."

He managed to stay at Auntie's house for four nights before she started dropping hints for him to move on. He squeezed out another three nights till she told him she didn't want to have to call the cops, but hey, you know.

He spent the following two weeks sleeping over at people's houses, begging for space on the couch or floor, once on an old lounge chair on someone's back patio. But eventually, everyone stopped answering the doorbell when he showed up.

He tried staying with Yolanda, but she wouldn't let him in the door. Her old man, Gabby's daddy, was back in the scene, and she was trying to make a go of it with him.

"You know he ain't sticking around for long!" Cal told her. "You're too good for him, you and Gabby. You should let me stay. We've always got along real good. Haven't we?"

She gave him a sad little smile and kept the door halfway shut.

"Look at you, Cal! What're you doing to yourself? When was the last time you ate? Or washed your clothes? C'mon!"

"I need a little mama like you to set me right. You know that. That's what you always told me."

She shook her head. "Go on now before Gabby hears you. I gotta try to make it work with her daddy. For Gabby's sake."

Stewart wasn't feeling him either. His dad got him cleaned up, and he started a new job. He couldn't risk letting Cal stay. He handed him a couple of twenties and looked away, like Cal had already disappeared from his life and just didn't know it.

Sometimes he got Eddy to front him enough dope to sell so he could put himself up in a motel for a few nights. But that didn't last long. When he failed to deliver the goods, Eddy went on the warpath, so he steered clear of him.

So, he headed down to Abel's Mall to check in with Wanda, the last of his band of brothers who he turned to when he was scraping the bottom of the barrel. But he couldn't find her anywhere. Gideon had taken took over her corner, a big black sonofabitch with a bad eye, who's not right in the head: Vietnam vet, his dad's age, three fingers missing on his left hand. He was in Wasco, the last Cal heard, doing hard time. Not sure when he got out or why. This used to be his corner before he was sent away and Wanda took over.

"Where the hell is Wanda!" he asked Slinky, one of Wanda's old cronies, a little guy, bald, with a habitual twitch that made him look like someone was jerking him around like a marionette.

Already, Cal's stomach was clenching, the stench of some foreboding filling his nostrils.

Slinky took one look at his face and hightailed it in the other direction. Cal chased him down and leaned him up against the wall to get him to talk.

"Hell, Cal. I don't know. Haven't seen her all week. I think Gideon did her. You know," he slashed his finger across his neck. "Wanted his corner back, but Wanda, you know her, she ain't sharing." Cal gave the guy a hard shake and lifted him two inches up the wall so he was dancing on his toes.

"I'll kill the bastard!" Cal told him, but all he felt was sick. Not mad, not even sad, just sick—like he'd been kicked in the stomach. Like it might be time to crawl away somewhere. No good left in the world.

First Mom, now Wanda?

He used to call her his street mama, only she wasn't old enough to be his mom, even though she looked older than his own mother ever did.

"Or maybe," Slinky offered, readjusting his collar once he was let loose and seeing how Cal's face had changed. "Maybe she got smart. Maybe her kids came and picked her up like they were always threatening to do. You never know." Slinky shrugged and sidled away.

Wanda, reduced to a shrug.

The hardness of it was almost more than he could bear.

That's what he'd be, too, if he disappeared, no more than a shrug. Mom wouldn't know. Dad wouldn't care. Kay . . . maybe she'd try to find him. Or not. Look at Mom. Not quite reduced to a shrug but moving that direction. He should have gone after her. Someone should have. But where? Where would you even begin?

I'm fine, she told Kay. *Tell Dad and Cal not to worry.*

Not to worry. *Right. Why should we? She's fine. We're all so fucking fine.*

After that Cal wasn't choosy where he slept, as long as he stayed away from his old stomping grounds, from anyone he ever knew, or who ever knew him. Solitude was what he sought.

One night he managed to sneak into the laundry room of some low-life trailer park and cozy up behind a dryer where he was half hidden. It wasn't too bad in there—at least it was dry, and when he got cold, he turned on a dryer. That heated things up pretty good. He stayed a couple of nights until the manager caught him napping.

The guy was nice enough about it. He invited Cal inside his trailer and fed him hot chocolate and a stale donut. He told Cal how he lived a couple of months in his car before his sister finally took him in and found him this job managing one of her trailer parks. But he couldn't risk losing his job to let him stay. He gave Cal a couple of bucks, some apples, and a big hunk of cheese he got from the government.

"Uncle Sam pays the corporate farmer big bucks so he can feed the likes of me on welfare. Never could figure out why he didn't give those bucks to me directly, why it must pass through his pocket."

"Go figure," Cal agreed. They shook hands when he left, and it felt good, shaking hands, man to man.

He tried getting into the local homeless shelter after that. He'd tried before, but it was always too full. Sometimes around the holidays, though, a few more beds opened up when people got invited home to spend Christmas with their families. But no go. He tested dirty and couldn't stay. One guy who was promised a bed took the yellow plastic poncho off his back and gave it to Cal.

"This will help keep you out of the rain, brother," he said.

"Hey, man, I can't take this. You'll need it."

"It's okay. The Lord will provide."

Another Jesus freak, Cal thought, but he thanked him anyway, shaking his hand before leaving.

After that, it was all downhill. One night he spent behind a Walmart dumpster and another at a construction site. The nights alone in the dark and cold were hard enough with thoughts of Mom and Wanda swirling around in his head as he hugged a thin blanket to his chest and rested his head on his backpack. Worse was tromping around all day in the rain, afraid to loiter too long anywhere, trying not to look homeless, trying not to look lonely, trying not to look as miserable as he felt. His feet were covered with blisters, so he had to stop every few blocks to rest them.

He began making the rounds of all his old drug haunts again, thinking he'd given people enough time to rest between visits. Sometimes they gave him speed or painkillers just to get rid of him, or because they felt sorry for him, or for old-time's sake. But no one let him stay overnight, knowing how hard it would be to get rid of him if they did. Most times they fed him something, and other times he either stood in line at a soup kitchen or shoplifted stuff from liquor stores, Mexican markets, and gas stations— small places that were used to clientele who looked like him. If he went into the big stores, the chains, they followed him around like vultures.

Funny how poor people, the dregs of the earth with nothing much to share, will give you the poncho off their back, and the people operating little, shitty, rathole types of businesses, if they think you're homeless, will look the other way when you sneak a Twinkie or fruit bar into your pocket. But the people who have more than enough, who drive around in gas-guzzling Hummers, even if they knew you once in better days, won't lend you squat. And the managers of the big box stores with their shiny floors and soothing music and rows of shelves stacked a mile high will give you the evil eye and get a clerk to tail you to make sure you don't take something they wouldn't miss and probably could write off on their tax returns.

Human-kind, they call us. Shit.

By this time, he was missing the good ole days sleeping in his old room. He hitched a ride to the old neighborhood. Maybe Mom was home by now, and he could move back in.

His dad's pickup wasn't in the driveway, so he tried the front door, but the house was still locked. Not wanting to break in like last time, he rang the doorbell—no answer.

When he turned to leave, he saw Mrs. Feinstein, an old neighbor Mom used to visit now and then, across the street. She was a lot older than his mom, skinny with a face pinched and drooping, caved-in chest, shoulders hunched and frail. But her smile was bright with red lipstick, and her hair looked freshly curled.

"Hey, I was looking for my mom. Have you seen her? Did she ever come home?"

"I didn't know she was gone. Has she been away?"

"Yeah, disappeared several months ago," he said, nodding solemnly.

"Disappeared? What do you mean?"

"Just took off, no note, nothing. Never came home again."

"Well, come to think of it, I haven't seen her at the mailbox in quite a while."

How sad is that, he thought, this woman who has lived across the street for the past twenty or more years, not knowing Mom was missing, not even missing her.

"Well, that's awful!" she said, looking alarmed, her forehead pinched. "Did you call the police?"

"The police!" The back of his neck stiffened the way it always did when he saw, heard, or thought of pigs. "What for?"

"To file a missing person report!"

"Oh. Well, no, I don't think anyone thought to do that."

She cocked her head and looked at him like he was crazy. "You didn't think to file a missing person report?"

"Well, no, I mean, she's not *missing* missing—not like that. She calls my sister and all."

She gave Cal that hard eyeball look, demanding answers. Under her intense scrutiny, he felt himself coming unglued and flailed around in his head for answers.

"Well, it's hard to explain. We're not your average type of family, I guess. We're just . . . a little weird, you know?"

He could see she didn't know, that until that very moment she had no clue. She pulled away from him then, physically—and emotionally. *Humanly*. He saw it in her eyes, that sense of alarm, of something not seeming quite right, that pulling back in her regard for him that he saw when people realized he lived on the street, had no job, no visible means of support. He stepped closer, trying to make amends, trying to pull her in.

"Not *weird*, weird, you know, not in a bad way, I mean. We haven't, like," he laughed, "cut Mom into little pieces and buried her under the rose bush, if that's what you're thinking."

"Well, I certainly didn't think so!" the woman said, but her eyes, full of fear, said otherwise.

He reached out his hand in apology. "Hey, I'm sorry. I was just kidding, you know. Everything's cool. Mom's not missing. I mean, I think she's gone to the store. She'll be back in a minute." Seeing her wary response, he started backing away. "No reason to call the cops, you know? No reason at all," he called out, deciding it might be time to hightail it out of there.

*****

Eventually, Cal found himself in a field near his parent's house, one he used to jog in years ago when he had his shit half together. He remembered once seeing a dense overgrowth of bushes and some toilet paper caught in the brambles. He figured some bum was hanging out there, and it made him mad to think of someone hiding in the bushes, maybe a pervert on the prowl for little kids or a letch, looking for some young, nimble female flesh jogging nearby. He imagined himself being there when the pervert jumped out of the bushes to grab her, how he'd rush in and stomp on the guy, pulling her to safety. She'd be some rich exec type looking for a good lover to take care of things on the home front while she went out making the big bucks. He'd start that novel Mom was always telling him he should write.

Now, he only hoped the bum had moved on so he could use his bush.

Sure enough, the place was empty, and the brush was thick enough to keep out most of the rain. He found some cardboard he could pull over him to help keep out the wind and drips and spent the afternoon searching the neighborhood for other stuff to weatherproof his new home and make a cold night in the rain a little more bearable.

He was feeling good the next morning when he woke. He'd been dreaming he was running with wolves, naked, free and fierce. The exhilaration of it was still pumping in his veins when he rolled out from under the bush, grunting and stretching.

That's when he heard her scream, a young woman jogger. Apparently, he startled her, roaring up like that—stopped her dead in her tracks. Her whole body was curled inward, convulsed in fear, dread, and disgust. He wanted to reassure her he was no pervert; he meant her no harm. But as he began to speak, she pulled out a can of pepper spray.

"Don't you dare! Don't come near me."

Then she sprinted away faster than anything he'd ever seen. He stood there with his mouth open, seeing himself through her eyes, through his own eyes not so long ago. He'd become the bum in the bush, the pervert who needed pounding.

Me. She's afraid of me.

Then he sat right down and bawled—not out loud or anything, but soundless heaving and howling in his mind. "I'm not a pervert," he whispered. "I'm not a pervert."

After that he couldn't go back to the bush. He spent the night walking the back roads in the rain, ducking off the street whenever he saw car lights. He walked in circles because he didn't know where to go. He hadn't eaten for two days, and his head was pounding.

That's how he found himself back at the old homestead again, standing in the dripping rain, gazing across the street at childhood memories.

After a long while, he forces himself to walk to the front door. He stares at the doorbell but can't ring it. He's stymied, frozen in time, unable to push the doorbell, unable to turn away, wishing he was anywhere but here but knowing he has no place else to go.

Suddenly, the door opens, and he's standing face-to-face with his dad.

"Cal!" he says, startled to see him there. He glances past him as if to see if he's with someone and then asks, "What are you doing here?"

"I dunno." Cal sucks in a breath and shakes his head slowly.

"Then why are you here?"

"I dunno. Guess I'll be going." He turns away.

"Wait!" his dad says. "I have something for you. Something from your mother."

12

CAL
Don't Mean Shit

Cal follows his dad into the house, removing his wet boots and dripping poncho on the entryway rug. He runs his hand through his hair, down his face, trying to remove some of the rain. Finally, he goes into the guest bath to dry off with a towel and tries not to look at himself in the mirror. Walking out, he catches a glimpse of an unbelievably old, dried-up bag of bones.

Me, he thinks. *Me*.

His dad stands over a stack of manila envelopes piled on the dining room table.

"These came for you about once a week, starting around the time you disappeared."

"I didn't disappear. I moved out," he tells him, eyeballing the stack of envelopes. "You haven't opened them?" He looks incredulous at his dad, who shrugs. He can't believe his dad never bothered to open them, never cared enough to find out what was in there.

"Your wife goes missing for five months, and she's mailing you this stuff, and you never open them?"

"Mailed *you* this stuff. You. Not me."

"Weren't you a little bit curious? How could you not open them?"

Dad looks at Cal, shakes his head, and walks away.

"I can't believe it," Cal mutters to himself and then says loud enough for him to hear, "You're a real piece of work, Dad!"

He opens the first envelope, postmarked a month after his mom disappeared. Then he opens the next and the one after that, sixteen in all. Each contains a single glossy 8x10 black-and-white photo.

"Photos! Nothing but photos!" he calls out disgustedly to his dad, who disappeared into the kitchen. "No notes, no 'Hi, how are you.' No 'Sorry for abandoning you.' No, 'Fuck you and go to hell.' Just photos."

His dad comes to the doorway. "Photos of what?"

"See for yourself." He watches his dad sort through the stack, looking as perplexed as he feels—photos of lizards, snakes, roosters, a cactus . . ..

"What does it all mean?" his dad asks as he shuffles through them.

Cal is startled by the question. It may be the first sincere question his father ever asked him, and he's disappointed he has no satisfactory answer.

"What does it mean? It don't mean shit, Dad. It don't mean shit."

*****

His dad invites him to spend the night since it's still raining, so he stays in his old room. Everything looks the same. All the stuff he didn't take with him is right where he left it. Only the pile of dirty plates and crumpled beer cans are missing.

His dad looks over his shoulder into the room.

"It's just how you left it," he says. "Didn't know if you were coming back or what."

Cal looks at him like he's crazy. "Coming back? You locked me out, Dad."

"What do you mean?"

"I came home one night, and everything was locked up tight. Even the windows were locked."

His dad cocks his head, looking surprised, and then nods. "Yeah, I remember now. There'd been a string of burglaries in the neighborhood. I figured you had a key. Why didn't you knock?"

"Didn't think you'd let me in."

His dad just looks at him.

"*Would* you have let me in?" he asks now, incredulous, startled to think he exiled himself for no reason.

His dad raises an eyebrow. "Well, son, I guess we'll never know now, will we?"

*****

Cal hides out in his room, only coming out to fix himself small snacks now and then when he gets hungry. His stomach has shrunk, and he finds he doesn't need to eat much. Mostly he wants to sleep. A week goes by, neither of them saying anything about it being time for him to move on. Neither saying much to each other at all, like the good old days, and there's a kind of comfort in that.

When the rain breaks for the season and the sun comes out again in late March, Cal gets nervous. He planned on taking off when the rain passed—head up to Oceano, hang out on the beach, take up with some campers who liked to party, and see if his old pal Fred had any odd jobs he could do in exchange for food and some of his pain meds. But now that he's settled in here a bit, he isn't ready to leave. So, one day he takes a bottle of Windex and a squeegee he finds lying around the garage and starts washing all the windows. He takes down the screens and hoses them off, pulls up the inside blinds and washes there, too, spraying heavily and wiping away the grime with sheets of old newspaper that crumble in his hands but keep the glass lint-free. He makes his strokes on the outside of the glass the opposite of those on the inside, a trick Mom taught him to tell where any streaks or missed spots might be.

He watches his dad out of the corner of his eye as he cleans the windows in the backyard. He's tuned a portable radio to an old sixties rock-and-roll station he thinks his dad will appreciate. Janis Joplin's gravelly voice belts out the blues, begging someone to take another piece of her heart.

Dad's been mowing the lawn and raking up grass shavings. Now he's sweeping the patio. Cal can't tell for sure, but he thinks his dad is pleased to see him working.

"So, what do you think," he yells across the yard. His dad stops sweeping and looks up.

"The windows! Think they're clean enough after all that rain spattered them?"

Dad grunts and gives a quick, clipped nod.

Now if it had been Mom, she'd be praising him up one side and down the other, going on and on about what a great job he did, how nice it looked, how much she appreciated how hard he was working to the point he'd want to strangle her and never do a damn thing around the house again. But his dad only grunts and nods, and he's not sure which is worse.

Fuck it, he says to himself and goes back into his room. He shuts the blinds tight to keep the sun from shining through those ever-so-bright windows he just, like a miserable suck-up, spent the whole morning cleaning.

But the next morning, when Dad is out back again trimming hedges and pruning trees, the ground piling up with twigs and branches, Cal tries again. He rakes up the hedge trimmings, putting them in the green waste can, cutting up the longer branches into small pieces so they fit nice and neat. It feels good working side by side with his dad, not talking, not needing to talk, working like they could read each other's minds and didn't need instructions, didn't get in each other's way. When they're done, Dad brings out two Buds and hands one to him. They sit in the patio chairs, looking out over the yard cleaned of debris.

"Looks good," Cal says.

Dad grunts and nods. This time, the response seems just right.

*****

After that, Cal gets into the yard and house work. He scrubs the walls and vacuums the carpets, moving all the furniture and using attachments to clean the drapes and window ledges. He empties the fridge, washing all the shelves, and defrosts the freezer. He helps his dad rebuild the side fence and clean out the gutters. He weeds the side yard and digs up a dead stump.

He likes getting up early, working hard all day, and going to bed tired and sore from the lifting and hauling. This is what he needed all along: time with his dad, working side by side like regular men. He thinks seriously about weaning himself completely off drugs and finding a job in construction or landscaping. He looks through the want ads in the morning paper, circling possibilities with a red pen and leaving it where Dad is sure to see. He cuts in half the portions of Vicodin he's getting from Eddy, going longer and longer without. He shaves off his mustache and trims his hair.

Life is looking good, he thinks. The future is starting to have some appeal.

That is, until one day in early in May when his dad comes home with a new pickup and camper shell and tells him he's headed north—to Alaska.

13

WALTER

To the Far Ends of the Earth

My Franny. That's how he thinks of her, affectionately, this way. My Franny, like she belongs to him, even while knowing she doesn't—like a cat, a pet you never quite own because it's so independent and unpredictable. And yet when she curls up in your lap and purrs—all that silky softness melting beneath your stroking hand—you think of her that way, like she belongs to you even when you know in another moment she'll disappear. Even when she's gone and wandered off to who knows where, and there's no telling when she'll reappear. Even when you know, finally, she's never coming home. Still, she remains, in your mind if nowhere else, in your heart, *my Franny. Mine.*

*****

Walter has been driving twelve hours straight now ever since leaving the KOA campground outside of Vancouver in the wee hours of the morning. He's headed toward a little town nestled against a bay in Alaska where he and his granddad went salmon fishing when he was twelve years old—their last trip together. He died soon after. Then, it was only him and Granny with her down-turned face left. His mom died when he was three, and he has no clear memory of her or his dad, who took off not long after that.

If it bothered his grandparents, their son leaving, never calling, they never let on. They hardly ever mentioned him except when Walter got into trouble. Then Granny was quick to warn him not to turn out like his dad. Mostly, though, he was quiet and reserved growing up, like his granddad. After he passed, that's when all his wildness came out, according to Granny—sweet as sugar one day, full of vinegar the next.

"I won't take your sass," she told him. "You can take off down the road like your daddy for all I care."

When he turned eighteen, he did just that. He joined the Marines. But he always looked after his granny, even when he moved to California to marry Franny. He'd drive up to Oregon twice a year to take care of the place, clean the gutters, trim the trees, mend the roof, whatever was needed. She'd put her arms around him and pat him on the back when he left.

"You're a good boy," she told him. *Not like your dad, after all*, is what he heard.

Now it's Franny who took off. She's been gone going on eight months now, traveling all the way to Cancun on the Caribbean Sea, according to the credit card bills he still gets. But she must be working along the way because her charges get smaller each month. He hasn't given up on her coming home. He won't. But he can't sit still and wait for her anymore either. He hasn't the patience. And knowing her, she wouldn't want him to.

He's been driving so long and at such a steady pace, watching the broken lines on the highway roll out before him, that he's entered a trance-like state where the passage of time loses all meaning, and nothing exists but the road ahead. Yet all the while, he's mindful that the road he travels northward also stretches south, toward the opposite end of the world, where Franny is headed now—her moving steadily away from him as he moves away from her. He feels the tension of that line drawn taut between them. With each mile he moves forward, each bend he rounds, he wonders, is this when the line will break? Does she feel it too?

He pulls over to the side of the road at a rest stop, the gravel crunching beneath his tires until the camper comes to a stop beneath a tall pine tree. He can't move yet, still feeling the trance of long-distance travel, the tiredness in his arms and neck, his foot still resting lightly on the gas pedal, his hand still on the clutch. He sits like that for he doesn't know how long. Eventually, the murmur of a creek catches his attention. In the brush ahead is a clearing, a faint path, and a glint of water beyond. He walks toward it through a maze of red chokeberry bushes, breathing in long draughts of perfumed air. The creek is shallow, about five feet wide, flowing swiftly around small boulders, creaming against the rocks, flicking tiny splashes in the air.

Kneeling, he cups the water in his hands, tastes it, and splashes it on his face. He stays there, hunched over the creek, smelling the sweetness of the water, feeling its cold breath on his cheeks.

Franny would have liked this.

He imagines her here now, laughing beside him. Watches her stepping out onto the slippery boulders, arms held wide as she balances herself, moving toward the opposite bank.

"Where you think you're going, girl? Get the heck back here!" He laughs, knowing she will pay him no mind and liking the sight of her looking back, that devilish grin on her face, daring him to join her.

He stares a long time at the bright spot in the middle of the creek where she disappears and then heads back to the camper. On the road again, he's driving faster this time, the tension between him and Franny growing tauter as he travels, carrying him further away from her as she is being carried further away from him, each to the far ends of the earth.

*****

The road ahead is open and clear with plenty of time to think, but he tries not to. He's never been prone to think long and hard about anything if he didn't have to. Things work out better that way. Even when he was busy at home mowing, feeding the hummers, or welding at work, he finds it all comes together better when he doesn't think, when he's on autopilot, as Franny used to say. She was right. He never realized that about himself until she put it like that. He knew right away she was right.

It took her a long time to figure that out about him, though. When they were younger, she was always asking him what he was thinking, and when he told her, "Nothing," she wouldn't believe him.

"No one sits there and thinks nothing at all! Something must be going on in your mind."

But there wasn't. She thought he was holding out on her, keeping some part of himself hidden. But truth was, he often sat with no thought in mind, just experiencing the air about him, the sounds, the scents, the feeling of being in his own body, without a thought at all. He figured everyone must sit like that.

She made him feel a secret shame that he had nothing to give her, no thought to offer up, no hidden depth or insight to share. Nothing but his presence, which seemed to be lacking, amiss. Not enough. Many mornings when she woke, she would reveal her dreams to him—long, complicated, fanciful, full of suspense and surprises, like watching a movie. But when she asked about his dreams, he had nothing to tell her. He never dreamed or never remembered them if he did.

When he was packing for the trip to Alaska, he found at the bottom of his sock drawer a stack of cards collected over the years—anniversary and birthday cards from Franny, Father's Day cards from the kids. Franny put them there—her, not him.

He sat on the bed and shuffled through them. Sometimes on special occasions, she'd slip a poem she wrote into the card. It amazed him that she'd write to him in a language he could not understand. That she'd give him something of herself so unexpected and indecipherable. But one time she wrote something that stuck with him and rang true. She said he was her anchor, holding her steady in the storm, and she was his sail, catching the wind that carried them across the sea. He saw them that way too—her as something otherworldly, ephemeral, prone to flight and him as that steadying hand keeping her grounded and safe.

Opposites attract, so they say. He and Franny were like that, attracted by the otherness of each other, yet striking a balance somehow. He liked the feel of her playful upward tug as she soared aloft like a skittish kite; she liked the feel of his calm hand holding her firmly to the ground.

He sat there on the edge of the bed with a handful of cards, realizing he'd always known someday she'd drift off like this. Their relationship was tenuous at best, and the fact it lasted this long was the most surprising thing about it.

Now, driving farther away from her, he wonders if she had the same feeling too, that someday she would drift away so far that his fingers would open and let her loose. But he knows now, now that the inevitable finally happened, that he will never let go, not completely. She will never drift so far that he will let her slip away for good.

As long as he holds on, she's safe. And he's safe. And his life has purpose.

14

KAY

Scattered

"So-o-o-o," he says, his eyes sweeping over Kay appreciatively, looking more like he's about to ask her out on a date than interview her for a job. "You're a Donner protégé."

Kay laughs, eyeing him as well—early thirties, athletic build, bronze face, streaks of gold in the dark blond hair tucked behind his ears—a surfer for sure. She can almost smell the sea salt and see the knobbies on his knees. Rob McDonnell is one of the founding partners at Cal-Lithix, an archaeological consulting firm specializing in environmental planning and development, one of the few working statewide.

"You, too, so Donner tells me. I wonder how many protégés he's had over the years."

"A select group, I'm sure," he says with a grin. "He was instrumental in helping Rabe and me get the firm going. Lots of our early work came from his recommendations. I'm sure he's told you all about it. One of the perks of having protégés is being able to bask in their success."

They walk the grounds downhill from the grassy knoll where Cal-Lithix opened a new office in an impressive professional complex on the outskirts of Sierra Madre. A light breeze molds Kay's navy-blue shirtdress against her thighs. She's glad she decided to wear her low pumps instead of heels for the interview.

"So, how's the dig at Rancho Viejo coming along? I was with Donner, you know, when we broke ground. What's new and exciting?"

She's tempted to tell him about the cave Miguel showed her. But she hasn't even told Donner. Somehow, even now, it feels like a secret she's been entrusted with, not hers to share with the world. So instead, she launches into her prepared pitch, telling how she's been leading the team under Donner's supervision this past year and about her own work in getting grant funding for the carbon-dating project.

She watches him as she speaks, calibrating his interest, diving into detail when he leans toward her or lifts his eyebrows, and skimming past when he looks away, which isn't often. At one point, his eyebrows squeeze together like he's puzzled about something.

"What is it?" she asks him.

He shakes his head. "Sorry. You remind me of someone. Have we met before?" His eyes sweep over her again, lingering on her face.

Kay laughs. "I get that a lot. Maybe at the movies? *Edward Scissorhands? Reality Bites?*" He cocks his head. "Wynona Ryder. People say I look like her."

Kay isn't sure it's a compliment. She's never understood why some people find Wynona, or Kay for that matter, so attractive. Mom was the beauty of the family. Kay took after Dad—dark hair, dark eyes, small stature. Although she has her mother's fine features and light, creamy skin, plus curves where it counts. That helps. But her eyes are all her own. "Lively and intense," Karl told her when she asked why he seemed so taken with her when they first met. "It's not any one thing," he explained. "It's the whole package. It's hard to look away. Like you'll miss out on something if you do."

Apparently, Rob feels the same, the way he keeps looking at her, which worries her. He's attractive enough, but he reminds her too much of her brother—the good looks, the confidence, the teasing eyes. They're about the same age, too, which makes her stomach squeeze. Cal should be like this: successful, well-off, not lost on the streets or hunkered down in the back bedroom of his parents' home. But aside from that, the last thing she wants or needs is a fling with the boss, assuming he hires her, which she suspects he will.

Rob grins at her now and snaps his fingers. "Yes! Wynona. That's who you look like! My fiancé and I saw her in the premiere of *Alien Nation* last week. He shakes his head at her admiringly. "Amazing resemblance."

Kay smiles, so relieved he's engaged.

"You've got the job. I'm sure you know that by now."

Kay lets the thrill of it shiver down her spine and tries to keep from grinning too hard. Instead, she asks teasingly, "Because of Donner? Or Wynona."

He throws back his head and laughs. "Neither! Because of that—that confidence and verve and the way your eyes light up when you talk about your work in the field. Donner helps, of course. He was pretty enthusiastic about you. Now I know why. I'm assuming, of course, you don't mind relocating to Sierra Madre. And you're willing to travel. This office will be handling most of our work in So-Cal, but we might need you to lend a hand occasionally up north.

"No problem there. I'm impressed with what I've seen of Sierra Madre so far, and I love to travel."

"Great! So how soon can you start?"

"Graduation is a month away, May 26. How about June 1?"

"Perfect!" He grins, opening the glass door for her as they return to the office to sign the contract. "Welcome to Cal-Lithix!"

*****

"Alaska? Are you out of your mind?"

Kay has returned to Northridge for another load of boxes in her move to Sierra Madre when her dad calls. She finally managed to find a place to rent that she could afford. Barely! Who knew the cost of living in Sierra Madre would be so much higher than a college town? But that wasn't even the worst part. Because it took so long to find a place to live, she had to push the start date at Cal-Lithix back a week. Rob was not pleased. Remembering the tone of his voice when she told him still makes her squirm.

And now Dad drops this bombshell!

"How could you leave the house in Cal's hands? How's he supposed to take care of it? He can't even take care of himself."

"He'll be fine," her dad tells her. "There's no mortgage, and I'll take care of the property tax. All he has to do is pay the utilities."

"With what? He has no money, no job, the last I heard!"

"Well, I guess he better get one if he wants to keep the lights on, don't you think?"

What she thinks is that her dad has no business leaving Cal in charge of the house unsupervised. What she thinks is that now she'll have to drive up there and check on him ASAP to make sure he hasn't destroyed the place or sold everything for drugs. She calls Cal as soon as she hangs up with Dad so she can read him the riot act, but the phone's been disconnected. Christ almighty! Did her dad not think to prepay the phone company?

She's trying to make a fresh start, for God's sake—a new job, a new apartment, a bright future. She doesn't want anything, or anyone, to ruin it. She sits down on one of the boxes she packed and leans her head on her hands. She misses the peace she felt in Baja, that cool, quiet pool of time. She imagines herself sitting on that bank again, her feet in the cool creek, and Miguel a watchful, comforting presence close beside her. She felt closer to her mother then, too. She was part of that larger pool of space that wrapped around her and supported her, like a larger body, her mind calm and all her senses alive. She wishes she could be like that again—in the stream of things—nothing extraneous, just clear, brilliant being.

Instead, she feels torn to pieces, bits of her flying off everywhere with no still point.

Her life is scattered in boxes across two counties. She starts her new job on Monday before she's even unpacked or feeling the least bit settled. Her family is scattered across two continents: her mother in South America, her father off to Alaska, and her drug-addled brother left in charge of the family homestead. She's not sure why this last part bothers her so much. She should be happy that her brother has a permanent place to live now, that her dad didn't boot him out onto the street, that he entrusted Cal with the care of his home. But that's the problem. Can *she* trust Cal with its care? It's the only home she's ever known, the only place that feels like home, that feels solid and safe. It's all she has left of her mother. And now it too seems precarious, in danger of slipping away. And there's nothing and no one she can count on to be there for her.

Stop this right now, she tells herself. She needs to head to Sierra Madre before work traffic starts again. She takes three long, deep breaths, letting them rise from her diaphragm, feeling the power that pools there, that steadies her. Then, she begins the long drive to her new home.

15

CAL
Suck of the Unborn

The bathroom door is wide open. Syringe, rubber tubing, candle, matches, bent spoon, and a baggie filled with heroin are spread along the counter like surgical instruments awaiting the almighty doctor, awaiting Cal. He can do that now, stand here naked with the door flung open.

Hell, he can leave every fucking door in the whole house open for as long as he wants. It's all his now, ever since Dad handed him a ring of keys and the remote to the garage, telling him the insurance, property taxes, all that's taken care of. All he must do is pay for the utilities, and he can stay as long as he wants.

"Keep an eye on the place for me," Dad said as he slid behind the wheel of the camper.

"Watch out for them burglars, eh, Dad?" Cal said, his voice dripping with sarcasm. "Sure thing, Pop!" he called after him as the camper backed down the driveway.

Cal should be bursting with happiness. He should be giddy with glee. He should be rolling on the floor in uproarious, glorious laughter at this boondoggle of a gift.

Hell, he is happy! Who wouldn't be? First Mom. Then Dad. Gone.

What's hysterical is how, for one brief, pathetic moment, he thought something good might come from his mom's disappearance, how he and Dad might become best buds. They'd joke together about how ditzy she was, taking off on vacation and leaving him behind by mistake.

The few times Cal remembers connecting with Dad growing up was when they were making fun of the girls, Mom and Kay. He'd make a funny little jab at Kay, and Dad would pick it up and run with it or vice versa. The two passed the ball back and forth, laughing at the girls, connecting in their love for the women in their lives through a kind of affectionate macho superiority that allowed them to poke fun at their flaws. He and Pop. Laughing together.

But that's all gone. It was gone a long time ago.

Slowly, methodically, he picks up the surgical tube, strokes it with his fingers like a strand of lover's hair, ropes it around his arm, pulls it tight, and makes a fist. He strikes a match, lights the candle, pours the fine white powder into a spoon, holds it over the flame, and watches the spoon glow and blacken while the powder melts. He sucks the liquid into the syringe and slides the needle into a swollen vein. Pushes down the plunger, pumping in the juice, and lets his head roll back, feeling the rush—the holy, holy, sweet, holy rush of heroin shooting through his veins.

Forget pot. Forget coke. Forget everything but this, his sweet Lady H, the love of his life, the one true thing he has God to thank for, that has never let him down. For all the time spent in rehab, twelve steps, counseling, and all the rest, for all the times he confessed his sins and begged and pleaded to be given the strength to give up this baby, he knows, he knows, deep down in his heart of hearts, that this is the one sweet love he never, ever wants to let go. He loves everything about his Lady—the mad, manic hunt to chase her down; the relief, thrill, and power of possession; the look, smell, taste, and feel of her rushing through his blood; the pure bliss of being carried away so high and so far from all his problems that they literally melt away with one sweet kiss.

It's what he lives for—this sense of peace and joy and power. Why would he—why would any sane person, for that matter—ever want to be free of that? And all the other crap—the pain of withdrawals, of broken lives and unfulfilled potential, his mother's grief, his family's disgust, lost jobs, lost friends, lost pride, homelessness, hunger, and a body wasting away—all of that, however long it lasts, however bad it gets, however much it shreds him apart, is nothing, NOTHING, as soon as the blessed white lady touches her hot sweet finger to his vein and lifts him into nirvana.

The truth is, he thinks, as he leans against the wall and slides to the floor, *I don't want this to stop. And now there's no reason why it should.*

*****

Cal wakes the next morning lying on the bathroom floor in a pool of vomit.

"What the fuck!" He scrambles to his feet. Did he have a mini-OD? Did he check out for a minute and pop back in again?

It wouldn't be the first time. He might want to get some party animals in here to keep him company, someone to haul his ass down to the ER if he starts convulsing again. He turns on the shower and steps inside, letting the room steam up and wondering how long he's been here, lying on the floor, living in the bathroom, like his mom used to accuse him of doing.

"You can't stay in there forever!" she yelled at him through the locked door.

"Ya wanna bet!" he yells back at her now. He damn well could now.

He's glad she hightailed it out of here, both her and Dad. If she was here, there'd be no peace. He remembers how she used to peck at the bathroom door when he was in there longer than she considered a normal amount of time.

"You okay in there?" she would ask, timid-like at first.

"I'm sitting on the shitter. Leave me alone," he'd tell her and grunt loudly to make his point.

After a while the pecks became angry pounding.

"What are you doing in there? Are you shooting up? Open the door!"

And he would open it finally, flinging it fiercely, glaring at her, pushing past and slamming the bedroom door behind him, seething.

She became the object of his self-loathing, the mirror against which he threw all his plates, watching them splinter against her face and slide to the floor, all his messes splattered over her. And still, she stood there, watching him, sometimes dissolving into tears, or raging in fury, or stony with disgust, but never backing away from the ferociousness of his attacks, standing her ground and taking it, bearing it, never retreating from his touch—unwavering, resolute.

The rage was okay. It was the tears that unmanned him. That killed him time and time again until he had to make it stop. He had to make her face the truth, that her tears were wasted on him, that he was a miserable fuckin' asshole who didn't deserve her love. And he'd prove it by ripping out her heart and holding it up for her to see until her tears finally did dry up in a rage that blew him away with its ferocity. A rage he fed with little bits of her heart and his heart until she fuckin' wanted to kill him and would too, if he didn't dance out of her way, laughing at her inept, futile rage, which didn't do either of them a bit of good—except in stopping the tears. Neither she nor he could survive the tears.

It's something he ponders but cannot fathom, the depth and folly of her motherlove, the obstinacy that thwarts his every attempt to shake it loose, even while he tests it mercilessly, uses it shamelessly, depends upon it endlessly—and wears it like ball and chain. Like an indictment stamped on his forehead: his total unworthiness of her unwavering love.

*****

Cal lives in a perpetual state of drug heaven now, his house a haven for all the lost, addicted souls in town, all the losers living with their parents who need a place to crash when they're loaded, all the bums who have no homes but wander from one flophouse to the next between stops at the beach, or a box behind K-Mart, or a bed at the shelter—all the derelicts like how he used to be before he had a house of his own. The feelings of power, of security, of having gotten away with something big, of winning the lottery, remain with him until one night one of the degenerates, the riffraff who live with him, stumbling in and out of the house at all hours of the day and night, tugs at his shirt sleeve while he's sucking on a joint.

"Hey man, did ya know there's a dude across the street spying on us with his binoculars?"

Cal looks up, startled, and then goes to the front window, tweaking the blind to peek out. Sure enough, from the front porch of the house across the street, someone is spying on him. He steps back in alarm and quickly surveys the room behind him.

It's the first time in weeks he's looked at the house as if viewing it through another's eyes, like his mom or his dad or the neighbor across the street. And he's astounded by what he sees— totally freaked out.

People are all over the place, and most of them he's never seen before. There's a naked dude lying on his couch scratching his balls. Another snores in the recliner, a beer bottle trembling precariously on his chest. A girl is curled into a corner like a fetus sucking her thumb, while a couple on the floor in front of the TV are going at it like frogs. Another couple is laughing it up in the hallway, saying inane, meaningless things.

"No way."

"Yes, way."

"You're putting me on."

"I'm telling you the god-awful truth. Would I lie to you?"

"You'd lie to your mama."

Piles of beer cans are stacked in the corners, and clothes scattered everywhere, like someone picked up a hamper of dirty laundry and sprinkled it about the room. Pictures hang crooked on the walls, except for one spot where an oil painting used to be. It's conspicuously missing. He looks around for more evidence of theft and finds it everywhere.

"Hey, where's my dad's stereo!" he shouts at the lot of them, so loud that for a moment, all is still.

"What stereo?"

"The one that was sitting right here, you moron," he says and kicks at the man sitting where the stereo used to be. "Out, out! All of you, out of here!"

They look at him like he's crazy. He picks up a poker from the fireplace and swings it, nearly cracking one guy in the head, catching him on the ear instead. The guy looks at the blood in his hand.

"Fuck it," he says and heads for the front door.

"Not that way, you idiot!" Cal shouts after him. "Out the back through the alley."

Some go out the back. Most leave through the front door, cursing him as they load into a car. He follows them into the street, waving his poker as the car peels away. Someone flings a beer bottle out the side window at him, which splinters into pieces on the pavement.

He looks across the street at where the binoculars used to be, but now he doesn't see anyone except maybe behind a chink in the blind.

"Nothing to worry about," he calls out to his neighbor, "just kids having fun. These young punks won't be back, so you can put those binos away. No need to call the cops. No need at all," he mutters as he putters back into the house and closes the door.

The girl in the fetal position hasn't moved, and he decides to let her be for the moment, let her sleep off whatever she has. She looks like a kid, lying there, blissfully unaware of all that's been going on. He leans down close to make sure she's still breathing, that she hasn't fuckin' OD'd on him, and he's relieved when he can smell her rancid breath still flowing.

She's wearing black stretchy jeans and a pink tank top, but she looks cold. He picks up a towel he finds on the floor and puts it over her bare shoulders. Then he scrounges for something else and finds a large T-shirt that he spreads over her bare feet, and then steps back to study his handiwork. She looks like she's as warm as she needs to be to make it through the night.

He wanders into his room to crash on his mattress, only to find another couple sleeping there. He's too tired to chase them out, so he grabs a quilt and curls up on the couch, but it smells like vomit, so he flops over onto the floor and falls asleep.

His head is throbbing the next morning, and he can barely open his mouth with all the dry mucus and who knows what else plastering it shut. He takes a long, hard drink from the bathroom faucet, but the face that shows in the mirror when he rises is not his own. It can't be.

The couple who'd been asleep on his air mattress has taken off, but the girl in the fetal position hasn't moved. He kicks at her foot to wake her up, but she only moans and waves him away. He kicks again.

"Go away," she mumbles and curls back tighter into position, really sucking away now on that thumb.

He studies her, thinking she looks like those pictures in sonograms, the unborn still curled blissfully in the womb, completely unaware of the chaos, treachery, and violence that swirl around her, waiting for her in the world outside. He wishes he could be there with her. He imagines himself lying down next to her, curling his body around her, melting into her skin: her breath his breath, her thumb his thumb, sucking the suck of the unborn, sleeping the sleep of death.

Instead, slowly, calmly, he reaches down, grabs her by the hair, wraps it around his fist, and jerks her violently to her feet.

She's instantly awake, the sleeping infant now a snarling medusa, her fists, elbows, knees, feet, teeth, striking at him like a nest of writhing snakes, cursing at him like he's the devil's son. He keeps his grip on her hair woven tight and fierce about his fist, raising her higher onto her tiptoes, his other arm wrapped around her chest, holding her close and forcing her in front of him, her head pulled back so far, she's snapping at him with her teeth. Then he goose walks her toward the door.

He feels a peculiar sense of satisfaction in doing this—in waking the beast and marching it toward the door—power, but no pleasure.

He takes his hand away long enough to fling open the front door and push her out.

"And don't come back," he tells her calmly, firmly, as she falls sprawling face first onto the walkway.

Instantly, she rebounds, all arched back, fierce claws and yellow eyes, springing cat-like toward him. He slams the door in her face, turns the lock, and stays there leaning against the door, each blow of her fists against the wood reverberating through his body, echoing in his heart. Pounding, pounding, pounding. He slides to the floor.

"I'll kill you, kill you, kill you," she screams.

"Do it, do it, do it," he urges softly to himself long after she's gone.

16

CAL
King of the Castle

Cal lifts a slat in the blinds and peers out: gray sky, empty street, all clear.

It's time to take another run to the corner store, maybe swing by the mailbox while he's out. Last time he looked, along with the usual bills and another photo from his mom, there was a refund check for his dad from some insurance policy that Cal was able to cash. Fifty bucks! Nothing to sneer at.

But he doesn't like going outside anymore and puts it off as long as he can. Just the thought of it makes his gut churn.

His days of pill peddling and wild parties are over. Survival lies in retreating into his own world and keeping everyone else out. He holes up in the house with all the windows and blinds pulled tight and ventures out only when he needs to replenish his supplies, just the basics: dope, weed, tobacco and beer, a few burritos, maybe a pint of milk, and Debbie Cakes. He figures he's as addicted to them as to anything else.

Paying for it all is the hard part, but so far pawning stuff has worked. He found a handy little shop close by, and the guy who runs it doesn't blink twice at what he brings in—Mom's jewelry, crystal vases, collector figurines, tools from the garage—mostly small stuff he can hoof on down there.

But there's the little matter of the utilities as well. The bills have been stacking up—first invoices, then warnings, then envelopes with red borders stating when the electricity, gas, water, and cable TV will be turned off. He better start saving some of the cash he gets from the pawnshop to keep the lights on. And the water. Squatting in a bush doesn't appeal to him anymore.

He shifts his backpack full of his dad's tools to a more comfortable position, slowly opens the front door, and peeks out. Even beneath gray skies, the light nearly blinds him. He pulls his baseball cap over his eyes and heads toward the street. It's ten blocks to the pawn shop, three back to Eddy's, then the 7-11, the mailbox, and he's home free.

I can do this, he tells himself.

But no. The front door of the house across the street opens, and shit, here he comes, the little bastard. It's like he sits there all day spying on him, like they're both facing off across the street from each other, peering through the blind slats, waiting for the other to show his face. He looks back toward the door, thinking to make a mad dash inside before the dirt bag can cross the street. *Fuck it*, he thinks and keeps going.

"When you going to mow that lawn of yours?" the man shouts at him from across the street. "Look at it, knee deep already. You think I wanna look at that every time I leave the house?"

"You and the damn lawn again. You ever going to give it up?" Cal says, moving down the sidewalk as fast as he can as the guy crosses the street toward him.

"Why do you want to let the place go to shit like this? What would your parents think? You're dragging down the property value." He's following him down the sidewalk now, shouting at his back.

"My parents don't give a shit about me or this property one way or the other," Cal says over his shoulder.

"Where are they then? You got them buried in the backyard? Wouldn't surprise me. I ought to call the cops on you."

"Go home, old man. You're making a fool of yourself."

"One of these days, I'm coming over there with my gas can and a lighter. See if I don't!"

"Wouldn't surprise me if you did," Cal says without looking back, knowing the old goat can't hobble fast enough to keep up with him. But the threat rankles. Not so much the part about burning him out as calling the cops. The last thing he wants to see is a couple of those fuckers pounding on his door, staking him out, following him off to Eddy's. You can never tell how far they'll go to find something to lock you up for. Bastards.

Fred at the pawnshop sends him packing after unloading only half his tools, and Cal's in a bad mood by the time he reaches Eddy's.

"You look like shit," Eddy says when he opens the door.

"So what else is new," Cal replies. Eddy bounces back to let him in. He's a small guy with a receding hairline and wispy goatee. A deep crease squeezes his eyebrows together like he's thinking something deep that doesn't digest well. But he has a bounce in his step and thick forearms, holdovers from his welter-weight boxing days.

"You eating anything? You're about walking out of those jeans," Eddy tells him.

"You my mama now?"

"Don't pull that. What'd I do if all my clients died on me? Ever think of that? Besides, we go back. How's Kay doin' anyway?"

Cal slings his backpack on the couch and throws himself down beside it. "Fuck if I know. Mom took off, then Dad. She's got no use for me now. I could eat shit and die as far as she cares."

"Women," Eddy snorts. He takes a chair across from him and pulls a bag of weed out of the drawer built into the coffee table.

"Sally still gone?" Cal asks, sitting up, eyeing the weed.

"Her mom's. I can see them now, buzzing around each other like little angry bees, talkin' shit about me. Claim I don't do squat for her."

"Women," Cal agrees.

Eddie lights a joint, takes a long hit, and passes it to Cal before retreating to a back room to rummage through his wares.

Cal leans back, sucking on the joint, surveying the room, all the furniture looking secondhand, like something he'd picked up at garage sales and thrift stores. No wonder Sally left him.

"It's all I got now," Eddy says when he returns, handing him a baggie of pills. "Junk dried up. Coke sold out a week ago. The trade's turning to shit. You heard about those big busts, right? Meth supply all gone. Everyone else spooked. You better make this last awhile."

Cal frowns, pulls the bills Fred gave him out of his back pocket, and peels off a few for Eddie. "Look, I got this job I hope you can help me with," he says as he hands over the money. "Need someone with a backhoe to come in and rip up my lawn, maybe throw down some rocks."

"What do you think I am, in construction?"

"You got connections."

"What you offering in exchange?"

He looks around the place. "How 'bout a new dining table and chairs? Got one of them cabinets for dishes too. Sally'd like that. You're still trying to get her back, aren't you?"

"You think a table and chair will win her over? What you smokin', boy?"

"You tell me!" Cal says, eying the joint he holds, and laughs. "Look, it's worth a try, don't you think? It's good stuff. Got the lion paw feet and all. Antiques. Must be worth $500 or so."

"Shitload more than that if it's got claws. Sally loves that stuff. Always dragging my ass into some antique store." He takes the joint from Cal and inhales long and hard. The crease between his eyebrows deepens. "Let me think on it."

*****

Eddy comes through in the end. He hauls away the dining room furniture in a pickup and, a couple of days later, sends over a guy with a backhoe. Cal watches while it tears out his lawn in big, mean bites like a hungry tyrannosaurus. Later, a dump truck pours a pile of white rocks onto the dirt. Cal spreads them around with a rake. The old man across the street stands in his front yard, watching. Cal gives him a big thumbs up.

"Bah!" says the man, throwing an arm at him before turning his back and shuffling into his house.

Cal stares at his back. "What the fuck?" he calls after him. No pleasing that prick.

At least he won't have to worry about him calling the cops now or burning the place down. He doesn't have to worry about a thing now. He's got everything he needs right here. Even managed to get the water turned on again after it stopped— Eddy's gift when he came to pick up furniture and got a whiff of the backed-up toilets. A bonus for helping get Sally back, he said.

"You're living like an animal," Eddy told him while eyeballing the place. Cal followed his gaze. He hadn't cleaned up much since he kicked out the last of the partiers: trash still everywhere, piles of soda and beer cans kicked into the corners—recyclables he can redeem for cash when there's nothing left to pawn.

"You need to get a woman in here to help you civilize things."

Cal snorted. "The last woman I had in here about scratched my eyes out." He didn't mention it was while he was hauling her ass out the door. "Besides, I'm good. Got everything I need."

Soon after that another package of photos from his mom arrives. He tacks the new photos up with the others on the wall of his mom's office or what's left of it. Her computer, scanner, and printer are all pawned now.

Sometimes when he's high, he comes here to look at the photos. He's sure there's some meaning behind them, something she's trying to tell him. He numbers them as they arrive and hangs them in order, as if they're letters of a word he can't understand, hieroglyphs from some ancient tomb. He paces, wandering from one photo to the other, muttering to himself. He thrusts his face within inches of the images, examining them for clues, thinking if he studies them long enough, hard enough, he'll see some sort of pattern or meaning emerge, some message, some trace of his mother and why she sent them, why she left.

Most are shot cockeyed, and some are blurry like she was careless or drunk when she took them. There's a close-up of a horny-head lizard with a mean face, wicked eye, and flash of tongue. But it's in the bottom corner of the photo, the rest all empty desert and empty sky, like she didn't know how to frame it right. She must have been lying on the ground to capture that shot. Why would she do that?

Then there's a photo of a nasty-looking rooster perched on top of a fence post, its wings in a flurry, beak open, eyes wild and furious. Another photo is of a dead tree, all bare limbs like outstretched arms, like someone shaking their fists at the sky or trying to tear it to pieces. And one of a window in an abandoned storefront. But looking closer, he sees in the window the faint reflection of someone—his mother holding the camera! He laughs, thinking how she accidentally left this trace of herself in the photo. Or was it an accident?

He looks more closely at the other photos and sees a thumb, the toe of a boot, and her shadow across the road. In others, he finds a candy wrapper, a half-empty Cola bottle, and a backpack. Could they be hers? Was she intentionally leaving traces of herself in every picture? What does it mean? What is she trying to tell him?

The lizard is his favorite. He looks startled somehow, like she snuck up on him when he was in the middle of his push-ups, one foot forward as if ready to scamper off. His eye is looking right at you as if he recognizes you and not sure he likes what he sees. All of it, the startled head, cold eye, raised foot, the empty sand and sky, gives the feeling of some fleeting, random moment captured for all eternity. He pictures his mother on her belly in the dirt, her camera poised before her face, waiting for the precise moment and snapping it up.

The rooster also looks startled, shot from below, wings a blur of motion as if caught off-balance. His eyes are fierce, glaring down at her. His claws dig deeply into the grain of the wood fence post. And in the corner of the photo is the blunt stub of his mother's thumb. Something about the rooster and lizard stays with him, flitting in and out of his mind as he goes about the business of keeping body and soul alive on the wing. Something about those eyes follows him everywhere. Sometimes he dreams about them. The photos are pieces of his mother she cut from her own body and sent to him to preserve, to piece back together.

"And all the king's horses and all the king's men . . .."

Snatches of the nursery rhyme about Humpy Dumpty run through his mind, in *her* voice, from *her* mouth, like she read to him when he was a kid. His mother, this patchworked woman scattered across the wall, is like that broken egghead. If Cal can piece her back together again, she's saved and he's saved, and she comes home. If he can't, they're forever doomed.

Sometimes when he stands back and looks at himself, the way Eddy did, he's disgusted by what he sees, holed up here in this house like it's a dark cave and he's some giant miscreant hiding inside. Like those fairy tales his mom read to him about some Cyclops or ogre living alone at the edge of the wild, away from good, decent folks. They are the things parents taunt their kids with and teach them to fear.

"If you don't be good, the ogre's gonna come down from his cave in the mountain and eat you alive."

Only, what they don't tell the little kids, which is worse than being eaten alive, is that if you aren't really good and careful, you'll become the ogre, doomed to live in the cave and feed off the innocence of the child you once were.

That's what he's become, Cal thinks, not the hero of the story but the monster. Here in his parents' home, he's become a giant ogre, gorging on the mutilated bodies of his parents, on all that's left of them. He's taken their perfectly ordinary, comfortable home and turned it into something dark and ugly—a festering sore, a blight on the community, a museum of the absurd and abnormal.

But he doesn't always feel that way. Sometimes he looks around and likes what he sees. Him, here, alone. Likes what he's become, king of his own dark castle, dungeon full of half-dead bodies. And he wants to chortle with delight because he's beaten them all—his mom, his dad, his sister, Eddy, the prick across the street, all those teachers back in grade school, all their hopes and expectations. He's beaten them all, and there's no stopping how low he can go.

"Fuck them," he says, leaning back now in his recliner, the one his father used to sit in when he was king of the castle.

"Look who's king now!" he crows to himself.

After a while, he nods off. He's dreaming of his mutilated mother screaming at him when her sharp claws tighten around his neck.

"Holy shit!" he yells, jumping up. His sister grabs him by the collar, pushes him against the wall, and pummels his chest.

17

KAY
Flying

It's late June before Kay finally has time to drive home to check up on her brother, only to find the front lawn missing and a pile of rocks in its place. Her scalp curdles at the sight, her mind ablaze as she heads inside. Cal is sprawled in Dad's recliner, snoring loudly with a half-eaten bag of corn chips on his chest. He looks like he hasn't shaved in days. The corners of the room are awash with trash, and the place smells like a sewer.

She leaves him sleeping and makes a quick tour of the house, her heart sinking with each door she opens, each room she enters. Her mother's jewelry is gone; her crystal collection, gone; Grandma's silverware, gone. Even the massive antique Victorian dining room table with the lion paw feet, matching chairs, and buffet cabinet are all gone, gone, gone! Her worst nightmare has come true.

She stands in the empty dining room, the rage rising inside unspeakable. She looks at her brother sleeping in the recliner and rushes toward him, screaming. Her hands close around his neck.

Cal jumps up away from her, but she lunges toward him, wraps her fists around the front of his collar, and drives him back against the wall.

"What have you done to our home? Where's the dining room furniture? The lion paw table? That was mine, you bastard! Mine!"

He looks dumbfounded like he's not quite awake.

"Mom promised me that. Promised! Now you've ruined everything. Everything!"

"Kay? What the fuck!"

"Look at this place. It's disgusting. You're disgusting. What would Mom think if she came home and saw the house like this? She'd turn right around and never come home again. *She'd never come home*," Kay wails, her face inches from his. Then she lets go, her fists falling to her side.

Cal wriggles past and turns to face her. She's hunched over now, hands on knees, head hanging down. Bile rises to her throat.

"You blame me, don't you?" Cal shouts. "Admit it! You think it's my fault. I drove her away."

"Yes!" she screams, unable to hold it back any longer. "Yes! I do," she says again, stepping forward, her hands shoving against his chest, shoving him away from her. "She hated seeing you like this. She tried everything to help you. And you wouldn't be helped. You wouldn't! You broke her heart, Cal. *You broke her heart!*" She gives him one final shove.

He staggers back and then regains his balance.

"But not Kay. Never Kay. Good Kay. Not you."

"No! Not me. I loved her. She loved me."

"Did she? Did she love you? If she loved you so goddamned much, then why did she leave you too? Why you, too?"

Kay stares at him, blood draining from her face as the question she's asked a million times is thrown back at her. *How could her mother leave her if she loved her?*

"She calls me." She can barely choke out the words. Her throat feels raw, raped. "She leaves me messages."

Cal is towering over her now, glowering down at her.

"She leaves you messages," he repeats, mocking her, his eyes wild, his head nodding as if beating a nail into the wall. "She leaves you messages, hmm now," he says. "Well, she leaves me photos. She leaves Dad credit card bills."

His eyes burn with suppressed rage. "And that's supposed to mean what, Kay? Messages, photos?" He grabs her by the shoulders, his thumbs digging into her flesh, his face so close to hers that all she sees are his eyes—the anger, the hurt, the defiance.

"Nothing, that's what it means!" he roars, shaking her, breathing his hot dragon breath onto her face, his eyes spitting fire. She blinks, trembles, feels herself visibly shrinking, knowing if it wasn't for his hands holding her up, she would collapse onto the floor.

"It don't mean shit. It don't mean shit! So don't go blaming me for anything! Not a goddam thing, I tell you! Nada!" Spittle flies out of his mouth, which twists and turns as if trying to find the words that express the bitterness, the rage he feels.

"It's all shit!" he repeats, then pushes her away and stomps off.

Kay stumbles against the arm of the recliner and sits there, trembling and weak. She still feels the hurt in her shoulders where he grabbed her, sees the pain in his contorted face, the anger in his eyes as he burned her with his breath. She sits teetering on the edge of the chair, unable to move.

*****

Kay is still shaking, still reeling from their confrontation, when she drives away, but she doesn't go far. She needs to sort things out, figure out what to do next.

She stays at a nearby Motel 6 where her Uncle Gerald and his girlfriend used to stay when they visited the family. At that time, it was painted bright pink with red shutters and red window boxes filled with pink geraniums. But now the pink paint on the stucco walls has faded to orange, and the red on the shutters and empty window boxes is peeling. Most of the rooms have missing screens, and the drapes are drawn tight like eyes whose pupils have rolled back into their sockets.

She shudders as the attendant, a Korean woman who smiles and nods, shows her to her room—a large, beaten-down bed and dresser with a small TV on top. The bathroom looks like it hasn't been updated since the 1970s. A blurry mirror hangs above a pink pedestal sink. Lime green tiles line a tiny shower with a stained plastic shower pan. She turns to tell the lady she's made a mistake and can't stay here after all, but the woman just smiles and nods as she backs out the door.

Kay is too tired and depressed for another fight. She follows the woman to the door and looks out. A scruffy-looking man with a long face and stooped shoulders unlocks the door across from her. He's carrying a hard hat and lunch pail. As he opens the door, a young girl with blond pigtails, no more than two or three years old, sits on a red tricycle and peeks out the door at Kay. Their eyes meet for a long moment before the door closes.

She lives there, Kay realizes. This is her home. This small, dilapidated motel room with the drawn blinds, beaten-down beds, and peeling window boxes is where this little girl, riding her trike, is growing up. There in the small dark room, her little legs peddle furiously around the dilapidated furniture, back and forth, around and around, endlessly.

Kay locks the door, pulls back the grimy-looking bedspread on the bed, and curls up in the middle of the sheets with her sweater jacket still wrapped around her. But she can't get the glimpse of the little girl out of her mind.

When she wakes, it's dark, and she turns on the lamp beside the bed. She's been dreaming—remembering more than dreaming—a scene from her early childhood that she's never been able to erase.

*****

She was three years old. The family was on one of its rare outings, a camping trip in Oregon. She and Cal sat at a picnic table in a campground shaded by tall, dark pines. Even now she feels cold shivers when she remembers, as if she were still there, as if it were happening again, this instant.

She watches in slow motion: her brother there beside her, teasing her like he always does with that rakish, infectious grin, poking, prodding at her again and again, as if he can't help it, can't stop himself. She pushes him away, petulant, sulky, whining for him to stop. But he won't. When she starts to cry, she hears it— a whooshing sound.

Her father, who has been sitting across from them, rears up. His face is huge, filling the sky as he rises. A look of pure malice strikes Kay full in the face as his hand, full-fingered, reaches out in slow motion toward her, coming down, down, down. She freezes, unable to move, waiting for the hand to fall.

But to her amazement and relief, the hand doesn't fall on her. It sweeps right by and catches her brother with a force so fierce it picks him up by the front of his shirt, drags him halfway across the table toward her father, then sends him flying over her head. He crashes with a thud and spray of dirt several yards away in the middle of the campground.

She watches it again and again: Cal dragged across the table. Flying over her head. His face is pinched in puzzlement—like it hasn't quite registered what's happening to him or what's to come. The impact of the fury that sends him flying, the rude landing that awaits, is as yet unimaginable. There's just this look of bewildered innocence as he gazes down at her, their eyes locked in silence for what seems like forever.

"Wha'd I do?" his eyes ask as he flies over her head.

I dunno, she silently replies.

135

Kay feels like she's been turned to stone, too shocked and scared to move or cry. She can do nothing but watch what unfolds. Her mother rushes forward, taking Cal into her arms, screaming at her father. Her father stands there as if he, too, is frozen, stunned by what he's done, by his own fury and his wife's furious response. As if he's astonished to find himself in this predicament at all—being at the center of a scene like this—a man who despises scenes, who more than anything wants always to be in complete control of his environment and yet completely unable to control either his young son, his own temper, or his wife's fury.

Kay watches from the sidelines. She is a part of and apart from it all—the catalyst, as it were, her tears being the spark that set off the explosion. She watches her brother being comforted in her mother's arms and wishes desperately to be there in his place, her mother's arms around her, not him—her soft cheek on hers, her gentle clucks and coos in her ears, her strong hands stroking her back, holding her close. How she craves the safety of those arms, the hallowed space near her heart that holds Cal.

In a moment, it's over. Her father is gone. Her mother has taken Cal into the tent to clean, to comfort. And Kay, still sitting there on the picnic bench, is alone, forgotten, still frozen by that look of pure malice, by that outbreak of fury, by the terrible guilt and jealousy squeezing her heart. She cannot fully comprehend what happened. Only later does the scene's meaning unfold in its constant replaying. It's become some terrible tableau hung like a tapestry on the wall of her mind. She knows it so well that she could depict it in oils, in stone.

Kay sits in the middle of the motel bed, shivering. She brings her knees to her chest and pulls the sweater jacket closer.

This is her family, how she has seen them ever after. Even during their happiest moments when everything was fine, even in the tender looks her father gave her, the comfort of her mother's lap, her brother's protective arm wrapped about her, even then, always then, this reel has played in her mind, stamped forever on her consciousness.

It's become the lens through which she sees each of them. Her father is forever the quietly ticking bomb ready to go off if you aren't careful. Cal is forever the explosion after, flying over her head, and that silent exchange (Wha'd I do? I dunno) is the link that binds them. And her mother—the buffer between her father and brother, sheltering each from the blunt force of the other, absorbing as many of the shocks as she can into her own body—is always the center of comfort and calm Kay aches for.

And where is she now, this brave woman? Has she, too, been blown away? Has she, who miraculously held them together all these years, finally, in some delayed reaction, been blown away by the blast of that day when Kay's world flew apart?

Wha'd I do? I dunno.

Things fall apart. The center cannot hold.

*****

The next morning Kay returns to the house, but Cal's not there. She finds the photos her mother sent him tacked onto the office wall. They mystify her as much as they do her brother. What do they mean? Why did she take them? She's trying to tell them something important; she's sure of it. She still receives comforting messages from her mother, having forwarded the old number to her new apartment. But none of her messages give any clue to decipher these strange, bizarre images she sends Cal.

Kay carefully removes the photos and takes them to Kinko's to make copies, which she tacks back onto the wall, keeping the originals. For safekeeping, she tells herself. Then she scouts through the house, removes everything of value left of her mother's, and packs it into the back of her car. She waits for Cal, not knowing what she will say to him but wanting closure.

In the evening when it starts to get dark, she flips on the light switch, but no light appears. She tries another room. Nothing. Apparently, the electricity has been turned off. She finds a stack of bills on the kitchen counter and puts them in her handbag. Then she looks for something to write on. All she can find are sticky notes. She writes one after another, sticking them on the refrigerator.

She locks the front door behind her as she leaves.

PART II

Making New

June 1998–March 1999

Sometimes I go about in pity for myself, and all the while, a great wind carries me across the sky.
—Ojibwe saying.

Everything is gestation and coming birth.
—Rainer Maria Rilke from *Letters to a Young Poet*

18

WALTER
Luther, Alaska

When Walter reaches Luther, Alaska, a small fishing village on Resurrection Bay, he knows he's come home. Who knows if this is where he'll plant his feet for good. But it's home in his heart, where his mind rests nice and easy between the granite-knuckled bluffs to the east and the bay curving gently westward; between the hemlock and pine-clad mountains rolling away to the south and that gleam of glaciers rising in the north.

It's where he and Granddad spent their last fishing trip together. What he remembers most is how it made him feel—cool, clean, quiet—out there on the water as he leaned on the bow, the wind's fingers raking through his hair as they flew across the bay. Later they camped ashore, standing side by side on the bank of a rushing stream, flicking their lines into the water. He remembers the rich, smoking scent of salmon sizzling on a camp grill. The low, haunting hoot of an owl outside their tent. The sight of a brown bear in the distance ambling lazily through splashes of warm sunshine and cool green.

What he remembers most about the town is what he and Franny saw watching a travel show years ago. She had to admit it looked pretty. He wishes she was by his side now to see it in person. Colorful clapboard buildings line Main Street, a red barn-like hardware shop holding down one corner and a blue-gabled post office perched on the other. Several home-style cafés, an antique store with a big ship's wheel in the front window, and other assorted souvenir shops are tucked between.

As he drives through the village, he almost hears himself saying to the woman missing at his side, "Here we are, girl, at long last." He's always imagined them growing old together in some wild, green place with deep blue skies and cold, clear water.

But she never saw it like that. The heat, desert, tropics—that's where she longed to travel. Something south of the border called her name. But Walter never liked traveling where he couldn't understand what people were saying, where their ways were strange to him and his to them. That one time they went south, camping by the Sea of Cortez, was largely a disappointment—too barren, too hot. He had enough heat welding day in and day out and, before that, in the jungles and steaming rice paddies of Vietnam. He was looking for cool: snow-capped mountains and icy streams, tall trees and deep lakes, places where you could wear knee-high boots and a parka, throw a line in the water, and bring up dinner.

He rents a room at a small motel, where half a dozen cabins lay in a semicircle beneath a canopy of red Alders. After off-loading some of his gear, he heads to a nearby restaurant called, oddly enough in these parts, Moondog Café. He takes a table by the window where he can look out toward the bay. When the waitress pours him coffee, he asks, "Where's the best fishing around here?"

"Oh, you got to ask Clay about that. He's got a bait and tackle shop at the end of the road there. Rents out boats, too. You can't miss it."

After a large helping of bacon and eggs with biscuits and gravy, he heads toward the bay, walking along the side of a road where his boots sink into the soft earth. The air is full of pine and salt and, beneath that, a deep loamy scent. Clay's Tackle and Bait

Shop lies in the hollow of a small cove. A dozen or so small boats are tucked into slips along a narrow dock.

He climbs the worn wooden stairs to a veranda, looking out past the boat slips to the open bay glinting on the horizon, and stamps his feet free of dirt before entering the shop. A "For Sale" sign is taped on the window. Inside turns out larger than expected. Under a high-pitched ceiling, an open loft is built across the rafters. Ribbons of light stream down through the high shutters. Below, the knotty pine walls are lined with shelves filled with all manner of boat gear—coils of ropes, engine parts, trays of feathered lures and silver spoons, a row of rods and reels, a barrel full of live bait, lobster and crab traps, tarps and tents, a freezer full of ice, and a small fridge of sodas and sandwiches.

A man sits on a stool behind the counter, reading a newspaper. He rises, leaning on a cane, and greets Walter.

"What can I do for you?"

"Are you Clay?" Walter asks.

"Born and bred," he answers. He's a big guy, a full head taller than Walter, topped with a thick thatch of silver. He has the look of an aging athlete, despite the cane. He has an athlete's good looks too, a wide grin, square jaw, crinkly blue eyes, and deep laugh lines burrowed into his cheeks.

"Walter Albright, here. In town to do a bit of fishing. Heard you're the guy to talk to."

"I'm your man. What you looking to catch? We got salmon, halibut, rockfish, ling cod—"

"Nothing big. What I can carry home and cook up sounds good."

"You might want to stick to bottom fishing then, rockfish and ling cod, I'd say." They spend the next ten minutes debating rods and reels, spoons and bait, then haggle on a price to rent a boat for four days.

"Your first time out in these waters, right?"

He nods.

"You better take Dawn with you then, show you around."

"I don't need no babysitter."

"You won't get one. Dawn don't like kids."

Walter grimaces, "I prefer being on my own."

"I hear you. She won't crowd you. You'll be on your own after that."

"Don's a she?" he asks as a woman comes out of the back.

Apparently, she's overheard him. "Dawn with a w—for woman," she tells him like she's been saying it her whole life.

"Walter here wants to do some bottom fishing. Told him you'd show him around."

Dawn looks to be around fifty, has cinnamon-colored hair cut short to her chin with bangs framing a square face. She's built like a brick: short, solid, and square, hardly any shape to her at all. Her face and hands are sprinkled with nutmeg-colored freckles.

She looks Walter in the eye and holds out a meaty hand. Her grip is firm, warm, and surprisingly soft, not manlike at all for all its heft and weight. There's something about her that immediately engages his attention and appreciation. He finds it not only in the four-squareness of a body built to last but in the sea-captain eyes—short, light-colored lashes framing a blue so fresh and sky-like that it makes him smile.

Their handshake lasts a few seconds longer than it would normally, and the look that passes between them seems to confuse her. A slow, pink blush spreads across her neck and face, the kind of blush that stutters somehow, showing her unfamiliarity with such things. This is followed by a grimace and a quick pulling back of her hand, which she buries in the pouch of her parka.

She clears her throat and looks down as she growls a polite, "Nice to meet ya."

"Same here," he replies, bringing his fingers into the palm of his hand, a soft fist. She sees the gesture and raises her eyes to meet his again, not blushing now, but in a sharp, studious way, cocking her head ever so slightly, as if gauging the measure of the man.

*****

The next morning, Walter picks up his tackle and bait from Clay and buys a ham sandwich and Coke from the fridge. He packs them into a portable cooler and heads down the dock to the slip Clay points out, where a sixteen-foot aluminum Lowe dinghy lies. Dawn is waiting for him, sitting in the middle of the boat.

"You driving or me?" he asks.

She smiles. "You're paying for this trip. I'm just along for the ride."

He loads the gear, unties the dock lines, and then climbs in and starts the engine. It takes three pulls, but Dawn offers no advice and no comment. She's sitting at the bow now looking out at the bay. When the engine catches, they motor out of the slip and putter down the channel, the Mercury outboard engine humming quietly as they head across the cove.

Dawn points out the channel markers, tells him where it shoals up and where the rip tide's strong, and guides him toward her favorite places to bottom fish. Her voice is low and husky, soft-edged against the humming motor, the slap of waves and cries of gulls. Her back is silhouetted against the bright horizon as they move forward, a hefty weight that keeps the boat on an even keel, even when he revs up the motor as they cross the channel, air-born mostly, skipping like a rock when it touches down. Beyond that, it's like she's not there at all, and after a while he forgets she is. The cold, keen air rushes around him and he feels rinsed clean, shed of thought and all manner of care.

By the time they return in the late afternoon, he's got three ling cods and two rockfish in the ice chest. He offers her one of the cods, which she accepts. He shakes her hand as they part, surprised again at how soft and solid it is. Her eyes now are a clear quicksilver gray, intense and lively, like the backs of the porpoises that played in the boat's wake as they headed out into the bay. They nod silently to each other before turning away.

He spends the rest of the week taking the boat out on his own, catching and releasing more fish than he keeps. He catches glimpses of Dawn now and then, up a ladder hauling down a box for a customer, kneeling on the dock in the distance coiling lines, pointing out the channel markers from the bow of another rental boat. Once he finds her running down the dock ahead of him and then crouching at the side of a young man who is busy by a boat.

As Walter approaches, he overhears her saying, "Awe, Randy. Wha'd you go and do that for? Didn't I tell you?" The young man kneels at her side, his wide eyes looking so comically confused that Walter suppresses a chuckle as he passes them, letting out a snort instead. Dawn glances up sharply at the sound, the gray in her eyes having a hard, keen edge now.

When his week is up, he goes to see Clay to settle the bill. As they say their goodbyes, Walter cocks his head at the sign in the window. "You leaving town too?"

Clay nods. "Back to Kansas. Wife wants to spend more time with the grandkids."

"Must be hard, leaving all this. You been here awhile?"

"Forty years. But it's time." Clay glances at his cane. "Don't get around as good as I used to—bad hip. And like Martha says, I had mine. Now it's hers."

"Fairs fair," Walter agrees.

"Why? You interested?"

"Naw. Just passing through. I'm headed up to Moosehead Lake. Spent some time with my granddad there when I was a boy. Taught me to flyfish in Salmon River."

"Some good hunting up there, too. Got me a moose once." Clay glances at the antlers over the cash register.

"I did enough hunting overseas. Think I'll stick to fishing," Walter says.

"I hear you. Best of luck then," Clay adds and shakes his hand.

But when he gets to the road, Walter looks back at the little shop tucked away in the cove, the small dock leading out to sea, and a small round figure with a flash of red hair.

*****

Walter spends three weeks at the cabin on Moosehead Lake, thigh-deep in hip waders, flicking his line out over the cold, silver-sparkled water of Salmon Creek, aiming to reel in the silver or coho salmon that coast the currents closer to shore. For the kings, he'll have to wade deeper and wait longer, plumbing the depths where they like to hide. He'd rather stay in the shallows, closer to shore. The hunt isn't the point so much as just being out here in the wild, his eyes ever watchful, following the dragonflies with their purple and turquoise iridescent wings as they skim above the silver stream, or marking the slow arc of the bald eagles circling overhead, or catching glimpses of moose with their long, stately legs wading into the shallows across the way to dip their noses into the drink.

He's come here seeking solitude. That's what he's wanted his whole life: a spot away from the crowds and confusion and all the complications that come from a life highly involved with others. It's what he would have if Franny hadn't come along and stolen his heart. Even then, he's kept to himself as much as possible, despite being a married man and a father to boot. His stint owning that welding shop, he realizes now, was an attempt to cut the clutter, to get out from working for others. But he was never able to make an income that matched what he brought in as a union worker, and he needed that pension, so eventually he let the shop go.

But the longer he stays out here by the lake, the more restless he feels. He's surprised by this and disappointed in himself. He thought he'd like being alone, nothing between him and God but sky and the surrounding forests. He thought he'd relish the stillness, nothing but the sound of breezes blowing through the timbers, birdsong drifting through the air, the rush of creek water spilling away below, or the whirr of the reel as his line flicks through the air and the cold-water hums around his thighs. And he does relish it, or he did, those first few weeks. But now it's too quiet standing here in the sunlight with his mug in his hand. The stillness has lost its luster and seems empty, barren almost, like he's listening for something not here, something missing, something he misses.

Although he's always been a quiet man at heart, a loner like Franny says, he's never been alone, not in the thirty-two years of their marriage and not even before that when he was in the Marine Corp and did his tour in Vietnam. His personal quietness has always basked in the ever-flowing sound of others, like a quiet eddy in an otherwise rushing stream of sound. In his life with Franny, the house was always full of noise—Kay bright and bossy with her bright and bossy bevy of girlfriends traipsing in and out, Cal with his loud outdoor-indoor voice and loose laughter chasing them about, Franny's cheerful chattering and soft, absent-minded humming. Even when they all managed to be gone for the day, the radio in his shop and the twenty-four-hour news on TV were a constant backdrop for the stillness in his head.

He misses his hummers in the backyard too, strange as that sounds, watching and feeding them, laughing at the way they attacked him with their long beaks when he took down the empty feeder and brought it back full of nectar, too impatient or ignorant to know he's the hand that feeds them. He misses his garden too, harvesting his fat beefsteak tomatoes and prickly squash in the half-barrel containers where he planted them. He's always been better at tending things than people. He could tend birds and gardens, tend houses and cars, tend the business of making and fixing things. It came natural, easy, to him. But people? How do you tend people? That always seemed a mystery.

He finds his thoughts returning to the tackle and bait shop— the warm rugged planks striping the floor, the high rafters filtered with sunlight, the heavy shelves packed tight with merchandise, the slap of water against the boat hulls, and that sandy curve of cove sheltered from the wind. He thinks of Clay with his head full of silver and the "for sale" sign hanging in the window.

His life isn't over yet. He needs something purposeful to do. He needs the rush of life to harbor his quiet, a world of work to carry his loneliness. He needs something to tend.

He leaves the cabin a full month short of his two-month lease and heads back to Luther.

19

WALTER
Weight of Gold

"Thought I'd see you again," Clay tells Walter as they shake hands.

"How so?" Walter asks.

"Can't say. Just get a feeling sometimes. Know what I mean?"

Walter nods, looking around the shop. "Think I might like to settle down here awhile. Your place still for sale?"

He's thought long and hard about this. With the right price, he could swing it. He still has the money from selling the welding shop in a CD that is ready to turn, and instead of renting out Granny's house, it's high time to sell it now that she's gone. He could always take out a small mortgage on their home if needed since he paid it off five years ago. He could also start drawing on his pension and taking an early retirement.

He and Clay talk shop as he shows him around, taking him up in the loft, in the back storage rooms, behind the shop where there's a portable lift, a few boats on cradles, and a large workshop. As they tour the dock, Clay points out the winners and losers in his fleet of boats. Then he takes him into his office and opens his books, telling him what he's asking for the whole kit and caboodle, as he says. Walter doesn't blink. It's less than he feared and more than he hoped for, but he could swing it.

"You got yourself a deal," he told Clay.

"You sure now? You don't want to take some time and think about it?"

"Can't say I do," Walter says, shaking his head.

Clay studies him. "There's one hitch though. And it's a big one."

"What's that?" Walter asks warily.

"Randy. Randy comes with the shop."

"What do you mean?" Walter's eyebrows pinch, vaguely remembering the young man Dawn was scolding on the dock that day.

"Randy's dad used to work for me. They lived up there in the loft. Bit of a lush, he was. Abandoned the kid six years ago when he was fifteen or so. Or maybe not. Maybe his body's out there somewhere at the bottom of the bay or frozen beneath some landslide. Hard to say. Anyway, when his dad disappeared, the whole town kind of adopted him. I gave Randy his dad's job, not that he's any good at it. He's a bit of an odd duck—not slow, just scattered, if you know what I mean. Mostly he sweeps the dust and cobwebs out of the shops, chases mice and sets traps, and washes down the boats. Dawn tries to teach him stuff, but he's forgetful and too fidgety to concentrate. Different town folk put him up for a while, but none wants to keep him long. He's made a nest for himself up in the loft now. This here's his home."

Clay looks him in the eye. "Bottom line—Randy comes with the shop. I'd have to have your word on it before I could sell."

"I don't know," Walter says, mind whirling, disappointment clouding his thoughts.

"He's no trouble. Sweet temper. Aims to please. Do anything you ask him or at least try. Discourages thieves because he's here day and night. Ran off a gang of vandals once. Brought back a boat some old geezer tried to run off with another time."

Walter looks around the shop, weighs the bulk and breadth of it, the high slanted ceiling, the shelves and barrels full of purpose and promise, a glimpse of blue water out the dusty window, and then stretches out his hand. He won't let one poor boy spoil his dream.

"You got my word on it."

*****

When Walter returns the next week to put down a deposit and sign papers, Clay is standing with Dawn at his side, and neither looks happy. Clay says something to her that Walter can't hear, and she nods. Then she looks at Walter, square in the face, her chin up, the muscle in her jaw flexing, before passing out of the shop.

He watches her go.

"What's that all about?" Walter asks.

Clay hangs his head, scratching at the back of his neck like there's something there he needs to get out, but he's not sure how. Then he sighs and looks up.

"Dawn wants to buy the place."

"But I thought we had a deal? Is she offering more?"

"That's the thing, she doesn't have the money. She can come up with half, wants me to carry the rest. I told her I can't."

"Then we still have a deal!"

"Maybe. I said I'd give her more time to see if she can borrow what she needs."

Walter's stomach clenches. He narrows his eyes and gives Clay a hard look. "I thought we shook on it. You trying to squeeze me for more?"

"Look, Dawn's as much a part of this place as Randy."

"Hell, she can keep her job. How much you pay her?"

"It's not that," Clay says and then leans toward him, eyes earnest. "She wants her own stake here. Something no one can take from her. Says she'd be willing to take a partner if needed. I think she can do it. If she can't get a loan, she'll find a partner. I know her. She will."

Walter doesn't know what to say. He's reeling with disappointment and looks away.

"She'll take you, if you'll have her."

His head snaps back. "What?"

"She said she'd be willing to partner with you to buy the place. Half and half. If you'll have her."

"I don't want a partner."

"I told her."

"First Randy, now her. You got some nerve." He is seething inside, trying to control his anger and his disappointment.

Clay winces. "It's not nerve; it's heart. If I had more nerve than heart, I'd be staying put."

Walter shakes his head and sighs. "So where does that leave us?"

Clay sucks in a big breath and lets it out slowly. "Well, it's like this. If she can pull it off, get a loan, find a partner, it's hers. If somehow that falls through, it's yours. I gave her two months."

"Two months! I don't want to wait that long."

"Then take a partner," Clay urges, leaning forward. "You won't regret it. If it turns out this life's not for you, she can buy you out in time. She knows everything there is about running this place. Knows everybody in town too. She's smart and fair-minded, easy to work with."

Clay leans back now and crosses his arms. "If you get this place without her, Dawn will eventually open up her own little operation on the side, and people will go to her." He shakes his head at Walter. "I'm telling you you're going to go bust if you don't get her and the community behind you. If you want this to work, you got to make her a partner. Let her buy a piece of the place and work beside you. Don't have to be a full partner, maybe a third, and then you can keep control. She doesn't want to grow rich. She just wants her own place, be her own boss, do what she loves to do, what she's good at. You'll find her an asset in the end. Worth her weight in gold. You'll see."

Walter thinks about what Clay's been saying and feels his resistance loosening ever so slightly. He thinks about Dawn, that look she gave him as she passed by, the four-square bent of her back walking away. A smile tugs at the corner of his mouth.

"Worth her weight, huh? That's a lot of gold," he can't help saying.

Clay chuckles. "That's a lot of woman."

20

KAY

Eyes Like Hands

Kay weaves her way through shoppers on a busy street in downtown Sierra Madre past colorful boutiques, vintage clothing shops, sidewalk cafés, and art galleries. She's shopping for a special gift for Bethany and Bill's first wedding anniversary. But despite what would normally be a pleasant pastime, she feels anxious and distracted.

It's been three weeks since that disastrous visit with Cal, and she still hasn't heard from him. She paid his phone bill, as well as water, electricity and gas, so you'd think he'd at least call and thank her for that. He's not the type to stay angry for long. She feels guilty about taking the photos Mom sent him, like she's stolen her brother's birthright, even though she left him with copies. But he's stolen her birthright, too, hasn't he? Selling her grandmother's claw foot dining table!

Still, she's worried. Usually, he's the one who calls first when they fight. For all his hot temper, he cools down fast and forgives easily. So, to ignore her calls like this isn't like him. If she doesn't hear from him soon, she'll have to start calling the hospitals, the jail, the morgue, for God's sake. That's what Mom used to do when she lost touch with him.

I can't do this, she tells herself. I can't do what she did. I won't. It's better not to know, to wait for him to call and trust he will—trust the worst she fears will not happen.

After an hour of shopping, she can't find anything she likes or can afford, so she heads to the car. On the way she pauses in front of an art gallery window, where a small oil painting of a sunset captures her attention. Maybe Bethany and Bill will like this.

Then she sees something that makes her heart stop. She touches the glass to steady herself. It's an assortment of black-and-white photographs, neatly matted and framed—her mother's. They must be.

Ever since returning from Cal's, she's been mesmerized by her mother's photographs. They are strange and deeply disturbing, unlike anything she would have expected her mother to take, unlike anything she did before. Yet, despite that, they are strikingly beautiful, the way stark images against a white backdrop can be.

And now, out of nowhere, her photos appear in a gallery window! How can this be? Her heart beats wildly as she leans closer to make out the signature scrawled in the corner. Gunther Ramon. It's not her mother after all!

She stands there dumbfounded before stepping inside. A bell on the door rattles as she enters. A clerk sits behind a counter, black-rimmed reading glasses far down on his nose. He looks up, nods politely, and goes back to his reading. Relieved that she'll be able to study the photos undisturbed, she wanders through a maze of small rooms until she finds the collection by the photographer featured in the front window.

The black-and-white images are mostly desert scenes shot from odd angles, heavy in contrasts, stark like her mother's with the same sense of incongruity that lends an eerie beauty—startling and disturbing. She is staring closely at one when she hears someone behind her. The clerk, she assumes.

"I like the way the light seems to lift each object to a new level of intensity," he tells her in a quiet, soothing voice, as if continuing a conversation begun long ago.

"I was thinking the same thing," she says. Turning toward the voice, she's startled by his nearness. He's dressed all in black—black faded jeans, black silk shirt, black leather jacket. His hair too is black, stylishly spiked. His forehead is high and so white between the dark brows and the dark hair that it seems luminescent. And his eyes—the intensity of those blue eyes cutting across her face makes her stumble backward. He catches her by the elbow.

"I'm so sorry. I startled you."

"Not at all," she says, realizing that in her whole life she's never said those words exactly that way, and wonders where they came from.

"So, you're a fan of Gunther Ramon's work."

"No, I've never heard of him. But his photos . . .." She turns to look again. "They seem familiar."

"They remind you of someone else's work."

"Yes, my mother's," she breathes softly.

"Ah," he says, letting the word linger in the air between them. "Your mother is an artist."

"No, no, nothing like that," she says, blushing, sorry somehow her mother isn't. "I mean, she's always liked photography, but she's not an artist."

"If her work reminds you of these, they must have some artistic quality."

"Well, they're odd. Beautiful in a bizarre way. But I don't know what they mean, what she's trying to say."

"Maybe she isn't trying to say anything. Maybe she's capturing something that speaks to her and letting it communicate its own message to the viewer."

"Maybe. But I sense she's trying to tell us something." She looks up at him.

"Have you asked her?"

She ducks her head.

"Forgive me. I didn't mean to pry," he says.

"No, it's not that. It's just that she's . . . not here anymore, and we don't talk, I mean, not in person. It's complicated."

Tears sting her eyes, and she blinks rapidly. She feels boxed in somehow between the mystery of her mother's photographs and this man's intense blue eyes. She must leave quickly, but she's not sure which way to turn, which doorway leads to the exit. In her haste, like a fool, she bumps against a doorframe. Her face burns with embarrassment. For a moment, the room seems to spin.

"Here," he says, taking her firmly by the elbow and guiding her toward a chair near the front entrance. She sinks gratefully into it.

"The artwork excites so much feeling. In such small spaces, it can be overwhelming," he tells her, lowering himself to her eye level. "I apologize profusely." His hand goes to his heart as he says this, as if he too is overwhelmed with intense feelings.

She watches him now, crouched there before her, looking genuinely distressed and vulnerable somehow, this serious young man with an accent she can't place.

There's something different about him, the way he moves, holds himself, looks at her, as if he's really seeing her, not thinking of something else—his head cocked just so, his eyes alight, listening. Even his breathing is palpable, as if he's drawing her into his body and sensing her through her scent. She wonders if this is what seeing is meant to be. Before this moment, she may never have truly been seen. In his gaze she feels naked and vulnerable, and gently caressed. Her own breathing is infected by his nearness, and she realizes she smells him too. She is breathing in his scent. The warm muskiness of him courses through her.

"You're not from here," she says in wonderment at this man who seems so different from everyone she's ever met. Then she blushes, realizing how impolite this must sound. "I mean, your accent . . .."

He smiles—a crooked grin that matches the scruff covering his jawline. But his eyes, which light up in amusement, are soft and tender. "I'm from Argentina," he says, pronouncing the name, the "g" and "t," softly. "Richard Verón. Ricardo, they call me at home. And you? What do they call you?"

"Kay. Just Kay."

"It's a pleasure to meet you, Just Kay." He smiles and holds out his hand, palm up and open. She lays her hand there and he places his other hand on top, pressing hers between his. She looks at her hand enveloped in his and feels its heat rising through her. She cannot look away.

"And you, where are you from?" he asks her, breaking the spell.

She looks up, surprised by the question. "Why, I'm from here!" she says, pulling her hand loose. "The United States."

He laughs. "Yes, yes, I know. I mean, do you live nearby, or are you visiting?"

She blushes. Again. "Oh! I thought you meant . . .." She takes a deep breath. "I live in Sierra Madre now. Just moved here from Northridge, the university."

"I see," he says, letting the words roll out slowly, as if they mean more than they say. "So, tell me about your mother."

And surprisingly, she does. It all comes tumbling out: her mother's disappearance, how unexpected and unlike her it was, the messages on the phone, the photos she sent her brother, how Kay stole them away and left him with copies, how guilty she feels.

She finds it all spilling out, all the mixed emotions and the terrible suspicion that she and her brother, all of them, drove her away. It feels like a confession, as if he's a priest and she's doing penance, confiding all her hopes and fears, although she has never been to confession and knows nothing of what it's like. Still, she senses it must feel something like this, pouring out your heart to a stranger who you know will not judge you.

He listens, nods, and murmurs things that invite her to continue.

"Maybe her leaving isn't about you or your brother or what you did or didn't do. Maybe her leaving is about her, a desire to travel, to photograph, to be on her own," he says.

She sighs and looks deep into those blue eyes. "I'd like to think that," she says. "You are probably right. She says she's happy." Her voice chokes.

"But you aren't happy with her gone."

"No. I don't do happy well, especially with her gone." She smiles wryly. "I worry too much. Question everything . . . myself . . . too much." She searches for words to explain what it is she wants, needs—that stillness, that pool of comfort her mother embodied for her.

He's crouched before her, balancing on his toes, the palms of his hands pressed together, his chin leaning against his fingertips, almost as if he's in prayer, a solemn pose, as if to show how closely he's listening to her. She can't stop the flow of words that keep coming, as if to hold him there a bit longer.

And she thinks: *I must stop myself. I must stop this very minute.*

And she thinks: *I don't want this to stop, this moment, this, this, just this.*

"I'm sorry," she says finally. "I must be boring you. I don't even know what I am saying anymore or why I'm going on like this. This is so not me." She starts to get up.

"No, no. It's been fascinating. Don't go." His hands touch down lightly on her knees, as if to hold her there. Her breath hitches, an electric current coursing through her, pooling in her center. She waits for him to say more, but he doesn't.

"Your poor legs, sitting there like that all this time. They must be numb."

"No, they're fine," he says. "See?" He starts to rise and then reels a bit as one leg gives way.

She reaches out to steady him.

"Well, maybe they are a little numb," he admits, laughing.

"I told you."

"Yes, you did." They smile at each other now, as if they're old friends. She moves again to rise, and this time he lets her, stepping back to give her room. He follows her to the door.

"We should meet for lunch tomorrow. You must show me your mother's photos. I could give you my professional opinion since they are so much like Ramon's, a fellow countryman. Maybe we can figure out what they mean together."

"No, no, I couldn't put you out like that. I've taken up too much of your time already."

"But you must!" he insists. Then seeing the startled look on her face, he laughs. "I mean, it's only right, no? After boring me with your troubles, as you say, and putting my left foot asleep." He shakes and stomps his foot now. "I do believe you owe me that much at least—to see these mysterious photographs you've been talking about."

"It would be nice to get your professional opinion," she admits and then laughs as he continues his comical dance. "Your poor foot. I'm so sorry."

"It's settled then," he tells her. They agree upon a restaurant down the street, and he opens the door for her.

"Wait!" he says before she walks away. "Do you have a card?"

"A card?"

"Yes, yes, you know, a business card, some way I can reach you." He hands her his.

"Oh yes, I think I do." The cards she ordered from Cal-Lithix haven't arrived yet, but she may have some old ones. She fumbles through her bag and pulls out a dog-eared card she had when she was teaching as a graduate student. "Wait," she says, scribbling her new number on the back before handing it to him.

His face lights up when he takes it. "Archaeology! How fascinating. Yes, yes, I see that in you. The desire to look beneath the surface of things, to ferret out meaning, to put the pieces of the puzzle back together again."

"You see all that?" she asks, bemused. Now that he's ventured into the area of her expertise, she feels more comfortable, more in control of her feelings, as if they moved safely away from a dangerous precipice.

He does not answer her at first, but his eyes rest firmly upon her like steadying hands.

"Yes, Kay. I see all that."

And the use of her name, the simple affirmation, the solemn way he says it, the eyes like hands, send her reeling again.

"I really must go now."

"Until tomorrow," he says, still holding the door for her.

She feels his eyes upon her as she walks away. After a moment, when her heartbeat slows, she's tempted to turn her head to see if he's still there. A panicky feeling rises at the thought that maybe he isn't. Maybe he hasn't been watching at all. Maybe as soon as she turned away, he returned to the gallery.

But when she glances back, he's still there, looking after her, his steady eyes holding her up.

21

KAY
Drowning

The next day Kay can't stop thinking about Richard. She takes out his card a dozen times, running her finger over the surface of the raised letters.

Ricardo Sarmento Verón
Verón Studio & Gallery

He's not a clerk, after all, but the gallery owner. An artist too? she wonders. Why is she so fascinated by this man she just met? It rarely happens this way, her becoming obsessed with them. In fact, she can't remember when it's ever happened. It's always their obsession with her that she feeds off, enjoys, and uses for her own pleasure.

She should be elated at finding someone who can help decipher her mother's photos. And she is, she tells herself. But somehow, the man himself has taken precedence in her mind and squeezed out all thoughts of her mother. All she can think about, and goes over in detail, is *him*—the way he knelt before her, the way his hands felt on her knees, the way he breathed her in. But even more was the startling blue of his eyes that held her as if she were his captive and he hers, that compelled her to pour herself out to him, that held her steady as she did so and safely embraced her after.

She's never felt this way before and has nothing to compare it with.

Is it only lust, after all? Is she so hard up that any guy off the street can cause her to blush and fill her thoughts with erotica?

She hasn't been with anyone since she and sweet Miguel lay together on that rock in Baja more than six months ago. Against her better judgment, she dated a couple of times: the cousin of a friend she barely remembers now and that cute jock from the gym. But halfway through the dates, she found the effort to connect, to inspire some spark of interest, too exhausting. A weariness fell over her like a blanket of ash, smothering any chance of sparking a fire.

When the jock dropped her off at her apartment, he reached nonchalantly across her to open the car door, saying, "I won't bother asking you for a second date since you weren't here for the first one."

She stared at him, stunned it had been so obvious, that her effort to go through the motions, to bring the night to a tidy, painless conclusion had been in vain. When she closed the apartment door behind her, she pressed her back against it, unable to move further. *Never again*, she promised herself. *Never again*.

She didn't want another man in her life, a relationship to worry about, someone she'd have to push away eventually or who would push her away, which would be worse. It's something she's managed to avoid all these years by choosing men she knew she could leave, if needed, with no regrets.

And yet, here she is, so aroused by the thought of seeing him that she must give herself a good talking to. *This meeting is not a date*, she tells herself as she prepares to meet him. *It's about your mother's photos, not your sex life. Under no circumstances, no matter how much he begs, will you sleep with him.*

And it's just as well because she can find nothing suitable to wear, nothing that makes her look the way she wants—careless casual and hot as hell. So, she settles for her best hip-hugger jeans, a black tube top, and a long-sleeved white cotton blouse that she leaves unbuttoned to play peek-a-boo with her belly button. She tops it off with a silver and abalone shell neckless and silver hoop earrings. Coral lipstick, black mascara, and she's done.

Then she dashes out the door, knowing she'll be at least fifteen minutes late. But that's okay, she tells herself. It's okay to keep him waiting—unless, of course, he's on a short lunch break and has no time to spend with her, or he thinks she's blown him off and leaves, or he's plain forgotten about her altogether by now.

By the time she arrives, she's a mess.

"I'm meeting someone," she tells the maître d'. "He's probably left already. I'm late."

He smiles at her. "This way please."

She sees him silhouetted against the light from the window behind him—the dark spikey hair, the aristocratic nose, the slender figure as he gracefully rises to greet her, watching her as she rushes toward him. He's dressed in black again, and she wonders if that's his signature style.

"Let me help you," he says, taking the portfolio she's holding that stores her mother's photos before pulling out her chair.

"I wasn't sure you'd still be here," she tells him breathlessly as she sits.

"How could you doubt me?" he asks, settling in his seat across from her.

"Only that I'm so late. I wasn't sure how much time you had."

He smiles and cocks his head charmingly. "Time is of no essence when waiting for a beautiful woman."

She blushes and takes a deep breath. "We're here to look at my mother's photos," she reminds him. And herself.

"But, of course," he assures her. "Still, I took the liberty of ordering lunch for us. And wine," he adds, pouring her a glass from the bottle left on the table.

"You shouldn't have. I don't eat lunch."

"But this is a lunch date, no?"

"No! This is not a date. This is me getting professional advice about my mother's photos."

"But, of course. Yet, it is lunchtime, and we are at a restaurant, so I assumed . . .. I can cancel the order if you insist." He looks so earnest, so confused, so disappointed, his blue eyes cloudy now, his smooth brow creased.

Fearing she's offended him, she touches his hand. "No don't. This is lovely. You've been so kind. How can I refuse?"

"I'm glad," he says, his eyes lightening, his brow smoothing, as he lifts his glass and touches hers. "To your mother then."

*****

When they finish their meal and the dishes have been cleared away, she spreads her mother's photos across the table. He studies each one silently.

"I see why Gunther's photos remind you of your mother's," he says. "It's more than the unusual composition. It's the strong light. Almost as if they were shot in a studio. See the shadow of the lizard, that rock there? How this dilapidated structure in the background is thrown into high relief by the strong light? How the deep shadow undercuts it?

"Your mother has captured that almost imperceptible distinction, that subtle quality of light that is so distinct in Latin America. There's a substantive, qualitative difference between the light in Latin America and in the north. A softer melting quality, very subtle, but distinct. It colors things in a unique way, almost as if, rather than refracting off the objects and illuminating them from without, it penetrates and lights them from within. You see here and here," he points at a photo. "That inner luminescence? It's difficult to capture that difference in a photograph, yet your mother, like Gunther, has done so."

He glances at her and seems surprised to see her looking at him with such amused skepticism. He leans back in his chair, the intensity by which he's been instructing her melting away. A slow smile surfaces. "Ah, I see. You don't believe me."

"No, no, it's just that . . . how can the light be different south of the border? Do you mean it changes as you near the equator?"

"It's a subtle thing. Sometimes Norte-Americanos, unless they are artists, cannot appreciate the difference."

"Ah, so now it's a cultural difference? Americans don't get it?"

"Unless they are artists, of course, or have an artistic temperament."

"Perhaps the difference lies in those who live in Latin America. When you come north, you lose the ability to see light in the same way you do in your native country in familiar territory. So, you think light has lost a qualitative difference when actually the light is the same everywhere." She waits to hear his response, smiling smugly.

He leans back in his chair, his forefinger lightly stroking his lower lip.

"You are very amusing," he tells her.

"*I* am amusing?" She didn't expect that. "No, I would say *you* are amusing."

"We are amusing together then."

"*No*. We are not."

"We are not amusing?"

"We are not *we*. There is no *we*."

"There is you. And there is me. Is that not we?"

He leans toward her now, and she hears him take in a deep breath, as if breathing in her scent, as if taking possession of some intimate part of her. His fingers reach across the table and take the tips of hers into his, folds them into his palm. She is totally unprepared and unable to answer him.

"Is this not we?" he repeats, holding her eyes with his as he lifts her fingers to his lips.

The kiss is so light she thinks she may have dreamed it. But his half-closed eyes as he holds her hand near and the deep breaths he takes as if drinking in her scent make her feel that she is the one who, with her hand in his, holds him up.

*****

That night she can't sleep. She keeps kicking the covers off as if she's having hot flashes, then piling them on again as she chills. She can't get Richard, Ricardo, out of her mind. Her dreams are full of her mother's photos, of Richard's face looming behind her, his hands searing her arms, that funny dance he did, shaking his leg awake . . ..

She rises. It's 3 a.m. She takes his card out again and reads each word, each letter, each space, as if it has something important to tell her, as if she really is, as he said, looking beneath the surface, trying to ferret out meaning.

Ricardo, it says, although Richard is what he calls himself, what she calls him. The doubleness of his name intrigues her.

"Ricardo," she whispers to herself, lingering on each syllable. This must be what his mother calls him. She imagines hearing his mother's voice. "Ricardo!" she calls. And he comes to her, a young boy with intense blue eyes.

The sound of the phone startles her. She nearly drops his card.

She thinks: *It's my mother.*

She thinks: *It's Richard.*

She thinks: *It's a wrong number.*

She picks up the phone tentatively and places it against her ear, hears the breathing.

"I couldn't sleep," he says.

She's sure she must be dreaming.

"You couldn't sleep either. I knew when you picked up so quickly."

"I'm holding your card," she confesses.

He sighs deeply. "Yes, I feel it."

They talk for hours.

*****

The following week Richard takes Kay on a real date. She figures the only way to get him out of her head is to get him into bed, as crazy as that sounds. She knows it's the last thing she should do. But she wants it, and doesn't, at the same time. And this crazy-making is making her reckless.

Just go with it, she tells herself. *See what happens.*

They meet at the gallery, where she leaves her car, and he drives her to an expensive Italian restaurant where they both eat and drink too much. He asks her about her work, and he tells her about his passion for promoting art, how he started with a gallery in Buenos Aires, then Santa Barbara, and now here. They talk music, what they love and don't love about Madonna, Springsteen, Nirvana, Santana, and Brubeck, discovering and appreciating their mutually eclectic tastes.

She's wearing strappy heels and a minidress this time, a soft, burgundy velvet that clings to her curves and ends mid-thigh. She loved the way his gaze, half-lidded, slid slowly over her when they met. He looks much the same as always, dressed mostly in black, a kind of casual sophistication that suits him, that you almost don't notice because he wears it so effortlessly. What she likes most are his eyes, the way he holds her with them, and his mouth, his sexy grins, his low laughs, his soft, distinctive voice with its otherworldly accent, like water washing over rocks, circling, gliding, gently lapping.

"I'd like to take you home with me, but we've drunk too much to drive that far," he tells her, opening the car door for her when they leave the restaurant.

"Where do you live?" she asks as he slides behind the wheel.

He points toward the roof.

She laughs. "In heaven?"

"No, silly." He leans over the dashboard, pointing outside. "Up there, in those hills, way back."

"You live up there? In a mansion?" It's the most exclusive part of town.

"No, no, a bungalow. A small bungalow at the top of the hill. Too far for tonight."

"So where are you taking me then?"

"We can go to the gallery—there's a small apartment over the shop. Or we can go to your place."

"No, not my place!" she says quickly, imagining what someone who lives on those hillsides would think of her cramped studio apartment.

"Why not? You seem so determined."

"I have a roommate," she lies.

"I see. Then we'll go to the gallery.

They drive in silence. She rarely drinks this much, and it feels strange, nice, like she's floating in slow motion. She lets her head roll back against the seat, while the drone of the motor lulls her to the edge of sleep.

"You're not going to fall asleep on me, are you?" He laughs softly and touches her knee.

She shakes herself and sits up.

As he leads her up the back stairs to his apartment, she thinks, *if he is truly honorable, he will realize I had too much to drink and take me home.* Then she remembers her car is parked right here if she wants to go. Or she can call a cab. *I'm not so drunk I can't stop this,* she tells herself as she trails behind him up the narrow stairs, her hand held lightly by his. Knowing this, she feels more confident, more in control.

But as they reach the landing and he lets go of her hand to unlock the door, a panic washes over her. *I don't want this to be happening. This won't end well.*

Then, as he turns to look down at her, his warm hand pressed against the hollow of her back as he ushers her in, she knows, *I want this to be happening.*

The brightness of the lights startles her before he dims them. She gets a glimpse of the living room, glass and stainless-steel tables, black upholstery, colorful murals on the walls. She moves through the rooms as if she's floating, as if she's not there, as if this isn't happening. He's leading her by the hand. His hand feels real. It's the only real thing in the apartment.

"I apologize for the décor. It was furnished like this when I bought the shop. I rarely stay here." He takes her into the bedroom with a round bed, black satin cover, red silk sheets, and mirrors everywhere.

"Are you sure you're not a gigolo?" she asks, giggling.

"A gigolo! What would make you think that?"

"Well, maybe not a gigolo," she says, realizing she's not sure what a gigolo actually is. "But this definitely looks like the apartment of a serious player."

"A serious player. Hmmm. I'll have to remember that. You are a very . . . interesting woman, Kay." His hands slide slowly up and down her velvet-clad curves. Then he sits her on the bed and kneels at her feet. He slips off her heels, caressing her bare foot, pressing his thumb against the arch, sending chills through her body. His warm hands slide up her calves to her thighs.

"I don't think I should be here," she tells him.

He reaches her panties and begins to tug at them. She shifts her weight to help him slip them off. He leans her back on the bed, peeling off his jacket, kicking off his shoes. He feathers her face with kisses and then claims her mouth. She moans against him. His hand reaches beneath her dress, stroking her stomach, smoothing her thighs, moving toward her center as his mouth devours hers. His fingers slip inside her. She lets out a soft mew.

"And where would you rather be?" he asks between kisses, his face rough against her cheek, his breath warm in her ear.

She arches her back.

*****

The next morning when she wakes, there's a note on the nightstand from Richard saying he's downstairs and they'll go to breakfast when she gets up.

Quickly, she dresses, looks around the bachelor's pad, and is dismayed—beyond dismayed. Why is she doing this? He will break her heart. It is already broken. *I can't do this*, she tells herself. *I can't.* She sneaks down the back stairs where her car is parked. She leaves quickly before she can change her mind.

But by the time she reaches her apartment, there's a message on her phone. She pushes "play" cautiously, not wanting to hear what she knows will be there.

"Why did you run away?"

She quickly erases the message and dashes to the gym. A good workout is what she needs. When she returns, another message is waiting.

"I'm not a gigolo. I promise," he tells her.

That night she's sitting in bed, trying to watch TV, trying not to think, trying not to think of him, when the phone rings. She mutes the TV and waits to hear the message.

"I'm not going to go away. I'm not going to stop calling. So, you might as well pick up." She holds her breath, waiting.

He whispers huskily into the phone, "Pick up, Kay . . . pick up . . . pick up . . . pick up." His voice sounds like a chant; it is so soft, so solemn, so full of longing.

She dashes to the phone.

"So, you are there after all. Why did you run away?"

"I didn't . . .," she starts to say.

"You didn't what?"

"I wasn't running."

"What was it then?"

"It was . . . it felt like . . . it feels like . . .," she sinks onto the edge of her bed, trying to understand what she's feeling.

"What Kay? What does it feel like?"

"Like . . . drowning," she tells him at last.

There's a long silence, filled only with the sound of their breathing.

"Kay, are you holding the phone? Do you feel it in your hand?"

She clutches it with both hands, pressing it to her ear. "Yes, I feel it."

"That's my hand. I'm right there with you. We're holding onto each other. I'm not going to let go of you. You aren't drowning. Not unless drowning means going down together."

"Are you sure we can do this?"

"It's already done."

22

CAL

Give & Get

So, what are you in here for this time, Mr. Dumbshit?

Cal stretches out on a jail cell bunk, hands tucked behind his neck, contemplating the question. He's wearing an orange jumpsuit and conducting this interrogation with himself.

For weaving, sir. Weaving on the road.

You mean you were driving under the influence and weaving through traffic?

No, sir. One would think that, given the charge, but one would be wrong. I was not driving. I was walking across the street.

You mean jaywalking.

I do not. I was in a crosswalk. But according to the officers who arrested me, rather than walking parallel to the crosswalk lines, I was weaving back and forth between them.

Weaving while walking—is that a crime?

No, sir, it is not. The crime is doing this at midnight with two bored cops at a four-way stop watching you.

And what kind of dumbass, Mr. Dumbshit, would cross the street with two cops in a cruiser watching you?

The kind so caught up in his own shit that he doesn't see the motherfuckers.

Are you saying it's Kay's fault you were crossing the street at that precise time?

I'm saying if she hadn't dumped a load of shit on me that night, I wouldn't have been going out to get a Ho-Ho and eighteen-ounce Bud at the local 7-11. No sir, I would not.

I'm not convinced that's the case, but saying it is, how can they arrest you for weaving while walking?

I asked the officers the same thing, at which one replied they can arrest me for drunken and disorderly conduct, to which I replied, "I ain't drunk, and I can prove it."

How so?

By blowing my foul, nonalcoholic breath in the officer's fat ugly face, at which he cracks me on the head and cuffs me.

For what?

Assaulting an officer.

With bad breath? Is that a crime?

No sir, it is not, which I patiently explain by saying, "That's not assaulting an officer. This is," demonstrating the difference with a head bang, after which he adds resisting arrest to the charge.

All that from walking across the street?

While weaving, don't forget.

Surely this could not stand up in a court of law.

Well, you almost got that right.

Cal swings his feet over the edge of the top bunk and hops down, picking up a pack of Marlboro's from the bedside table. He grunts and holds up the pack at Rollo, his bunk mate, who's stretched out on the lower bunk reading a comic book. Rollo nods his approval, and Cal taps one out and lights up, still thinking about that day in court.

He was sure he'd be able to talk the judge into giving him time served, once he heard the whole story, and the judge almost went for it. But that damn DA came waltzing in, gave Cal the evil eye, and rolled out his rap sheet. The big guy's had a hard-on for him for a long time. He also gave the judge his tox report, showing traces of every illegal substance known on both sides of the border in his bloodstream when they arrested him—but no alcohol.

So, Cal restated his argument that because he wasn't driving under the influence, had no illegal substance in his possession, and weaving while walking isn't punishable by any law he knew, he should be released for time served. The DA recommended ninety days and one-year probation for assaulting an officer.

"With bad breath?" Cal exclaimed.

"No, with a head-butt!" said the DA.

"Quiet!" the judge reprimanded both. Then, after some head-shaking deliberation, he compromised, giving Cal two months, time served, and six-month's probation, which Cal countered with three months, time served, and no probation.

"Look, your honor," he said, "I'd rather serve time than do probation. If you give me probation, you'll be seeing my sorry ass back here every couple of weeks or so over the next year or two for countless probation violations. It's a proven fact. Look at my record. Me and probation don't dance. Give me my time straight up."

So, he did—ninety days on top of time served and no probation.

"Thank you, sir," he said, but couldn't help muttering as he turned to go, "Ninety days for weaving while walking. Taxpayer dollars well spent once again."

The judge was livid. "Do you want me to hold you in contempt of court, son?'"

"Contempt is too mild a word," he replied.

"Get him out of my courtroom," the judge roared. Cal gave the DA a big wink as they led him away, knowing that with ninety days and the crowded jail conditions, he'd be out in half that time, say forty-five days max—piece of cake.

*****

Cal doesn't mind doing time once he's gotten through the worst of it. The worst is the withdrawals, cold turkey: the vomiting, the shits, the shakes, the gut-wrenching pain that leads to banging your head against the bars in a futile attempt to end it all now. But he already suffered through the worst of that while waiting for his arraignment. The next part is a stroll in the park by comparison. He's done it enough to know the ropes, even doing a short stint at Wasco Prison, which he preferred to county jail: better food, roomier accommodations, bigger yard, and more equipment for exercise. Jail's smaller, louder, more intense, but personally less threatening. He's had to prove himself in both places when needed, but mostly he tries to keep his head down and stay out of trouble. He figures this time, with only forty-five days, he'll breeze by. But you never know. That's the joy of the jungle, both on the inside and out, the unseen danger. You never know what punk might want to cut his teeth on you.

A week into his sentence, a big bruiser he's never seen before seems to take a shine to him. Cal can smell it coming. Whether the guy wants to bounce him against the wall or take him in the shower, he's not sure. Either way it's clear he's going to have to go on the offensive.

But he's not worried. He's got it all figured out. If he sees a series of incidences going down that looks like it's leading to heads bouncing, he makes his move. He scopes out the opposing gang members and finds a riser, someone who wants to prove himself, move up the ranks. It's got to be the right riser, big enough and mean enough to impress but not so big or mean he'll get slaughtered. Then he makes his move, bumps up against him, and asks, "What's your problem?"

He knows he's going to get hurt. There's no way around that. You resign yourself to the fact and think of it as investing in the future. You take your punches now so you can live longer and easier later. You got to be willing to give and get. Give and get.

Cal's not the toughest fighter, nor the strongest or fastest, but what he's got that others don't bet on is endurance and pure holy rage. He fights like a wild man and like he's having a wild time doing it. He gets knocked down again and again, and when they're walking away, thinking it's over, he rises with a roar and goes at it again. They might outfight him, but they can't keep him down, and soon the crowd around them is cheering him on. Even his opponent's homies are cheering the pure audacity of a guy who doesn't know when he's beaten and won't let it go. In the end, it's either the inmates or the guards holding him back, trying to bring the fight to an end. After that everyone leaves him alone. The consensus is clear. There's no beating this guy and no glory in trying.

He finds his mark, Chewy: shaved head, beady eyes, hard and wiry, talks a lot. He's about Cal's size and looks mean as shit, but it's the talking that gives him away and clinches the deal. Talkers aren't fighters. This is almost always true. It's not that they can't fight, not that they don't want to. They prefer talking their way out of most of the messes they make, so their heart's not in it, not in doing the most damage possible in the least amount of time, only doing enough to win or to get the other guy to give in.

Cal sees him across the yard, and their eyes meet.

"What you looking at?" Cal says, crossing the space between them. Chewy looks behind him like he's not sure who Cal's talking to.

"What's your problem, Whitey?" he says, seeing he's Cal's target.

"You, you wetback greaser with the roving eye."

"Say what?"

And so, it begins. Their homies line up behind them and cheer them on, the Mexicans behind his mark, the white boys behind him, but poor Chewy doesn't have a chance. Although he holds his own against Cal, and even beats him down a couple of times, he doesn't stay down, and each time Chewy thinks he's laid him to rest and walks away, Cal roars up like a madman, grabs him by the ankles, and throws him to the ground again. And on it goes until the guards decide they've had their fun and pull them apart.

When it's over, the big guy who'd taken a shine to Cal and who could have done serious damage steers clear of him, and he and Chewy shake hands after the welts start to heal.

Cal gets a week in solitary, and his early release is revoked, but he's not complaining. His time here has been good for him. He's been reading, working out, putting on muscle, and planning his future. By the time he's out, he'll be three months drug-free, and he means to stay that way. Even that gash above his eye, the bruises and welts across his body, feel good, feel real, feel right: tender, clean, and pure. Like some madness has been beaten out of him and he knows who he is again. Like he's pulled himself out of the sewer or some stinking quagmire by his bootstraps and is standing tall again.

When September rolls around, he hitchhikes home and finds a garage sale going on down the street from his house. The front door is locked, so he climbs through a back window. Stuck on the fridge door is a flurry of sticky notes from his sister saying she took some of Mom's stuff, including the original photos, leaving him with copies, and paid up all his utility bills for two months.

"You have a good thing going here, the house all to yourself. Don't screw it up. If you can't find a job to pay the bills, rent out a room."

Cal laughs at his bad luck—utilities paid during the time he's been away. Staring at the empty fridge and his sister's note, he's reminded of something else he needs, which is long overdue. He drags the ping-pong table they rarely used out of the garage into the driveway and props up a homemade "for sale" sign. With the garage sale down the street bringing in a steady stream of bargain hunters, it's sold within the hour. Then he heads off to the 7-11 for that Ho-Ho and eighteen-ounce Bud he's had his heart set on for the last ninety-odd days.

23

CAL

Wide Awake

Cal kicks back in a lawn chair, legs stretched out, feet propped up on a cooler full of beer, soaking up the warm October sun and burning away some of that jailhouse pallor. He's sitting in the driveway with the garage door open, dressed in a tank top and cut-off jeans, eyeballing the strangers who pull up to the curb in their pick-ups and four-doors to mosey up the driveway and view his wares. It seems garage sales are a lucrative business in this neighborhood, so every time a neighbor puts up a sign, Cal opens up his garage and drags out a few more pieces of furniture and whatever else he can find that he hasn't pawned yet: filing cabinets, bookcases full of books, a crock pot, waffle iron, lamps, rugs, and other stuff he finds at the deep end of the closets and kitchen cupboards. He sets up things nice and neat on blankets, drives a good bargain, and finds he's good at it. Eventually he'll make enough to get all the utilities turned back on. Already he's stocked up on beer and burritos.

Kay will be proud of him, he thinks. He's staying clean and sober, hauled away most of the trash in the house, and cashed in a pile of recyclables. He's even put up a "Room for Rent" sign, as his sister suggested.

She's right. He has a sweet deal here and shouldn't be fucking it up. The sound of her scream and the feel of her sharp fingers squeezing his neck he thinks of now as an alarm clock with claws strangling him awake.

He feels wide awake, too, more alive than he's felt in a long, long time. It's like he's been walking in his sleep for years and probably has been, stumbling around in that drug haze. But he's done with that now. He is. He knows he's said that before—how many times, he's not counting. But this time feels different. For one thing, he has a house now. It still amazes him. A place to sleep at night, no one to bug him, no rent to keep up, no landlord to dodge, no dad giving him the evil eye, no mom wringing her hands over him. He's as free as he's ever been. And he owes it all to his little sister for that visceral wake-up call.

Maybe he has Mom to thank, too, for leaving him high and dry. And Dad, for handing over the keys to the house.

Now all he must do is figure out how to hang onto what he has and how to spend the rest of his life. The most ambitious he ever got was when he was working that recycling gig as a kid. An entrepreneur, Mom called him. That still appeals to him, being his own boss, but doing what? That piece of the puzzle isn't falling into place.

What he really likes is just this, what he's doing now, rummaging and selling. He even went digging through some dumpsters behind a thrift shop where they throw stuff they don't have room for, looking for something with unseen potential he can add to his garage sales. He's not sure if you can make a living doing this. But maybe it's a way to get by. That's all he needs right now. And he's got Baby Kay to thank for that.

He's always been more afraid of Kay than his mom or dad. Mom he could always manipulate, Dad avoid, but Kay, his baby sister—there is no escaping the fury of her wrath or her demands. She is the one he could always count on for the truth. When she calls him out on his shit, he sees it through her eyes with absolute clarity—an unforgiving mirror. What he sees there is not always pretty but always instructive.

Unfortunately for him, Kay never had any interest in being her brother's keeper, and she distanced herself from his troubles as much as sisterly possible a long time ago. She wanted no part of his bullshit, as she politely put it to both him and Mom whenever they tried to enlist her help.

Still, when he did manage to obtain her attention with his bullshit, her wrath was a beautiful thing to behold. So much so that sometimes in moments of pure insanity, he deliberately provoked her to bear witness to that burst of "holy shit" rage. A fury as cold and bright and sharp as the knife she chased him with that day when she was only eight years old. He teased, tormented, and whipped her into a rage so frightful she could not contain herself any longer. She grabbed a long knife out of a kitchen drawer and went after him with a vengeance—her raised arm, glinting knife, and deadly eye fused into one beautiful fury.

Their parents had gone out for the night, and Gina, their anorexic teenage babysitter, was jumping on the couch like it was a life raft tossed about in a raging storm, screaming, "Stop it! Stop it! Stop it!"

He was laughing his head off as he dodged his knife-wielding baby sister, dancing out of her way, feeding her fury and feeding on it, cranking up his adrenaline so high that it might have been his first taste of drug heaven. He was astounded by what he had wrought. With equal parts delight and fright, he danced around the furniture with his wild-eyed sister, singing, "Holy shit! Holy shit! Holy shit!"

He smiles now, thinking about it. Baby Kay! He picks up the portable phone his dad always kept in the garage, now that he's got service again, and leans back in his lawn chair to give her a call.

"Where the hell have you been, Cal? I've been calling and calling. Didn't you get all my messages?"

"Well, no. I just got the phone turned back on."

"But I paid it up for two months when I was there last."

"Yeah. Right. About that. Unfortunately, I got locked up right after you reamed my ass and—"

"Jail? You were in jail, again? Good God, Cal. So, all that money I spent helping you out was a complete waste!"

"I wouldn't say that. It's the thought that counts, right?"

"When are you going to grow up, Cal, and stop this shit?"

"Well, that's what I was calling about before you jumped down my throat, to tell you the good news. I've quit that shit. Down to smoking pot, mostly."

"Mostly? Am I supposed to applaud that or what?"

He laughs. "Well, you could. A couple of claps, at least. It's progress, isn't it? I even hit up a couple of NA meetings with Mikey recently."

"Mikey, huh?"

"Yeah, he's trying to trim down the hard stuff too. Got kicked off his auntie's couch into a sober living home."

"Why can't you say, 'I'm done with it all,' and let that be the end of it?" she says.

"Just like that?"

"Yeah, just like that. Like pulling off a Band-Aid, quick-like, and you're done."

"It doesn't work like that, Kay. Addiction. Even for booze or cigarettes, let alone the hard stuff. You ever hear of a smoker quitting like that?"

"Mom did. She said when she was pregnant with you, she lost all desire to smoke again and stopped cold turkey."

"Mom," he shakes his head. "And you believe that shit? She was full of fairy tales, Kay, and you know it."

"You saying I can't trust my own mother to tell me the truth?"

He laughs. "Can't trust . . . hmm. C'mon Kay. Where's Mom now? She's been gone . . . what? A whole year now? Yeah, she's someone you can count on."

There's silence on the other end.

"You're a shit, Cal. You know that?"

He laughs again and hears the loud click.

Well, it's a start, he thinks. He's glad he called. He's got to start somewhere mending the fence. Now that he's wide awake, bright-eyed, and bushy-tailed again.

24

KAY
Fitting In

Kay slams down the phone, still fuming at her brother, the way he pushes her buttons—every time! The way she lets him!

Still, she's relieved she's finally heard from him, that he's been in jail all this time, safe and sound. That's how she and Mom saw these time-outs. He always comes out clean and pumped up, motivated to do something positive about his disastrous life. If only it sticks this time. She's not holding her breath.

Within minutes of hanging up, Richard calls, reminding her she has something new to worry about besides her brother. After dating all summer, he's persuaded her to move in with him. The thought excites and scares her at the same time. Thinking about all the time they could spend together in bed, in each other's arms, makes her bones melt. But the thought of how well she might actually fit into his life, and he in hers, makes her stomach drop to her knees. She doesn't like putting herself in such a vulnerable position. She made Karl move in with her so she wouldn't have to be the one to move out when things fell apart. Clearly, she can't make Richard move into her tiny hovel. She doesn't even want him to see it! But she can't resist his entreaties to live with him either.

He'll be here soon to take her to see his home for the first time, his "modest bungalow," as he puts it, set among the luxurious hillside homes of Sierra Madre. What if she doesn't fit in with his lavish lifestyle? What if he doesn't like domestic Kay? What if this ruins everything?

"This is so wrong. This is too rash. We barely know each other," she tells him now, tucking the phone under her chin as she finishes packing a few toiletries into a small bag.

"Yes, yes, it's all wrong. That's why it feels so right. I'm coming up. I'm just outside. Which apartment is yours?"

"No, you're not! You can't be here already. I wasn't expecting you this soon." Her hands fly to her ponytail, pulling her hair free. She looks down at the dirty sweats she's wearing and then at the mess in her apartment.

Kay doesn't do neat. Karl never minded, happily picking up after her as she kicked off her shoes by the couch and flung her jacket on a chair upon returning home. But she can't imagine Richard doing that or being comfortable living in such disarray. She has a horrible vision of him reacting to her apartment with the same disgust she felt for Cal when she saw the state of her parents' house on her last trip home.

"Tell me you're kidding. You're not really here. Not yet. Please." She peels off her sweats and squirms into a pair of jeans.

He laughs. "It's true, I'm really here."

"Then wait down there. I'll be out in a few minutes," she tells him, kicking her dirty sweats into the closet.

"I'm already coming up the stairs." His voice, soft and sensuous, continues in her ear. "I'm walking down the corridor."

She looks wildly around her studio and sees it through Richard's eyes—how cramped, cluttered, and extremely messy. And so horribly ordinary. She's certain once Richard sees her as she really is and not as he imagines her to be, he'll find her terribly pedestrian and boring. *I will learn to do clean*, she tells herself, as she throws a half-eaten apple and bag of chips into the garbage.

"Is this it? 205?" Richard asks, still talking to her on his cell phone. "I'm at the door."

She freezes at his knock.

"I know you're there. You must let me in."

"I can't."

"You must."

Slowly, she goes to the door, unlocks it, and then backs away, holding her breath, waiting for him to enter.

Slowly, he turns the knob and pushes the door inward.

They stand facing each other.

"What were you afraid of? This?" He rushes toward her, and she jumps into his arms to keep from being knocked off her feet, throwing her legs around his waist. He lurches and then carries her to the bed, which is only a few feet from the door. It's hours before they come up for breath. He lays back naked against the headboard, his arm around her shoulders, and looks about him for the first time.

"So, this is where you live? This tiny, crowded studio. What a mess! How can you live like this?" He's laughing, his eyes shining.

She bats him with a pillow. "Don't look! You were never meant to see it this way."

"But don't you see, I love it! It's so . . . so . . . so Kay!"

"I hate you! I bet your house is spotless like your apartment, the closets all color coordinated, full of neatly stacked shelves."

"Yes, yes, exactly like that. Everything in its place. My mother taught me well. You will never fit in. I'll have to give you your own private room to squalor in."

"Squalor! You're calling me a squalor-er?" She bats him again. He pushes the pillow away and pins her down on the mattress.

"It's nothing to be ashamed of. We all have our faults."

"You beast! Now I know why I hate you!"

"No, you don't."

"Yes, I do."

"No, you don't," he insists, his eyes still shining, but his face suddenly serious as he reaches beneath the covers, caressing her breasts, moving between her thighs. "Tell me," he whispers into her ear.

"No, I don't," she whispers back.

*****

The lavender sky deepens to violet as they drive through the hills toward his home, past expensive homes nestled among giant oaks and glimpses of mansions down secluded driveways behind iron gates. The higher they drive, the more anxious Kay becomes, her stomach clenching.

"Please don't tell me you live in a mansion!"

He laughs. "A modest bungalow, at best."

She pictures it now, the home filled with expensive ornate furniture, priceless works of art, rare artifacts collected from his travels, expensive oriental carpets covering marble floors. *I'll never fit in. I'll never fit in*, she tells herself, trying to draw her hand from his, where he holds it firmly on his lap.

"Don't," he says, squeezing her hand tighter. "It will be all right. You'll see."

Finally, they turn up a driveway, the wheels crunching gravel, and she catches a glimpse of the city lights below. When they step out, she smells pines and a whiff of lavender. He takes her hand and leads her up a stone pathway lit by tiny lights to a house half hidden among trees and dense foliage. They step through an archway into a small courtyard. A red lantern casts splinters of light across the flagstone, revealing a small fountain and urns full of blooming flowers and ferns. He unlocks the heavy, rounded door carved into thick adobe walls. She fingers the fronds of a large philodendron by the door, its leaves long and luxurious, reminding her of the one half-dead fern in her apartment, the one Richard laughed at and then watered with a cup from the kitchen.

"He looks thirsty," he told her apologetically.

"I know, poor thing," Kay said. "I don't do plants well either."

Now he pushes the heavy wooden door inward and lets her cross the threshold before him. He switches on a light. A small, curved entryway opens into a larger room, the soft recessed lighting glowing against the creamy walls, illuminating a room choked with heavy, carved furniture, sprawling plants, and stacks of books and magazines on the tables and floor. Photographic equipment is piled into a corner, and a heap of matted photographs leans against a chair. Pillows are everywhere in careless disarray. A cup and plate of crumbs sit on the coffee table. The ornate furnishings and objects of art she imagined are all here, half hidden in the clutter.

"You see, what can I tell you? I know squalor when I see it. You'll be right at home. Or perhaps a housekeeper is in order, no?"

It turns out his home is a bungalow, as he claimed. Besides the combined living and dining room, there's a small kitchen, a sun porch facing the garden, one large bedroom with a tiny office built into a loft, and a smaller room used for storage.

"Is this where you were going to put me, in the loft, to squalor alone?" she teases.

"No, not at all. I need my office. But this walk-in closet is quite large. I thought you would fit here nicely, hidden away in my drawers."

"Your drawers!" She laughs. "And what will the housekeeper think?"

"Who cares," he says, taking her into his arms.

25

WALTER
Damn Weather

Walter finds it surprisingly easy starting over in a new place with a new business and new partner. By the time escrow closes in late September, he has a firm grip on running the shop. With Dawn there to ease the way and shorten his learning curve, it's no time at all before it seems like he's been doing this forever. The work divides easily along natural lines. Dawn keeps the books, does the ordering, stocks the shelves, and takes customers out in the boats, showing them around the bay. He keeps the boats and engines running, keeps reels and rods in prime working order, and makes sure the dock and slips are shipshape. He also pays the bills, balances the checkbook, and does the banking.

If there's a fly in the ointment, it's Randy. While he's an asset when it comes to sweeping up, cleaning toilets, or taking out the trash, he's a nuisance in most other ways. Often, he's underfoot, clamoring to take on tasks he isn't equipped to do and chattering nearly nonstop about mostly nonsense, as far as Walter can tell, who tunes him out as much as he can.

Dawn's patience is stretched near the breaking point too at times, but she manages to reel herself back in. The situation reminds him of Franny and Cal—her endless patience with him and her ability to overlook his most glaring faults, her eternal faith that, in the end, he'd amount to something they'd be proud of.

For Dawn, though, since Randy isn't her son, it's not blood that binds him to her. It's something else that Walter can't quite get a grip on. Her belief in him, maybe, in his worthiness as a human being, flawed and all, whether he'll amount to anything or not, and most likely not. Her belief that she, they, the whole goddamn town, it seems, has an obligation to look after him. Community, Dawn calls it. Randy's part of their community. Tribe, he thinks. This little town and the people in it are like a tribe that takes care of its own.

Walter's time in the Marines may have been as close to a tribe as he's ever known—until Franny and the kids. That was his tribe. Maybe that's why he kept letting Cal move back in with them, even when he was grown, even when Walter knew it was a bad idea, even when he was sure it would only make their son weaker than he'd have been if they said no.

But how long did that tribe last? Franny left. He left. His boy and girl scattered across California. Where's their tribe now?

Franny's been gone a year now—a whole year! It doesn't seem possible she could have been gone this long, and there's no indication when, or if, she will ever return. Last he saw from her credit card charges she was in Columbia. Still heading south.

Kay has called him twice now since he got here, once early in the summer to see if he'd heard from Cal, who apparently disappeared again, and a couple of weeks ago to say Cal was back and to give him her new address. It seems she moved in with a new boyfriend. He didn't even know she had broken up with Karl! Franny was always the one who kept track of the kids, made sure they were okay, or, in Cal's case, took on the chore of caring for him when he couldn't look after himself. He supposes he should be doing that now, keeping an eye on the kids, but it doesn't come naturally to him, talking on the phone. He always feels like he's intruding on people, prying. He's thought of calling Cal to check up on him, but that's what it would sound like and feel like, too—checking up on him. Wasn't he always telling Franny to let the boy be? Isn't that what he should be doing now?

None of it makes any sense. You come into this world alone. You go out alone. Maybe along the way you hook up now and then. You join the service. You marry. You have kids. But when it's all said and done, you all go your separate ways. It's no one's fault, really.

He was never sure it was in his nature to be a family man any more than his dad was. But he tried. For Franny. For the kids. Hell, how could you not when you meet someone like her?

*****

During work hours, he rarely sees Dawn except in passing. In the evening, they help each other close down, cash out the register, and swap stories about the day's events and what's needed down the road. Sometimes they slip on over to the Moondog Café with Randy in tow, dining together like the small family they seem to be.

The first time Dawn invites him to join them for dinner at her place, he passes. When he turns down a second offer a few weeks later, Dawn looks him up and down the way she has of doing that makes a man feel like he's forgotten to zip up.

"Suit yourself," she says, mouth grim. He can tell from her tone that his refusal will be bad for business, or at least bring a chill to the shop, so he changes his mind.

"Think I'll take you up on that offer, after all," he says.

Her house is the old craftsman style, gray with green shutters. Two big pots filled with red geraniums stand on either side of the front door. As he stands there waiting for her to answer the doorbell, the spicy scent reminds him of something comforting and long forgotten. An image of his grandma drifts into his mind, her crinkled hands snipping away dead blossoms.

Randy's wide grin greets him at the door as he ushers him in.

"He's here, Dawn, like I said he'd be," he calls over his shoulder. Turning to Walter, he confides, "She thought you'd make up some excuse not to come, but I told her it wasn't so, and I was right. Weren't I, Dawn? Dawn!"

"Randy, stop your chattering and bring him into the kitchen where it's warm."

It's dark inside. Passing through the living room, all Walter can make out is a large, comfy-looking couch set in front of a dark fireplace before entering a bright kitchen. Dawn is leaning over the oven, her backside big and broad, pulling out a large pan, her hands covered with quilted mitts. The warm scent of oregano and mozzarella fills the small room. Dawn looks over her shoulder at him as she puts the pan on the stovetop.

"Take a load off, why don't you? Randy, fetch him some beer."

She swipes at her forehead with her mitt and takes a swig from her own bottle.

"I know you're supposed to serve wine with Italian, but I don't care for it myself, so I don't keep any handy."

"Beer will do fine," Walter says, taking a bottle of Bud from Randy.

"Hope you like lasagna. Never knew a man who didn't, but you could be the first."

"I'm not. Smells mighty good. Liked those geraniums by the door too. My granny used to grow them."

"About all I can grow. But I like a bit of color on the porch. I hang red mittens out there in the winter when it's too cold for flowers."

"You don't say?"

"She's messing with you," Randy says as he pulls out a kitchen chair and turns it backward before taking a seat.

"Is she now," Walter rallies, leaning back in his own chair.

"That means she likes you," Randy adds in what passes for a loud whisper.

"Randy, do you ever grow up? I swear you're still in high school." Dawn shakes her head at him but otherwise looks placid as pie as she sets the pan of pasta on a crocheted owl in the middle of the table. "Get the parmesan from the fridge," she tells Randy. "And grab the salad while you're at it." She puts a handful of breadsticks into a tall mug and sets that on the table too.

No one talks much as they eat, aside from "pass the salt" or "have another helping."

After dinner, Walter helps Dawn with the dishes while Randy disappears into the front room. The sound of canned laughter from some TV show, along with Randy's loud guffaws, drifts around the corner.

Dawn washes, and he rinses, stacking the dishes into a wooden rack.

"Sure you don't want me to dry them? I can, you know."

"Why bother? The air does fine."

"Haven't had a home-cooked meal like that in a long time," he tells her.

Dawn looks sideways at him. "You divorced or widowed? I don't see a wedding band."

"Never wore one. I was a welder. Didn't mix well with machinery."

"So, you still married?"

"Yeah," he nods. "Separated, I guess you'd call it."

"She leave or you?"

"She did."

He stands with his hands under the warm running water, waiting for another dish to rinse, wishing he had something to dry.

"Never married, myself," she tells him. "Most men take me for a dike."

He about chokes, trying to swallow a laugh, and she laughs too, patting him on the back.

"Glad you find that funny. Had one for a while. A man, I mean. Thought we'd eventually get hitched, but neither of us was in a hurry, so we never did. He went offshore on a rigging job a few years ago and never came back. Heard later he finally got hitched. Just not to me." She laughs again, and he joins her.

After that it becomes a weekly ritual. He comes over on Wednesday nights for a homemade meal, and on Saturdays he brings pizza. Most nights Randy joins them for dinner, then leaves to watch TV, often falling asleep on the couch. After doing the dishes together, he and Dawn sit at the dinner table, drinking beer and playing cribbage or Chinese checkers. On Saturday nights, they trade shots of whiskey. They play mean and hard, whooping it up when they are winning, cursing when they aren't. Neither are good losers. But once they put the boards away, it's over. All's forgiven, even if grudgingly. Yet often, curiously, something of that tension remains crackling in the air between them after, making them eye each other oddly. It's something Walter can't quite identify.

One night in late October after belting back a shot, Dawn places the glass on the table and looks at him. "You never told me why your wife left."

"You never asked."

"Never thought it was my place to do so."

"But you do now?"

"Must be the whiskey talking." She reaches across the table and touches his hand. "You don't have to answer, you know. Like the phone. Just because it rings, don't mean you have to pick up."

"Or the doorbell. Never answered it if I was home alone. But the kids or Franny always did. Thought it was impolite not to. Never could figure that out."

"That your wife, Franny?"

"Frances Adelaide Miller. Miller was her name before we married. Always the prettiest girl in the room."

He swings back another shot and pours one for Dawn.

"Don't know why she left. Don't know where she is. Haven't heard from her since. Kids haven't either, aside from some phone messages and photos. Me, all I get is a trail of credit card bills. Well, I guess I do know where she is. Was. She bought a ton of film and stayed a couple of nights in Cartagena last month."

"Mexico?"

"No, that's where she started out, but she's in Columbia now, still moving south, almost on top of the equator now. She likes the heat. I like it cold." Then he adds, smiling, "Guess we were doomed from the start."

"That damned weather, always screwing things up," she says, nodding.

He snorts a laugh and toasts her. "To the damned weather!"

Later that night she looks him straight in the eye and cocks her head. "Seriously, you pay her credit card bills? Why? That's worse than answering the phone when you don't have to."

He can't answer that and stares out into the room with a puzzled look playing over his face.

"You still love her."

He's silent a moment then nods. "I can't imagine not loving her. She's half my life. Half my history. Who I am."

"That bad," she muses.

"That good, really." He picks up his glass and then sets it down.

"But it's not the way you're thinking. I'll never stop loving her or stop supporting her if she needs me. But . . . I like it here.

And she likes it wherever she is, I guess. There's no turning back. I knew as soon as I bought the shop. What surprises me is how easy it is—moving on. I suppose she felt the same way after she took off or she would have come home by now."

Dawn picks up her glass.

"To Franny," she says, touching her glass to his.

"To new friends," he answers.

*****

Randy is sound asleep on Dawn's couch when Walter is ready to leave. Usually, he walks Randy home to the loft in the shop, which is on his way back to the motel. Walter tries rousing him, but the boy moans and curls up tighter into a ball. That's when he sees the bottle of bourbon hidden behind the cushions. He hands the half-empty bottle silently to Dawn as she comes up behind him.

"Son of a gun! I was saving that for a special occasion."

"I'll get him home," Walter tells her. He puts his arm around Randy's shoulders and lifts him to a sitting position. "Time to go, son. Hold on now. We'll get you ready."

Dawn helps Randy bundle up and pull his boots on, while Walter puts on his own coat and scarf. Then he gathers Randy in his arms and pulls him up. They stumble toward the door, Walter's arm wrapped around Randy's waist.

As they head out the door into the moonlit night, he glances at Randy.

"You okay, buddy?" All he can see is that mop of dark hair hanging in the boy's face and a curve of cheek. The hair and the fine features, delicate like a girl's, remind him of Kay. She's fragile looking too—but looks can deceive. Of his two children, she reminds him more of himself. A mind of her own, suffers no fools. Same as him. And certainly not one to get so plastered she can't find her way home. Same as her daddy. Same weakness, too, it seems. Her mother. She could do no wrong in both their books.

Cal's the one Randy reminds him of most often—now, more than ever, seeing him in this state for the first time and wondering how often he drinks himself stupid. Did he inherit his daddy's taste for liquor? Is he an alcoholic in the making? The thought makes his stomach wrench. He thought he got away from all that. It's way more than he bargained for.

He knows, despite his promise to Clay, that Randy isn't his problem. But once you start letting someone depend on you, and seeing how there's little hope he'll grow better than he is, doesn't that make you responsible for him? If you allow him to lean on you and get comfortable with it, and then remove your support, aren't you at least partly liable for his fall? Is that how Franny felt about Cal?

Funny, he's never felt that kind of responsibility for his son. Cal was always Franny's. They understood each other in a way he never could. It only seemed right to let her deal with him because she knew him so well. And once he turned Cal over to her, even when he didn't like how she was handling things, how could he interfere? It was her call by then, and the only way he could help was by getting out of the way. Gritting his teeth and bearing it if he had to, standing back, not interfering.

But it's a wonder to him now, stumbling through the dark with Randy leaning on him, how he's never worried about Cal the way Franny did. Somehow, he always saw Cal as a survivor. And that's how he differs from Randy. The whole town knows Randy needs propping up to survive, and they all pitch in to make sure he does. It isn't that part that reminds him most of Cal. It's the goofy grin, the way he likes to play around, his loud voice and louder laugh, the way he likes to tease and pester people past their patience.

In some ways Cal reminds him of himself, too, but it's not a side of himself he likes to think about, a side he tried to beat down—and did most of the time—till Cal shook it loose. He knows he has no right to blame the boy for his own devilish nature, his short temper, what Walter inherited from his father and Cal inherited from him, he supposes. Walter held it down, that dark side, most of the time, but it wasn't easy, pushing it down again and again. Then, without warning, there it was. Out in the open. Surprising Walter as much as anyone.

It was like his granny used to say when he was young, how he had a devil on one shoulder and an angel on the other. One minute they'd be baking chocolate chip cookies together, having a good old time, and the next she'd be cursing and chasing him out the door with a broom.

"What the devil got into you, boy?" she'd call after him. But he never knew. Had no clue. Cal was like that.

"Our wild child," Franny called him once when he was only two. She had no idea what fear that phrase conjured up in Walter, the thought that the wildness he beat down but still stirred inside him might rise in his son. It scared the shit out of him and drove a wedge between him and his boy whenever he saw that devilish spirit emerge.

The military is what saved Walter. Cliché or not, it's the truth. In the jungles of Vietnam, the angel on his shoulder took off, and the devil took over, saving his ass more than once. And when he returned home, the angel flew back wearing Franny's face, and he beat the devil down with the same fierce-faced discipline his drill sergeant had used on him—until Cal egged it out. But it wasn't the boy's fault. It was in Cal's blood. His son got bit, same as he had. And his son would beat it down, same as he had. He's a survivor, like his dad.

But Randy! God help Randy, he thinks as he settles him on the couch in the shop office, knowing he'd never make it up the stairs to his loft. He bundles up the blankets off Randy's bed and carries them down to tuck around him. Then he stands back watching him sleep, his long, dark lashes curled against his cheeks. Randy isn't Cal and never will be. The thought wells up a measure of pride and relief on one side, seeing his son as a survivor, and a whole lot of worry and grief on the other.

"You poor S.O.B.," he whispers, looking down at him. Then he turns out the light and heads home.

26

CAL
Drinking the Kool-Aid

It's late November. It might even be Thanksgiving Day for all Cal knows or cares. He's in the front yard with a can of Round-Up zapping the grass and weeds sprouting up among his clean, white rocks. It turns out you're supposed to put down a plastic tarp as a weed barrier before you lay down rocks. *Too late now*, he thinks, as he points and sprays his poison.

He stops a moment to light the cigarette dangling from his lip and looks around, taking in the neighborhood, growing dim in the waning light. The sun is almost down, laying a band of gold beneath the pearly gray sky. The scent of smoke from a nearby chimney drifts his way, and he pictures a bunch of kids and parents gathered around a fireplace, roasting marshmallows or chestnuts or some such crap.

Kay invited him to spend Thanksgiving with her and her boyfriend at her new digs, but he declined. He's never much liked holidays. They always seemed to lead to heartache one way or another. He never made it home when promised, leaving an empty plate at the table to haul away, or he showed up high and no one liked that much either and let him know. He'd be happy if there never was another holiday.

He's been staying clean and keeping the lights on at the same time, selling almost everything he finds in the house at garage sales and doing a couple more painting gigs for Lou. He's feeling good about himself, productive, and really likes his rock lawn. Not sure why. Maybe because he made it. Or because he likes coming out here and spraying the weeds away, sticking it to his dad who loved his green lawn. That might have something to do with it, too. Or maybe he just likes rocks.

Across the street, the string of Christmas lights beneath the eaves comes on, blinking red and green. Lights are already up at other houses on the block, too. This is one of those streets they write about in the newspaper, where all the neighbors have been competing for years, trying to outdo each other and other neighborhoods on the number of lights and decorations they can squeeze onto their tiny lawns. How his dad hated that—the constant parade of cars streaming by their house. Their home was one of the few holdouts on the block, which used to embarrass him and Kay, their dad being the neighborhood Scrooge.

Cal gives his can another squirt and watches the old guy across the street carry a box to the curb and prop up a "free" sign. He crosses over to check it out. Ever since he's covered the weeds over with rocks, he and his neighbor, Mr. McCloskey, have been on friendlier terms.

"You want these? I got more in the back. Got enough decorations to fill the yards of five houses, I bet. But lots of stuff is broken."

Cal rummages through the box.

"You thinking about joining the Christmas Club this year?" McCloskey asks. Cal gives him a blank look. "You know, decorating your house, putting on a show for the neighbors and all those little kids."

"I dunno. Hadn't really thought about it."

"Come here. Let me show you something." He takes Cal into the backyard and opens a large shed, filled top to bottom with decorations. "See anything you like?"

McCloskey pulls out a metal relief of Christmas carolers, about four feet tall and six feet long. All the carolers are dressed in fur-edged coats and boots, tall black hats and Sunday bonnets, holding onto songbooks and singing their hearts out. Every one of them has a mouth as round as a donut.

"This one's almost an antique—vintage they call it now. Don't make stuff like this anymore. It needs mending though. The stand that props it up broke off. If you have a soldering iron or welding gear to fix it, it's yours along with anything else here you want. Not for your garage sale though. You got to put it up in your yard. I can help you string some lights too."

Cal listens with one ear as he pokes through the shed, looking at the reindeer and snowmen made of wire, an angel with a missing halo, and a fat plastic Santa.

"So, is it a deal?" the man asks again.

Cal looks at him, remembering his dad, the old miserly Scrooge that he was. Last he heard from Kay, Dad was up in Alaska somewhere, freezing his nuts off. Even bought some tackle shop! Think he'd invite his unemployed son to come work for him or take a spin in one of his new boats? Hell, no. Cold-hearted bastard.

"What do you think?" McCloskey prods him. "We got a deal?"

"Hell, yes," Cal tells him and holds out his hand. "It's a deal!"

"Take that, you old-motherfucking Scrooge!" Cal chortles to himself as he lugs the boxes across the street, imagining what his dad would say about what his son was doing to the old homestead.

*****

When his dad sold his welding business, he brought a lot of his equipment home and set up a shop in an old shed out back. Cal used to watch him out there with his welding hood pulled down over his face, looking like some medieval knight surrounded by thousands of tiny blinding sparks, like an arc of shooting stars. Or he's hunched over an anvil hammering away on a piece of metal, his arm rising and falling with earth-quaking, ear-splitting bangs. It was part of his mystique, Dad in the shed, dressed for battle with his hood and gloves and leather apron, surrounded by arcing fire and flying sparks, squeals of grinding metal, angry hissing, and violent pounding. He was fierce and unapproachable, doing mysterious, manly things. Things he had no interest in sharing with his son.

Once when Cal was about thirteen, after persistent pestering and his mother's urging, his dad showed him some of the basics of welding and let him have a go at it. But it was a disaster. Whatever he was doing was wrong and a waste of his dad's patience. He finally threw a dog-eared book about welding at his son and said, "Come back after you've read this." Cal left the book on the ground where his father tossed it and stomped off. He had no interest in welding after that, at least not so anyone could tell. But the images of man surrounded by flying sparks of fire stuck with him, along with the mystique of flowing red-hot metal being pounded, molded, and shaped.

Cal takes the boxes of Christmas decorations to Dad's old shed and pries off the lock to see what's left in there. It's chock full of tools and welding equipment and would have brought in big bucks if he ever thought to come out here to pawn or sell the stuff. The Sears 120v 80-amp inverter welder is still here, along with a huge anvil, a grinder, a set of torches, and chisels. Hanging on the walls and scattered across the workbench are more tools and equipment—hammers and pliers, safety glasses, earplugs, welding rods, a hood, and gloves. He even finds the welding manual he scorned in his youth and sits down in a shop chair to study it.

After a while he fires up the welder, assembles some tools, pulls the welding hood down over his face, and sets to work repairing the carolers, mending the seams holding them together, and creating a stand to prop them up out of scrap metal he found in a box under the worktable.

It looks good when he's done. Feels good, too, seeing it stand there, straight and firm. He pokes through the boxes McCloskey gave him, looking for other stuff to mend. He adds a missing halo to the angel, makes Rudolph a bigger nose, and finds more scrap metal he can weld into a sleigh for the plastic Santa to ride. Working there in the shed making stuff, armored and helmeted, his gloved hands clasping metal, bending it to his will, a fountain of sparks flowing from his fingertips, he feels grounded and alive in a way he's never felt before. It's like one of those sparks flying around the shop found its way through that hole in his heart and lodged there, lighting up something deep inside.

Well before Christmas arrives, his yard is as decked out as any of the others in the neighborhood. A string of colored lights that McCloskey helped him put up is dangling below the roof. The carolers, mended and repainted, stand front and center in the yard, lit by a floodlight and surrounded by a trio of wire reindeer sparkling with tiny lights, Santa in his sleigh, the angel with outstretched wings and halo, and an elf he designed and welded all by himself out of scrap metal he picked up at the junkyard.

Several neighbors from down the street come by to give him a thumbs-up and welcome him to the Christmas Club. They stay to talk shop with each other there in his front yard, assessing the pros and cons of different types of lighting and the newest line of decorations. Cal doesn't say much; he just listens and nods, taking it all in, feeling like he's part of something he doesn't quite understand and not wanting to spoil it.

One of the guys stays behind when the others leave.

"Cal, right?"

He nods warily and shakes the man's hand when offered.

"Buzz, here. Remember? We were in high school together. My folks lived down the street, a block over. I took over the place when they retired and moved away. Looks like you did the same thing. Any kids?"

"No, no. Still single," Cal says, wracking his brain and then remembering. Buzz was a tall, lanky guy on the basketball team, a couple of grades below him. They didn't hang out, but they ran into each other around the campus and neighborhood and waved or stopped to chat now and then.

"Me, four girls. Can you believe it?" He shakes his head.

Buzz seems surprised when Cal tells him he's still unmarried. He asks Cal where he works and nods in sympathy when Cal tells him he's between jobs. A few guys at the place where Buzz works got laid off recently too. Damn shame.

The crazy thing is, Cal realizes, Buzz thinks he's just a regular guy like him, only better because he's still single and has all his options open, no one to hold him back, no extra mouths to feed.

"I wish I'd done like you did. Holding back awhile, not getting married so young. Not that I'd trade Marsha or the girls for anything. We have a good life here, but sometimes I wonder, you know, what it would be like if I'd waited before settling down."

Cal watches him walk away and gets a weird feeling—a guy like that who has it all envying him, even if it's a fake him he envies. For a minute, it's like he sees two Cals, the one he's been living these past several years and the one this guy sees. Two Cals walking down parallel paths, and for a moment the trees between them thin, and they get a glimpse of each other. Two startled faces looking at each other.

Later that night Cal sits in a lawn chair on the front stoop, half hidden in the deep shadow, hugging a quilt to keep out the cold. Cars stream by slowly, the windows rolled down, little kids leaning out, oohing and aahing over his handiwork. Sucking up the Kool-Aid, he smiles to himself. A warm, slushy, glow spreads through him, pours out onto the misty lawn and into all those faces, lit by the spirit of something he helped create—in one of those parallel lives that crisscross the universe.

27

KAY

Mother of All Mountains

It's New Year's Day, 1999, and Kay is carrying over a tradition from her childhood, taking down the Christmas tree while watching the Rose Bowl Parade on TV—with Richard this time instead of her mom. She rescued favorite childhood ornaments on that last trip home—the felt elves and reindeer she and her grandmother made together one Christmas, some tiny crystal angels playing harps that she now wraps in tissue paper, and the red velvet bows her mother hung last to fill any empty spaces left after everything else was hung. She invited Cal to spend Christmas with them, as she had with Thanksgiving, but he declined, which was just as well. The thought of him and Richard in close proximity makes her nervous.

She and Richard have been living together for five months now, and it's working out better than she expected, despite the fact they both have crazy jobs that take them away from each other. Richard travels often to meet with artists and buyers and to check up on his other galleries. Kay surveys building sites all over southern California, looking for archaeological resources that might need to be protected before building permits are granted.

She still receives her mother's calls, having transferred her landline number to her new home, a line dedicated to her mother. The calls come sporadically—sometimes several within a few days and then nothing for weeks or longer. She's not obsessed about the calls like she once was. But still, every time she sees the red light blinking on the phone, her heart quickens. The sound of her mother's voice and the soothing things she shares send a wave of relief and comfort coursing through her body.

Now Kay is leaving messages on the phone too, so when her mother calls, she hears the recording of her daughter's voice sharing tidbits of news about her life as well. Sometimes they respond to each other's comments, as if carrying on a conversation. She tells her about Richard and her new home in the hillsides of Sierra Madre, about her new job and funny things that happen at work, things she thinks her mother will enjoy.

She tells her about Dad moving to Alaska and Cal living at home alone. But she doesn't tell her how Cal sold all their furniture and tore out the front yard. She doesn't tell her that even though Cal assures her he's staying clean, her stomach still knots when she thinks of him. Or how scared she is to visit him again, to see what else he's done to the house. How it's become a shell of what it was when Mom was there—when they were still a family, not four people flying off in different directions.

And she doesn't tell her to come home like she wants. Or ask her why she left. She bites her tongue and tells herself: No. Don't spoil this—whatever this is—these sweet conversations running through the airwaves, stitching them together.

In some ways, Kay feels she's coming to know her mother better in her absence than her presence. These messages being extracted through the airwaves are a distillation of all she loves about her mother, giving her a more distinct sense of her essence than she got in person when daily concerns and distractions cluttered the space between them.

"I think we understand each other so well," Richard tells her now as he packs away the last of the Christmas ornaments, "because we both have strong, loving mothers we adore."

"What about your father? You don't talk about him much."

"This is true. We don't get along all that well, like Cal and your dad, I suppose." Kay doubts very much that his relationship with his father is anything like Cal's and Dad's, but she doesn't say so.

Richard is an only child. His parents never married, and he spent his youth traveling from one continent to another, his mother in Argentina, his father in Portugal. His childhood seems so exotic compared to Kay's. She loves hearing about it, but it makes her uneasy too. Are they too different? Do they really fit together?

His father is some kind of financial wizard who divides his time between Europe and the United States. He was the one who insisted Richard learn English, the universal language of commerce, he claimed. Although Richard visited his father often as a child, his home was with his mother in Buenos Aires.

"I was the only child of parents in lust who couldn't stand each other outside the bedroom. Or so they contend. In truth, they are devoted to each other. Although they can't live together, not even on the same continent, they can't live without each other either. They are constantly drawn back, in and out of each other's lives, circling each other endlessly."

His mother is an artist, he tells her, working mostly in textiles and collage. She inspired him to live his dreams rather than becoming the financier his father had been training him to be.

"I wasn't an artist like her," he tells Kay. "But I loved her work. I studied art history, as well as finance to please my father. Then, I realized how this knowledge might be useful to promote the arts. I became obsessed with helping my mother gain the recognition she deserves. Women artists are notoriously neglected in Argentina as elsewhere."

He started off marketing her work, helping to get it shown in major galleries and museums. Then, he began doing the same for other artists whose work had been neglected. Eventually, he opened his own gallery in Buenos Aires. When a colleague who owned a successful gallery in Santa Barbara told him he was closing, Richard bought him out. Later, he opened a gallery in Sierra Madre. By then, his father had taken an interest in what he was doing and was encouraging him to expand to San Francisco.

"My father always said, 'You're just like me, son. You have the soul of an artist, the spirit of an entrepreneur, and the mind of a mogul!'" Richard laughs. "I don't know about the mogul part, but the other two he has right."

"Why did you end up staying here, managing this shop, rather than the one in Buenos Aires?" she asks.

"Or Santa Barbara?" he says. "That's what my father always asks. Why here?"

"So, what do you tell him?"

"Him? Nothing. It's none of his business. But if I were to tell him, I would say I like it here, beneath these mountains, away from the noise and confusion of the big cities yet close enough to an international airport so I can manage my affairs easily. That's what I would tell him. But . . . .."

"What?"

"I'm not sure that's the real reason." He turns to look at her. "I think it was kismet, my coming here. Meeting you. Us. This."

"Kismet, huh? So romantic!" She gives him a saucy grin and leads him to the sofa, where she curls up beside him.

"So, tell me, sweet Lothario, just when did you fall for me? When did you know you were fated to be with me? Was it lust or love? I want all the details. Don't skimp on anything."

"So demanding!" he says. "Okay, let me think. Well, I might have begun to fall for you—a tiny bit—the moment you walked into my shop. You looked so intense and hopeful at the same time. You looked like someone on a mission, the way you breezed by me with barely a glance.

"And then when I found you standing in front of those photos, you turned toward me with a look of wonder in those big, brown eyes, so wide, so open, like I could fall into them. That's when I felt myself falling for you, toward you. Just irresistibly drawn."

She wriggles with pleasure beside him.

He looks at her and laughs. "You like this, don't you?"

"I love this!" she agrees. "Go on, go on."

"Okay, so there you were all open to me. But then!" he says. "For no reason I could see, you suddenly closed down! A look of alarm came into your eyes, and you started backing away. I didn't know what was happening, and it appeared you didn't either. So, I grabbed your arm and led you to that chair.

"Then you looked at me with those big, brown eyes, tear-filled, and it all came spilling out, everything you were worried about, all you had been holding back. So much feeling! Wave after wave! I felt drenched in all that emotion. I wanted to take you in my arms to comfort you. To show you I was there for you. And then I had this erotic vision: You sitting naked in my lap, me stirring beneath you. I knew then that I had to have you. No question." His arms tighten around her.

"And that's when you fell in love?"

"No, silly. That's when I fell in lust. But it wasn't only physical; it was emotional too. I wanted all that feeling you were pouring out. I wanted that poured on me."

"So, when did the love happen?"

He rubs the scruff on his chin and twists his lips as he thinks.

"In the restaurant, I think. The day you showed me your mother's photos. When you began to talk about your work and your face lit up. I remember thinking, I want more of that, what was going on in your mind. Then when you reprimanded me about the quality of light below the border, arguing with such self-assurance, I loved that! I thought, this is someone I could argue with forever and never tire of."

Kay tisks her tongue in disbelief. "*That's* when you fell in love? When we argued?"

He cocks his head. "A little. Not all the way. But falling, yes.

"So, when did you fall all the way?"

"Oh, that's easy," he says as his soft, ardent lips find hers, and she's swept away into this red-hot, melting, erogenous zone where their mouths meet.

When he finally lets her go, when they both come back to themselves, he says, "That's when I fell all the way. When I tasted you for the first time in my apartment. Every cell in my body drew you in, lapped you up, devoured you. I knew then I was lost forever. I pushed you back onto that ridiculous round bed and peeled away your clothes. You lay there so still, so patient and pliant as my eyes feasted on your flesh, the stark whiteness of your skin against those red sheets as you looked up at me in wide-open wonder. That's when I fell all the way. In love. In lust. Devouring your body for the first time, every inch of you. And knowing every inch was mine and would be forever. There was nothing you or I could ever do to change that."

They look at each other now, deeply, darkly, and Kay feels as if she's drowning again.

She swallows hard. "But then I left."

He laughs. "Yes, you did! You tried to run away."

"But I couldn't."

"No, you couldn't. Because we were fated to be together. That's why I settled in Sierra Madre. The name drew me—Mother of All Mountains. I knew this is where I would find you. The mother of my children."

Her heart is thumping wildly now.

"You want me to be the mother of your children?"

"But of course. What did you think?" He looks at her, his eyes soft and puzzled.

"I didn't know."

"How could you not?"

She takes a deep breath. "Are you proposing?"

He cocks his head and smiles. "I suppose I am. Should I get down on one knee? I will if you want."

He moves from the sofa to the floor, as if to kneel before her. But then he reaches up and pulls her down beside him, turns her back toward him, cradles her in his arms, and nuzzles her neck. "I prefer proposing this way, with you in my arms."

"Me too," she whispers.

"So, it's settled." They rock together like that, silently, for a long while.

28

CAL
White-Hot Flow

Cal pulls the welding hood down over his face and watches flame meet metal through the dark visor, his hands twisting and turning the iron to match the images in his mind. It's not like he has this clear idea of what he's creating. Not yet. It's more like a germ of an idea, a felt sense of something that bubbles up from his subconscious—something that wants to be that he's giving birth to, pulling into the world with the sheer force of his will and the fire's might. Sometimes it starts with a memory or a fragment from a dream or nightmare—a demon that's been haunting him or some sweet yearning calling to him like a siren's song. Whatever it ends up being in the end—a wild-eyed rooster, a hunched-backed ogre, or an angel with lifted wings—it starts out the same: hands, metal, fire. Cal's just the conduit, surrendering himself to this thing moving through him.

He's been at this since before Christmas, since he first opened his dad's shed and made it his own, since he realized: *I can do this. I can make something out of nothing. I can weave my dreams and hopes and fears into something fierce and tangible.*

He's on a roll now, caught up in what he thinks of as a white-hot flow. The creative juices feed him for two, three, four days at a time. He's been holed up in the shed, welding and sculpting with barely a moment to eat, piss, sleep. And even when he must, he does so grudgingly, worried that any interruption, however slight, might break the spell and end the white-hot flow that feeds his work.

Cal realizes his new obsession is the kind of hyper-focus related to his ADHD. Those hunters in the wild scanning the horizon, looking for game, had to become hyper-focused once they sniffed out the scat of some prey and followed its tracks. The hunt could last for miles, days, weeks before they finally chased it down. It was like those days when he was rock hunting in the riverbed with his sister, his attention never wavering. He was like a bloodhound, his focus clear, intense, pure.

Welding is like that, only he isn't interested in being a workman welder like his dad. He wants to bend metal and flame into the images that surge through his imagination, the monsters and gargoyles, angels and devils, of his dreams and nightmares wrought to life by his hand and hot metal. He searches through piles of books at garage sales and thrift stores for books on art, anything to help him understand and channel his desire to create. Even when he isn't in the act of creating art, it's in his head—all day, all night—when he dreams, when he wakes, when he makes himself eat.

Cal on a tangent. Cal obsessed. Cal throwing the weight of his will into whatever activity grabbed hold of him—this is how his mom and sister would see it, how he's always been since he was a kid, grabbing hold of something and beating it to death. Not letting go . . ..

So be it, he thinks now. *It's how I'm wired. I can't do a thing about it. And, for once, I don't want to.*

For the first time, he knows exactly where he wants to be and what he wants to be doing, 24/7, for the rest of his life.

*****

More and more Cal finds himself drawn into his mother's office to study her photos.

Is it art? Is she an artist? Am I?

217

Over time the photos have changed. They've become more fluid, spacious, panoramic: Clouds drifting across a desert sky. A mosaic of rocks, twigs, and water in a rushing stream. A tapestry of moss stitched along the trunk of a gnarled oak. Sunlight filtering through leaves. Things connected rather than things askew. And they're not only photos of nature or wildlife anymore, but people too: young couples holding hands, kids playing on the beach, scenes from street markets.

But something about those earlier, weirdly angled photos won't let go of him. They remind him of a photo his mother gave him when he was a boy. A photo that disturbed him even then. It's driving him crazy.

He digs through a box of stuff his mom saved for him—letters from his grandmother, postcards from summer camp, school report cards, wrestling trophies, arrest records, articles on AIDS and hep C, lists of sober living homes . . . all her love and worry piled together over the years into a cardboard box. Cal. Her son. What she'd have left of him if her worst nightmare came true, if she received that midnight phone call that haunts the hearts of all mothers.

And then he finds it. He sits back on the floor holding the photo he'd been searching for, his stomach clenched, his breath thick and heavy. Hot, hot tears he will not release gather behind his eyeballs.

It's a picture of his mother he took when he was five years old. He was playing with her new expensive Minolta camera, even though he was warned not to touch it. But as soon as his mother turned away, he picked it up and held it to his face the way she had. There she was, caught in the tiny aperture. Excited, he called out. She turned, a look of horror on her face as she dashed forward, bending to grab the camera from his hands. Before she could, the shutter went off, capturing for all eternity her fear, her anger, her disappointment in her son.

The photo looks like those she first mailed him, pictures of things partial, up close, and askew. A hazy close-up of her face fills three-fourths of the frame. You can see her skin, grainy in its closeness, one dark eye, a curve of cheek and chin, a haze of hair backlit by the overhead lamp. The rough closeness, the blurred intimacy, the hovering presence capture his mother better than any portrait could. That's how he experiences her, then as now: Partial and incomplete. Too close to see clearly, to know fully. Hovering at the periphery of his awareness wherever he goes. Silently demanding. Her disapproval, huge and heavy, presses down on him.

Yet, once she developed the film, she proudly showed the photograph to her son, wrapping him in a hug.

"Cal's first picture!" she said, beaming as she gave it to him—a gift—this picture of her dark displeasure. This glimpse into the underbelly of her motherlove.

*****

Now when he's welding and stops to take a swig from the water bottle he keeps by his side, when he lifts the hood and wipes the sweat from his forehead, his gaze drifts to the photo of his mother taped on the wall—no frame, no fuss, just jagged strips of masking tape crossing the corners, holding it up.

It's not even a picture of his mother, he realizes now. It's not even her he's glancing at. Hell, how could it be? He has no idea who she is. In the place his mother once occupied remains this mystery. That's what he's glancing at, touching base with. It's what she's come to stand for in his mind—the mother of all mysteries—this creative angst, this burning desire, this vital urgency that feeds his art. Whatever it is that runs through his mind, that appears, disappears, reappears, and has no name. That's just past knowing. That's what he glances at continually as he works, what fuels him and pulls him forward: the mystery in the midst of things. That's what keeps him, keeps all of us, searching, reaching for this "something more" that underlies all longing.

29

CAL
Tats

Not long after the New Year rolls in, Cal drags some of his metal sculptures out into the driveway to bulk up his garage sales—the wild roosters and coiled snakes ready to strike, the hunch-backed ogres and angels with lifted wings and flowing hair. He makes practical things, too—potholders that look like old-fashioned tricycles with their big wheels, scorpions whose curved tails are hooks that can be hung on the wall, and large sunflowers to decorate a garden.

People seem to get a kick out of these strange creations, and it does his heart good to see them going to new homes. Aside from his artwork, his garage sales now consist mostly of undervalued items he's picked up at other garage sales or in thrift shops since he's pretty much sold all the extraneous stuff in the house.

Now nearly the only things left from when his parents lived here are his mother's coffee table—a chest she brought home from some thrift shop, sanded down and varnished—and his dad's green recliner. He's not sure why he hung onto the chair aside from the obvious: It's damn comfortable, a good place to lean back, kick up his feet, and survey his kingdom like his dad used to do. Sitting there is like claiming something he never thought he'd have for himself: A home of his own, a place where he belonged. More than that, a place that belongs to him.

He tried getting Grandma's dining table and cupboard back from Eddie for Kay. But Sally wasn't having it. "She loves that shit," Eddy told him. But if they ever upgrade or Sally leaves again, Cal can buy it back, he said. Seeing as how Eddie and Sally's relationship has always been stormy, Cal figures there's a fair chance he'll get it back one day.

He's maintaining his recovery too, or what he calls his recovery. Sometimes he even goes with Mikey to his NA meetings. Mostly he sits in the back, arms folded across his chest, legs kicked out, listening. Sorting out the bullshitters from the real devotees.

Mikey keeps prodding him to share, and one day in mid-January, he finally does. He stands there at the podium looking out at that sea of sad-sack faces and tells his story: Mom leaving, Dad leaving, Kay's wake-up call, jail, McCloskey, welding, Christmas Club. All leading up to his pronouncement that he's six months sober now—meaning he's not shooting up or using the hard stuff anymore. A six-pack now and then, a couple of joints—no harm in that. In fact, he sees that as part of his recovery. It takes the edge off when he's leaning in the wrong direction.

But he can't share any of this at the meetings. They'd say he wasn't sober at all, that he was fooling himself, taking shortcuts, not doing the hard work, not finding his Higher Power. But he thinks he has found it: his artwork, fire and metal, purpose and passion. That's his Higher Power, something from within welling up and flowing through him. It's what motivates him to steer clear of the hard stuff that could derail all that. His new love keeps his old love, Lady H, at bay.

*****

One afternoon when Cal is refilling his water bottle in the kitchen, the doorbell rings. He freezes. The old paranoia kicks in, and he weighs the pros and cons of answering. Cops? Nosy neighbors? Avon lady?

What the fuck, he thinks. *I have nothing to hide from.* He slams down his bottle and heads to the door. A young woman stands on the front stoop. She looks familiar—definitely not Avon, he thinks, looking over the small, slim blonde. She's dressed in jeans and a long-sleeved gray jersey. Tattoos peek beneath the shirt at her collar and wrists.

"I know you," Cal says. "I've seen you around."

He remembers her from that NA meeting where he spun his story. She was wearing a dress then, leaning against the back wall, ankles crossed in front of her. The first thing he noticed were the tats running up and down her bare arms and legs. The second thing was the way she held herself aloof from everyone, even after the meeting. She was friendly enough, shaking hands and exchanging greetings, but there was something about her that set her apart.

"Who is she?" he asked Mikey as they followed the crowd out the door and he stopped to light a cigarette. A real one. He was done rolling his own.

Mikey shook his head. "Dunno, new around here. Heard she sleeps in her van."

Sure enough, as they were watching, she crossed the street and opened the door of an old two-toned VW bus, where she was greeted by a big, blond Labrador. She stood there a moment, kneading the dog's ears, saying something low and friendly, before squeezing in behind the wheel and driving away. Her eyes met Cal's as she passed.

"I remember you too," she says now. "Cal, right? I'm Ivey. Mikey said you had a room for rent."

He looks her over again. "You clean?" he asks. "Don't want no users. Trying to quit that shit. Pot's okay, booze too, but nothing harder."

She cocks her head. "You're not clean if you're smoking pot and drinking."

"That's a matter of opinion," he replies.

"No, it's not." She lifts her chin and looks him straight in the eye.

He snorts a laugh, her reminding him of every sponsor he's ever had, and then looks her up and down. He's not sure he likes what he sees, but he admires her spunk. He's both fascinated and repelled by the tattoos leaking out from under the edges of her jersey. Aside from that, she wears no ornamentation, not even earrings to fill the three holes on each earlobe or the one that lay on the side of her nose like a wayward freckle. He wonders where else she might be pierced. Her hair brushes her shoulders, pale and fine as corn silk, which she tucks self-consciously behind her ears as he watches. She is short and thin—too thin for Cal's taste, who likes his women softer, rounder, with something to grab hold of. She looks hard and dried up, like she's been left out in the sun too long. Definitely not his type. Which is good, he tells himself, this being strictly a business transaction.

Ivey's been giving him the eye too, her eye not as friendly as before. "I'm four years sober. Four years, five months, thirteen days."

"That'll do," he says as he waves her through the door. "Don't want you preaching though," he adds as she sashays past him.

"I don't preach."

"See that you don't," he says, pushing his advantage as he closes the door behind them.

He shows her the living room, dining room, kitchen, laundry room, all still mostly empty, although he's added a used couch and small TV to go with his recliner and Mom's chest. Slowly he's been replacing the furniture he sold in garage sales, now that he has the utilities covered and he's been able to make a bit of profit selling some of his sculptures. Then he leads her down the hall, opening each bedroom door.

"This is my room," he says. A full-size futon and small dresser have replaced the air mattress and boxes. He holds the door open and looks down at her as she peeks inside. He likes the way her hair parts down the middle, a strip of pale pink showing through the blond.

"This is my mom's old office." He opens the door next to his room, empty now except for her photographs tacked on the wall. Then he heads to the end of the hallway.

"Here's where you'll be, private bath and all," he says, showing her his parent's bedroom. It too is empty.

She looks inside and then up at him. "You don't like furniture much, do you?"

"I like a clean, streamlined look," he says with a smirk. "So, what do you think? Still want to rent?"

"I have a dog. That okay?"

He shrugs. "Why not? Housebroken, right?" She nods. "Well then," he says, leaning against the bedroom doorway. "Let's make it six hundred even. You have full use of the house, kitchen and all."

"Can't do it," she says, shaking her head.

He looks at her. "Five hundred?"

She looks back.

"Four?"

"You got a deal," she says and sticks out her hand. He shakes it, suspecting he got played but figures four hundred is better than nothing.

"I'll need that first month's rent upfront," he tells her, firm now, like he means business.

She reaches into the canvas bag slung over her shoulder and pulls out a fold of bills. "Here's first and last. Eight hundred." She peels off the hundreds one by one into Cal's hand. "I'll need a receipt."

"Don't have one."

She pulls out a yellow receipt book and hands it to him. "Now you do."

He laughs. "Ain't you the Girl Scout, all prepared?" He takes the pen she hands him and fills out the receipt. "So, when you moving in?"

"Right now, if you don't mind. Got all my stuff in my van."

"That's right. You've been living there a while, haven't you?"

"Long enough. Got a steady job now working at the animal shelter."

"Good for you. Need help bringing in your stuff?" He hands her the receipt, which she studies before sticking into her bag.

"No, I'm good."

He walks her to the front door and watches her go out to the van and bring in an air mattress and pump. Then she brings in two plastic crates full of bedding and books, a backpack, and a giant green suitcase on wheels. Her yellow Lab, who she introduces as Buddha, follows at her heels. Cal sticks out his hand for the dog to smell and nuzzles her behind the ears. He likes the thought of having a dog around. Dad never wanted animals in the house, so he and Kay went without childhood pets, aside from a pair of parakeets Mom brought home one day. But they didn't last long. Flew the coop when she was airing them out in the backyard and forgot to latch the door. He and Kay chased them around the neighborhood for a week, trying to get them back. To no avail. That was the end of their pet experiment.

Now he kicks back in his recliner and turns on the sports channel, as if he has nothing better to do while waiting for her to unpack her van. He doesn't want to return to his welding until she's moved in. Letting a stranger roam around his home when he's not here doesn't feel right yet.

After a while she brings in two bags of groceries. "You said I have full use of the house, right? Can I put these in the kitchen?"

He follows her in, and they divvy up kitchen cupboard space and shelves in the fridge. That night she cooks up curried rice with carrots and offers him half. She sits on the couch while he leans back in the recliner and turns on the TV. The news pops up with photos of Monica Lewinsky's blue dress and a newsreel of President Clinton denying the allegations of an affair. Cal looks over at Ivey and quickly switches the channel. He's not sure why. Normally, he likes following the unfolding melodrama, his sympathy totally in the Clinton camp. He flicks through several options and finally settles on watching reruns of *Cheers,* where a saucy romance is brewing between Sam, a swaggering bartender, and Diane, a new high-brow, uptight employee who thinks she's way too good for him. Soon he and Ivey are both shaking their heads and chuckling over the unlikely antics of this mismatched couple.

He likes the way she laughs, light and carefree, like the tinkling of piano keys at the high end of the scale. It breaks down the hardness in her face and the stiffness of her body, making her seem like she never had a tattoo stitched into her skin, never lived in a van, never had a mean day or bad break in her life.

*****

The following week Ivey invites him to go grocery shopping with her. "I've noticed you don't have much left to eat in there."

He grins at her. "You don't want me mooching off your stuff, do you?"

"Well, there's that too," she admits with a sly smile.

He follows her to her van and slides into the front seat beside her. Buddha's not too happy being relegated to the back, but she circles herself onto the floor and looks up at Cal with big eyes before laying her head on her paws. He's been enjoying having a dog around. He likes the way Buddha greets him with a soft wag of her tail when he comes into the room, sniffing his clothes and hands when he reaches down to pet her. When they arrive at the store, she gets to her feet, tail twitching with excitement, ready to join them.

"Sorry, girl," he tells her, feeling her disappointment and scratching behind her ears in consolation.

Inside, he and Ivey part company. Each grabs a cart and heads in opposite directions. She goes toward the fruit and vegetable section, while he heads toward the frozen food. A couple of times they pass each other in the middle of the store. The first time he hops up on the bottom rail of the cart, gives it a push, and sails past her, grinning. She shakes her head and bites her lip to keep from laughing. The next time they merely give each other a nod and a casual, appreciative glance over, not saying anything. He likes that, the way they connect without speaking.

But once they get home and he watches her step up on a stool to reach a high shelf, even while he's admiring the shape of her calves showing beneath her capris, he's put off by the tattoos. Why'd she go and spoil herself with all those scrawls?

"What?" she asks as she steps down and catches him staring at her.

"Nothing, really. Just . . .."

"What?" she asks again.

"What's with all the tats, anyway?" he blurts out.

"What do you mean?"

"I mean, why did you . . .," he wants to say abuse, spoil, ruin yourself that way, but changes it to, "cover yourself up like that."

She looks at him—a hard, pointed look. Then she turns her back and digs down into her shopping bag for more to put away. Like she's going to ignore him.

"What?" He throws up his hands. "I'm not supposed to ask that. It's impolite or something?"

"No, it's just personal," she says.

"Personal! It looks pretty public to me."

He's expecting her wrath now, indignation, maybe a "fuck you." So, he's surprised when she laughs.

"Yeah, I guess you're right. I don't know." She stands there with her hands full of canned soup, her head cocked. "I think it's like bringing what's inside outside. Our bodies are pretty much an accident of birth—what we look like, our gender, skin color, all that. This is a way to take what's inside and put it on the outside, to show who we are and what matters to us." She turns and stacks the cans on the shelf.

"Yeah?" He watches her and then adds, "Well, sorry to say, all I see is a body covered with scrawls."

She stops and turns, looking him full in the face. "Sometimes you're a real shit, Cal."

He laughs. "I know, I know. My sister tells me that all the time."

"You're sister, huh?" She eyes him, curious.

"Yeah, Baby Kay."

Her eyebrows rise, and a smudge of a smile tugs at the corner of her mouth as she looks him over. Like she's just figured out something.

30

WALTER
Lighting a Fire

Walter's not prepared for winter in Alaska. He thought he was. The tamping down of summer into fall, the shortening days, he welcomed all that. Hell, he was glad to see the dark arrive when it should, instead of staying light until almost midnight. He liked it when the sun started dipping at ten, then eight, then five.

But when it starts going down at four, then three? When it doesn't grow light until nearly noon? When the sun never rises higher than the mountains, drifting along the treetops like a half-deflated balloon? When the air is so cold a sneeze will explode into splinters of ice that fall tinkling to the ground like broken glass? That's something else. Something he can't quite wrap his mind around. That feels dangerously out of kilter.

It isn't only him, either, or just the cold and dark. It's the way the whole town tamps down, too—the energy and laughter and lightheartedness of summer draining away, leaving behind a lethargy that spreads over everything. Like everyone is wading through thick molasses or everything is buried beneath a blanket of melancholy, resigned to settle into semi-hibernation. Getting up and getting out the door seems like a chore too cumbersome to negotiate.

Most folks in town create their own ways of handling the gloom. Some fill their homes with "happy lights" that emulate natural sunshine. A few spend time in tanning booths. Some hightail it to Hawaii. Others become hyperactive, taking up dogsledding, or snow skiing, or ice hockey. Some drink themselves happy or bury themselves under the covers, fornicating like crazy. Birth rates always spike around September and October in Alaska.

Others—the less manic—settle into the slower, colder, grayer days reading long books and taking longer naps. That's how Dawn settles in and the way Walter's drifting. Only he isn't a big reader, so instead he catches up on countless TV documentaries. Randy, though, is an entirely different beast. He's too hyper to hibernate, and the dullness of their days makes him edgy and drink more. There isn't much work to be had by mid-November. By then, all the boats have been hauled up, put through the annual maintenance routine, and then stacked on cradles to wait out winter. Most of their work now is maintaining their fleet and fixing what the wind or snow tears up or breaks down.

But as the days grow darker and colder, Randy's "heebie-jeebies," as Dawn calls them, get worse. By mid-January the poor boy seems likely to jump out of his skin.

"Why don't you go put on those cross-country skis I got you for Christmas and go hiking out Bullnose Canyon?" Dawn suggests to Randy while teaching Walter to play pinochle. "You've hardly used them at all. Maybe take a sled and bring us back more firewood."

"Maybe it's time for me to take off to Anchorage," Randy says. "There's a dogsled race I want to see come February, and Billy Buckley should be back in town. I sure do like the way he picks that fiddle. You should come with me, Walter. You haven't seen any sledding, have you? And I know you'd like the way Billy plays."

"I thought Albert was going with you this year?" Dawn says.

"No, Gemma's down with something, and he said he can't make it."

"How 'bout Harry Steffen? Didn't he go with you last year?"

"Yeah, but he said he'd never go with me again. Said I about talked his ear off. So, what do you say, Walter?" He gives him a soft slug on the shoulder. "You and me and the big city."

"That's kind of you to invite me, but I think I'll stay put. Me and big cities never mixed well. Don't like crowds much."

"Who else do you have to go with, Randy?" Dawn asks. "You can't go by yourself."

"Why not? He's old enough," Walter says. "It will do him good. Being on his own."

Dawn shoots him a dark look. "Randy likes company, don't you, Randy?"

"You think I could? Go by myself?" Randy asks.

"I don't see why not," Walter says before Dawn kicks him under the table. "Unless Dawn here knows something I don't?"

"I don't think it's a good idea. You'll find someone to go with you. I'll give Ed Summers a call. I know he likes the bright lights."

The next day Dawn makes some calls, but Ed can't go either, and neither can Mackie or Marcel. "Damn it," says Dawn when she hangs up the phone. "Clay always went if we couldn't find anyone else to babysit him. Looks like I'll have to go."

She's at the shop with Walter where they spent the afternoon doing inventory.

"I don't see why," he says, putting the ledger back in the desk drawer. "Let him do this on his own."

"If you don't see why, you're blinder than a bat."

"What I see is that too much coddling ruins a boy, keeps him from developing what he needs to make it on his own."

"You speaking from experience?"

He looks at her, his mouth grim. "My son," he says. "Franny coddled him too much. It didn't turn out well."

"Randy's not your son. You don't know what he needs."

"I know he's not a boy. And I know he won't ever be a man if people keep treating him like he needs propping up. But you're right. I don't know him like you all do. You do what you want."

By the end of January, Dawn still can't find anyone to go with Randy and can't talk Randy out of going or into taking her along for company.

"Hey, Dawn. No disrespect, but you don't like to party as much as I do," Randy tells her. "When I go to Anchorage with Clay or Billy, we hit the clubs. I can't see you doing that. And what if I want to bring someone back to the room for a drink? How'd you feel about that?"

They are sitting around her kitchen table. Dinner dishes have been cleared away and washed, and Randy sits backward in his chair like he likes, watching Walter and Dawn play Scrabble.

"I wasn't thinking about bunking up with you," Dawn tells him. "You'd have your own room. Besides, when was the last time you brought some girl back to your room? I can't see Clay putting up with that."

"That's my point. I'm not a boy anymore. Right, Walter? I don't need propping up."

Dawn gives Walter a look that makes him wince.

"Whoa, now!" he says, throwing up his hands. "I didn't say anything to him. I swear!"

"He didn't, Dawn. I overheard you two talking the other day. And he's right. You all always treat me like a baby. Some Peter Pan who never grows up. Don't think I don't know."

"Some people should keep their fat mouths shut." Dawn stares menacingly at Walter. Then she turns to Randy. "Do what you want then. I wash my hands of it. Of both of you." She pushes her chair back and stomps off, slamming the bedroom door behind her.

"I've never seen her that mad," Walter says, looking after her.

"I have. She'll get over it."

"You sure you want to do this? Go on your own?"

"Sure do!"

Randy's grin reminds Walter so much of his kids, then—Kay with that mop of dark hair and Cal with that goofy grin—it makes his eyes smart. Damn weather, he thinks, linking this unlikely display of sentimentality with that. That and the damn gloom. And Dawn stomping off, mad at him for the first time ever. And Randy here, grinning like a little kid, like he has no business going off to Anchorage by himself. But it's too late to back away. He's set something in motion, and it's moving on without him.

And the truth be told, he can't help thinking he's right. His kids are out there on their own, aren't they? They're doing fine, as far as he can tell by what Kay says when she calls—better than ever, now with Franny gone and him gone too. Cal's getting clean, keeping the lights on in the house. Kay's got a new job, new boyfriend. And so it will be for Randy.

He follows Randy into the mudroom and watches him bang out the back door, his boots crunching through the snow, the moonlight soft on his shoulders. He watches him until he disappears around a snow-capped hedge and then watches the hedge long after that. He should be heading home too. He gathers his coat, scarves, and galoshes and sits on the bench to pull on his boots. But he doesn't have the energy to do it.

Something is weighing on his mind, and he's not sure what. It could be how all this reminds him of Franny and the fights they used to have about Cal. It makes him wonder if he should have stood up to her, taken down some of that propping up, the way he's doing now with Randy. Or maybe he should have kept his mouth shut and let Dawn have her way. Maybe he's gone and ruined things by interfering. You're damned if you do and damned if you don't.

But he knows that's not what's really bothering him. It's not about Randy. It's about Dawn. He can't stop thinking of her stomping off like that, her bitter mouth, her downcast eyes. The urge to follow her down that hall is strong. He sits there till a chill grabs him, and noting the stand of logs stacked in the corner, he snatches a few, takes them into the living room, and begins laying up a fire.

He's poking at the logs, getting the flame to take hold, when he hears a noise behind him. He stops and looks over his shoulder. It's Dawn in a long, white nighty and red woolen socks.

"What are you doing?" she asks. "I thought you'd be home by now."

"Home? I don't have a home, Dawn. I have a cabin at a motel. That's what I got." He rises now and faces her.

"So, you planning on staying here all night?" The light from the fire flickers over her white gown.

He cocks his head. "I hadn't thought that far ahead, but it sounds like a good idea. You inviting me to stay?"

She crosses her arms over her chest. "Hope you like the couch."

He smiles. "I would if you join me. For a little while, at least." He holds out his hand and, amazingly, she takes it. He pulls her into a dance embrace, dips her, and grins.

"And Franny says I can't dance."

"Could have fooled me," says Dawn. He draws her down on the couch beside him and leans back, his arm still around her soft shoulders.

"I can light a fire though," he says, looking at how the flames have spread and feeling its heat.

"That you can," Dawn agrees, looking straight at him.

It's as easy as that. He moves in the next day. The spark that was lit when they first met, that lay dormant all this time as they sized each other up as business partners and settled down into a comfortable friendship, is rekindled and keeps growing until they both feel enveloped in its warm glow—a comfortable fire, not huge or blazing, but steady and sure.

31

CAL

Keeping the Lights On

The first time Ivey comes out to the workshop while Cal is welding, he scolds her.

"Hey, you want to go blind! Wear these if you're gonna watch." He tosses her a pair of black welding glasses. She puts them on and sits on the floor, back against the wall, watching.

He likes it when Ivey watches him. She doesn't talk; she just sits there and watches in a way that shows him she's interested. Not in him, in what he's doing—man and his fire, making it, using it, bending it to his will. He remembers watching his dad out here and filters her watching through his. He's not self-conscious. He knows what he's doing, and what he's doing absorbs all his interest. After a while, he forgets she's there. When he looks up, she's gone.

A couple weeks after Ivey moves in, she hands Cal a large manila envelope she found in the mailbox. Cal gives her a funny look before peaking inside at the photos he knows will be there. These aren't too bad: mountains, sherpas in striped serapes on burros.

"What is it?" Ivey asks.

"Something my mom's been mailing me from wherever the hell she is these days."

"Looks like she's in Peru from the stamps," she tells him, looking at the row of papayas and other tropical fruit spread across the top of the envelope.

He hands her the photos. "These are beautiful," she says.

He nods. "Yeah, but you should see the crazy stuff she used to send me." He takes her into his mom's office where those first photos are still tacked onto the wall.

Ivey takes her time studying each photo like she's a visitor in an art gallery. Cal leans against the doorframe, watching her.

"Wow. These are amazing," she says, looking at him. "She's really good, Cal."

He comes up and stands beside her. "You think so? But what do they mean? I used to sit here all night sometimes, staring at these things, trying to figure out what she's trying to tell me. But they make no sense."

"Why would she be trying to tell you anything? Maybe she's trying to show you something."

"Like what?"

"Something about the rooster or the snake, there in that moment. Something that speaks to her. That she thinks might speak to you."

"But why send them to me, not Dad or Kay?"

"Maybe because you're an artist, like her, and she wants to inspire you. Look at your welding: the roosters and snakes and lizards. She's done it already."

He shakes his head. "But I wasn't creating anything when she left. She wouldn't know that."

"Maybe she *did* know. Maybe she saw it in you." Ivey turns to the photos, looking closely at them. Then she looks at Cal, and again at the photos, and laughs. "I know what she saw here. You!"

She looks intently at the rooster. "I know these eyes. These fierce, defiant eyes, and that head, the way it's cocked like that." She moves to look at the photo of the coiled snake, its raised head staring solemnly into the camera. "So lofty and lethal. And this one—see how the paper bag is caught in a gust of wind? How sudden and unexpectedly beautiful, just blown away like that, without meaning to be at all."

She looks at him. "It's you, Cal. These pictures are you."

His head shoots back, his eyes going hard, mean.

Ivey laughs. "Yes, just like that!"

"You think that's funny? My mother seeing me as some . . . some . . . low-life animal? A piece of trash floating around, and you think that's funny?"

"No, Cal, no," she says softly, touching his arm, which he shakes away. "That's not what I see when I look at these. It's not what your mother saw when she took these photos. What I see is, what they say to me, is something so . . . human, you know? They're about what it means to be human. Something beautiful and terrifying at the same time. Proud and unflinching. Fragile and fleeting. They show something in us that wants saving. That's worth capturing on film and savoring."

He looks at Ivey and then at his mom's photos and doesn't know what to think. But something about these images does speak to him, some wildness there, something defiant and undefeatable. Some craziness he identifies with, and feeds on, and for all its potency, longs to let go.

That night Cal lies in bed thinking about his mother—that loving, hovering presence who comforted and cajoled, threatened and rewarded, encouraged and shamed, who looked into his eyes like she was looking into his soul and loved what she saw, who cherished and championed him when no one else would. He's trying to reconcile all that with what she's become now—this mute, mysterious absence, this woman who sends him these strange photos as if trying to tell him something important.

Is she, like Ivey thinks, showing him pieces of himself, what she sees in him—something wordless but emphatic? Maybe she's sending photos instead of calling like she does Kay because, when it comes to him, she's all talked out.

*****

Eventually Cal and Ivey settle into a comfortable routine. Sometimes on the weekends, he goes with her and Buddha to the beach, where she sits on the sand laughing as he and Buddha crash through the waves together and wrestle over the Frisbee she throws.

Lately she's been driving Cal to thrift stores and garage sales, looking for underpriced merchandise to resell at a higher price at his garage sales. Like him, she has a keen eye for a good deal.

Along with stuff to resell, he's always hunting for anything made of metal that he can incorporate into his art, like old spoons and forks, cuff links, boxes of bolts, or coils of wire. Ivey's good at spotting things he misses.

"You know, you could probably get a lot more for your art if you took it to a swap meet or flea market," Ivey tells him. "I could help you with that. You'd need to stock up first, though, so you have a nice selection of wares."

"You think so? What will sell best?"

"Small stuff mostly, the scorpions, geckos, roosters. A few potholders and coat hooks. Maybe one or two larger pieces for the collectors—you know, to show off what you can do."

He feels like he's stepped up to a whole new level of enterprise, selling his artwork from a stall surrounded by other merchants. People eyeball him with a new respect, like he's somebody doing something productive. But in his heart, he feels like a fake. Because the artwork, the creation of it, surrounded by fire and spinning out his dreams, that's all for him, his own sweet satisfaction, nobody else. It's like when he was doing drugs, going for the high and trying to stay there, in it, as long as possible. Only this is cleaner, simpler, and more satisfying, even when the high fades.

Selling the stuff is the same as selling pot—supply and demand. Only now, he doesn't worry about the cops coming after him. Selling stuff is what keeps the lights on in his home. But creating stuff is what keeps the light on in him. And what keeps him hungering for more.

32

CAL
Lost & Found

Life is good, Cal thinks, watching Ivey vacuum around his recliner one wet Sunday morning in March. The sliding glass door is streaked in rainy rivulets as NASCAR engines rev up and roar around the track on TV. He lifts his feet on demand as she plows under.

She's around five-one, five-two, no more than a hundred pounds, he guesses. Skinny legs and arms, barely any tits. Yet for all that, she's finely sculpted. The bones and muscles in her bare arms and legs, her thin shoulders and slim hips, are lean and tightly crafted, as if an artist's eye drew them with loving precision.

He likes having her here in his home, the way they've created a shared life together, helping each other yet staying out of the other's way. He likes the cleanness of it—no strings attached, no messy emotional connection to muck things up. All business, pure and simple.

But sometimes it bugs him too, how she shows no interest in him as a man, only as a landlord, roommate, or business partner. He's not used to women ignoring the man in him that way. He's used to having his good looks and boyish wiles wear away at a woman, even the most resistant, until she finally softens and opens. *Like petals in the sun*, he likes to flatter himself. But his warm rays seem lost on Ivey. He assumes it has something to do with her tattoos, with the hard life she's led. It's like the strength she's acquired in overcoming her addiction makes her immune to his charms, to people like him who have used drugs for so long it's become part of their personality, part of the way they look at themselves and relate to others.

It's not like he's attracted to her either, he reminds himself. She isn't his type at all. Ivey is nearly all bone. But bones so slight they are likely to break easy, he worries. Although on second thought, nothing seems easy or easily broken about Ivey, hard as she is, all meat and muscle.

Still, he must admit, there's something vulnerable about her too, something that, when caught in the right light, in the right mood, makes him ache for her. Makes him feel no one can ever break her, for she's already broken up inside. And that broken-up-ness makes her seem defenseless and invincible at the same time. This is what fascinates him about her, the something more he cannot name.

Hell, maybe I am attracted to her, he thinks now, watching her move across the room unselfconsciously, her body slack, soft. The terrycloth shorts are riding up her butt, a pale moon of cheek peeking out. The strap of her crop top slips oh-so seductively down her arm. When she leans past him to reach for something, her hair falls across her face like a veil, and the smell of her breath is musty and sweet. But the tattoos are off-putting. Too hard, too trailer park trashy. He likes his women clean, unstained.

He squints at the tattoos now, trying to decipher the colorful, intricate designs. But he can't. The lines and shapes fade together, or else his eyes, overwhelmed by the complexity, refuse to focus, and the images stream together. Still, there's plenty of clean, white space between all the commotion, and he lets his eyes rest there: On her bare midriff and creamy thighs. On the small of her back that dips and rises, spreading across the creamy lobes of her hips. On the faintly fluttering pulse in the hollow beneath her throat. There—between the tattoo boots that rise over her calves and the cloak that spreads across her shoulders and back—she seems naked. Shockingly, tantalizingly, exposed. There, her skin is startlingly white. Not even white, he decides, but bright—creamy and luminous like vanilla ice cream.

Some shadowy thing that was clouding his vision, darkening his perception, melts away. Ivey doesn't look dried up and lost anymore the way she had before. Ivey looks found, like something brand new in this world, something bright and hard and fine and so far out of his reach it's like she's living on the moon rather than right here in front of him. He doesn't know how to touch her, how to move across the space that divides them and holds her there and him here and keeps them separate and apart. He feels that if he ever attempted to cross that divide, the space beneath his feet would open like an abyss, and he'd never stop falling.

He sits there staring at her with his freshly peeled eyes as this realization takes shape. But the more he watches her vacuum, the more appalling he finds her placid disregard of him. It's like he's not here, or he's a piece of furniture—not a man with lusty eyes and sweating palms. *How does she do that?*

What makes him crazy though, what drives him absolutely wild, is how when she leans over, her little butt cheeks show beneath her shorts like two halves of a ripe peach, looking so soft and succulent that he wants to reach over and grab it between his teeth.

"Goddam it, girl, can't you see I'm trying to watch the races!"

"So, watch them," she says, rising and glancing nonchalantly over her shoulder at him. "I'm not stopping you." Then she bends over again, exposing the globe of her cheeks, fresh and raw, beckoning, begging—begging to be bitten.

He groans loudly, pushing himself from his chair and strides into the kitchen. He holds the refrigerator door open as he reaches for a beer, lingering there in the coolness, letting the frigid air finger his face.

But then, one night, it happens. They are watching another rerun of *Cheers*, sitting next to each other on the couch, sharing a bowl of popcorn she holds in her lap. They're both laughing at something ridiculous happening between Sam and Diane, laughing hard, their sides shaking, their mouths cracking wide open, their eyes streaming tears. They eye each other while laughing, enjoying the companionship, the common bond, the comfort of being in each other's company. It feels good, laughing like that, clean and sweet.

When the laughter is spent, they sit there still looking at each other but in a strange way, like they discovered something new. Like the one has just unpeeled the other, and each sits there naked and open.

Then he reaches for her, across the divide that has separated them forever, across the abyss that opens beneath his feet, so he feels like he's falling, and she leans toward him, catching him as he tumbles into her arms. They're all over each other now, sudden and fierce, going crazy, tearing at each other's clothes. But the couch is too small, and they're falling off. Her knee knocks the coffee table and makes such a god-awful cracking sound that they spill out laughing again.

But this time he picks her up, surprised at how light she is, how easy to hold, how right in his arms, and takes her to his bed, which is still unmade, unwashed, still smelling of his night sweats, but not caring, not caring at all. For all he wants now is to drink her up. Just open his mouth and drink her up. And he does. He does. He opens his mouth and she falls in.

*****

Afterward, they fall asleep in each other's arms. He wakes up and goes to the bathroom, almost tripping over Buddha, who is sprawled across the bedroom doorway. When he returns, Ivey is awake.

"Hi," she says softly, shyly. "I thought you left me."

"I did," he says, "but I'm back now." He turns on the lamp beside the bed before climbing in beside her.

"Why are you doing that?"

"I want to see you. I want to see everything about you." He pulls back the covers, turning her this way and that, to see all she is. His fingertips trace the colorful scrolls that roll and collide and converge on her skin.

Up close the tattoos are a kaleidoscope of changing colors, lines, and forms. If he could unreel it and lay it flat against a wall, it would lose its charm—the rhythm of its contours, the way it embodies her, or she embodies it, the way they flow together. It's the essence of living art, an art that changes as she moves her body and he moves around her. Impermanent, partial, potent.

But when he leans back to look, what he sees is like a page from a book of fairy tales, a living tapestry. He sees now how the tattoos he once viewed as harsh, as evidence of a hard life, aren't harsh at all but beautiful and haunting and strangely familiar. They portray images from a forgotten past, from fairy tales he heard long ago. There are dragons and mermaids, wolves and unicorns, Red Riding Hood with her basket tucked under her arm as she wanders through the wild woods, Rapunzel leaning out the window with her long hair streaming down the tower wall, Rumpelstiltskin dancing before a fire, Beauty wrapped in the Beast's arms. He turns her this way and that as he reads the stories of his youth painted on her arms and legs, scrawled across her back.

"Why fairy tales?" he asks.

"I dream in fairy tales," she tells him. "They're never about real life, you know, but filled with these strange creatures from another place and time. Always tales of danger and dragons, elves and fairies. Funny, huh?"

"My dreams are like that, too. But darker, more sinister."

"Tell me."

He lies back on the bed, one arm tucked around her, the other behind his head.

"Devils and demons. Goblins and ghouls. Bats fluttering around outside my windows, over my head. Sometimes I see myself as this Cyclopes, you know? One huge eye staring out from the middle of its face, hulking around in its cave, lonely like, pathetic, stumbling in the dark."

She presses her naked body tightly against him, throws a protective leg over his.

"Weird, huh?" he says. "We're two fucked-up people, aren't we?"

He hears her swallow, feels her heartbeat quicken. "I wouldn't say that," she tells him, her voice husky with feeling. "Maybe we're just lost. Like in the forest, you know? It's not so uncommon. Not such a bad thing, really. All the heroes, the heroines, they all go through that. You have to be lost before you can be found, right?"

He thinks about this, staring up at the dark ceiling half hidden in shadows.

"Maybe so," he says, looking down at her lying in his arms, his eyes bright, hopeful. "We found each other."

"Yeah," she whispers, her fingers lightly tracing his face. "We did."

PART III

The Gathering

March 1999–March 2000

I will gather them from the ends of the earth, the lame and the blind, the mother with child: . . . And their soul shall be as a watered garden.

—Jeremiah 31:8, 12

33

WALTER
The Deer

It's the easiest thing Walter's ever done, falling in with Dawn this way. Is it love? He doesn't want to name it, what they have together. It just feels right, like it was meant to be.

If it's love, it isn't what he had with Franny, a love that felt more like trepidation. From the start, he never believed he deserved her, like she'd taken up with him by mistake and might not stick around if he didn't play his cards right. But he never knew which cards to play, and the fact she stuck around anyway seemed more like good luck on his part or plain laziness on hers. He knew she could do better, and why she didn't was a mystery.

He can't quite believe it, the fact he's falling for someone else, someone who isn't Franny, who isn't anything like her.

Franny always said they fit together perfectly in each other's arms. And they did. That was the beauty of it—on one level, everything fit. But on another, it didn't. Something didn't quite click. He was a serious, practical-minded man, as hard on himself as he was on others, like his son or those who worked under him—people he was responsible for who weren't living up to what was needed. But Franny, she wasn't practical-minded at all. And she was too easy on people: on him, on the kids, especially on herself. She was damn smart, though. If she applied herself, who knew what she could accomplish, what she could become?

But with Dawn—deserving, not deserving—that never comes into play. When he's with her, he feels at home, like he's where he belongs.

*****

Randy leaves for Anchorage late in February, driving Dawn's old four-door sedan, the one she lets him use so often he's begun to think of it as his own. The snow is deep, but a patch of clear weather is forecast for the next ten days or so. Anchorage is only 150 miles away, a three-hour drive that winds through deep forested canyons before hitting a four-lane highway.

Dawn's become reconciled to the fact that Randy has to do this on his own. He's excited about the trip and calls her as soon as he gets there and then every few days after to share some enthusiastic tidbit. Sometimes Walter listens in and can't help thinking what a boy he still is, despite his twenty-two years. Some people never grow up, never grow old in their thinking, never lose their enthusiasm for life. Randy will be one of those. Walter wishes he'd been more like that back in the day when his kids were growing up, sharing more of the small pleasures of life.

Dawn hangs up the phone and returns to the kitchen table where she and Walter have been playing another game of cribbage. Chili is simmering in a big black pot on the stove, and a pan of cornbread is in the oven. Sweet-spicy aromas fill the room.

"Randy," she tells him. "He'll be home tomorrow."

"I figured. No one else can bend your ear that long."

"He's so full of himself. Had a grand time apparently. I guess you were right. He needed this."

Walter nods, not willing to give the appearance of saying "I told you so."

She takes a deep breath and lets it out slowly, as if letting go of something heavy she's been carrying around since Randy took off. "It's like he's coming home after being away at camp. Or college. Is this what it feels like, having an empty nest?" She looks up at Walter as she deals out another hand of cards.

"I guess so. We never had an empty home for long. Kay was always coming home for breaks and summer, even after she went off to college. The same is true with Cal, showing up with his backpack or big black plastic bags full of whatever he managed to hold onto when he got kicked out of some halfway house. They were both coming and going so often, it felt like they never left sometimes."

"It's been so quiet around here with him gone. You can hear yourself think."

"Are you saying I'm not much company?" he asks, pretending offense.

She grins. "No more than me, I guess. I like that."

He nods. "I miss him though. You never know what will come out of his mouth."

She laughs. "Remember how he was telling you all about me that first time you came to dinner, like I wasn't even here."

"He never learned how to whisper, did he?" He cocks his head. "You were sweet on me back then, too, weren't you?"

She frowns as she slaps down another card. "Who says I'm sweet on you now? If I don't win this hand, you'll see how sweet I am!"

He laughs and then gets serious, looking her straight in the eye. "Feels like we've been doing this forever."

"What?"

"Just this. Us." He looks at her, full in the face, and catches the answering spark in her eye.

*****

The call comes well after midnight like they always do. Dawn is wrapped in his arms, her long nighty twisted around his legs, her head damp and heavy in the crook of his elbow, cinnamon hair moving with his breath. She's a heavy sleeper. He reaches past her to pick up the phone, to spare her waking. "Who's this?" he asks.

"Dawn?"

"No, Walter. Who's this?"

"Deputy McCallum. I'm sorry to have to tell you this. We received a call from a state trooper about an accident forty miles east of here in Copper Canyon. Dark blue Impala sedan went off the road. Hit a deer it appears. Has Dawn's license plates but I know Randy always drives it. One male occupant. No survivors. Clay was listed as his next of kin, but since he's not here, and it's Dawn's car, we thought she should know. He was like a son to her too."

"Jesus," he says. "Jesus."

Dawn is stirring beside him now.

"Who's that?" she asks, still half asleep.

He looks down at her but can't speak. She has to pry the phone from his fist.

*****

By the time they reach the scene, the sun is throwing a few red gleams through the fir trees, casting long shadows across the snow. State troopers and an ambulance are already there, red flares set along the road to close off one lane. They pull off onto the side of the road next to a patrol car. A trooper comes over to greet them. Dawn talks to him in the hushed, somber tones that accompany death. A deer is lying on the side of the road, a doe.

Her large dark eyes are glazed over, fur stiff with frost. A bloody trail is frozen into the snow.

The car fell into a ravine about thirty feet below the road. They watch while Randy's body is hauled up the bank on a stretcher. His clothes and skin are crusted with ice. His dark hair and eyebrows and that stubble on his chin gleam where the sun hits. His long eyelashes are dusted with snow, and the blue below looks like tiny frozen lakes.

Dawn puts her fist in her mouth and crumbles. Walter grabs her, holds her up, while the boy he's come to love is zipped into a body bag and lifted into the back of the ambulance.

*****

"You were right. I should have gone with him," Walter says on the ride home, his hands gripping the steering wheel.

Dawn gives him a sharp look. "Why? So, there'd be two of you brought up in body bags?" She looks small and fierce sitting there, pushed against the passenger door as far from him as she can get.

"It might not have happened if I'd been there. If I'd been driving."

She grimaces and looks straight ahead. "That deer. You would have swerved too."

"But we may have missed it." He glances at her. Her dark face is silhouetted by the sun, an orange glow striking the window beside her.

"Don't you do that," she says, still facing straight ahead.

"Do what?"

She looks at him now. "Make me choose. Absolve you or hold you responsible." She looks away. "He belonged to all of us. We bear that weight together."

And so, they do. The whole town turns out for his memorial service, Clay and Hilda too, having flown in the day before. They crowd into a small church with Randy there in the casket, all slicked up, looking like he's ready for another night on the town.

The ground is covered in four feet of snow, frozen down to the permafrost as early March storms, one after the other, assail the town. They must wait until the ground thaws to bury him. It's during that long, dreary wait while the world is still frozen solid that Walter realizes Franny's gone missing again, too. She hasn't charged her credit card since December, three months ago. And he hasn't even noticed till now. The last charge was for a motel room at the foot of Machu Picchu in Peru.

*****

He calls Kay a week after Randy's memorial service. Usually, she's the one who calls him, so she sounds surprised to hear his voice. He sits on the edge of the bed, next to the phone on the nightstand.

"You still with that fellow you moved in with?" He wonders if he should tell her about Dawn, moving in and all, but decides not to.

"Yes, Dad, still."

"He treats you right?"

"He treats me fine."

"You getting married?"

She laughs. "Probably. Yes. We've talked about it. What's this all about, Dad? Why are you calling?"

"Can't a dad call his kids?"

"Well, sure, but you rarely do. And Cal says you never call him."

Walter scrubs his hand down his face. "I know, I should, but . . . how's he doing? Is he okay?"

"Yeah, you leave it up to me to keep track of him now, like you always left it up to Mom before."

He has nothing to say to that. She's right. He always left everything to do with Cal up to Franny. And now he's doing it with Kay. He picks up the phone with its long cord and starts pacing.

"Cal's fine, Dad," Kay continues. "Staying clean or so he tells me."

"We've heard that before."

"I know. But he sounds more upbeat than usual on the phone. He's welding too, he tells me. Using your old shop out back. He does metal sculpture."

"Cal's welding?" Walter stops pacing.

"Yeah, says he decorated the house for Christmas with angels, reindeer. Joined the neighborhood Christmas Club."

"McCloskey got to him." He shakes his head.

"Cal says they're buddies now, he and McCloskey."

Walter laughs. "That old busybody. Always nosing around. Well, I guess Cal's keeping the place up then. If he wasn't, McCloskey would let him know."

"Well, I wouldn't count on that if I were you. But he's got a boarder now too, a girl, so he says."

"He always could get the girls. I'm glad he has someone. And you, too."

"But what about you, Dad? How're you doing?"

He can't answer right away. An image of snow on Randy's frozen eyelashes flashes through his mind. He sinks down on the bed again.

"Dad?"

"Yeah, I'm fine." He runs a hand over his face and takes a deep breath. "Lost someone recently, though. A boy who worked for me."

"A boy?"

"Well, not a boy. Young though. Too young." He leans his forearms on his knees, hunched over on the bed.

"He died?"

"Struck a deer. Went off the road. Probably . . . probably froze to death laying there overnight. Too hurt to get out. Get help."

"Gee, Dad, I'm so sorry,"

"Yeah, me too. He reminded me of Cal. You sure he's okay?" He grips the phone tighter, gets up, and starts pacing again.

"Cal's fine, Dad. I promise."

"Okay, then. Okay. You too, right?"

"Me too. We're all fine. Promise."

"But your mother. You heard from her lately?" He stops his pacing, and his throat freezes as he asks the question.

"Well, yes, I think so. It's been a while. But I got a message maybe two weeks ago."

"You sure it wasn't longer? A month or more?"

"I'm sure it hasn't been that long. Why?"

"Did she say where she was? Last time she called?"

"The last time she mentioned anyplace she was in Peru. Why? What's wrong? Have you heard something?" Panic creeps into her voice.

"No, no. I only . . . I wanted to make sure. I worry, you know."

"I know."

"Well, I better go."

"Me too."

He stays on the line waiting for her to hang up, not wanting to be the first to let go. Only when he hears her soft click does he put the phone back on the cradle. He stands there for a long while, feeling as if a shroud has been cast over his head, like he might suffocate. Like if he doesn't do something soon, he might lose everything that ever mattered to him. If it wasn't for Dawn . . . .

She comes up beside him. He wants to reach out and wrap himself around her, make a warm, safe cocoon. But he doesn't. Things never fell back into place between them after losing Randy. She must have seen that look of longing in his eyes, for she reaches for his hand and squeezes.

"You all right?" she asks, looking into his eyes.

He swallows a hard breath. "I've gotta go find Franny," he says, squeezing her hand tighter as she goes rigid beside him.

"I know," she says. "I know you do."

"When the ground thaws. After we lay Randy to rest."

34

KAY

Couches on Curbs

"You're not wearing that, are you?" Kay asks Richard when she sees him dressed in the same black silk shirt and leather jacket he wore when she met him.

They're getting ready to drive up the coast to San Domingo to visit her brother, to check up on the old homestead. To make sure Cal hasn't torn down the walls to sell for scrap lumber or isn't curled up in a ball somewhere, wasting away. Ever since that weird conversation with Dad, Kay's been more worried than usual about him. She feels her own stomach curling up into a ball like it always does when she lets her thoughts linger too long on her brother, despite his cheery phone calls apprising her of the progress he's made. And now there's this new tattooed lady he told her about to check out, too.

On top of all that, she's late! Which almost never happens. She should have started her period two weeks ago, and now it's mid-March. Yet, she's too chicken to test. If she hasn't started in another week, though, she'll have to. She glances now at Richard, guiltily, wondering if he's noticed she's late.

He looks down at his clothes and up at her. "Why? What's wrong with this? I thought you liked this shirt?"

"It's too dressy and expensive. My brother will probably wear sweats. He may not have showered for days."

"So, you want me to wear sweats too? Go without bathing?"

"No, I just want—" She doesn't know what she wants and struggles to answer. "I want him to like you, to feel comfortable around you. He's all I have left in the way of family. Nearby, anyway. Now that Mom . . . and Dad . . .."

But she knows it's not only Cal being comfortable around Richard that has her bothered. It's seeing her childhood home empty of all that made it home. It's Richard seeing where she grew up, comparing it with his own childhood home.

When they finally arrive, Kay's dismayed by how tawdry the town looks, how rundown and uninspiring. San Domingo could be a poster child for urban sprawl with its patchwork of big-box stores, four-corner gas stations, strip malls, and drive-through fast-food restaurants. She remembers the drive up to Ricardo's bungalow that first time and how misplaced she felt. Will Richard feel that way? Her stomach is queasy now, the same way it was then. Maybe she should prepare Richard for what to expect.

"Turn here," she says when they reach the corner with Pappy's Oak Furniture store, a few fat recliners and fake-leather couches drug outdoors for a parking lot sale. They move away from the main drag toward a residential area. At least the homes here are a bit bigger and nicer than where they are headed. She wishes she could have him turn into the driveway of that cute home with the red door and green shutters and lush lawn—not a yard full of rocks, for God's sake. As they continue driving, the homes become smaller and less tidy. The cramp in her tummy tightens.

"You know," she tells him testily, as if accusing him of something, "we're very middle class. We live in a forty-year-old tract house. Most people don't take care of their yards, and they keep their Christmas lights up all year long. They wash their cars on their lawn and drag their old couches out to the curb to give away. And people take them! It may not even be middle class at all. It's probably lower than middle—"

"You're poor? You live in a ghetto?" Richard asks.

"No! Not a ghetto—just nothing like you're used to."

"Why are you telling me this? Do you think I'm a snob?"

"No, but—"

"You Americans!" Richard says, waving a hand in the air. "You say you live in a classless society, but you are more class-conscious than most! You realize this, don't you?" He glances sideways at her.

She purses her lips and stares back. "I don't like it when you say, 'you Americans' like that!"

"Like what?"

"Like you're lumping us all together . . . like we're all the same."

"In some ways, you *are* all the same. People from all nationalities are. They share common characteristics, typical way of expressing themselves, and thinking about the world–"

"There!" she says, snapping her fingers at him. "Bingo! Typical ways! You're stereotyping us!"

"I'm saying you're more class-conscious than you admit. Who was it just now worrying about how low her class is?"

"Richard, I know how you grew up, jetting back and forth from Buenos Aires to Portugal to New York. I've seen photos of your home. You had servants, for God's sake! I want you to know what to expect."

"You already told me how your brother sold all the furniture and sleeps on an air mattress. Now you're telling me you live in a slum?"

"Not a slum!"

"A tenement then? A trailer park?"

"No!" she says. "A lower-middle class housing tract."

"Cars on lawns. Christmas lights up all year. You think this will shock me? You think I'm too delicate, too superior, for middle-class white trash like you?"

"Richard?" She is glaring at him now, her voice low and dark.
"Yes?"
"Shut up!"
He grins at her. "Yes, that's more like it."

*****

As they drive through the neighborhood where she grew up,
Kay sees the smallness and the shabbiness through Richard's eyes.
Or maybe it's through her own eyes from her new perspective
living in a bungalow on the top of a mountain. Maybe she's the
snob. She's become too delicate for the tawdriness she sees
around her. Her heart contracts as they pull up in front of her
childhood home, the front yard full of rocks.

She's ashamed of being ashamed. She's ashamed for never
having realized until now that there was anything to be ashamed
of in her old neighborhood. That lower middle-class housing tract
was the world to her when she was a child, America at its finest.
And now it looks tired and sad.

"Kay?" Ricardo says as he opens her door. "Are you
coming?"

Once inside the house, she's relieved to find it's much
improved from the last time she visited. There's furniture now at
least—nothing good but, still, furniture. The trash piled in the
corners has been hauled away. The blinds are open, sunlight
flooding the room. Out the patio door, the birch trees are still
bare but beginning to bud. Cal is much improved too. He's
smooth-shaven and dressed in clean clothes, a faded denim shirt
and dark jeans. He shakes Richard's hand enthusiastically and
introduces Ivey, like he's showing her off.

"Baby Kay," Ivey says as she steps forward to give Kay a
quick hug. "I've heard all about you."

Obviously, Cal's relationship with his "boarder" has evolved into something more intimate since Kay last talked to him. She looks for the infamous tattoos, but they are hidden beneath Ivey's jeans and blousy, peasant-style tunic. They look good together, Cal and Ivey, she must admit, comfortable with each other and with them. Ivey offers them something to drink. She brings out beer for the guys and 7-Up for her and Kay.

"Sit, sit," Cal says, inviting them to take the couch.

"I can't yet," Kay says, still too nervous, too pent up from the long drive to sit. She puts her hands on her hips, arching her back. "I need to stretch my legs a bit."

"Then let me show you what I've been up to." Cal leads them out the sliding glass door into the backyard and opens the doors to his shop. The light from the dusty window falls on an assortment of metal sculptures.

Kay recognizes their mother's influence right away when she sees his collection of roosters and lizards. She doesn't know what to make of the troll-like sculptures, the weird monstrosities with gaping eyeballs and twisted mouths, and finds them disturbing. Richard takes particular interest in these as the two men kneel before them and talk. She looks away. Something about being here with her brother in their dad's old shop makes her uncomfortable, as if they're trespassing. Like any moment someone will grab them by their arms and yank them away.

She wishes she could kneel there beside her brother and gush about his artwork like Richard is doing, seeing him as this budding artist. But she can't. She can't trust herself, or him, to see him as anything other than the way he's been these past—what—ten years? That long? She still sees him as this screw-up, this irresponsible boy-man who tortured their mother with his addiction, who drove her away, and who, for as long as she can remember, was always monopolizing her attention. Something ugly lurches inside her. Jealousy? Anger? Shame?

Fear, she thinks. Fear that this good spell he's going through won't last. That she'll get her hopes up again, thinking things are better, that he's hit bottom and is now moving up the scale. But she thought that before, and it didn't last. She looks away toward the door, her eyes stinging, and catches Ivey watching her.

"Let's go back," Ivey says, taking her arm. "I have something simmering on the stove that needs stirring." Gratefully, Kay follows her into the house. But she's no more comfortable inside than out. Apparently, it wasn't Richard's comfort level she should have been worried about or Cal being comfortable with him. It was hers, she realizes. Her being comfortable in her old home with her parents gone and her brother taking over the place. And now, this stranger stands before the stove where her mother once stood, looking so at home.

Ivey strikes Kay as one of those rare women who is totally comfortable in her own skin and without pretension. She can't help feeling impressed—even a little intimidated. Ivey seems to have no airs or qualms, no agenda, nothing to gauge her by. She doesn't seem to care if Kay likes her or not. Yet she appears interested in her, listening to her, quietly, intently, as Kay chatters away about the trip up here and how the town has changed, just to fill the silence, to keep her from thinking about the last time she was in this kitchen putting sticky notes on the fridge when Cal went missing.

Ivey doesn't say much in return, but she reveals herself in other ways, like the way she cuts fresh rosemary from the herb garden on the windowsill, strips the leaves from the stem, dices them, and crushes them in a mortar. Then, she carries a pinch of the fragrant herb on her fingertips for Kay to smell. Kay breathes in the heady aroma while Ivey sprinkles the crushed leaves into the pot.

She watches her stir the sauce.

"I like what you've done to the place," Kay tells her, glancing about the kitchen. She notes the cleanly swept floor, the windows you can actually see through now, and the countertops cleared of clutter. It isn't as spotless as her mother kept it, but it's a vast improvement over Cal's neglect.

"You can't imagine what this place looked like the last time I visited. Or maybe you can? I mean, *I'm* messy! I'm no neat freak, believe me. But this place was filthy!" She stops to let Ivey chime in, but the woman continues stirring with a noncommittal look that is disconcerting.

"I mean, you couldn't even see the floor beneath the trash. The worst part was the smell, the way he kept everything locked up so tight, never opening a window and hardly a blind."

Still no response.

"I don't know how you stood it. To live here, I mean. Before you cleaned it, that is." *Someone stop me*, she thinks as Ivey turns to the sink and runs the hot water until the window steams. The moisture spreads through the room, flushing Kay's cheeks.

"I don't know how you could stand it," she says again when the water stops, "to move in here. With him. My brother."

Ivey turns to her. Kay is breathing hard now, feeling as wild-eyed as her brother sometimes looks. She's not sure why she is pushing this, why she's ruining it between them. Ivey gives her a knowing look and dries her hands slowly on a towel. She faces Kay head-on, and not unkindly.

"Your brother saved my life, Kay."

She hadn't expected this and doesn't know what to say.

"He saved my *life*," Ivey repeats, slowly but firmly, as if to let the words sink in.

Then she touches Kay's shoulder and turns her away from the kitchen. "Come, let's sit while the sauce simmers."

Ivey leads her into the living room. A couch is pushed against the wall, and Dad's old recliner sits perpendicular to it, with Mom's

266

coffee table holding them together. The recliner and the chest are the only furniture she recognizes from when Mom still lived here. Across from them, a small TV—not the one her parents owned—rests on a stand. All of it is terribly shabby and sad looking. Ivey curls up in the recliner, which leaves Kay the couch. She looks at it suspiciously. It seems clean enough, but the arms are worn, and the cushions are soft and sagging. It's so old and beaten down looking, it could be one of those couches left on the curb she told Richard about. Who knows who might have sat here and what they might have been doing on it. She sits at the edge, feeling queasy as she breathes in its musty odor. Then she scoots back awkwardly against the limp cushions, trying to look relaxed. Ivey watches in silence.

"Look, Kay," Ivey says finally, "Your brother's life is nothing new to me. I've been living the same way most of my life. My parents were junkies like he was, like I was by the time I dropped out of high school. It's all I knew.

"I grew up with trash piled in the corners and no place to sit because of the clutter. I understand the paranoia of closed windows and blinds tweaked from peeking to see what's out there. I tried to get away from all that when I grew up. And I did for a while. I got clean, met a good guy, and got married. Even had a kid of my own."

She smiles now, shyly. "A beautiful little boy! I was so happy. We had a nice house. I kept it clean. I cooked. I gardened. But I couldn't—"

Her voice breaks, and her face darkens. She looks down at her lap and then up again. Kay can't help staring at her, like she's watching a runaway train and can't pull her eyes away.

"I couldn't keep it all together," Ivey continues. "I started using again, keeping it secret for as long as I could. But it grew worse and worse. I couldn't hide it anymore, and I couldn't stop. Finally, my husband kicked me out."

She stops again and looks away. Kay sits in silence, stricken by this confession. She doesn't want to be here. But she can't move.

Ivey looks at her now full in the face.

"I lost everything, Kay. Everything. But I didn't care because none of it mattered. Only the drugs. I didn't even try to get a life. I lived in my van. The same one out there in the driveway. I lived there longer than I care to remember, traveling around the country and mooching off people who tried to help me until they figured out they couldn't and let go. But by then I'd found someone new to help. And then . . . one day—" Her voice catches, and she stops to take a deep breath.

Kay watches her, wide-eyed, holding her breath as if to keep from breathing in this woman's pain. *I don't want to hear this*, she thinks. *I don't want to hear this*.

"And then," Ivey continues, "I became obsessed with seeing my son again, being with my baby. So, I went home. And I stole him away. I was so fucked up I didn't know what I was doing. I had him for three days, they told me, three whole days before they found us and took him back. And I don't remember any of it. But he does. I'm sure of it. I'm sure my baby still has nightmares about what I put him through."

Ivey pushes herself up from her seat and goes to the glass door, staring out at the birches whipping in the wind.

Kay isn't sure if Ivey's done or has more to say. She doesn't know how to respond. She's overwhelmed with a sense of horror and pity. It's all there on her face to read, so she leans forward, elbows on knees, hands over face, forming a mask that covers her nose and mouth, trying to hide what she feels or make it disappear.

"I cleaned up after that," Ivey finally continues, calmly now, still staring out the window. "I stopped cold turkey. I wanted to die, and I thought stopping like that would surely do it."

She looks at Kay and then crosses to the couch to sit beside her, one leg tucked under her as she leans closer, earnestly, as if to underscore the importance of what she's saying.

"I swore on the life of my baby that I would never use again. I would never take the thing that made me do to my baby what I did when I stole him away. And I didn't. I never used again. And I never saw my baby again. And probably never will. Because to him," she swallows hard, "I'm just this nightmare, you know?"

Kay is crying now. Silent tears stream down her face. The ball in the pit of her stomach, the one she has worked so hard to keep down below where she can't feel it, is churning, churning. Ivey takes her hands and squeezes.

"Your brother doesn't know any of this. He doesn't need to. Not yet. But I want you to know, Kay, how he saved me. I'd given up on life, on having a real life, in a real home. In loving someone and being loved. I didn't think I'd ever have that, didn't think I deserved it, and it was okay until I moved in here with your brother. And that's when I saw it."

"Saw what?" Kay asks, tears still streaming down her face.

"I saw something of myself in your brother. Something wild and reckless like I used to be and something sweet and kind like I want to be. Something that wants saving. Seeing that, knowing that, is what saved me." A smile of wonder plays over her face. "I didn't think I could ever *love* again. Or be loved. But now I know I *can*. Your brother did that."

Kay squeezes Ivey's hands back, not trusting herself to speak.

"That's what this sad story of mine is all about. Your brother's going to be okay. He is. He really is. You need to believe that."

Kay looks at her, her lips trembling. "My mother used to tell me that. But I never believed her, Ivey. I never *believed* her."

Then, the fear and despair she kept balled up in the pit of her stomach breaks loose in broken sobs.

269

"But you believe me now, don't you?" Ivey asks.

"I do, I do!" she says as the two women hold each other.

35

KAY
Door Number Three

When it's time to go home, Kay gives Ivey a big, long hug. She almost doesn't want to let go; it feels so good. When she pulls away, her hands slide down Ivey's arms and grasp her hands, giving them a final squeeze before letting go.

As much as Kay loves Bethany, her best and oldest friend, she's never been able to talk to her about her brother or confess all she feels. Beth always regarded Cal with a touch of scorn and skepticism, brushing away any hopes or fears Kay had about him. Which was the same way Kay always responded to her mother, she realizes now. She didn't want to hear about him, didn't want to get sucked into that drama. But now, Kay has Ivey to talk to, someone who loves Cal and believes in him the way Mom did. And the relief is palpable.

"Thank you," she whispers into Ivey's ear. "Thank you!"

As she and Richard are driving home and the sky is fading along the horizon from bright champagne to pale salmon, Kay begins to question herself. Is she doing to Ivey what she did to her mother? Is she just relieved she has someone else to worry about her brother and take care of him now, so she doesn't have to?

The truth is, even with Ivey there, Kay doubts she will ever be able to let go of the uncertainty that lies like a damp, dull blanket over every thought of her brother. She's done the research. The recovery statistics for heroin addicts are extremely low. Even after years of sobriety, addicts can relapse suddenly without warning. "Recovery" is like a Shangri-La fantasy—a misty, romantic vision of some hoped-for utopia for those who love addicts. A wistful yearning. A dream to stave off the horror of what our loved ones have become and what lies in their future.

In truth, there's nothing hopeful about heroin addiction. The hope her mother insisted upon that Ivey is offering now, always comes with an asterisk: a maybe, a probably not, a don't go there, don't look at that. A kind of dread.

Cal has lived behind Door Number Three in Kay's mind for nearly her whole adult life. Neatly walled off, boxed in. She allowed herself only quick, furtive peeks inside. What she saw there was Cal in jail, Cal on the streets, Cal in rehab, Cal starting a new job, and now, with a new girlfriend—waymarks along a road full of hope that he would survive his addiction and dread that he wouldn't, that he'd never have the bright future they always envisioned for him. Statistically, a heroin addict is more likely to die of an overdose before he turns forty than to live long enough to collect Social Security. It was unbearable to contemplate.

So, there he went, behind Door Number Three, where she didn't have to look at or think about him for too long. But she couldn't do that anymore. She would not do that to him or Ivey.

What is needed, she feels strongly now, isn't hope or worry, but trust. Trust that Cal has what's needed to pull himself through this. Trust in his strength, his courage, his love, his passion. She doesn't want to see him as hopeless or helpless anymore, as needing to be propped up, as Dad always accused Mom of doing. She doesn't want to lock him behind a wall of worry. Instead, she will be there for him as much as she can. She won't hope for the best but trust in him. And maybe that's what her mother is doing now, why she left. Not to escape him. But to allow him, trust him, to do what's needed to survive.

Can Kay trust like that? She isn't sure. But she won't shut him away because he's too painful to look at or abandon him to someone else's love and care. She will keep the door of her heart open. Mom couldn't save him; she could only love him. It's the same with Ivey, with Kay. *Keep the door open, open, open*, she tells herself as she peers out the car window and watches a dark indigo curtain fall across the pale sky.

*****

In the days after they reach home, Kay has a new Door Number Three dilemma to contend with. Is she pregnant or not? She's afraid to find out. But all her fervent hoping that she isn't pregnant does no good.

Kay sits on the toilet with her jeans heaped around her ankles and stares at the pink plastic tube in her hand. It's the third one she's peed on in the last three days. How can this be? She's on the pill, for God's sake! She's not ready for this. They talked about having kids someday. In the distant future—not now!

She groans in frustration as tears well to the surface. She can't help thinking about Ivey's long, sad story about her lost son or the fact that her own mother took off the way she did. Being a mother, having that responsibility, that heartache, she's not ready for that. Everything has been going along so beautifully between her and Richard, as well as her career. She loves her job! How will a child affect that? What about their plans to go to Baja this winter to join Donner at the dig? She was so looking forward to showing Richard around, taking him up to that secret cave in the hills with the mother-child handprints. Will they be able to do that? She counts forward on her fingers from when her last period was. My God! That's when the baby will be born, around December, right before winter break. Scratch off that trip. She groans again. Her chest heaves, and her breath catches. Soon she is choking back sobs.

"Kay! Are you all right?" Richard knocks at the bathroom door.

"Go away," she says. This isn't the way she wants to tell him.

He pushes the door open anyway and, seeing her collapsed on the toilet, rushes to her. He kneels at her feet and feels her all over. "What's wrong? Are you sick? Tell me."

He finds the plastic tube in her hand. "What does it mean?"

"It means I'm pregnant!"

He reels back. "Pregnant! Are you sure?"

"Of course, I'm sure! Would I be crying if I wasn't?" She pushes him away and pulls up her jeans.

Richard rises with her, looking confused. "But this is good, no?"

"No! This is not good."

"I don't understand. Why wouldn't this be good?" He takes her by the shoulders. She leans against him.

"I can't do this. Not now. We're not ready," she says, her voice muffled against his chest.

He pushes her back so he can see her face and shakes his head in wonderment. "But why?"

She can't answer. He wouldn't understand. She barely understands herself. Besides, what would be the point? It's not like they have a choice anymore. It's done.

He brings her close again, rubbing her back, his wide, firm thumbs running along the length of her spine the way she likes. She waits for them to begin circling each disc and they do.

"You're not alone, you know," he whispers, his chin resting on her head, his breath stirring her hair. "I'm here too. We can do this."

She hugs him harder. He feels so solid and reassuring in her arms, the hugeness of him bending around her, his wide back and strong arms wrapped tight. His warm breath wafts her cheek as he leans down to rub his face against hers, his tender hands kneading her back in all the right places. She presses her pelvis hard against him, wanting to feel more. He grinds back in response, already growing hard. He's so easy! She laughs through her tears.

Mine, all mine, she thinks rapturously, hugging him tighter. *And this, whatever is growing inside me, cradled between us, is ours. His and mine. Together. We can do this.*

36

WALTER
Something Unseemly

It's the longest winter Walter's ever endured and the coldest. Winter that swallows March, storms into April, and marches toward May. Waiting for the ground to soften enough for Randy's burial. Waiting for the ice to melt between him and Dawn.

They still sleep in the same bed but back-to-back now. She says she doesn't blame him for Randy's death. But saying and believing are two different things. Her head tells her so, but her heart doesn't believe it.

He doesn't believe it either. He lies there beside her and cannot sleep.

Franny always blamed him, too, for Cal's addiction. She never said so, in so many words, but he saw it in her looks, heard it in her accusations—how he was too rough on him, too critical, too distant. She may have been right. Now he figures the best thing he ever did for Cal was to back away, leave him in Franny's hands. If he hadn't—if he refused to let him stay at the house, if he held her back from helping him—would his son be in the morgue now, too?

He kicks off the covers and sits hunched at the side of the bed, his head hanging. Dawn stirs beside him. He knows she's awake. Can't sleep. Like him.

"I can't stay here," he tells her. "I'm no good to anyone. I should never have come."

She says nothing, so he gets up.

The living room is dark and cold, but moonlight falls on the floor from the window, a square of light like polished stone or a sheet of ice. He sees the doe's eyes again. Randy's frosted eyelashes. Boy and doe.

He lets his body slump on the couch. There's no place to go. He has no home. The place he made here is gone, the one with Franny gone. The wood he stacked in the fireplace before going to bed is ready to light. But he can't move, can't make the effort.

Dawn appears by the hall doorway, the moonlight dusting her nighty. She's wearing the same one, the same red socks, she wore that night when she fell into his arms. *Lit at both ends by fire*, he thinks—red hair, red feet.

She kneels by the hearth and lays a long match to the kindling. They watch it catch together, the wads of paper, small twigs, flaring up, flickering, spreading, then poof! A flame rises, strong and steady at the center.

She sits on the couch beside him—not close, a full foot away, and that, more than anything, breaks his heart. The distance between them.

"It's not your fault," she tells him.

"You don't believe that."

"I blame me, not you."

"For listening to me, for letting him go alone."

"For not loving him more while I had him. For not insisting I go too. For wanting to stay here with you more than go babysit him. I was so tired of babysitting. *I wanted to let go. I* did. Me." Her voice breaks. A strangled cry, like a dying deer, comes from deep inside her.

It scares the hell out of him. He wants to hold her. He doesn't know how. The strangled cry is crushing him. He cannot breathe. And then it ends. As suddenly as it came, it ends.

All is still. Even the fire, without stirring, has nearly gone out. He rises automatically, without thinking, and pokes it until it flames again.

When he turns around, she's gone. His heart stops.

This is the end. This is how it ends.

An icy draft crosses the floor. He watches a flurry of snow melting in the moonlight on that polished square of stone.

The front door is open. She is standing on the porch in her nighty and red socks, her red hair frosted in moonlight. He comes up behind her and wraps his arms around her, forcing her back against his chest. She stiffens and then lets her body go soft.

"I can't lose you," she says. "I can't lose you too."

"I'm not going anywhere," he answers.

*****

But when May arrives and they bury Randy, Walter knows he must try to find Franny, what's become of her, and the chill between him and Dawn returns.

He finds himself mentally pulling away from her more and more as he prepares for the trip. Now when he looks at Dawn, he's not sure if he's looking at something more from his past than his future, and the uncertainty unsettles him. It's Franny more and more at the forefront of his mind—his guilt at letting her go and this urgent need to find her. The line drawn taut between them as they moved further away from each other has snapped at last, and he's left holding onto something that dangles uselessly in his fingers, unfinished, incomplete.

Losing Randy has made the loss of Franny more real. Maybe she, too, will never return.

"I'll be back," he tells Dawn as she watches him packing his suitcase.

But he doesn't sound convincing even to himself. He's tired, and his head feels muddled by the long winter's dull fatigue, by worry, guilt, and loss. It's not only Franny he's worried about. It's Kay and Cal, too. He can't lose them the way he did Franny. The way he did Randy. He feels the fragile ties that bind them slipping.

Dawn stands in the doorway. "What will you do if you find her?"

He glances over his shoulder at her and then back again, adding a pile of socks. "I don't know. Make sure she's all right."

"That's all?"

He stops packing and looks at her. "I'll be back," he repeats.

He wants to tell her he loves her, to reassure her somehow with words he's never spoken. But how can he? Nothing seems settled, certain, anymore. All the easiness that flowed between them before the accident has pooled up into something else, something slippery and disturbing. They still sleep in the same bed. But something sleeps there between them. Randy's ghost? Franny's? It's something unseemly and uncertain. Something that makes him afraid to hold on too tight.

"Don't make promises you can't keep," Dawn says, lifting her chin, a bitter edge in her voice, her gray eyes sharp as ice.

"I *will*," he tells her, he tells himself, wanting, needing, to believe it.

"We'll see," she says and walks away.

37

CAL
Rocks & Ducks

A warm May breeze ripples through Cal's hair as he stands in his front yard zapping weeds with his trusty can of poison. He can't believe how many of the little suckers are sprouting up all over, their sneaky green heads peeking out of the white rocks. It's like guerrilla warfare, the way they hide out and then spring up when he's not looking. Keeping his rock patch weed free has become a point of manly pride.

But the yard has been looking bare since he took down the Christmas decorations, and he needs something to fill it. The new sculpture he's working on might look good where the angels and carolers once stood. It's his most ambitious sculpture yet, Don Quixote riding his donkey and slashing at windmills. He chuckles every time he sees the old, deluded knight, reminding him of someone he used to know—himself, back in the day, the way he's been most of his life, slashing at windmills, at stuff that should be easy to control and is for most people, but not for him. That is, till now. He seems to have life more or less under control these days, and he likes the way it feels—he and his handy spray can and fountain of fire shaping the world to his own design. And Ivey at his side and in his bed, filling all the cracked places in his soul.

Speak of the devil! Who's charging up the driveway on her white horse to greet him? His own sweet Dulcinea. Only she doesn't look too sweet as she climbs out of the van and stands there, hands on hips, giving him the evil eye. She's been unusually edgy these past couple of weeks, looking around the house and yard with squinty eyes, like there's something that needs doing that's not getting done.

"Say, what's up, girl? Looks like you have trouble on the mind."

"It's those rocks, Cal. They've got to go."

At first, he's confused, thinking she's saying *he's* got to go, or maybe she's got to go. Something she sees she sure as hell doesn't like. His mouth goes dry, and he feels the rocks shifting beneath his feet as if a huge hole is about to open up and swallow him. He steps back sharply onto solid ground.

"What do you mean?" he asks warily.

She opens the back of the van. "Look." Plastic pots of pink rosebushes, trays of trailing ground cover, and big bags of bark are lined up inside. She pulls out a rosebush and sets it on the driveway.

"What are all these for?"

"Landscaping the front yard. The rocks are an eyesore. We need to get rid of them."

He stares hard at her and shakes his head. "No way. The rocks stay. They're mine."

She stares back, frowning.

"You don't know what I had to give up to get them," he tells her, thinking of the claw foot table and cabinet he traded for the backhoe and rocks. The way Kay went psycho about losing them. But it's more than that. He loves these rocks. He did this. He did. "You should have seen what the yard looked like before I put them down."

"They look trashy! They're all stained with that stuff you keep spraying. Don't you want something green and growing out here?"

"You think my rocks look trashy?" He can't believe what he's hearing. His eyes narrow to slats as he crosses his arms. "The rocks stay."

She throws her hands up. "What is it with you and those damn rocks? They look like crap!"

The words hit him like a slap in the face. He steels himself and moves toward her, shoving his face within a foot of hers. "Yeah? Well, it's my crap, Ivey! Mine! I made it."

She does not back away.

"You're not the rocks, Cal," she says firmly. He clenches his fists and looks away.

"Look at me," she says. "Look at me, Cal."

He looks at her. His whole body is trembling, and it takes all his strength not to show it.

Ivey pulls herself up on her tiptoes, stretching all five feet two inches of her frame to bring her face within inches of his. His breathing is hot and heavy.

She repeats it slowly, emphasizing each word. "You're . . . not . . . the . . . rocks."

He stares at her, blinking hard. Then storms off.

He sleeps in his old bed that night, not hers, as they've been doing ever since that first night together in his room. If sleep is what you can call it as he twists and turns. His dreams are edging backward to the good ol' days with Freddy grinning at him from the window.

He keeps hearing Ivey's voice: "What's with you and those damn rocks, damn rocks, damn rocks . . ." like an endless echo.

Who does she think she is? Who does she think he is?

He wakes early the next morning and drifts about the house in the semi-dark. Then he goes out front to suck on a cigarette. He sees the garbage can on the curb where Ivey drug it, waiting to be picked up. Sees something sticking out and goes to investigate.

A rosebush! He opens the lid, and it's all there—the bags of bark half ripped apart, the trays of groundcover upended, the rest of the bushes, still whole but looking sad. He wants to sit down and cry.

If the rocks are him, then these are Ivey, and they don't belong here. He pulls them out and gently pats the small plants back into the trays and pots. Then he gets a steel rake from the garage and begins moving the rocks back away from the center of the yard to create a long oval of bare earth. He lines that with plastic garbage bags he's cut up for a weed barrier. Then he rakes the rocks back over, thicker than before, creating a little island of rocks at the center of the yard. He piles the rest of the rocks into a wheelbarrow and wheels them out back to save for later.

When Ivey comes out, she silently begins helping him spread weed barrier over the now bare earth that surrounds the rock island, pour the bark over that, and plant the rosebushes and ground cover—all to soften the effect of the hard rocks still at its center. They do not speak but work comfortably side by side.

When they are done, he drags out some of his metal sculptures to display on the rock island until he finishes Don Quixote. For now, a four-foot-high rooster with upraised wings and beady eyes and a three-foot-long lizard with a curled tail and flashing tongue will have to do. They stand back on the sidewalk to view what they created together—a compromise.

"See," she says, hooking her arm through his. "It looks nice, doesn't it?"

He looks at the yard and remains silent.

"Well?" she insists, giving him a little hip bump.

He glances down at her with a wicked smirk. "I like the rocks and rooster," he says.

She purses her lips.

"You're not the rocks, Cal," she tells him, playfully now, an insider joke.

"But I'm the rooster, right?" he says in his best little boy voice, full of yearning.

She laughs and shakes her head.

"Yes, Cal," she assures him. "You're definitely the rooster."

*****

A couple of weeks later while he and Ivey are unloading the van after returning from the swap meet where they've been selling his artwork, he notices two bulky lawn bags secured with twist ties half hidden behind the driver's seat.

"What're these?" he asks Ivey.

She peeks inside to see what he means, and her eyes go wide. With an effort she resettles her face into a look of nonchalance.

"Oh, those. They're nothing. Don't worry about them."

"Looks like a shitload of something to me." He nudges one with his boot.

"C'mon now, leave them alone!" She jumps inside the van but not before he's grabbed a bag and squeezed it. A loud quack startles them.

"What the . . .?" He shoots a look at Ivey, whose face turns white. Then he tears open the top of the bag. A rubber duck falls out, followed by a brown and white Teddy and a long-necked spotted giraffe.

"Toys?" He picks up the duck. "You've got bags full of toys? What the hell, Ivey?"

She grabs the duck and stuffs it and the other toys back into the bag.

"They're my kid's," she says, not looking at Cal.

He stumbles backward. "Your kids! You have kids?"

She looks up at him from where she's kneeling, twisting the tie. Her face is contorted like she's trying to keep from crying.

"Kid. One kid. A son."

The revelation hits him like a kick in the gut. "You have a son, and you never told me?"

She stares at him with that half-defiant, half-scared look on her face.

"I can't believe you never told me you have a frigging kid! So where is he? This son of yours?" He looks around the van like he's hiding somewhere.

"With his father."

"And?" he says, eyes bugging out, waiting for more. "Why aren't you with his father? Or with him for that matter?"

"Because I'm not, that's why!" She stands, staring him full in the face and then pushes past him. He grabs her arm.

"No, no, no . . .. You can't drop this on me and not explain."

"I didn't want to tell you like this." She tries to shake her arm loose.

"Well, it's too late for that!" He steers her toward the back of the van and sits her down on the edge next to him.

"Now, tell me," he says.

And she does. She tells him everything she told Kay and more.

"I'll kill him," Cal says when she's done.

"Why?" she asks, surprised.

"He kicked you out!"

"He had to. He tried. He really did. I wouldn't be helped. Not then. And when I took Bailey, he could have pressed charges, but he didn't. It was the DA who charged me with kidnapping and endangering the life of a child. My own child!" She's shaking now and takes a deep breath to steady herself. His arm closes tight around her as he grinds his teeth.

"You went to jail?" he asks, incredulous,

"Prison. Two and a half years."

"Jesus!" To think of her locked up that long with those animals about kills him.

"It's okay," she says, "I needed to be there. When I got out, I knew I was done with all that. Drugs, booze, sex. Everything." She looks at him. He sees she means it. She's okay. She's a survivor. He thinks about what she said and cocks his head.

"Sex, too, huh?" he teases. "I think you might have fudged on the sex part."

"Well, until I met you," she says shyly, pinching his arm. Then she adds, "I have a picture. Wanna see?"

She grabs her canvas bag and pulls out her wallet, showing him a photo of a solemn-faced boy around three years old. He looks a lot like Ivey with wheat-colored hair hanging down to his shoulders.

"Bailey," she tells him, smoothing the photo with her fingers. "He was three then. Now he's eight."

"You haven't seen him in five years?!"

"I mail him presents every birthday."

"That's crazy! You need to see him."

"Don't," she says, putting the photo away. "It's okay. He has a nice family now. He's better off with them."

"Them?"

"His dad and stepmom. Has a little sister too, I heard."

"Yet you carry around all his toys?"

Her shoulders cave. "It's all I've got left of him."

"Bullshit! You have a right to see him!"

She shakes her head. "No, I don't. Not after what I did."

"But you're not like that anymore. He's your son. A son needs his mother."

"I don't want to talk about it." She hops down and heads toward the house.

But he won't let it go. Over the next few days, he keeps badgering her about how it's not right, she's paid her dues, he's her kid, he needs her, and she shouldn't give up on him. Or herself. In time, he wears her down until she agrees to at least call her ex and ask about Bailey.

When she does, she paces in the living room as they talk, staying on the line for a long time. Cal busies himself in the kitchen, wanting to respect her privacy, but glancing out from the doorway every couple of minutes. Her head is down, her hair falling forward so he can't see her face. She talks low and soft, and he only catches a few words here and there. "I don't know about that . . . It's been so long . . . You think so?"

When she puts the phone back, he asks, "What did he say?"

She turns toward him, tears streaming down her cheeks.

"I'll kill him," Cal says, clenching his fists.

She touches his arm and smiles up into his face. "He says the only thing Bailey remembers about the time I took him was when I painted clown faces on us before going to the fair."

Her eyes are bright. "He wants me to come see my boy."

38

CAL
Pearl & Bailey

"There it is," Ivey says, looking up from the map. "Turn right here."

They drive up a dirt lane to a large, newly built house set back on a dusty, un-landscaped lot. Three Harleys are lined up in the side yard, and a shiny jeep with a trailer holding a pair of jet skis is in the driveway. A little blonde girl sits on the front porch. She jumps up and runs yelling into the house as they park in front. A boy on an ATV comes roaring up the driveway, its fat tires skidding in the gravel as he brakes in a flurry of dust. He glances over his shoulder at their van and then dashes into the house, his light brown hair flying out behind him. Cal recognizes the hair. It's darker than in the photo but just as long. He reaches across the car seat, takes Ivey's hand, and squeezes.

"That's my son," she says softly, her voice filled with pride.

He knows she's as nervous about meeting her son again as she is excited, and it breaks his heart. He's nervous too, not about her son but about her ex, the bastard who covered her body with tattoos and abandoned her. No matter what Ivey says, he should have stood by the mother of his son. Just thinking about that makes his gut clench.

As they walk up to the house, hand in hand, a man comes out the front door to greet them—Vince, Ivey's ex. Cal's surprised by how big Vince is, bigger than Cal, who stands just under six feet in his bare feet. He never could quite stretch up that extra notch, although he tells everyone he has, as if reaching six makes you more of a man—more than his dad at least, who's five-eight or nine at best.

But this guy is huge, six-four or five, and built like he used to pump iron, although the flesh covering his arms, and probably his chest too, has gone soft. Still, from what Cal can see, what's beneath his T-shirt looks solid enough.

Vince's head is shaved or bald; Cal can't tell which. Either way, his skull has a mean gleam, and his eyebrows are dark and fierce. But his weak chin, looking like someone forgot to pull his face all the way down, spoils the effect.

Like Ivey, he's covered in tats. Although they looked trashy on her at first, on him they look just plain mean. He has the appearance of a man not to be messed with, and he knows it, judging by the way he stands there looking down at Cal, all solemn faced, as Ivey introduces him.

Cal grins up at him, rolling back on his heels and rubbing his hand slowly over his own finely chiseled jawline while looking the man hard in the eye. They stand there like that, a half-second longer than they need to, eyeballing each other, before Vince offers his hand and Cal accepts it.

"C'mon in," Vince says and leads them inside and down a long hallway to the family room out back.

The house is bigger than Cal's and brand-spanking new. So is the furniture. It all matches like they picked it up off a showroom floor. The hallway is lined with an assortment of photos, most that feature the big guy. Turns out Vince, despite his tats, is a respectable businessman, a regular pillar of the community, it appears, who owns a chain of tattoo parlors and, more recently, a Harley dealership. There are photos of him surrounded by city council types cutting ribbons in front of his new shops, and one with him donating a big check to the local Boys and Girls Club.

Apparently, Vince also is some hot-shot marine from the first Gulf War, Cal discovers, seeing a photo of him with his buddies kneeling in the desert sands, all decked out in fatigues holding machine guns. He learns all this within five minutes of entering the man's home and walking past a history of his respectability lined upon the walls. All of which makes Cal think Vince probably isn't as respectable as he wants people to think, given he has to make a big ass show of it.

The family room is huge. A pitched ceiling lined with heavy wooden beams stretches twenty feet high at the center and a stone fireplace dominates the far wall. Built into the corner stands a large bar with a thatched roof, no less. They hang out inside the entrance of the room, waiting for the kid's return.

"I told Bailey to wash up and put on a clean shirt," Vince tells them. "Kid sure loves his ATV. Got it for his birthday last month."

"I know when his birthday is," Ivey says. "Did he get the book I mailed him?"

"Not sure. You'll have to ask Greta. She takes care of all that."

Cal hangs back, watching Ivey and Vince go at each other in that polite, subdued way exes have when they want to make nice but score points at the same time. Vince towers over Ivey. But she's got that plucky, chin-up way of defending herself, which about breaks his heart watching her. Then there are all those tattoos on both, underscoring their history. Seeing the tats plastered on their bodies brings it all together in Cal's mind. Vince was practicing his trade on her, honing his skill with the needle. All the odd-looking tattoos on Ivey—the ones that don't quite fit in with the fairy tales, the ones that pop up in odd places on her fair skin—were him trying out new designs. And her letting him. Letting him use her like that. The thought of it makes bile rise to his throat and his belly grow hard as a fist.

Vince's wife, Greta, comes up behind him. She's blond like Ivey but a dumpy-looking thing, not the fragile wonder of his Ivey. She's a plumper, washed-out version of Ivy, the way Ivey might look if she let herself go and lost her luster. But Greta is noticeably lacking in tattoos. Vince must have gotten his trade down practicing on Ivey before he met Greta. Cal's face goes hot thinking about it, and his hands begin to itch. He's not sure how long he can contain himself or even if he wants to.

That's when he catches a glimpse of the little girl sitting on the leather couch across from them. She can't be more than three or four, a little blond cutie hugging her knees and grinning hard like she knows a secret she's bursting to tell. He lets out his breath, shakes his hands, and wanders on over toward her. Out of harm's way.

"Hey, Sweetie, mind if I sit here?"

She scooches over.

"My name's Pearl," she tells him. "And that's my brother they're waiting for. He's not a full brother, only half, because we have different mamas. That there is my mama," she points hard at Greta and then points to Ivey, "and the other one is his."

Greta is watching this. "Put your hand down Pearl. It's not polite to point."

Pearl sticks her finger in her mouth and looks up at Cal, grinning sheepishly.

"What a crazy world we live in, huh!" he says to her, and she nods hard in agreement.

Greta sits down in the arm chair across from them, taking her time on the way down, as if the distance between her ass and the seat is mighty steep. A big part of her plumpness, Cal now realizes, is belly.

"How long you got?" he asks.

She looks puzzled at first. "Oh, this?" She rubs her belly. "About three months. A boy," she adds proudly.

"That right? I forgot they could do that. Tell in advance."

"They been doing that a while now," she tells him.

"How 'bout that," he says, not sure where to go from here.

"Must be hard," she says in a low voice, glancing at Ivey on the other side of the room talking with Vince. "Not seeing your son for so long."

He's not sure if he should take offense on Ivey's part, so he doesn't say anything. He nods solemnly as if it's something that needs pondering.

They all look up when the boy reappears, a bit breathless and looking nervous, still tucking a checked shirt into his jeans. Vince puts an arm around his son's shoulder, and the boy looks up at him in the adoring, trusting way that Cal has always envied and yearned for in vain.

The boy is all Ivey. He has the same slight body, pale face and arms, and vulnerable, serious-looking face. His fine loose hair is a couple of shades darker than hers.

"This here's Ivey, your birth mother, Son," Vince tells him.

Cal wants to jump up and ram his fist down Vince's throat for calling her Ivey instead of Mom. For acting as if a birth mother isn't a real mother but a shoddy second best.

"Hi, there," Ivey says softly and holds out her hand. The boy takes it, shyly, and she holds on, cupping his hand between both of hers, holding him there as if she may never let go. He looks up at his dad as if to ask if this is okay, if he can take his hand back from this woman they say is his mother, whom he barely remembers.

Slowly he slips his hand from hers. Ivey takes in a hard ragged breath like she's holding back a sob. Cal half rises from the couch to go to her, but Greta catches his eye. She gives her head a little shake, letting him know she thinks he should stay put. He's not sure what to do, so he sits back down.

Ivey reaches out again and lets her hands wash over her son's head and hair in the tenderest way Cal has ever seen hands move. Even the son must feel the love pouring through, judging from the way he's looking at her now. When her hands come down on his shoulders and gently pulls him toward her, he lets himself be moved. His head falls against her breasts as her arms come round him. Her head bows against his as if in prayer. They stay there like that for what seems like forever, the son leaning soft and slack against his mother, and her hands washing over his hair.

Finally, Ivey and the boy head out down the hall with Vince following. They are off to get something to eat at I-Hop, Vince tells them before leaving—time alone to talk and get reacquainted.

"You hungry?" Greta asks Cal. "I'll make some lunch."

She heads off to the kitchen, and he plays bunnies with Pearl. He pulls finger puppets onto his thumbs and makes them talk to each other and to Pearl. She jumps up, laughing and dancing around the room in her excitement, eating it up. He's always been good with children. They can't get enough of him.

He doesn't know how he does it, how girls as young as this take to him so keenly. Maybe they see something in him that brings out the sweetness in them. Something that gives them license to poke at him, hold up their dolls and demand his total attention. Or cuddle up on the couch with him, as Pearl has done now, sliding a leg over his, leaning close, stroking his chin, while he pokes fun at her and makes her laugh.

"Leave him be, Pearl!" Greta says when she comes back with a plate of tuna sandwiches. But her voice is soft and easy, and both Cal and the girl know she doesn't mean it. She's playing the mama part as she sits there, enjoying the show, watching her daughter charm the socks off this man.

Feeling good, Cal takes a sandwich and looks over at Greta, thinking to charm her too. But there she sits all plump and pale, naked almost, her skin clean of tats, glowing in the sunlight spilling through the windows, all warm and luminous. It makes him want to throttle Vince all over again, as he's imagined himself doing ever since he got here. Make him pay for the way he used Ivey like a wall he could scrawl on and vandalize, like boys out back in the alley with their spray cans, while he keeps Greta here, all clean and untouched.

For a moment he's possessed with the urge to jump up and rake his fingernails across her skin to leave his mark, make her as scarred as her husband made Ivey. But the sudden intensity of that thought somehow alerts the girls. He feels the young one retreating, pulling away, ever so slightly, and the mom leans back now, too, away from him, and crosses her legs. That's all it takes to drain the meanness out of him, seeing those innocents back away like that, feeling that gap open up between them and the shame pouring through.

"I love her, you know. Ivey. She's been hurt bad," he says, staring hard at the mother, by way of explanation, or apology, or maybe in defiance. A test to see what she'll say, if she deserves his shame.

She hurt herself, he almost expects her to say, and if she had, he's not sure what he would have done. But instead, her eyes go soft, and her little girl leans back in.

"He misses her, Bailey. He never says anything, but I know he does. The boy misses his mama," she says.

Cal nods. Something washes across his face and catches in his throat—hot like tears, soft like gratitude. Pearl takes his hand and looks into his eyes, doe-eyed like her mama. He leans down and bops her head lightly with his, making her laugh. He watches her, all that laughter spilling out over them. Then he picks up her hand—tiny, soft and white—and kisses it.

By the time Ivey, Vince, and the boy return, Pearl is sitting in his lap, having just proposed to him and he having happily accepted. She jumps up when she sees her father and runs to him. He pulls her up into his arms.

"I'm going to marry *him* when I grow up," she declares loudly to her dad, pointing hard at Cal.

"You can't do that," Bailey scowls. "He's already married. To her!" He points at Ivey.

Ivey and Cal exchange glances.

"Well, not yet," Cal says, looking at Ivey. But he knows in the way she looks back at him that if it's the last thing he ever does, marry her he will.

"If she won't have me though," he tells Pearl, "I'll marry you for sure!"

"See," the girl says to her brother and sticks out her tongue. "He does too want to marry me! So there!"

The boy shakes his head, disgusted. But when it's time for them to leave, he seems sorry to see them go.

"You'll come back?" he asks Ivey, as he walks her to the van.

"You want me to?" she says, as if for the pleasure of hearing him say it again. "Then I'll be back. Wild horses couldn't stop me."

He grins at that and looks up at his father. "You'll let her, won't you?"

He nods at his son and looks at Ivey. "Yeah, you're welcome back, Ivey. Any time. You too, Ken."

"Cal," he tells him, and they shake hands again.

"Hear you're a welder," Vince says as they shake. "Always looking for good welders in my Harley shop."

"He's not that kind of a welder," Ivy tells him, adding proudly. "He's an artist."

"A weld's a weld," Vince replies.

"Not really," Cal says, "but I appreciate the offer."

He opens the door of the van for Ivey—the first time he's ever done that. He imagines Greta giving Vince a hard time later, wondering why she never gets treated so well.

Ivy smiles her appreciation at him as she ducks inside, and he closes the door behind her. As they drive away, she rolls down the window and leans out, looking back and waving. The boy jumps on the back of his ATV and follows them down the road a ways and then stops, disappearing into a cloud of dust.

"You okay?" Cal asks after a while, reaching out to touch Ivey's cheek with the back of his fingers.

She scoots closer, nestling her face against his shoulder. "I'm more than okay," she says looking up at him. "I'm blessed."

39

CAL
Wings & Claws

After Ivey's reunion with Bailey, Cal spends the rest of the summer locked in his shed, welding. Sometimes he goes with Ivey when she visits her son, twice a month now. But mostly, she goes without him. Ever since she told Vince that Cal was an artist, he's becoming more serious about his work.

Don Quixote was Cal's first large-scale sculpture. He follows that with the Old Man and the Sea's struggle with the giant marlin. Perseus holding the head of the slain Gorgon, Medusa, comes next. All are self-portraits, Cal writ large. In some ways, all his artwork is like that, he realizes. Certainly, the roosters are and the lizards and gargoyles. Even the small stuff—the scorpion hooks and frog plant stands—hold pieces of him. But after the series of big, free-standing sculptures, something shifts in his work.

One day when he's heating a flat, thin square of metal, it begins to melt. The whole surface begins to blur and blister in long, fluid welts. He stops and steps back to examine the damage. It reminds him of a windowpane streaming rain or a steamy mirror that's starting to run. For a second, he glimpses his own face reflected there looking back at him, blurry behind the wet surface—his face running with rain, dripping with steam. Immediately, he works the metal until he sees it, this bewildered face half hidden below the surface, looking out.

After that, he starts a series of self-portraits. Not him writ large in myth or symbol but him writ small, twisted and turned inside-out—the way he saw himself, the way others saw him not so long ago. Him, fucked up and falling apart; him, piecing himself back together again. He uses squares of metal with screws for eyes, fuses for mouths, and knobs for noses. Jagged pieces of metal overlap each other, so you get the full face and its profile at the same time. What he sees is something alien and terrifying or studious and curious, looking back at itself. He does not display or attempt to sell these. He hangs them on the wall of his mother's office next to her photos, which he's matted and framed now.

Later when he's rummaging through a junkyard, he comes across an old porcelain electrode, round and stubborn, like a nose, and Wanda's face flashes before his mind. He gathers more materials—a mess of copper wiring for her hair, a set of screws for her teeth. He welds together her face, this impossibly strong and intimidating face with eyes like a god, like something that sees right through your soul.

Gideon is next with his wandering eye, mottled complexion, and motley beard, a look like he'd sooner eat you than look at you. Then he does Mikey, so thin and comical and goofy, so trusting and gentle that it makes you want to laugh and cry at the same time.

If you look at these faces one way, they're nothing but junk—odd bits of scrap metal, useless garbage, obsolete car parts thrown together. But if you look at them another way, you see the fierceness, the vulnerability, the loneliness. You see something interesting and unique. You see faces torn apart and reassembled, as they must have been, time and time again, every newborn day.

He hangs these, and more like them, on the office wall with his self-portraits. Now when he opens the door, it's like he's looking into a crowd of people staring back at him—strange and wild and broken, but so infused with emotion it's like a wave breaking over you, a wave of faces tumbling over and through you. His heart feels good, standing there, looking at them. Like something true that needed saying got said.

In late August, a buyer comes to his garage sale who looks different from the other weekend shoppers and looky-loos. He isn't from around here, Cal can tell right away. He goes right for the sculpture of Don Quixote, which is now displayed front and center in his yard. Cal's not surprised by this—his big pieces are getting lots of attention. He's sold a few already for a lot more than he ever gets for his yard art. After studying it awhile, the guy comes into the garage where Cal displays most of his metalwork. His eye lingers on a rooster, its strained neck and beady eyes, its wild wings and open beak, like a terrible noise is tearing through its throat. He stops. He kneels. He studies.

"What do you think?" Cal says, coming up beside him.

The man rises and looks at him. "I like it. I heard you had some interesting welds, and they were right. I like Don Quixote out there too. Not quite what I'm after but close. You got anything else?"

"What do you have in mind?"

"I'm looking for dark. Edgy. Off the radar."

Cal looks him over, a guy who knows what he wants. He's a bit on the scrawny side but with big forearms and paint under his nails.

"You a painter?" he asks.

"Murals, mostly"

Cal takes him inside and opens the office door. The guy steps in and stops, staring at that sea of metal faces hanging on the walls.

"Shit!" He glances at Cal. "This is wild."

He spends some time wandering from one metal portrait to the other.

"People you know?" he asks.

"You could say that. Or getting to know. Self-portraits, mostly. The rest, street people. Some I know. Some I wish I never met."

"For sale?"

"Depends. How much?"

The guy looks them over again, then points to three: Wanda, Gideon, and one of Cal. "I'll give you $900, all three."

"Make it twelve and you've got a deal."

He looks again at the work and then nods. "I know a few people who might be interested in more of these. I'll send them your way if you want."

Cal finds three boxes that he flattens out, putting a metal portrait inside each and securing them with masking tape. Then he helps carry them to the guy's car, an old classic BMW, and loads them in his trunk. The guy writes him a check and hands him a business card, the background a crazy quilt of color and his name, Juan Valdez, in bold black scrawled across it, an artist from Oakland.

"You ever get up my way," he tells him, "drop by."

Cal hesitates and then asks, "Would you do me a favor? Look at something else I've been working on? Not for sale. Just want to know what you think."

He leads him back to his workshop.

Cal doesn't know what to think of this piece. Doesn't know what to do with it. All he knows is the joy it brings just gazing at it, so he hangs it from the rafters of his workshop. It started with a roll of thin, silvery, lightweight metal about twelve feet long. When he unwound it, he had a vision of wings. Wings spread out so far you almost lose sight of them, and you wouldn't know it was wings, a bird, at all, except at the center, two tiny trident-clawed feet hang down, and above that is a parted beak.

When he opens the shed doors, the light catches the edge of the wings and shimmers through it. He watches Juan's mouth fall open.

At first glance, all you see is this ripple of light, like a wave playing out in slow motion across time. You think it's this abstract, ethereal thing until, pow! Smack dab at the center you see it—these tiny, terse, reptile markings. The audacity of it! All that beauty held together by claws and beak.

You almost don't notice them. The feet and beak are so disproportionately small, seemingly inconsequential, they're like apostrophes and commas bisecting a wave of words, like they're not important at all, like you don't even want to see them. You don't want anything to stop your eyes' joyride across the ripple of light. But once your eyes get snagged, you can't turn away from them, these hieroglyphs from some ancient past, the thing that grounds it, names it, makes it come alive. The thing that turns this ripple of light, this undulating wave, into wings.

"Holy Mother," Juan says softly as he walks beneath and around it. "You sure it's not for sale? I could get you some big bucks for this."

Cal closes his eyes and breathes deeply. Then he looks at Juan and smiles. "That's all I needed to know."

"What?"

"That someone with an eye sees what I see."

*****

Later that night, Ivey falls asleep on the couch where they've been watching TV, her head on a pile of pillows, her legs pinning Cal down. Gently, he scoots free and goes into the kitchen where he keeps his stash high on a top shelf in a coffee can. Mostly, it's only the pot he uses now, and even that, not so much anymore. He knows Ivey doesn't like it, and while she never says anything, he's hearing what she's thinking in his mind, and it sort of takes the pleasure out of it. Still, his kit is there too, just in case, clean needles and all; you never know. She doesn't know about the kit.

But tonight's special. He feels like celebrating after selling those portraits and seeing Valdez's face light up when he saw his wings. He feels like he's turned a corner, passed a milestone. The way before him is pure and clear. He wants to kick back and savor the good feeling and maybe amp it up a bit.

He takes the stash out to the back patio and sits at the table. He opens a bag of weed and takes a deep, heady breath, savoring the rich pungent smell. But instead of rolling a joint like he planned, he pulls a pack of Camels from his shirt pocket and lights up.

He's been heroin free since he went to jail last summer for walking and weaving. It's been over a year now, nothing to sneer at. He suffered through the agonizing withdrawals during those first two weeks in the can, and by the time he was released it was out of his system—physically at least. Since then, he's been able to burn off whatever residual life-sucking-cravings he's had with his welding and his weed. Welding and weed, that's the recovery that's been working for him. A little beer on the side, his smokes, and Debbie Cakes round out his regimen. But mostly it's the welding, getting into that frame of mind where all his yearning, craving, and pure craziness is driven into his art. He powers up his tools, pulls the hood down over his head, and gets sucked up into the intensity of that fire—that's what saves him every time.

Why does everyone get so hung up on AA or NA as if it's the be-it-all cure for addiction? As if even trying to find some alternative to that Holy Grail is sacrilegious. Almost all the rehabs he ever got into were pushing that shit—find your Higher Power, work the steps, total abstinence. Maybe it works for some but not enough, not for most.

It's not like he never tried the Higher Power path, either. Shit, he's gotten down on his knees, he's shouted to the heavens, he's pounded his head against a wall—please, please, please. But nothing spoke to him. No message from heaven, no sweet saving grace ever answered his prayers.

The closest he ever got to feeling some God-like serenity was out on the ocean in his surfing days, suspended between sky and sea, the sun warm on his face, the rush of the wave moving beneath him as he paddled like hell to catch it, slipping into the curl, melting into that wave of energy, all one raw molten motion—no thought, no thought, just this wild-ass bliss.

But it never stuck. It receded into this hungry yearning for something missing, out of reach. Sometimes in his drug-obsessed days, he found himself at the beach, looking to reconnect with what he lost. It always felt like something gnawing inside him—a hungry mind craving for what was out there in the sound of the waves, that rush of raw power and mind-crushing beauty—out there, out there! He couldn't get hold of it. Couldn't bring it inside. He could only crave what was lost—until he plunged that needle down and felt it coursing through his bloodstream. Then he felt it. God, how he felt it. Then it was there, here, inside, and he was it.

It's what he could never understand—how something that felt so good could be so bad. How could that angel turn into a screaming demon that sucked his life away?

Now when the craving comes, he fires up his welding and funnels all that holy-shit yearning into his flame, the metal that moves beneath it, and the wonder of what he's wrought. It's like something greater than his own miserable self is moving through him, using him, and he willingly, eagerly, submits. He lets go and surrenders his all.

He taps his cigarette on the ashtray he keeps out on the patio these days and thinks about the roller-coaster ride he's been on and where it finally led. Hell, maybe his art is God's answer to his prayers. Maybe he's been ministered to all along and never knew it. Maybe that old fart who lives across the street with his box of Christmas toys is an angel unaware. Is this what his mother meant when she told him so long ago how the grace of God rains down, unasked, unearned? He shakes his head. Mysterious ways, they say. What does he know? What does anyone know for sure?

All he does know is that he's right where he wants to be for the first time in his life: Home. With his art. And Ivey.

He can see her through the sliding glass door where she's curled into the corner of the couch sleeping, her hands folded together, tucked beneath her cheek like a child in prayer. Something immense moves inside him, like a sleeping giant stirring almost to wakefulness, then turning over and slipping back into unconsciousness.

He used to come outside to smoke when his mom was still here, watching her through the glass door like he watches Ivey now, filled then with this fierce affection and gut-wrenching guilt, along with a bitter resentment at having been banished outside to smoke. As if he and his filthy habits had no proper place within her home—as he was banished, it seemed then, from every worthwhile and wholesome activity he ever pursued.

And yet, now that he can smoke inside, he has no inclination to do so. He likes savoring the contrast of the warm smoke in his mouth and the cool air on his face. He likes sitting here in the dark, hidden among the shadows, watching the people he loves sleeping inside. He likes how the light spills across the patio, inches away from where he sits in darkness.

The utter blackness of the staggering sky leans over him with its pinpricks of stars winking through the branches of the birches, like Disneyland lights in the trees lining Main Street. He takes immense pleasure in the way the constellations—Orion, the Big

Dipper, and Arcturus chasing the Seven Sisters—mark the massive darkness.

His father taught him the names of the constellations. He must have been eleven or twelve, stretched out beside his dad in the cool damp grass one warm summer night, staring up at the dark sky. His father's voice was soft as his finger traced the constellations, shaping them in Cal's mind, spelling out their names, and Cal repeating them, his voice hushed with wonder.

"You'll never be lost if you know the names of the stars," he told him. "You'll always be able to find your way home. By day, you've got the sun to count on to know east from west. But say you're lost in the woods at night—all you have are the stars. And there are so many, and they look so far away, you think they're no help at all unless you know their names and shapes. And now you know Orion and the Big Dipper and how to find the North Star."

Cal is touched and stunned by this forgotten memory.

"Think of that!" he marvels to himself. "The old man never taught me shit—how to throw a baseball, or ride a bike, or change a tire—but he taught me the shape of the stars, how to find my way home in the dark."

He takes a long, deep drag on his cigarette, musing wryly about how, out of all the worthless rubble in his memories, he somehow lost track of this one gleaming gem. He wonders at the mystery of things—at the immensity of the universe breathing down upon him, at the warmth and tenderness of Ivey sleeping under that halo of lamp light, at that ripple of wings hovering over his workbench. His thoughts settle into a cool, quiet place. A comforting presence washes through him, rinses him clean, and when it's done, he sits in utter silence and stillness.

You don't have to do this anymore.

The thought comes unexpectedly, like a stray pebble pinging against the side of a steel pail, the sound clear and unmistakable.

It comes like the ring of truth, like something always known but long forgotten.

You don't have to do this anymore, he repeats silently to himself, letting the words sink in, echoing down, down, down through his whole being.

When the feeling washes away, he takes one last drag on his cigarette and stamps it out in the ashtray. Then he walks his stash out to the back alley and buries it deep in the garbage can, where it's always belonged—not out here in the cool air and wide sky with the stars beating their music down on his head, not with Ivey right there, sleeping her sweet dreams.

He goes inside and kneels before his sleeping beauty, slipping his arms around her.

"I'm done, Ivey. I'm done."

She stirs, opening her eyes and looking deep into his. She looks puzzled at first, not sure what he means, and then she knows. Her face softens, and she touches his cheek. "You sure?"

"I'm sure," he tells her.

She nods sleepily and pats him reassuringly. "That's good, baby. That's good."

40

WALTER
Ghosts Among the Ruins

The small plane circles the airstrip twice before landing. The jagged edges of the Andes are scattered to the southwest, while a sea of green treetops falls away to the north. Walter flew ten hours straight with a two-hour layover in LA and three hours in Mexico City. Then he spent two days at an airport hotel in Lima before catching this puddle jumper to Cuzco. From there, the only way to Aguas Calientes, the town at the base of Machu Picchu where Franny disappeared, is a four-hour train ride. To get to the peaks where the ruins lie, the stones he knows Franny must have haunted, a twenty-minute bus ride awaits him, or a steep hike by foot up the rain forested slopes.

So far away, he thinks, looking out the blurry window of the plane.

*****

He takes a room at the Paqarini Hotel, a quaint hostel-like residence off the main thoroughfare in a small courtyard. Purple and blue petunias tumble from an assortment of terra-cotta pots gathered at the side of the front entrance. It's the place where Franny last used her credit card, where he hopes to find her still. She often lingered at or returned to places she once visited, so the expectation he might find her here is not without reason. At the least, he hopes to find clues about where she's going next or why she stopped using her credit card. Beyond that is the hope that by being where she last was, seeing what she last saw, stepping into her footprints and following her like a shadow, he might discover at long last why she left in the first place. And, if not that, who she is or has become.

The young hotel clerk doesn't recognize the photo he shows of Franny, but he produces a ledger with her signature, a childish scrawl that dips carelessly below the line, almost indecipherable, as if her signature isn't important, a minor obligation she dashes off absent-mindedly.

He asks for and is given the same room she stayed in. The walls are sea blue, and a white chenille bedspread embroidered with red roses covers the bed. A matching nightstand sits beside it, and across the room is a dark dresser beneath a shadowy mirror. A wardrobe stands in the corner. He opens the door but finds only a few wooden hangers and a wadded receipt lying among the dust bunnies on the floor. He unfolds it but cannot read the writing. He has no idea if it even was Franny's. White lace curtains billow in a slight breeze from the open window. Below in the courtyard, a dog wanders listlessly in circles, tied as it is to the handlebars of a green bicycle spilled upon the cobblestones. He pictures Franny looking out this window, holding the curtain just so, as he does now, drinking in the blue sky above the red-tiled rooftops, listening to a young couple arguing on a balcony across the way.

Sleeping in her bed that night, he feels her bones beneath him and hears her breath overlapping his. Rather than following in her shadow as he thought to do, she will lead him to her.

*****

At first light he's up, wandering through the streets of Agua Calientes, strung together by walkways and foot bridges, for there are no cars, no vehicles, no roads leading into or out of town, only train tracks and walking trails. The town lies along the winding Urubamba River, hemmed in by steep mountains and dark rainforests. Wild orchids grow beside the road, and rainbow-colored birds dart in and out of gardens. The air is thin and hard to breathe at such a high elevation. A morning squall has left everything sparkling with silver teardrops, reflecting everything around them in the morning light.

He takes the first bus up the mountainside to the ruins—eighteen switchbacks in all as the road climbs higher. Mist, like flimsy gauze, weaves in and out of view as he catches glimpses of the river far below. Its raging white-water wash grows smaller as they climb.

He has the uncanny sense of Franny beside him as he wanders among the ruins with his guidebook in his hand—not because he's sightseeing but because he must leave nothing unseen, no place where she might have been, or might be yet, untouched.

Even so, what he sees is impressive. Buildings made from irregularly shaped stones fit together perfectly without mortar. Trapezoid-shaped doors and windows with rounded corners are built for strength and stability. He's worked in construction long enough to know what craftsmanship is needed to build something this big with this much precision—and all without modern tools or means of moving earth and rock. This alone excites a sense of awe in him as well as timelessness, as if Incan ghosts walk in the mist among these ancient stones with him and Franny, who walks at his side as if she's just another ghost among many.

Yet by late afternoon as the crowds thin and visitors begin their long treks down the mountainside, Franny is still nowhere to be seen, and her ghostly presence at his side has disappeared as well. As dusk falls, Walter returns with the last of the tourists for the final descent, feeling as if he's left Franny up there somewhere among the mists and fallen stones. And he knows he will return.

The next morning Walter rises before dawn, determined to hike to the ruins this time instead of taking the bus because it's what Franny would have done. The climb is more difficult than he expected, as he's not yet acclimated to the high altitude. As he wends his way up the mountain, each breath is shallower than the last, as if he cannot take in enough oxygen to fill his lungs. But he likes the feel of the earth beneath his feet and the scent of rain-washed trees and rocks, wet with moss. He relishes the sound of the river gushing below, even though most of the time he cannot see it, and when he does, it's only a glimpse of white froth among the trees.

By the time he crests the ridge, the sun is streaming fingers of light through the mists, streaking the dark stones with an amber glow. He stops to catch his breath and take in the beauty that surrounds him. For a moment he forgets all about Franny.

That's when he sees her—at the edge of the ridge next to a low rock wall. Her back is toward him. She's crouching there with camera in hand, taking photos of the view, the shutter rapidly click-click-clicking. She rises, moving around the edge of the wall. Her hair is blonder than he remembers, longer, softer. As the breeze blows it across her face, she shakes it free and keeps on clicking.

He cannot catch his breath. It still burns in his lungs from the steep climb, and now it quickens in his chest with his pounding heart, as if breath and heartbeat are welded together.

When he walks up behind her, he has no thoughts. Her body is like a blow to his mind, and he cannot think. But behind her blond hair, her clicking camera, he catches fleeting glimpses of Dawn: Dawn's red hands, Dawn's red hair.

He reaches out with his hand but is afraid to touch her, afraid to break the spell, afraid doing so will shatter her, shatter him, shatter all he's come to love.

"Franny," he says, his hand brushing her shoulder.

She turns. Her face is round and curious. He freezes, startled. "Oh! I'm sorry, I thought you were . . .." She reaches up and removes a strand of hair blown across her face—her hand, gestures, intense blue eyes—all Franny. "Are you?"

"Franny?" She smiles and relaxes. "No, Alissa—Franny's doppelganger, judging from your face."

"Her what?"

"Doppelganger—her double. They say everyone has a twin in the world."

Seeing he's speechless and bewildered, she beckons him to come sit with her on the edge of the wall looking down on the green terrace stairs. He sits beside her and lets her talk. Being with her is like being with Franny and not being with her at the same time. His mind is reeling, trying to grasp how she could be so like her and not her. Her voice is soft like Franny's but lacks her lisp. She has an accent, but he can't tell where from. Sweden, maybe? Switzerland?

No, she's from Denmark, she tells him, on assignment for a travel magazine. She's not married and has no children. "I have no time for that. Too busy. I want to be everywhere at once! See it all, do it all. This right here," she strokes her camera, "this is my baby, my work. When I look through this lens, I am all that I see. All this," she says, sweeping her hand across the terraced hillsides, "all me, in here," she says, touching her heart. "You understand?"

"Now it's your turn," she tells him. "Tell me all about her, this Franny."

And he does: their life together, her leaving, her phone messages and photographs, her credit card charges, why he's here, and Dawn. He tells her all about Dawn waiting for him in Alaska.

311

"This Dawn," she tells him. "I wish I could meet her. She sounds like someone I'd like."

"You would. Franny would too."

She shakes hands with him when they part and holds him there a moment looking deep into his eyes. "This Franny, my twin, if she's anything like me, she's fine, you know. You don't have to worry about her anymore. Truly."

*****

The plane slowly rises as it takes off, taking him with it. He rubs his fist against the cold glass and looks down at the still clouds, stark against dark green mountains flowing beneath them. The plane circles twice, and he catches a glimpse of the rugged Andean peaks and the sea beyond, what well could have been Tierra del Fuego, the tip of South America, had they been further south. It looks like the end of the world. Then the plane completes its circle and turns northward, heading for home, his home, on the far side of the earth.

41

WALTER
Dawn Again

He doesn't tell her he's coming home. He takes a shuttle from the airport to Luther and walks from the drop-off point to her house. The geraniums by the front door are beginning to bloom again, tight nibs of crimson clasped in green. Memories of his grandma and Dawn roll together in his mind, warm, simple, soothing. Good, solid women, he thinks and lets the thought drift away as he turns his key in the lock and pushes open the door.

A loud clattering of curses and the smell of something burning greet him.

The morning sun spills across the kitchen countertops, splashes against the white fridge, and warms the worn wood of the little table where they used to eat and play cribbage, trade shots of whiskey and stories from their past, sculpted and embroidered through time and shifting memories. The aluminum foil peg he crafted to fit the one short table leg to keep it from wobbling is still there. And somehow, that tiny detail fills him with hope.

He stands in the kitchen doorway and watches Dawn bending over the oven, pulling out a pan of burnt corn muffins. A haze of smoke escapes the oven and fills the air.

"Damn!" she says again. "Damn it all to hell."

He wants to laugh. She looks like she did that first day he entered her home, bent over the oven like that with Randy tipped backward in his kitchen chair laughing. His heart squeezes and releases. She turns and sees him. Her face lights up for an instant, her clear blue eyes dazzling. Then the clouds roll back and turn stormy, her mouth a grim line.

"I'm back," he says with a weak smile.

When there's no response, he adds, "Like I told you."

Something soft and vulnerable washes across her face before she turns her back to him and sets the pan down on the tiled counter, softer than he thought she would.

They stand their ground a moment, each still and silent. Then she asks without tuning, "So. Did you find her?"

He shuffles through his mind. "No . . . yes. Maybe."

She glances over her shoulder at him, and what he sees there before she looks away turns his mouth dry. His heart stutters, but he presses on.

"What I mean is, I didn't find her, but I found out she's fine. She doesn't need me. She's moved on."

"Good for her," Dawn says, all ice.

He winces and takes a deep breath.

"I found something else too. You. Up there on that mountaintop. In my mind, always. Everywhere I looked."

He moves softly, slowly, toward her as he speaks, his hands rising ever so slightly, as if she's a wild thing he doesn't want to scare away.

"I found out she's not who I want to be with. She's my past, not my future."

His hands come down gently on her soft, warm shoulders as he leans in, brushing his face against her hair, breathing her in.

"She doesn't fill my heart the way you do, Dawn."

He turns her in his arms. She lets him.

Her eyes are wide and bright with tears.

"She's not home. You are. You."

*****

That summer he and Dawn buy a piece of property on the edge of Caribou Lake, outside Luther, and begin building a cabin together. All summer they work, and he watches her. She works like a man, squatting, sweating, grunting now and then. She walks like a man, too, stiff and full of purpose, confident and strong. But she tastes just like a woman, like that old song that plays in his mind when he watches her. He stops to taste her often. Taste the look of her red hair moving through the green pines. Taste the smell of her damp neck bending before the lake. Taste the feel of her rough hands splashing cold water on her warm, open face. Taste her lips, her tongue.

In early September they stand at the edge of the lake and exchange rings. Although no one is there to witness the act, they feel like they've been married forever. When the cabin is finished, he tells her, "It's time for you to meet my kids."

42

CAL
Hanging On & Letting Go

"So-o-o, how 'bout Pop?" Cal asks Kay soon after learning Dad is coming for a visit. The last he talked to her, he found out he was going to become an uncle. That was a kick all by itself—Baby Kay having a baby! Then he learned she got married and didn't even invite him to the wedding.

"We wanted to keep it simple, a little chapel in Sierra Madre," she told him. "If we invited you, we would have to invite Dad and Mom and Richard's parents too. Who knew if or when any of them would be able to make the trip? It would have become a big, complicated mess."

Cal gets that. That's how he'll do it, too, when the time comes. It's the news about Dad visiting that bowls him over, and he wants to know if it affected her the same way.

"Yeah, how 'bout Pop," Kay agrees. He hears the squeak of a treadmill in the background.

"I about shit my pants when I heard. I thought he was coming to take his house back. Then when I realized that wasn't what he meant, he dropped another bombshell. Said he's bringing a 'lady friend'! Can you believe it?" he asks, egging her on.

"Un . . . be . . . lieve . . . able," she says, through puffs of breath, finally giving him what he wants. "He's married, for God's sake! He has no business bringing his girlfriend to visit us!"

"Well," Cal says, feeling magnanimous now that he knows where Kay stands, "maybe we should give the guy a break. Mom left him, remember? It's been two years already."

"Even so, why bring his girlfriend here? Why do *we* have to meet her?" The treadmill sound stops, and a moment later he hears water running.

"She must be important to him. Someone he wants us to know."

"I don't know if I can handle it."

"What did you say when he told you?" Cal asks.

"When he told me he was bringing his girlfriend? What could I say? It's not like he *asked* if it was okay. What did you say?"

He stops to think. "I asked what her name was."

"What did he say?"

He laughs and tells her. "Dawn, with a 'w,' like sunrise."

"Like *sunrise*? He *said* that?"

"I swear," he insists.

"Jesus! *Jee*-zuz!"

"I know, I know."

*****

By the day of their arrival, Cal's so nervous his skin itches like it used to when he was strung out. The urge to use is fierce. Instead, he pops the cap on an eighteen-ounce Bud and gulps down big, cold draughts, hoping to ease his anxiety and wishing he had something stronger to soothe the conflicting emotions that swirl and surge in his mind. He's glad he ditched his stash, glad there's no temptation close at hand he's got to dodge.

It will be the first time he's seen his dad since he was handed the keys to the house and told to take care of it. Cal's proud of the home he and Ivey created, but he doubts Dad will see it that way. How will he react? Will the ridicule fly? Or the fireworks?

And, more importantly, how will Cal react to his reaction, to seeing his dad, face-to-face, again? Will it bring back all the old hurt and shame and anger?

Around two that afternoon, he hears a car door slam out front, and his stomach lurches.

Ivey is watching him warily, so he takes a deep breath and forces a smile for her sake.

"Here we go," he says, giving her hand a hard squeeze. As they head toward the front door, he looks down at her. She's wearing a long, gauzy skirt and blouse open at the neck. Her blond hair curls softly around her cheeks. She squeezes his hand back and rubs her thumb over his in a steady, soothing rhythm.

His dad shows up in the same camper he left in, and none the better for the wear, bearing the dents and scrapes of a rough life in the wilderness. Dad doesn't look much better. He's shorter than Cal remembers and not as lean and wiry as he used to be. His hair has thinned and is nearly all gray now.

Dawn isn't much to look at. She has the ruddy, weathered complexion of a farmer or logger. Her dark red hair, cut Dutch-boy style, makes her square face look even squarer. She's wearing comfy jeans and a long-sleeved plaid shirt buttoned up to the neck. A brown corduroy jacket tops off her attire, giving her a four-square, work-wise look. Next to her, Dad looks almost puny.

"You made it!" Cal says, trying to sound more enthusiastic than he feels. He lets go of Ivey and steps forward, sticking out his hand. Walter takes it and looks him over. Then he pulls him in for a hug. Cal is surprised by the hug and how long it lasts. Just the feel of Dad's bony back beneath his hands, that physical contact, makes his eyes smart.

His dad introduces Dawn, and Ivey—picking up Cal's slack—introduces herself and holds out a slender hand to each of them.

"I like what you've done to the place," Walter says, eyeballing the yard and all the rocks piled in the center. The lawn he worked so hard to keep green and weed-free is gone.

"Sure, you do, Dad. Sure you do." Cal forces a laugh, while his stomach squeezes, wondering what direction this will turn.

"No, really. Less watering."

Cal nods, following his dad's lead. "And mowing."

"That too," Walters agrees. "What about that iron in the middle? That your work? Kay says you're welding now."

Cal looks out at his sculpture of Don Quixote. "Yeah, that's mine. But the landscaping around the edges—that's all Ivey."

"Green thumb," Walter says, giving Ivey a nod. She gives him a thumb-up.

The four stand there for a moment in silence, looking each other over. Ivey is tucked beneath Cal's arm again, and he's proud of the way they look together. The other two, Dad and Dawn, stand side by side, shoulder to shoulder, not touching, but still a twosome.

Maybe I don't have anything to worry about after all, Cal thinks, hardly recognizing this older, smaller, gentler man standing before him. They aren't the same people anymore—Cal or Dad. Some ancient, disquieting longing and resentment that's always occupied the space between them slide sideways for a moment. He looks down at the top of Ivey's head, that path of pale pink parting the waving wheat of her hair. He dips his head toward hers and drinks in the smell, the memory of her curled beside him as they lie naked in bed, the sweet and heady scent of her filling his lungs.

He takes her hand and leads the party up the walkway to the house, lifting one of Ivey's green thumbs into his mouth for a quick suck. She pulls it out and gives him a hip bump. Their laughter carries them across the threshold into the house.

"You drink beer, Dawn?" Cal asks as they enter the living room.

"The colder, the better," she says.

He returns with three cold Coronas and a Pepsi for Ivey. They are still standing, Ivey and Dawn making small talk.

"Sit, sit," Cal says, settling back in his recliner. Ivey takes the winged-back armchair across from him that they bought after Kay's last visit, the lush green pattern of fern leaves feathers around her. Dad and Dawn take the couch, which sags a bit in the middle under their weight. Time to replace the couch too, he thinks. The only furniture left that his dad might recognize are Mom's old coffee table and Dad's recliner, where Cal is sitting.

Holy shit! He jumps up, realizing his mistake.

"Hey, sorry, Pop. You take the recliner. I almost forgot this is your spot."

His dad cocks his head and gives him a puzzled look. "No, no, we're fine right here," he assures Cal as he picks up Dawn's hand and holds it. "Besides, that chair suits you better than me these days."

"You sure?"

Cal lets out the breath that's been gripping his gut and settles back into his chair, letting the conversation pick up around him, Ivey and Dawn mostly. Dad joins in with an occasional grunt or clarification as Dawn relays the rigors of their long trip down the coast from Alaska. Slowly, the last of the strain Cal has been holding in his shoulders and neck all day drains away, carried off by the comfortable chatter in the room.

When the women go into the kitchen to prepare something to eat, Cal takes Dad out to the welding shop. The backyard has been weed-whacked and watered enough to keep everything green, but it's not much to look at except for the birches spilling gold against the dark blue sky. They duck their heads as they walk beneath the trailing branches.

Cal searches for some appropriate small talk.

"You been getting those rent checks we've been sending?" he asks.

"You didn't have to do that, you know."

"I know, but Ivey . . .," he begins and then wants to kick himself, wishing he hadn't let on it was her idea, not his. "We thought we should."

"She seems like a good one, Ivey."

"She is," he agrees, a lump growing in his throat as he pushes a delicate, whip-like strand of birch away from his face.

"Glad you found her," Walter says.

"She found me. It was all her."

"You hang onto her then. Don't let her get away, like I did your mom."

Cal nods. "What about Dawn?"

"She's a good one, too."

"So, you're . . .?"

"Hanging on," Dad tells him.

They stop in front of the workshop. Cal digs the keys from his back pocket and stops to look his dad in the eye. "What about Mom? If she comes home?"

"Where, here?"

"No. To you."

Walter shakes his head. "We've all moved on. Her more than any of us. If she comes home, it won't be to me."

"How do you know? Kay said you never found her down there."

"I know. But I don't think I was meant to find her. Don't think that's what she wanted when she left."

"So, it was a wasted trip?"

"I wouldn't say that. I didn't find Franny, but I found something else."

"Like what?"

"Peace of mind," his dad answers. "And a way to let go."

Cal nods. "Amen to that," he says as he pulls the shop doors wide open.

*****

The workshop is banked in shadow when Cal enters the weekend after Dad and Dawn leave to visit Kay. Only a pale wash of early morning sunlight seeps through the windows, lighting up a ghostly display of dust motes that fill the room like hovering spacecraft. He stops to turn on the portable gas heater to burn away some of the damp cold.

His dad seemed impressed by his artwork and enjoyed looking at all the crazy stuff Cal welded, shaking his head and chuckling sometimes. Other times, asking technical questions, one welder to another. Cal gave him the sculpture of the Old Man and the Sea, and he seemed pleased by that. When they were leaving, Dad made Cal promise he and Ivey would visit and go fishing with them sometime.

Cal's been putting off calling Kay about how her visit with Dad and Dawn went, not sure he wants to know. He hopes she wasn't too hard on them. She could be a dick when she wanted. He snorts a laugh, realizing it's one of the things he enjoys most about her. He kicks back in his swivel chair, pulls out his cell phone, and flips it open. Then he gives the chair a big push and leans back as he twirls, gazing up at that dust-mote galaxy swirling above him.

"So-o-o," Cal asks when Kay picks up, "how'd things go with Dad and Dawn?"

"Well-l-l," Kay answers, "she's nothing like Mom, thank God! I couldn't stand seeing him with a Mom-light. Still, it's weird. Seeing him with anyone at all. I always thought of him as a lone wolf, you know? As completely self-sufficient. I thought he was heading off to Alaska to become a hermit, living in the wild, not becoming a small business owner! With a dike-y girlfriend, for Christ's sake! It's like I don't know him at all."

Cal laughs, still spinning lazily in his chair. "So, what did you talk about?"

"Mom, mostly."

"Mom!" Cal puts a brake on his spin, aghast.

"Well, I thought she should know what she's up against. What she's getting into. I showed her their wedding album, how beautiful she is. And her photos, the ones we framed and hung in the hallway."

"Geez, Kay, I can't believe you did that!" *Poor Dawn*, he thinks. "What did Dad say?"

"Oh, he didn't know. He was off with Richard somewhere. Besides, what's he going to do? Ground me? Disown me? Anyway, she liked it. She seemed grateful I showed her."

"Sure, she did," he says, doubtfully. *What were they thinking, leaving Kay alone with her!*

"This is just *so hard*!" she says. "Wasn't it hard for you? Seeing Dad with another woman?" Her voice is sad and wistful.

"Yeah, it's hard," he agrees. "But I *liked* her. Didn't you?"

"She's okay," Kay says grudgingly. "What about you and Dad? How'd you get along."

"A lot better than I imagined. He seemed smaller somehow. He liked my welds though. Took the Old Man and the Sea sculpture home with him. Said he was going to set it up in front of his shop." Cal gives his chair another spin. "You and Richard still coming up next month for Ivey's birthday? We've been getting things ready for you. Even got a whole new bed set from McCloskey for the guest room. Just in time for Dad's visit too. Who knew we'd need a guest room?"

"We'll be there, don't worry. With bells on."

Cal frowns. "What does that mean, anyway? Mom was always saying that."

"Heck if I know. Go ask Mom!"

Cal hangs up, still thinking about his mother and the silly things she'd say sometimes, like she was still a kid. Snatches of songs and nursery rhymes would come out of nowhere and she'd clap her hands when she was happy. It was embarrassing growing up, and kind of endearing now, when he thinks back on it.

He realizes he's never known her apart from his relationship with her, the mother-love he so heartily depended upon and so carelessly abused. There was little reciprocity in that relationship. Its whole purpose was bounded by *his* needs—what he wanted from her, what she wanted for him. He didn't *see her*, who she was apart from him.

But all that's changed. Since she started sending him her photos and he started welding, he understands better her need to get away, to create and do what she loves. He doesn't think her leaving had anything to do with him now.

He's not worried about Dad anymore either, or their history together. They'll never be best buds or close the way he wanted when he was a kid. But he doesn't need that now. He's got what he needs—same as Dad, same as Mom.

He takes one more wild spin in his chair, then heads into the house to find Ivey.

43

KAY
Little Raft of Love

Kay hangs up the phone after talking to Cal and lies back on the sofa, her feet propped up on pillows, now that her daily treadmill turn is over. She's still wearing the long, pink T-shirt and panties she slept in. A lazy weekend at home. She will be so glad when this baby is born! Dad looked so funny when he first saw her big belly, like he'd forgotten she was pregnant and didn't quite know what to make of her. He hugged her from the side, steering clear of her womb. Mustn't touch!

Actually, the visit wasn't as bad as she made out to Cal, even though she was kind of shocked when she first saw Dawn. She was expecting some pretty little thing hanging on Dad's arm—a Mom-light, like she told Cal. But she ended up liking her. Telling her all about Mom was *her* idea, not Kay's. She kept asking questions, so Kay got out the albums to show her. She thinks Dawn is still trying to figure out how she fits in with all that's gone before. She didn't seem jealous of Mom, or worried—just curious, wanting to know more about her. Kay can see Mom and Dawn being friends someday. Mom liked people like her—straightforward, candid, and unselfconscious. She can see why Dad likes her, too. Maybe he and Mom never were a good fit. Maybe Mom knew, and that's why she didn't stay in touch with him, so he could let go of her more easily.

Kay groans when the baby—Amma, they named her—starts doing somersaults and kicks a kidney. She watches in amazement as her tummy becomes a molten mass of shape-shifting movement.

Richard wanders into the room from the study where he's been working, his reading glasses halfway down his nose like the first time she saw him in the gallery. Only now, he's bare-chested, and those silk pajama bottoms he likes to wear on lazy weekends ride low on his hips, showing off the light trail of dark hair that leads so enticingly below. Maybe she can lure him into joining her on the sofa.

"Amma's turning into a shape-shifting monster. Wanna watch?"

"Hmmm?" he asks, distractedly, digging through a pile of papers on the floor.

"Amma, your shape-shifting daughter," she repeats.

He finds what he's searching for and turns toward her, eyebrows raised. She nods at her tummy. But, of course, Amma has ended her performance by now. He drops an absent-minded kiss on her belly and turns away, heading back to his study. All on autopilot. But she isn't ready to let him go.

"Wait!" she says. He looks back at her, eyebrows lifting again.

"Come here." She smiles seductively, fingers beckoning.

She reads the indecision in his eyes, the inner struggle as the part of him on a mission, wanting to return to his study with the item he just found wrestles with her clear invitation. She shifts again. His gaze leaves her face and follows her body stretched provocatively before him, like he's seeing her for the first time lying there, her legs bare, knees bent, pink T-shirt askew, pulled tight across her breasts, nipples raised. She sees the precise moment when the struggle ends. His eyes mellow and then burn. A slow smile spreads as the animal of his body moves with a slow rolling motion toward her. She can already feel the heat of his hands, his soft mouth moving lazily over her. Her whole body purrs.

*****

Two weeks later, Kay wakes up in San Domingo, feeling groggy after the late-night celebrating Ivey's twenty-ninth birthday. She eases out of bed, so glad Cal bought that bed set off McCloskey. She doesn't think she could handle an air mattress at this stage in her pregnancy. She pulls on a robe and waddles to the kitchen. That's how she thinks of it as she navigates her big belly around the house these days. Richard is already there with Cal and Ivey. She's surprised to see her brother so dressed up— for church, Ivey tells her.

"We were hoping you'd join us."

Kay looks at her brother. "Since when did you start going to church?"

He grins at her. "Yeah, ain't it a trip?"

Of all the members of their family, Cal has been the most hostile to anything remotely religious, which always surprised Kay, remembering how much he enjoyed the stories they told in Bible school those summers Mom made them go, thinking Bible school should be part of everyone's education. Mom rarely went to church then, but when Cal was deep into his addiction, she started going more often and tried to get him to join her.

"Ivey's idea," Cal tells her. "I went along to keep her company. But . . . I don't know. I liked it. What can I say?"

*****

Kay is nervous about going, never having felt comfortable in a culture of angels and prophets and parting seas. She had no grounding there, no way of making sense of it, apart from the fairy tales her mother used to read her and Cal—stories she sensed expressed deep truths that couldn't be told any other way.

She's not surprised to see that the church Cal attends isn't the conventional type with a steeple and stained glass. It's a storefront church, the dusty glass window painted with white crosses and a black Bible.

Inside, folding chairs are positioned in rows on the rough linoleum floor before a makeshift stage. Nothing is hidden. Speaker wires snake across the room and up the steps to the stage, held in place by gray electrician tape. A small keyboard set in the corner of the stage exposes a backside full of plugs. The varnish on the wooden podium in the center of the stage is lashed with small scratches. But bright yellow chrysanthemums in foil-lined pots adorn either side of the stage, and the light streaming from the front window, flowing on a trail of dust motes across the room, strikes a sign on the back wall above the podium that reads, "Come unto me, all ye that are heavy laden, and I will give you rest."

The room is crowded with people of all ages, races, and ethnicities. What they have in common, Kay thinks, is a kind of rough-hewn appearance. Their faces and features, the clothes they wear, and the way they wear them reveal a lack of artifice, a raw frankness underlining the piety. There is hardness beneath the humility, an edginess lacing the vulnerability. These are people, it seems to her, who haven't known much kindness in their lives except for the kindnesses, perhaps, they find in each other's company. She senses a true brotherliness here—not the polite kind you see on the green lawns of conventional churches but the prodigal kind, where you gather each other up in your arms to keep from falling.

It's so strange to see her brother here in this church, earnestly shaking hands with the pastor and deacons, exchanging warm greetings with the people they pass. Cal leads them to aisle seats near the front of the room—Cal, who always disdained anything spiritual or religious, who insisted the whole purpose for NA meetings was to give drug addicts a place to look good for their parole officers while they scored new connections, who called God, on more than one occasion, the biggest motherfucker of them all.

Yet here he is now, sitting near the front row, holding hands with Ivey, who leans against him, his head tilting to touch hers. Cal stands with a little hymnal open in his big hands, singing in that big, boisterous way he used to belt out outrageous rock songs to irritate her when they were teens. Singing in a loud, clear voice about the little Lord Jesus, about grace pouring down on their heads like rain. And when the singing is done, he sits listening closely, intently, to the sermon, his head cocked, his eyebrows squeezed together the way they always did when he was listening hard, trying to remember something he knew he shouldn't, he mustn't, forget.

The pastor is strutting around the stage like some holy warrior. He's dressed in a shiny, black robe that covers all but the tips of leather work boots. His neck is stretched, the muscles taut and strained as he strides across the stage holding the big black Bible in his right forearm, pumping it like a weight, thumping it for emphasis. The Lord's word is a hard, taut thing on his tongue, belted out loud and clear in hard words.

"And God said, 'Behold! I will gather my children from the far ends of the earth, the lame and the blind, and the woman with child.'"

"Do you hear? What God promises?" He glares at them.

"He will *gather us*," he says with emphasis, "*gather us all* and bring us home. You and me. Your brother. My sister. He will bring us from afar, gather us like children onto his lap, and bless *us*, everyone.

"Now, let's see if we've got this straight," he says, his hard eyes surveying the room. "Did God say He will gather us only if we are willing to come?"

"No-o-o!" the congregation roars in unison, startling Kay, the word rumbling beneath her feet like an earthquake.

"Did He say I will gather you only if you have not strayed too far?"

"No-o-o-o!" comes the answer, echoing against the walls and reverberating in her mind.

"Did He say I will gather *this* brother and *that* sister but not *you*, brother Terrance, not *you*, sister Teresa?"

"No-o-o!"

"And when He has gathered us there on his lap, what will He *do*? *To us, for us*?"

"Bless us," cries the congregation, feet stamping the floor, creating a tidal wave of emotion that sweeps through the room.

"Say it again; say it till you know it, till you feel it! What will He *do*? For *you*? For *me*?" the pastor asks again, his fierce eyes piercing each heart.

"Bless us," Kay whispers, trembling, with the others. "Bless us."

Then she buries her head in her hands, letting the tears flow from a place deep in her heart. "You okay, little sister?" Cal asks, leaning toward her, taking her hand, bending to kiss it.

She squeezes his hand in answer and raises her head. Richard is looking at her like she's been struck by lightning, making her laugh, so she reaches for him too, squeezing his hand. And she realizes, the four of them and her unborn child are all joined together, all holding onto each other, holding each other up, forming a little raft of love and affection, afloat in a sea of thundering voices.

44

KAY
Getting to the Heart of Things

Kay slowly lowers her body onto the sofa and stretches her legs on the cushions. It's December 14, and she's ten days late now, two weeks into her maternity leave from work. She spends so much time on the sofa now, it's like a second home.

She looks down at her lap, a giant beach ball, drum tight. All day she's been having the strangest sensations, every twenty minutes or so, a gradual tightening, holding, then letting go. She can't be in labor. There's no pain.

"It isn't always painful," her mother told her only last week. "The fear makes it seem so, but when you let go of that and just feel what you feel, it's not so painful. Lean into it and breathe. It's all natural. Flow with it."

They've been talking more and more in real-time, making "dates" so her mom can plan to be someplace where a phone is available. But since she's often traveling in remote areas, it's difficult to find places to make long-distance phone calls, aside from expensive hotels. Mostly, she lives in her camper. Often, she's "on assignment." After cutting her credit card in half so she wouldn't be dependent on Dad anymore, she's been working as a photographer to support herself. That's why she can't be here for the baby's birth. An important assignment she's obligated to fill falls right during this time.

After a couple of these harried conversations about her phone problems, Kay misses the leisurely, breezy messages Mom used to leave before Kay's urgent need to talk in "real-time." Good one, she tells herself.

When Kay was little, her mother used to sit on the sofa like this, her legs stretched, her knitting in her lap. Even then, Kay was jealous of anything that took her mother's attention away from her. Her mother seemed to sense that, so whenever she climbed up beside her, her arms would open and then close back over her again, like a wave parting and washing back.

She remembers one day when she was around ten years old, leaning back against her mother's chest, head nestled against her shoulder while her mother continued knitting, needles softly clacking as an afghan grew around them.

Something classical was playing on the stereo full of long, rapturous arpeggios. She lay there, feeling her mother's breath moving beneath her, feeling her arms, her knitting, her music wrapped around her. The light of late afternoon filtered through the room, buttering the walls. Through the sliding glass doors, the birches danced with the breeze. Kay felt perfectly at peace, as if the boundaries of everything around her melted away, and she was cradled within some vast, luminous womb-like existence.

And yet, when she stepped away out of her mother's arms, when the moment passed and she was just Kay again, everything shrank around her, even her mother. She was this small woman whose forehead creased as she counted her stitches, who shooed Kay away to set the table for dinner, who pounded on the wall for Cal to turn down his music, and who whined to Dad about the broken garbage disposal. When she was back into the ordinariness of life, her mother, her real mother, seemed to melt away. It was as if her mother forever morphed between these two visions Kay held of her: the expansive one she craved and longed for, and the narrower version that seemed so cramped and frazzled.

Now Kay is a mother. She's joined this long line of life-givers that includes her mother, grandmother, and granny—going all the way back through time to that mother in the cave so long ago and even before that. A begetting that stretches back to when? The first woman? Or back to the begetting of everything, the original womb from which all this evolved? She places her hands around her own taut womb.

She's become the thing she's always craved—but for her daughter now: the safe, warm blanket wrapped around her. She's what needs to be the still center at the heart of all her daughter's exploring, the place she comes home to, until she finds her own still center.

That's when she feels it—a sharp prodding right below her heart. She cries out in alarm.

When Richard rushes to her side, she looks up, wide-eyed and wild. "She's coming! She's coming."

"Finally!" he says as he scoops her from the sofa.

*****

Kay stirs in her hospital bed and opens her eyes. A ceiling fan turns slowly overhead, a softly whirring motion. Beside her, someone is humming. Cal sits in a rocker next to her bed holding Amma, five hours new, in his arms. He leans forward.

"You awake? Richard and Ivey went to get something to eat while you were sleeping. I said I'd wait here with you and Amma. I didn't want to put her down until she was asleep."

Kay pushes the remote control on her bed so she's sitting up and looks down at her daughter, a pink bundle in her brother's arm. The tiny face is luminous, like a pearl, her dark eyes captured by the flickering movements of the fan overhead.

"I can't believe how tiny she is," Cal says looking down at his niece. "All that dark hair. She's a beauty."

"Isn't she!" Kay reaches down to caress the velvety smoothness of her daughter's cheek. "She didn't seem so small coming out though. Seven pounds! I can't believe I . . . you know . . . pushed her out like that. Poor baby! Squeezed like toothpaste through that tiny hole."

Cal chokes a laugh and holds up a hand. "Please! I don't need to hear about the logistics."

"Well, it's a good thing you weren't there. Although Richard didn't seem to mind, capturing it all on video. God! I can't imagine what it's going to look like. There will be lots of editing, I can tell you that much."

He shakes his head. "You're too funny, you know."

She smiles. "I know. Actually, I was luckier than most. Only six hours' labor! The nurse said I was born to have babies. These wide hips! I take after Mom, I guess. Her births were easy too."

"She told you that?"

"She's been staying close to a phone these past few weeks. It's weird. I don't miss her now, not like I used to. It's almost like she never left us. Like we still have her, only she's giving us different pieces of herself now."

He nods slowly. "Different pieces. I used to think that. Like those photos were pieces of her, a puzzle to put back together."

"Do you still feel that way?"

"No, now it's more like she sent me pieces of myself to put back together. I have a photo of her up on the wall of my workshop that I look at all the time. It's like she's become my muse."

Kay smiles. "Your muse and my birthing mentor. Maybe she's helping both of us give birth to something." They sit quietly, comfortably, for a while and then she touches his hand. "Look at Amma. She's sleeping. You should lay her down now before your arm falls asleep."

He lays her gently in the bassinet and then plops down in the rocker. "Too bad Dad couldn't make it."

"I know, slipping on the ice like that! Dawn has her hands full keeping him off his feet till that leg mends. I told her to wait until Amma's christening. I'm glad you're here though," she adds, taking his hand and twining her fingers in his.

"Me? Why?"

"You've always been sweet to me. Even when we were little."

Cal laughs and squeezes her hand. "No, I wasn't. Not always. But I'm glad you think so."

She studies Cal, a deep crease growing between her eyebrows. He was her big brother for so long, the one she looked up to, who walked her to school and protected her from neighborhood bullies. Then somewhere along the way, the tables got turned. He seemed to slip and then fall, and she couldn't grab onto him. It was like he was drowning, and she was afraid to swim out far enough to help him for fear he'd pull her under. So, she let go. She just let go. Her face crumbles.

"I should have helped you, Cal. When you were struggling with addiction. And even earlier when we were young. Dad was too hard on you. I should have stood up for you more."

"What could you do? It wasn't your fault."

"But it was! Sometimes. And I'm sorry, Cal, so, so sorry!"

"Hey," he says, leaning over her, his thumb smoothing the crease between her eyebrows. "What's this all about? You didn't do anything."

"But I did!" She sees a flash in her mind, Cal flying over her head. Hot tears wash behind her eyes.

She takes a deep breath and plunges forward. "Remember that day Dad threw you across the campground? I did that. If I wasn't such a whiney baby, he wouldn't have done it."

"Dad threw me?"

335

She looks at him, incredulous. "You don't remember? How could you not?"

He leans back in the rocker and shakes his head, thinking hard. "I got nothing."

"When we were out there camping in the pines that summer. Oregon, I think. You were teasing me, and I was crying, telling you to stop, and then Dad reached over, and grabbed you, and threw you over my head."

"Holy shit!"

"You don't remember that?"

"I remember something. I remember him being mad. But he was always mad at me."

"You don't remember flying over my head? You looked down at me, and you looked so surprised, so puzzled, like you were asking me, 'Wha'd I do?'"

Cal throws back his head and laughs.

"Why are you laughing? This isn't funny. This has traumatized me my whole life!"

"I'm sorry, I'm sorry," he says, trying to contain his laughter. "It's just so typical me. 'Wha'd I do?' Like I didn't know. Like I was never to blame for all the bad things that happened. Couldn't own up. But I'm done with that shit, Kay. Done."

"But it wasn't your fault! You were just a little boy. You didn't deserve to be thrown like that." Her voice breaks in a sob.

He brushes her bangs away from her forehead.

"Kay, Kay. It's all right, I'm all right. I don't even remember it. You got to let it go. Really!"

She stares at him, dumbfounded. "You don't remember all the times Dad was mean to you?"

"I didn't say that. I remember other times." His face grows hard. "I remember him shoving me up against the wall once, his fist balling up the collar around my throat, calling me motherfucker. I remember that."

"Jesus!"

"Yeah. I was fourteen then. Almost as big as him. That's when I was on the wrestling team, and I knew my stuff. When he shoved me to the wall, I was thinking, *I can take you, you bastard.* And I was ready to do it too. I was aching to. Only I saw Mom's face. She'd come up behind us yelling, 'Stop!' Just like that. I thought she was talking to me, like she knew what I was about to do."

He pauses and takes a deep breath. "But I know now she was telling him to stop, not me. He let go of my collar, and I squirmed away. Then I turned around and screamed, 'I hate you!' Like a little kid." He stops and laughs. Then he looks at Kay. "But I was really talking to her, you know? It was her I hated then, not him."

"But why her? I don't understand."

"For being there, for seeing that, I guess." He thinks some more. "For being the one to stop him instead of me. For keeping me from doing it. Like she stole that from me. She robbed me of that right."

"But why not Dad? Why not hate him too?"

"Because I saw his face, Kay. After Mom yelled at him, when he saw what he was doing, he looked so shocked. And crushed. Like I'd been the one who'd pounded him. Like he'd been in some god-awful fight and had just got his butt kicked. I never saw a man look so defeated."

A sad smile plays at the corner of his mouth. "It changed me though. I never lost a fight after that. Any guy who crossed me, bam! I would *not give in.* Not ever. So, he gave me something. She took it away, and he gave it back."

"And that's how it ended?"

"Pretty much. He turned away, and I turned away, and—" He stops and huffs a laugh. "I guess you could say that was a turning point in our relationship. He never got onto me after that. Never yelled at me. Never confronted me. He stayed out of my way, and I stayed out of his. And that was that."

"What about now? You seemed to enjoy his visit."

"I did," he says. "We had a good talk. Sorted out some things. He told me about his time in Vietnam. About his mom dying, his dad abandoning him. I think he was fighting his own demons back then, like me. But he's moved on, and so have I. He doesn't loom so large in my mind the way he used to. But what about you and Dad?"

"Me and Dad!" Somehow the question shocks her. "I don't know. We weren't close growing up either. I felt sorry for him sometimes, like he was an outsider, never a part of us—you, me, and mom. But . . . I don't think I can ever forgive him for the way he treated you."

"Shouldn't that be between him and me?"

"No," she says, looking at him defiantly. "It shouldn't. It affected all of us. I wasn't at the center of it, but I was there too."

"Collateral damage?"

"Something like that."

"But he loves you. You know he does."

She bites her lip. "He tries. He does try."

Cal laughs. "You'd think we'd grown up in a war zone the way we talk!"

She smiles sheepishly. "Not a war zone, maybe, but a cold war? An uneasy truce that could explode at any time?"

"Well, either way, Lil' Sista, there's no reason to feel guilty about that time in the pines. All I remember from that trip is the fishing. One of my best memories of Dad. Caught my first fish too. A little snapper—probably five inches long." He laughs. "And, miracles of miracles, I didn't tip over the boat or nothin'. Win–win all the way around."

She smiles at him, happy he's able to let go. She wishes she could too. While she might not be ready to forgive Dad yet, the images of that day she's been carrying for so long begin to soften around the edges and dissolve a bit in her mind.

"Now, if you want to feel sorry about something," Cal says with a wicked gleam in his eye, "how about that day you chased me around the house with a butcher knife? Remember that? Scared the shit out of me. Now that's something you should feel sorry for."

"That? I'm not a bit sorry for that! You deserved it. God, I was furious. I wanted to kill you. And I would have if I'd gotten hold of you."

Cal laughs. "Remember Gina, our babysitter? Jumping up and down on the couch, trying to stay out of our way."

"I remember! Like we were mice scurrying at her feet."

They are both laughing now.

"God, I hated her. She was such a prima donna," Kay says.

"Wasn't she? I think we staged that whole scene to get rid of her. She never came back, you know."

"I know!" She's laughing so hard now that she's holding her side.

They look at each other until the laughter dies.

"We had some good times, didn't we?" he says.

"Yeah, good times," she agrees. "Chasing each other with knives!" They laugh all over again.

He gets up finally and kisses her on the forehead. "I'll see if I can find the others, let them know you're awake. I love you, Little Sis."

"Me too," she says, blowing him a kiss as he leaves.

45

KAY

The Gathering

Dawn is the first to arrive for the baby's christening. She stands in the front courtyard with a bag in each hand, looking like an orphan someone dropped off on their doorstep. Kay greets her with Amma folded snugly into the shawl she wears across her chest, the way Alma, Richard's mother, showed her when she arrived for the baby's birth three months ago.

"Where's Dad?" Kay asks looking past Dawn.

"He's out there with Richard. The car we rented at the airport was making a clunking sound as we rode up that last steep hill, and they're seeing if they can figure out what's wrong."

"Come, sit," Kay says, leading her to the sofa. The bags Dawn sets on the floor are full of brightly wrapped presents. "Are these for Amma?" Kay asks, pulling one out.

"Yes, but you can't open them yet. Your dad will want to be here for that. He did most of the shopping."

"Dad? That's a shocker. This should be interesting." She puts the present aside and unwraps Amma, smiling at Dawn. "Would you like to hold her?"

"No, no. I'll watch from here. I've never had a young one. Don't know much about them."

"Me neither!" Kay laughs. "Till now. We're learning together, huh Pumpkin?" She bends to kiss the baby's bare foot. "You'll learn too. You and Dad together," she tells Dawn.

"I suspect your dad knows a good deal more about them than I do."

Kay raises an eyebrow. "Oh, I don't know about that. Dad was never a hands-on guy when it came to us kids. Mom was always the one who cared for us. Dad was always out in the garage with the cars, like now!" She laughs. But something doesn't feel right. The last time someone told her dad was out in the garage, he was actually in backyard watering the fuchsias.

The phone rings just then, and Kay jumps up to answer it, taking the baby with her. "Where are you? I thought you and Cal would be here by now." She chuckles at Ivey's reply. "Typical, typical. Why does this not surprise me? Okay. Drive safely, and we'll see you when you get here."

She hangs up and turns to Dawn. "Cal's lagging as usual, still scrambling about getting organized. Then they have to pick up Bailey. It's his weekend with them. It's a wonder they ever made it here in time for Amma's birth! Richard called them around midnight, and three hours later they were here. Ivey said she'd never seen Cal move so fast! He was so sweet with Amma. The third person in the whole world to hold her, he kept saying. Streaming tears! Her first shower, I told him."

Dawn laughs and then frowns. "We felt horrible about not being able to get down here then! Such bad timing, your dad slipping on the ice that way."

"I know. Poor Dad. But you're here now. Things were hectic at her birth, especially after Richard's parents arrived. Between Alma and Cal, Richard and I barely had a chance to hold her!"

Richard's parents are flying in this afternoon, and the whole family will be going out to dinner tonight, the first time they all will meet. Kay's a little nervous about that. How will Alma and Alfredo, Dad and Dawn get along? She can't think of four people less alike.

Tomorrow morning they'll all meet at the little chapel where the christening will take place. Richard was the one who wanted a christening. Kay resisted at first, but after that day in church with Cal and Ivey, she warmed to the idea. They found a Unitarian minister, a woman, who will officiate. Kay likes the idea of a woman, another mother, being the one to bless her daughter and welcome her into the world. It reminds her of the ritual she imagined taking place between the mother and child in that cave so long ago. The only mother who won't be here is her own.

"I'm so sorry I won't be able to get back in time for the christening either, but my heart will be there," she told Kay. Yet, instead of being disappointed like she thought she might be, Kay is relieved. If her mother came, everything would change. The center of attention would shift away from her daughter to her mother, who was gone for so long. Uncomfortable questions and feelings might arise between her and Dad. Where would Amma be in all that? No. It's better this way. Her mother's heart is here, like she said. Already, Kay sees something of her mom in Amma's round, mobile face, the expressions that pass over it like wind through trees—the sense of calm and wonder that envelops her and that Kay feels when she looks at her.

That's mother enough for her now.

Kay looks up when Richard and Dad come chattering up the walkway. She stands to greet them, holding Amma in her arms. Dad looks flushed and excited as he enters, his eyes brightening as he sees her. "This is your granddaughter," Kay says proudly.

Walter puts his finger in the baby's hand. Her dark, solemn eyes take in his face, and her mouth moves as if searching for something to say.

"Here, let me hold her," he says, reaching for the baby. Kay freezes, startled by his movement.

"Are you sure, Dad? She's so little"

"It's okay, I've got her." He takes Amma gently into his arms.

342

"Be careful! She's getting pretty wriggly." Kay's voice is shrill even to her own ears.

He looks quizzically at her as he snuggles the baby. "Settle down, Mama. I know how to hold a baby. I had two of my own, remember?"

Yes, but you never held us, she accuses him silently. *You never held us.*

Yet even as she is thinking this, a flood of half-forgotten memories comes rushing to mind, as if she's flipping through the pages of some long-lost family album revealing photos of her father holding them when they were young—cuddling her when she was no older than Amma, bouncing Cal on his knee as a toddler, grabbing each of them under an arm as he ran into the house to escape a swarm of bees in the backyard. Images of him holding them, as he is holding Amma now, with confidence, care, and love in his eyes.

Why has she always assumed he never held them? She wonders for the first time if she knew her father any better than she knew her mother, if any of her childhood memories could be trusted, or if they all were filtered and distorted through her worst fears and most urgent needs, like the one of Dad and Cal in the pines.

She looks at her father now as if through her mother's eyes. He was the stalwart man she married who she could always count on being there, providing for all of them, even when she left—not the arms wrapped around them, not the hands propping them up, not the safe place, but providing the space that made all that possible.

She watches her father now as he rocks his granddaughter in his arms with such affection and assurance, cooing at her, showing her to Dawn, grinning at Richard. The pride, the tenderness, shine in his eyes. And she's blown away. She doesn't know how else to describe this feeling she has now, watching her father, *her father*, holding her daughter in his arms.

Something deep inside moves as she watches him. Something sharp and disjointed realigns itself to match this new realization— what she sees now and knows in her heart must be true. Something painful shifts and falls gently, smoothly, into place with a soft, resolute click.

She realizes now that her father, in his own quiet, awkward way, was holding all of them all along, all these years. The light of her mother's love overshadowed his to the point where she didn't see it for what it was. It doesn't excuse his harshness toward Cal or the unease that permeated the household. But it was there, nonetheless—his love too. And she may never have realized this if not for her mother leaving.

Kay is in the bedroom changing Amma's diaper when Cal and his crew finally arrive. She carries Amma to the doorway and waits there, watching. Cal stands in the center of the room, tall and shiny, grinning like a banshee, his arm tucked around Ivey, who is holding Bailey's hand. His voice is big and boisterous, crackling with good cheer and corny jokes; his very presence seems to radiate light and energy, a childlike glee. *Same old Cal, always the center of attention*, she thinks, but affectionately now. There's an order to things, a design, and within the dynamics of their family, each fills an essential space.

Cal sees her and the baby and wraps them both in a big bear hug. Then he takes Amma and holds her over his head, bringing her bared belly to his mouth, making loud smacking noises that fill the whole room with laughter.

*****

A few weeks after the christening, Kay is sitting out on the back patio with Amma, basking in the sun's drowsy warmth, when Richard lays a thick pile of mail on the patio table beside her.

"What's this?" she asks.

"See for yourself," he says with a mysterious grin on his face.

She hands Amma off to him and shuffles among some bills and advertisements. Then, she sees the letter from her father—well, from Dawn, most likely, she thinks, as she rips it open. Out falls a photo of them perched side by side on some rocks overlooking the lake where they built their cabin. They each hold a fishing rod and wear identical green parkas as they glance sideways at the camera. It's such a picture of togetherness she has to laugh.

"Look," she says, showing Richard. "Like two peas in a pod, aren't they?"

He nods and then pulls a brown manila envelope out from the remaining pile of mail. "What about this?" he asks. "It's postmarked from Argentina."

"Your mother sent me something?"

"Not my mother."

Her eyes widen as she unwraps the package. It's a *National Geographic* magazine. On the cover is a dramatic photo of Tierra del Fuego, an archipelago at the tip of South America. A walrus and her pups lie on rocks against an ocean backdrop. Something about the photo, the light on the dark wet skin, the curious cock of the mother's head, the twin pups curled below her raised chest, the wild stormy seas at their back, catches at her throat, stings her eyes. Below the photo are the words "Story and photos by Fran Albright."

She flips through the article. On the last page she finds a photo of her mother looking out at the sea, a beach of walruses sunning below. She's wearing a heavy blue parka with the hood down, pale hair blowing across her face, one hand raised to hold it back, revealing her high cheekbones and round, firm chin.

"She said she was working on a special assignment, but I had no idea how special!"

A flurry of emotions swirl through her as she gently touches the image of her mother and then holds the photo of her father next to it—her two parents, flung to the far ends of the earth, now gathered in her hands.

"It's time for her to come home," she tells Richard. "She's at the tip of South America, for God's sake! Where else can she go?"

"So, tell her."

She smiles ruefully. "Sure. Call my mother home."

"Why not? You're a mother now. It's what mothers do."

She stares at him, startled by the possibility. Tell her mother to come home? The one thing she's always wanted to say but was afraid to? She looks at the photo of her mother again, standing there with that faraway gaze, staring out at sea. Then she shakes her head, her eyes bright.

"No. There's no need. She'll come home when she's ready, like Dad always said. I can wait till then."

46

CAL
Seeing & Being Seen

Ever since the christening, Cal has been obsessed. He's been welding in his workshop for days, weeks, it seems, rarely leaving. Ivey is like a light, a ghostly presence who wanders in and out of his consciousness, bringing him water, food, murmured encouragements, giving him the space he needs to create this thing, this image that wells up in his mind and flows out through his body, through fire and metal into something else, something new in the world.

He's on a roll. He cannot stop. He does not want to.

He lifts his hood to wipe the sweat from his forehead. The arcing flame pops. Splinters of light surround him. A bursting sun blinds.

Out of the light, he sees a faint figure far away. The sound of rushing air fills his ears and carries him toward her. He feels like he's traveling at warp speed, spinning through space.

A woman in a blue parka stands at the edge of a cliff, looking out to sea. Her back is toward him, her body limned in fiery light. She turns slowly now as if she hears him coming. Her hair blows across her face. She brushes it away.

She sees me, she sees me!

She always has.

Reading Group Questions and Topics for Discussion

1. This novel was written from the viewpoints of the three family members left behind when the mother disappeared. How do each of them see Fran and cope with her absence based on their relationship with her? How do they differ?

2. Kay wonders at one point if she ever really knew her mother. Have you ever felt that way? Can we ever truly know our parents? Or do we see them filtered through our own needs, fears and prejudices, as Kay wonders?

3. What clues does the prologue give about why Franny left? How did you feel about her leaving? Did those feelings change after learning more about her through the perspectives of Kay, Cal, and Walter? Have you ever felt the need to get away from your family? What are our responsibilities to our own self-actualization?

4. Kay mourns her mother's absence, even though she knew from her mother's messages that she was alive and well. What was she mourning? And why didn't Cal or Walter react the same way?

5. The novel is entitled "When Things Go Missing." Besides the mother, what else was missing in the lives of Kay, Cal, and Walter?

6. Addiction is a major affliction in the lives of so many families. Does the portrayal of Cal's addiction ring true to you? How does his addiction affect other members of his family? Did his mother's leaving help or hurt Cal?

7. Homelessness and addiction often go together. Yet Cal says early on that he always felt homeless, even as a child.

Why do you think that was? Does feeling at home (or not) in one's body, one's family, one's community affect one's sense of wellbeing? Is this a societal problem?

8. Why do you think the mother leaves messages on her daughter's phone, but does not call her son or husband? Why does she mail photographs to the son but no one else? What does she give her husband—if anything?

9. Part II of the novel is titled "Making New." Kay, Cal, and Walter each find a loving partner in this section. Which love story, or love partner, did you like best, and why?

10. Did your view of the main characters change over the course of the novel? Did they become more sympathetic or less? Which was your favorite character and why?

11. Walter's random bursts of temper traumatized Kay and Cal when they were children. What caused Walter to be so angry and take it out mostly on Cal? How did his temper affect the other members of the family? Toward the end of the novel, how did Kay's and Cal's feelings for their father shift? Do you think it was warranted?

12. What factors contributed to Cal becoming drug-free eventually? What things might trigger a relapse? Do you think he will be able to stay clean?

13. At the end of the novel Kay, Cal, and Walter each accept the mother's absence and do not "miss" her anymore. Why do you think that is?

14. Art and archaeology play important roles in this novel. How do they impact and inform its themes and plot?

15. What do you think Cal meant when he says in the last chapter of his mother: "She sees me, she sees me. She always has." What did she see? Why was this important to him?

Note From the Author

When Things Go Missing was an intense labor of love that spanned many years, sometimes needing to be set aside before picking it up again. Many people helped me as I wrote it.

I want to thank the NightWriters group in San Luis Obispo for looking at the very first chapters, as well as the beta readers who followed: Liz, Gina, Jill, Cynthia, Laurel, Kerri, and especially Dianne. She not only supported me throughout the process but introduced me to her literary agent, whose support, encouragement, and belief in the novel that she heralded as "about everything that matters" meant the world to me.

I am grateful to my editor, Dana Isaacson, who understood my vision of the ever-present-but-absent mother and helped me bring it to fruition. And I wouldn't be where I am today without the help of Jody Dyer and her team at Crippled Beagle Publishing. A big thank you to Owen Gent for designing the brilliant cover.

I am forever grateful to my lovely daughter Kelli, whose expertise in archaeology was a tremendous help, and to my sweet son Chris, who has always enthusiastically encouraged me in all my writing. And my dear husband Dale, what can I say? Your love and support through all of this made everything possible. I couldn't have done it without you!

I also want to extend my gratitude to you, the reader. I'd love to hear what you thought of *When Things Go Missing*. You can email me at *seastonepress@gmail.com*. If you enjoyed the novel, please recommend it to friends and family, and leave a review on Amazon and Goodreads or wherever you bought the book. Reviews are critical to authors' growth and help readers like you discover books they'll enjoy. Come visit me at my website/blog *www.DeborahJBrasket.com*. I'd love to hear from you!

About the Author

Deborah J. Brasket spent six years sailing around the world with her husband and two children before returning to California. She now lives with her husband among the rolling hills and vineyards near Paso Robles where the elk and wild turkey play. She has been writing creatively and professionally all her life. Her stories, poetry, essays and articles have appeared in literary and academic journals, as well as sailing magazines.

She earned her master's degree in English at Cal Poly University in San Luis Obispo and taught literature and composition before entering the nonprofit sector. As the executive director of SB*CAN*, she was a strong advocate for affordable housing, public transportation, and preserving open space and the environment.

When Things Go Missing is her debut novel. She invites you to subscribe to her newsletter at *www.deborahbrasket.substack.com* and visit her website *www.deborahjbrasket.com Writing at the Edge of the Wild,* where she shares her stories and poetry, and writes about art and literature and sailing around the world on *La Gitana*. You can also find her at *www.facebook.com/ DeborahJBrasket/*

www.ingramcontent.com/pod-product-compliance
Lightning Source LLC
Chambersburg PA
CBHW050513110726

47899CB00005B/1442